I0685052

Stricken (Quantum of Revenge)
Copyright © 2016 Joseph W. Bebo
Copyright © 2004, 2009 (as In the Belly of a Flea) Joseph W. Bebo
Published by Joseph W. Bebo
(An imprint of JWB Books Publishing)

All rights reserved. No part of this publication may be reproduced or used in any form or by any means, graphic, electronic or mechanical, including photocopying, recording, taping or information and retrieval systems without written permission of the publisher.

This is a work of fiction. Names, characters, businesses, places, events and incidents are either the products of the author's imagination or used in a fictitious manner. Any resemblance to actual persons, living or dead, or actual events is purely coincidental.

Joseph W. Bebo
PO Box 762
Hudson, MA, 01749
Email: joewbebobooks@gmail.com
Editor: James Oliveri
Interior and Cover Design: Elyse Zielinski

Library of Congress Cataloging in –Publication Data
Joseph W. Bebo
Stricken (Quantum of Revenge) /Joseph Bebo – First Edition

ISBN: 978-0-9819724-9-7
Techo-Thriller; Science-Fiction

Stricken

Quantum Of Revenge

Joseph W. Bebo

CHAPTER 1

PALO ALTO, CALIFORNIA, JULY 26, 2036, 1:00 AM

The gears of Dr. Linda Rayburn's Lithium battery-powered Volvo down-shifted automatically as it took the exit ramp off the freeway. It had been another smog-filled, gray California day. The evening was no different. Linda had barely noticed the car slow down. Fortunately for her, the latest model luxury cars could drive themselves. Linda Rayburn was completely oblivious of her surroundings, preoccupied as she was with the universe of her inner thoughts. Lately that universe had become extremely troubled.

An unusually gifted research scientist in the field of quantum physics and microbiology, Linda hid her lithe figure behind frumpy clothes, her pretty features behind thick-rimmed glasses and a pageboy hairstyle. She never wore makeup on her pale skin, and was especially ashamed of her hands, which she thought too big and unfeminine. In spite of her lack of care in her appearance, Linda never lacked for male companionship, although she had never been in a real lasting relationship. She just couldn't relate to men, and went through life seeing only the terrible things they did to women. Casual sex was another matter, however. Her father had taught her that at an early age.

Dr. Linda Rayburn shut down the car's auto-pilot and used the undersized steering wheel to maneuver it into the deserted parking lot of Quantum Corp, located along the Silicon Valley parkway. Until sixteen hours ago, Linda had worked for this up and coming company, leading a small group of researchers in the development of an advanced new type of computer of her own design, something so far ahead of its time, so advanced, that not even her own peers and superiors fully understood it. Even the revolutionary organic computers introduced less than a decade before seemed insignificant in comparison.

Dr. Linda Rayburn had been on the threshold of creating the first fully functional quantum computer. Made up of millions of atom-sized elements, it was capable of holding more information, and executing more instructions per nanosecond, than anything made before, all on a machine invisible to the naked eye. Only she had the right combination of skills and knowledge to pull it off, work thought by many to be all but impossible.

It had been slow going, even though she had been working on it since her doctorate, which dealt with sub-atomic computer architectures, programmed by manipulating the very electrons themselves. Few other scientists could follow the complex twenty-first century mathematical underpinnings of her work, let alone those managers and executives to whom she reported and who had the final decisions as to what projects got funded and which didn't.

As time went on and results came slower, more voices were raised in opposition to her project and her detractors grew in numbers, yet she toiled on. If she'd had more political savvy, she might have seen the warning signs. How, slowly but surely, research assistants were taken off her project and placed on others, until she was working virtually alone. Then they replaced her manager, the only person in the company who believed in her, with the dick-head who until he called her into his office this morning, had not said two words to her except to cancel every meeting they had ever scheduled together. Not to mention the vaguely worded hints of cutbacks, of how the company's board of directors could not continue to support research that didn't pay off in a reasonable period of time.

She should have seen it coming, and in a vague way she did, but she refused to recognize the obvious. She had her inner world of thoughts and dreams. All she saw were the endless possibilities for humankind, the infinite potential for good, the countless benefits to society, with her name married to it, written down in history for all to see. Surely then her father would notice her.

Yes, she should have seen it coming, but she was too busy, too self-absorbed to notice the abyss she was heading toward. She had pushed herself relentlessly, beyond human endurance, working long hours on little sleep and less food, spending all her spare time pursuing the challenging perplexities of the problem. Now they wanted to take it all away, to steal it from her!

The phone unit on her console had indicated an incoming call that morning before she even had time to take her first sip of coffee. She answered it distractedly, slightly surprised and annoyed to hear her new boss on the other end of the connection.

"Hello, Linda, this is Jack Veldt," he had said in a formal voice. "Would you mind coming up to my office? I'd like to talk to you, right now if you could."

She left her lab feeling numb and weak with apprehension, and walked unseeing down the corridor to her boss's office. She was sure that they were going to try and cancel her project, but she was determined to find a way to change their minds. When she knocked and entered, and saw the manager of Personnel sitting in the chair next to the desk, her heart sank along with her stomach. This was not going to be a normal business-as-usual meeting, not with that passive-aggressive jerk sitting there. The HR manager stared at her sullenly as she sat in the chair opposite the desk. Its hard plastic seat and curved back seemed to pitch her forward uncomfortably when she tried to lean back.

From the moment the interview began she had been suspended in some sort of limbo, wrapped in a cocoon of silky deadness, all sounds muted, all sights dimmed. She barely heard their words although she saw their mouths move and knew what they were saying. "Sorry but... Can no longer afford to continue... Need to make some tough decisions... I'm afraid we're going to have to cancel the project... Don't worry about coming in, we'll send you your personal belongings." She had vaguely understood the terms of the severance documents she signed, fourteen years of her life wiped away in a moment, fourteen years of her blood, sweat, and dreams shattered with one swipe of the pen.

In a state of shock, able to utter only a few scattered monosyllables, she was escorted out of the building by security in front of all her peers, carrying a cardboard box with her meager collection of personal effects. That had been nine o'clock the previous morning. It was now one am, long after normal office hours, but not at all an unusual time for Dr. Linda Rayburn to be working.

Even though they could have locked her out immediately, which they in fact attempted to do by disabling her personal accounts, they would have had to take down the entire system to keep her out completely. Bureaucratic red tape and incompetence ensured that this didn't happen until the end of the workday. For the rest of the day she had virtually unlimited backdoor access to the company's administrative computers, including the molecular-based master operating system itself, the brains of the entire complex of machines and one that Linda knew like the back of her eyelids. By the time they did take the system down at the end of the day, it was as good as hers. No matter what they did to try and keep her out after that, Linda had full access.

When the system was reinstalled that evening, supposedly clean of any trace of her having ever worked there, Linda's programs woke up and started to perform their tasks, each one synchronized with the master computer's atomic clock, which she also reprogrammed for her purpose. All was set for this very hour.

The sense of hurt and indignation at what they had done to her motivated Linda to take this fatal step. She focused her prodigious intellect like a laser beam on the target of her revenge. All her life she had been deprived of affection. All her life she had lived without love. She was through being the one getting hurt all the time, the brunt of the bad intent of others. Now she would be the one doing the hurting.

She parked the car in a handicap space and got out, a handbag hanging on her shoulder like a holstered gun. Pinned to the strap of her bag was a new homemade ID badge. She knew old Pop Wineman would be on duty tonight. The old man would be paying closer attention to his magazines than to her. Thanks to her preliminary work, the second shift security personnel would have no specific information concerning her termination the previous morning. She checked her watch. She was right on schedule.

While it was easy for her to duplicate the shiny blue employee badge displaying her picture and ID number, it had been much more difficult to duplicate the keycard access code. That had been a time-consuming process taking weeks to accomplish, something she had done in advance. Using the facility's high-density lasers, she first deciphered the key code and then etched it into her homemade card. Linda Rayburn might be oblivious of some things, but she thought ahead. She lived in the world of her own thoughts, past, present, and future all mixed together like a kaleidoscopic fragment of colors.

The heel-clicks of her long, rapid strides rapped on the concrete pavement as she entered the building. Flashing her homemade ID in front of the card reader next to the inner door too fast, she caused it to misread. A small light next to the unit flashed red. She waited for the light to turn green again. Not having a prior opportunity to test it, she hoped this time her card would work. Before she had a chance to try it again, the night watchman, Pop Wineman, came hurriedly from around his desk and opened the door for her.

"Sorry, Dr. Rayburn, she must have misread your card." So far so good, she thought. He had no idea that she had been fired.

"Thanks, Pops. How are you doing?" she said, hooking her badge back on the strap of her handbag, subtly screening it from view.

"Not bad. Nothing a little nip wouldn't cure," he replied, going back around the desk and flipping the after-hours log open absentmindedly for her to sign.

She took her own pen and signed her name, entering her badge number along with the time, checking her watch again in the process. She was still on schedule.

As she had gotten out of her car and walked across the parking lot, the little programs and procedures she had written earlier the previous day, hidden deep inside the security system's critical operating files, secretly and invisibly woke up. Each subversive routine, programmed to first duplicate and propagate itself throughout the system like a living virus, started executing, one statement after another in a cascading fashion. By the time she thanked old Pop and started walking down the corridor to her office in the basement, every administrative computer in the building, all eighteen of them, controlling sensors, video cameras, security doors, and consoles, among other things, were doing her bidding.

Immediately, some of her software agents, tied to the building's security systems, started to modify these systems so that any activity logged against her ID was immediately deleted. The computers controlling the video cameras were also modified to block out the next sixty minutes of time, virtually snipping an hour out of the visual record. There would be no sign of her being there once she left. Every visage of her activity and presence would be wiped out like footprints in the sand.

She donned her clean-garb and entered the lab where her new, not quite completed quantum computer was kept. Locking the door behind her, she stared at the incubator-like contraption enclosing her sleeping machine, her brainchild, her only child. She was tempted to smash it so that no one could have it. Instead, she would content herself with removing a few key pieces of its subatomic logic arrays in a manner that no one would notice for quite some time, sabotaging any chance they might have had of somehow continuing her work without her.

Going over to an equipment-covered bench, she called up an electron-microscope scanner to view the quantum internals of the machine, pulling out the key elements and components needed to make it complete. These she recorded on a portable memory unit that she had devised for just this purpose.

The anger at her humiliation came to a boil as she relived the events of the previous day. No, she couldn't leave without doing something more. She went to the interface unit for the bank of Organics and sat down, contemplating disrupting the intricate molecular reasoning of the biological computers and shutting down the whole system. But she realized it would announce that she had been there and only cause a minor nuisance, as they'd have the system re-installed by the end of the next day. She had to do something better than that. Then she considered of what she had daydreamed about earlier and dismissed as an aberrant fantasy. Now she wondered if it might not be possible after all.

"Yes, this just might work," she said to herself out loud, suddenly feeling better, as if a giant spring wound tight in her stomach had suddenly gone lax. Not only would she get her child back, but those who had tried to steal it would pay, and pay dearly.

Her mind finally made up, she called up Stanford University's Genome program, where the genetic codes of various viruses and bacterial organisms were kept for research and identification purposes, a kind of database of germ blueprints.

Viewing the building blocks of each organism in turn, she searched for one that would suit her purpose. The genetic code she settled on was an ancient bug thought to be eradicated in most of the world and not considered worth researching. That would soon change.

Chosen because of its simplicity and ease of manipulation, the code she selected had once been the scourge of the medieval world, feared more than the rampaging Turks. The choice was as much a matter of chance as intent, the germ's common name being early in the list of codes. Linda knew it was the one as soon as she saw it, like she knew she was going to have sex with a man as soon as she saw him. It was just so fitting, to sting them with something so deadly and ancient.

Calling up the interface to the central Organic from the command console, she started manipulating the colored patterns of pixels on the bio-machine's graphic display screen. Adjusting the thresholds of several key parameters, she changed the conditions controlling which nodes would fire, when and how. In this way, by tweaking the small patches of undulating colors on the screen, she modified each Organic's state-transition rules ever so slightly, imperceptibility preparing them for the package she would soon be delivering.

Once this was done, she copied the genetic code of the organism, consisting of thousands of three letter words, to the Organic's biological memory arrays, the whole operation taking less than a minute. When she left, there was no sign of her activity, the normal security logs erased by her earlier programs, which were still running in the background.

By the time she left the building, waving bye to Pop Wineman as he looked up briefly from his magazine, all trace of her visit had been wiped away. Moreover, her little package lay sleeping in the internals of the central Organic like a bug in a bowl of soup, invisible to the slightest detection, even if it had been known about, just waiting to be activated. In addition, she had backdoor access to virtually every major part of the system, via her network hookup at home. As a parting shot, Linda had transferred company funds to her own bank account, sums quite a bit larger than her $170,000 severance payment. That was nothing, however, compared to what she would soon unleash on her unsuspecting ex-employer.

Her scheme, as mad as it was, would not have been feasible without the new Organic computers, whose innards resembled tanks of Petrie dishes more than machines. They would be a suitable host for her package, and the fiber network that strung these clouds of organic computers together would be the vector, moving her germ from place to place with the speed of electrons.

As Linda Rayburn drove out of the parking lot and merged into the late night traffic of the Parkway, the ink she had used to sign the after-hours log started to evaporate, erasing the last sign of her visit, except for a few confused images in the mind of an over-aged security guard who should have been retired years ago. The thought made her smile and almost laugh out loud. The little touch of low-tech evaporating ink was the one thing that she enjoyed most of all the evening's activities.

SALT SPRAY MOUNTAIN, JAMAICA, JULY 26, 7:15 AM

A hot Jamaican sun beat through the thin drawn curtains, flooding the bedroom with filtered, golden light. Dr. Peter Danvers turned over one last time, trying to snatch another minute of sleep before giving in to the bright new day, not that he had gotten much peace during his slumber. His dreams had been disturbed by cruel images of suffering and death, steaming with undercurrents of sickness and despair. He woke sweating too much for the coolness of his air-conditioned room, with a vague feeling of uneasiness.

Without bothering to put on a shirt, still in his cotton briefs, he went to the window and pulled back the curtain. Lifting the shade, he was instantly blinded by strong, yellow light, which spilled into the room like a blast of liquid fire. He had to shut his eyes momentarily against the glare. When he opened them again, the beauty of the lush landscape surrounding him filled him with delight, dispelling the nightmarish images of the evening before.

Everywhere he looked was a symphony of color, a riot of vivid greens covering the mountainside and splashing against the clear sky. In the distance below he could see the off-white sands of the many beaches that dotted the shore, contrasting sharply against the deep blue of the Caribbean, broken here and there by long lines of white surf. He would never get used to the beauty of this place.

Dr. Peter Danvers was just a shade under forty, tall and angular, with thin, wispy blond hair that receded slightly from his high forehead. Intelligent blue eyes looked out from a sunburned face. A perpetual smile played on his full, hairless mouth, which parted in a wide yawn.

He moved lazily to the living area of his small bungalow on the mountain, a semi-circular, single-story dwelling, which clung to the hillside nest-like, all but hidden amid the flowering bushes and trees that covered the house like a devouring host of man-eating plants.

Pete Danvers, doctor of Computer Science, MIT, retired, went out to his small patio with a cup of quick-brewed Jamaican coffee and surveyed the scene in front of him. His neatly-manicured lawn, with its well-kept tropical plants and exotic flowers, quickly gave way to a wild tangle of trees and colors, a rampage of vegetation that marched down the hillside from the mountain peak behind him to the sea below. The familiar smile widened across his still unshaven face. He thought again how fortunate he was and what a wise decision he had made, against all the advice of his friends and family, to leave the rat race and move here to Jamaica.

Until a year ago, he had been the founder and president of a breakthrough computer manufacturing company. Organic Computers, Inc. or OCI, was a leader in the area of organic computing, a fast growing segment of the computer industry in the early twenty-first century. Peter was one of the leading experts in this relatively new and advanced field, combining knowledge of parallel computer architecture and engineering, with cellular biology and chemical engineering. That was before his voluntary retirement, however.

Holder of several patents for various biological computing devices and architectural protocols, head of a manufacturing firm of 1400 people, guest speaker around the world at conferences and symposiums, husband, father of two, Peter Danvers had been at the prime of his life, the apex of his career. Then he chucked it all and moved to this island paradise, leaving the computer industry, the multi-million dollar business, the huge house in the suburbs, the wife and the kids, to live the carefree lifestyle he had always secretly craved.

Call it burn out, call it disillusionment, call it what you will, he had walked out on the whole thing and didn't regret it one bit. The pressures had increased with each new achievement. Each new invention brought fresh worries. With each success there was more riding on the outcome of his decisions, more people depending on his work for their livelihoods, their very survival. He could have taken that, along with the back-stabbing, two-faced, lying crooks he had to deal with every day, but when he caught his wife and business partner in bed together, that had been the last straw. So he quit the business, divorced the wife, and moved to Jamaica.

Peter's invention had revolutionized the industry, changing the way the world interacted with computers forever. Early in the twenty-first century, the giant internet companies like Google, IBM, and Yahoo started building giant banks of computers, all tied together with fiber-optic cables, cooled by miles of water pipes and kept going by massive generators. These computers were built to implement a concept called 'cloud' computing, where banks of machines supplied computer time and storage to thousand of users. Peter's invention made these blocks of computers, with their massive consumption of electricity, obsolete almost overnight.

The importance of biological computing had mushroomed since his college days at MIT, with the approach of the theoretical limits of the silicon chip at the end of the first decade of the twenty-first century. As more circuits and arrays were stuffed onto these silicon wafers, the physical limits of how many electrons could occupy a given space and how fast they could be moved around were quickly being reached. Moore's law – that the amount of computing power doubles every two years - was no longer valid. With this limit, the astounding forward progress of technology at the end of the twentieth century would be virtually halted. Peter's breakthrough, a massively parallel, self-programmed computer made up entirely of biological, cell-like molecular computer chips, was a stunning achievement in technology, ushering in a whole new era. While there were still banks of computers, they now used practically no electricity at all and generated little heat.

Even winning the Nobel Prize for physical chemistry in 2024, however, could not make up for the pain and disappointment he felt at the betrayal of all his dreams and hopes by the dishonesty and greed of friends and associates.

Soon banks of the new Organics, as they were called, were servicing the needs of millions of people, managing the vast sea of information that flowed around the world daily. Of course, conventional computers were still in use, traditional computers with silicon chips, but they were relegated for the most part to palmtops and PDA's, or embedded in automobiles and appliances. A few were hidden in the basements of old-time hackers who clung to the twentieth century like reluctant house guests who should have left long ago. They were few and far between.

With the advent of the new global, high-speed fiber-optic network, connecting virtually every house, corporation, government agency, and institution in the country, and eventually in the world, the vast power of these new computers would soon be at the fingertips of every man, woman, and child on the planet.

While Peter had accumulated quite a fortune over the years, as demand for his product soared, most of his liquid assets went to his wife and children in the divorce settlement, including both houses. Other investments and company stocks were sold off, much of the money going to charity or held in Trusts. He lived on the few hundred thousand left over, using a portion of it to buy a small villa on the side of a mountain overlooking Lucea harbor, only thirty minutes from Negril. With twenty thousand more, he was able to buy a boat and some water-jets and set up a small business on the beach renting them out to tourists. He lived comfortably off the interests from his savings and what he made from the jet-ski business, employing a housekeeper and a chauffeur-gardener to help around the place. He had everything he needed - almost.

Peter finished his second cup of strong-brewed coffee and went inside to shower and change. Afterward, he called Stephen, his groundskeeper, driver, guide, and side-kick. Soon they were driving Stephen's Russian-made Lada - with the steering wheel on the right-hand side - down the winding mountain road into town. After doing some shopping and errands, they would head down to the beach to check on Peter's rental business.

While much of the world was being wired through the ubiquitous fiber networks and communications satellites, much of it still lingered in the late twentieth century, especially after the trade-wars. Most of the poorer, less industrialized countries of the southern hemisphere still relied on older technologies, and even these were marginal. That's why Peter had chosen Jamaica for his escape. It was close enough to the states – and his kids - to be comfortable, but light-years away from the fast-paced, frantic world of the turned-on, permanently connected generation.

Peter was not exactly happy with the way his invention had been applied, the way it had been exploited by short-sighted entrepreneurs and government officials; how it had proliferated through society with the speed of a stampede, instead of the orderly fashion he had envisioned. There was something obscene about changes so far-reaching happening so quickly. There was still so much they didn't know, so much still to learn. Now that was no longer Peter's problem, even though it intruded on his peace of mind every now and then to cloud his otherwise untroubled existence.

"Hey, slow down!" he said to Stephen, who was tailgating a large truck ahead of them full of sugarcane in his rush to get down the mountain. "We're in no hurry. You're too close. You trying to get us killed?"

"Sorry, boss," said Stephen, who was driving with his right hand and shifting with his left. He let out the clutch along with a sigh. "That darn truck pulled out ahead of me, and now he's shuffling along like a donkey."

He applied the brakes and let the truck move slowly away, belching black smoke in the process. Soon they entered town where they parked the car and went to the market.

In spite of the beauty of the day, Peter's thoughts had turned sour. It was getting so he no longer had control of his own mind, but then Peter never did feel in control, even when making his greatest discoveries. It always felt to him like he was in a tiny raft being tossed about in mountains of waves, holding on to some thought-experiment like Einstein on a beam of light, working in agony to tear the truth out of some obscure problem like a bloody fetus. No, discovery for him was more like giving birth than science.

Just when he should be enjoying himself the most, at peace with the stunning scenery around him, he was troubled by vague fears and phantom worries lurking at the edge of his brain. The frightening pace and proliferation of the fiber network, with its huge banks of Organic machines, taking over virtually every aspect of modern life, from the home to the office, from entertainment to warfare, concerned him deeply, as did the poverty and what it spawned. Peter had urged caution when the first all encompassing plans had been published for the new technologies, as billions were funneled into research and manufacturing. But no one had listened.

Of course, the massive sudden changes wreaked havoc among many in the rich northern countries. Companies involved with the old technologies went bankrupt overnight and had to close their doors, throwing hundreds of thousands out of work. Many soon found themselves on the streets, becoming part of the migrating homeless as unemployment hit record levels, living in the growing shantytowns and slums that spread from the edges of the larger cities like fungus on a rock. Peter had seen it all coming and urged the government to pass laws limiting the dissemination and use of the technology so that they could study the impact, and everyone would have a chance to adjust, re-train, and re-tool. But that flew in the face of the enterprising American spirit. They accused him of trying to monopolize the technology for himself. A few of his associates even began to cast doubt on his mental stability. So in the end, no one listened, including those governments of the world with the money and wherewithal to realize the immense potential of the new discoveries. They diverted all their wealth into the new invention at the cost of programs to help the poorer nations, or even their own disenfranchised citizens.

By the time they reached the beach, Peter was in a grand funk, despite the beauty of the day. The sun sparkled off the clear water. Palm trees swayed gently in the warm breeze. His heart was heavy with the weight of the world, a world that held the fate of his two little girls. He had often toyed with the idea of bringing them down, but knew their mother would never agree in a million years. He was sorry he hadn't contested custody, although he could see them whenever he wanted, as long as it was in the US. He couldn't bear the thought of fighting over them in court, making some lawyers rich at their expense, though he missed them terribly. He made a mental note to contact Sandy first chance he got.

Taking off his shoes, he waded in the gentle surf, letting the cool water wash over his feet. Even at this early time of day, the sun burned his bare forehead. Sitting down on the sand, he surveyed the scene before him. His guys were already out on the jet-skis, checking out the equipment and drumming up business in their inimitable way.

Peter was starting to feel better. Naturally good-natured and optimistic, it never took long for the surf and sun to wash away any troubling thoughts. He was soon smiling and enjoying the day, waving to one of the guys as he sped by on a jet-ski, the troubles of the world a million miles away, in a place his thoughts refused to be drawn. The blue sea sparkled in the bright sunlight like a bowl of cut diamonds, giving no hint of storms brewing beyond the horizon.

MINIMUM SECURITY FACILITY, BULGARIA, EASTERN EUROPE, JULY, 27, 11:45 AM

Eddie Pavloski, otherwise known as the *Dark Enigma*, carelessly munched a ham sandwich, the bulk of which ended up on his rumpled shirt and unkempt jeans. He punched a few keys on the small, old-fashioned laptop sitting on his bunk with his free hand. Eddie, while no longer youthful, was tall and well built, with an unshaven face, long black hair and dark penetrating eyes hooded by thick brows. Given better circumstances and more attention to personal hygiene, Eddie Pavloski might have been considered handsome, but under the current conditions, in a rotting East European prison cell, he was a physical mess. His mental state was something else entirely.

Eddie had once been king of the computer hackers, claimed by some, including Eddie himself, to be the best virus writer ever. Back in the heyday of these intrusive programs, at the end of the second decade of the new century, his innovations had revolutionized the art.

What inspires hackers like Eddie more than anything is the challenge, the same impulse that causes mountain climbers to risk life and limb. A hacker is motivated by a computer's security system because it's there. The better the security, the bigger the challenge and the louder the acclaim from admiring fans when it's been breached. Of course, one must leave a calling card, a reminder of the conquest like a flag on the summit of Mt. Everest. That had been Eddie's undoing

Just as in real world of biological viruses where new vaccines were daily being discovered, as anti-viral programs became more adept at fighting the worms, the virus writers rose to the challenge and became cleverer themselves. They created programs capable of hiding and disguising themselves in ever more ingenious ways, until in Eddy's day the virus writers reined supreme, holding the computer industry at their mercy. Then Peter Danvers' Organics came along, with their biological circuits and massively parallel architectures, and its brutally complicated programming. While conventional computers and hybrids were still susceptible to the hackers, they were unable to crack the secrets of the Organics, which remained immune to their onslaughts. Slowly but inexorably, as the Organics took over, the hackers were put out of business - until now.

As every dedicated hacker knows, there was simply no such thing as a foolproof system. All systems were made to be broken, just like every mountain was made to be climbed, it was just a matter of how hard you were willing to work and how much time you had, and Eddie Pavloski had all the time in the world.

Eddie peered intently, his thick eyebrows furrowed in concentration, at the green screen of his small laptop, a long obsolete Dell machine with a few Gig of memory and an ancient CD player. Eastern Europe was still ten years behind the West in computer technology, but even by their standards his machine was antiquated. That's why he was able to get his hands on it while serving the seventh year of a fifteen year sentence for computer theft and espionage, albeit in a minimum security prison on the shores of the Black Sea. Not that the innocuous hacking Eddie had been engaged in could fairly be called theft and espionage. No, as far as he was concerned, he had been shafted, given a royal screw job.

While Eddy's crimes had not been as malicious as some of the other computer hackers of the time, he was one of the most notorious of the lot, responsible for not a few multi-million dollar pranks at the expense of some giant corporation or other. He was the one who had been caught, so he became an example, to deter all the other would-be hackers and computer thieves out there. His sentence had been harsh by any standards, probably because the brunt of his practical jokes and mischief had been the all-powerful Global OptiComm Corporation. His 'prank' had cost an estimated 200 million dollars in damages and lost productivity. As enlightened as these giants of industry were, Eddie Pavloski and those like him were considered public enemy number one.

Early in his prison term he had been in touch with one of Europe's largest publishing houses, which expressed interest in his memoirs and the inside story on computer viruses, of which he was a leading practitioner. They in turn put pressure on skeptical politicians and prison officials to allow Eddie access to a computer for this purpose. When the judge assigned to the case asked Eddie why he should be allowed to have a computer after using them for such malicious and anti-social purposes, he answered that he wanted to expose the secrets of virus writing once and for all, so that it would never again plague the world. He wanted to atone for his crimes against society. Maybe by reading about his story, others with similar talents and urges might be dissuaded from following his path to self-destruction. Anyway, he argued, what could he do, even a computer whiz like himself, with a small antiquated computer, with no way to connect it to the outside world, no modem, no telephone, no wires, no antennas. He was totally isolated and cut off. The judge agreed and within a month Eddie had a tiny, old-fashioned, rebuilt laptop barely powerful enough to function as a fancy electronic typewriter. Eddie had feigned disappointment at the verdict, even though he was so excited he could hardly contain himself. He knew that was all he'd need to achieve his comeback.

All precautions were duly taken. The machine was checked for any possible means of connecting to the outside world. The tiny and now obsolete thumb drives he was forced to use to transfer his data were examined carefully before being brought in and after being removed from his cell, to verify that they indeed contained only what they were supposed to - his memoirs.

Eddie typed away softly on the antique keyboard. While he did spend some time writing hogwash about the history of virus writing and the more mundane tricks of the trade, he spent most of his time in other pursuits, ones more in line with what had got him into prison in the first place.

He had been caught not so much because of the ever more aggressive computer security methods and law enforcement, but because of his overpowering ego and need for recognition. His decision to go after the biggest of them, the Goliath of international giant corporations, Global OptiComm, had been bad enough, but his repeated provocations and attacks, accompanied by ever more infuriating cues and taunts proved to be his undoing. In his efforts to establish the authorship of the intrusive viruses he was unleashing and to add to his own self-serving publicity, he finally led the authorities right to his front door, which at the time was located just down the street from the Bulgarian Embassy in Budapest.

For five years now, every waking moment, every sleepless night, Eddie had been plotting his comeback, his great coup. He would strike from within the confines of this very prison, at the heart of the new system, the Organics themselves. He would show those toady Eastern European bureaucrats, the stiff barristers and stiffer judges, the richly-dressed corporate lawyers who worked so hard to persecute and malign him. He would show them all.

In the past twenty-four months he had studied everything he could get his hands on relating to the new Organic computers, including its maker and inventor, whose doctoral theses - which read more like a biology textbook than one on computer science - lay neatly on a homemade bookcase next to him. He knew all there was to know about the machines, perhaps even more than their inventor himself. In the process he'd had to study cellular biology and molecular engineering, and learn the secrets of DNA. Now he was putting that knowledge into use.

Eddie smiled in appreciation as he thought about the inner workings of the organic computers, whose violation he lusted after, from his bitter home on the dreary shores of this barren sea.

At first he had been stumped by the massively-parallel architecture and the bizarre molecular programming, with proteins and enzymes in place of logic arrays and electric circuits. Then one night, as he was reading one of Peter's books, it hit him in a flash. The whole thing was like a computer game he had experimented with in college shortly before he had to drop out for lack of funds and passing grades. It was called the *Game of Life*.

In this game the pixels on the display screen were programmed to turn on and off according to certain rules. The pixels turning on – turning some color - represented life. A pixel turning off – turning black say - represented death, thus the name, *The Game of Life*. Programming the rules involved setting thresholds of activation that determined when a pixel would turn on or off, based on the state of its neighbors. The whole group of pixels that are on at any one time is called a population, and these populations change as pixels are turned on and off, giving rise to undulating, constantly changing patterns, some of which are quite interesting and go on for a very long time. Different algorithms or rules give rise to different populations. Some lead to very short-lived groups, where everything stops or dies in a few minutes. Some go on virtually forever, the dots never ceasing to switch on and off until you stop the program or turn off the computer. The concept had fascinated Eddie, but the leap from that simple game to programming a massively-parallel computer using protein activation and enzymes, the languages of our DNA, was huge. Eddie Pavloski had recently breached that gap. Now it was just a matter of building the delivery mechanism and sending it out. That was the easy part.

Eddie's anti-social streak was directed not so much against technology, which he excelled in and enjoyed, as against the arrogant people who used it so casually and the fat-cats who ripped off the public selling it when it should have been given away for free. Then when the US had built their huge banks of Organics and connected it all together with fiber-optic cables, spending billions of dollars, money that could have been used to greater benefit elsewhere, like feeding starving children, only to make increasingly obscene profits in the end, he had been even more ticked-off, especially since the new machines promised to put him out of business overnight. That's when he had unleashed his last masterpiece and shut them down even before they had a chance to get the Organics started That had been almost a decade ago, just after the trade wars. Now the Organics were fully operational in the US, the Fiber connecting the whole place together like a single office, and they were about to do the same thing in Europe. Well, not while Eddie Pavloski had anything to say about it. They could do anything they wanted in the States, but they weren't going to pollute Eddie's neck of the woods.

He tapped away in the semi-darkness on the old-fashioned keyboard, still favored by aged hackers everywhere, testing his latest code. The screen undulated and swirled with patterns of changing colors, as the pixel display simulated the neural networks Eddie was constructing, which he copied to the thumb-drive as bitmaps hidden in the text of his innocuous memoirs. The rules of activation were thus hiding in the character set of the document itself, so that each component of the virus was hidden within another, as a multi-dimensional vector, until the final piece was found in the most deeply nested part of the worm, thus its name - the *Trojan-horse* virus.

"Warden on the floor. Warden on the floor," came echoing up the hall in whispers. Quickly hitting a few keys, Eddie changed the display to show his manuscript, which had been held in abeyance while he worked on his virus.

"How you coming with the memoirs, Pavloski?" asked the warden, a clean-shaven, well-dressed man about Eddie's age, but opposite him in appearance, with short blond hair and soft blue eyes. Appearances could be deceiving. There was nothing soft about John Hidemaster, who would have given the old Stasi a run for their money given half a chance. Lucky for the inmates and guards alike, the prison was highly scrutinized and regularized, but that didn't prevent him from making their lives miserable.

"Good," said Eddie. "I'll be finished soon."

"You're not fooling anyone, you know," said the warden. "I don't know what you're up to, or how you got that judge to let you have a computer, but you're not going to get away with anything on my watch."

"I'm not trying to get away with anything. The court ordered you to let me have this machine. The money I make with this book is going to charity and the people I harmed, all of it. I'm not making a dime. I'm doing it to make up for the trouble I've caused. I know you can't understand this, but my motives are honest."

"I've heard it all before," said the warden. "I'm watching you like a bug under a microscope. I'm even examining your documents myself. You may get something by some of these guys, but you're not getting anything by me. And if I find one bug, one out of place period, I'm going to fry you for good. You got that, Pavloski?"

"There's no reason to be so hostile, John. I'm not trying to pull anything. I've learned my lesson. You can do whatever you want to those disks, but I have a contract. Once you've checked them, you've got to send them to my publisher. Otherwise you'll be in breach of contract. You know the rules."

"Yeah, Eddie, unlike you and your kind, I know the rules. And I know you. Once a hack always a hack."

"Sorry you feel that way. I hope I can prove you wrong."

"Hmmph!" said the warden. "Give those disks to me when he's finished," he ordered the guard, as he moved away to find someone else to harass.

What the warden didn't know was that as soon as Eddie's thumb drives were loaded and scanned by the antiquated anti-virus software - the East European prison could not afford the newer tools – his tiny programs would activate and invade the scanning program itself, corrupting it so that other viruses that followed would go undetected and be transmitted to his publisher, who would unwittingly unleash them on the world.

LOS ANGELES, CALIFORNIA, JULY 28, 3:00 PM

Stan Bellows had just convened the board-of-directors meeting. Sitting in the plush glass-enclosed conference room, overlooking the marble floor of a vaulted lobby twelve stories below, were perhaps the ten most powerful men and women in the world. That power came not from political office or wealth, but from the computer network that these ten people controlled.

They were the directors of Global OptiComm, a giant international consortium of computer and telecommunication companies that together controlled the largest network of Organic computers in the world, along with the optical fiber cabling that connected them. Virtually all the world's computing, public and private, business and pleasure, took place over this network.

Along with advances in computers like Peter Danvers' Organics, breakthroughs in telecommunication and computer networking technology had also revolutionized the industry. In the year 2036, buying a computer was virtually a thing of the past, except for large, special-purpose super-computers used in advanced research, or miniature handheld machines, ubiquitous as calculators of old. Now, instead of buying a computer, one bought computer services from giant Organic computer vendors much like subscribing to cable TV in the past. These services were delivered to the home via the television set, which was really just a high-resolution digital display device, connected through two-way, fiber-optic cables to large banks of Organic computers, distributed throughout the country.

Stan Bellows was chairman of the board of OptiComm, the one that made it all happen. He was the one who controlled the high-powered executives and PhDs sitting before him with their giant egos. Like a centurion controls the horses of a chariot, he pulled one this way, another that, sometimes using one's weight against the other's to make things go the way he wanted. Stan Bellows was an expert at his craft, always knowing the right amount of pressure to exert, when to use finesse, when to use force, though you would never know it to look at the small, wiry man with the graying crew-cut, dressed in the coarse, rumpled brown suit. That is except perhaps for his cold, piercing-blue eyes.

Those eyes surveyed the men and women sitting around the large oval, highly-polished, rosewood table. Business analysts, scientists, engineers, and telecommunications experts, these were the people who ran the giant global fiber-optic network of Organic computers, which would soon link virtually every home and institution, in every city, state, and country in the world.

"Gentlemen," began the chairman. "I'm afraid we have a problem, which if not resolved immediately will seriously delay the implementation of our plans." Everyone in the room understood that this would not be allowed to occur. *Problem* was not a word in the lexicon of Stan Billows.

Stan was used to being in a position of authority. In the first years of the twenty-first century, he had been just another ECO scrambling for a piece of the telecommunications industry pie, until gradually, one by one, he had bought out or bankrupted most of the competition, not always in the most legal of ways. Stan Bellows was as ruthless as he was ambitious.

In the years leading up to the tariff wars, he had been a strong and vocal proponent of free trade and global competition, one of the few, and had repeatedly warned of the consequences of trade sanctions and high protective tariffs. The domestic market, however, was under heavy competition from China and Europe, and the politicians and officials, pressured by highly-paid lobbyists, refused to listen. The outbreak of the trade-wars and subsequent great depression, while devastating most of the world economic systems, did much to raise Stan Bellow's reputation amongst the public as someone who knew what he was talking about. He had even run for the country's highest office, on the Republican ticket in the 2024 presidential elections, but his blunt style and lack of social charm made sure he polled a dismal showing in the primaries. In spite of the huge sums of money poured into the campaign, he eventually had to pull out. Now he held the reins of power from behind the scenes.

The US phase of his plan was all but complete. Just a few more blocks of cable needed to be connected, a few additional hubs installed, and it would be finished, his dream a reality, the entire country relying on his network and computers for their every need. Soon, the world would be singing to his tune.

The European linkup, scheduled for next month, would combine the computer power of the two continents, equivalent to all the human brain power in the world, all eight billion of them. With Asia, to be completed a few months later, the combined power of the networked machines would surpass human intelligence on the planet. With that type of computing power, who knew what discoveries awaited. Stan Bellows would be the master of it. Except for a few small last minute snags, everything was on schedule.

"Ted Samasota, our head of Field Operations, has informed me there's been some minor cases of sabotage out near Boston. Nothing we can't handle, but the sites attacked were key gateways to our European hubs, so we have to make sure they're clean before we go ahead with the hookup. The culprits have been caught and will be prosecuted to the fullest extent of the law. This just goes to show you what we're up against. Some people out there will stop at nothing to throw us all back into the dark ages."

There was a suitable murmuring of outrage from around the table that anyone would stand in the way of progress like that, obstruct something that was obviously such a benefit to mankind, not to mention their own pocketbooks.

"After what we did to that Pavlosky character, I'm surprised anyone had the nerve to mess with us again," said Bellow's VP of security. "We fried him good. As a deterrent to others his harsh penalty was the best thing that could have happened. Maybe we didn't go hard enough on the guy."

Bellows did not return his subordinate's leering grin.

"If I'd had my way we would have given him the death penalty," said the chairman. "Are you sure they can't infect the Organics with these new viruses they're writing?"

"No, sir," said the security chief, parroting what he'd been told by his experts. "They can only get to the hybrid hubs with their silicon components and arrays, and we've got fixes for that now. No hacker can invade the biological security of the Organics, sir."

Bellows wasn't as sure as his chief of security seemed to be, but nodded his approval all the same. One problem at a time. For now he had an empire to finish building.

CHAPTER 2

PALO ALTO, CALIFORNIA, JULY 30, 2036, 6:00 AM,

Linda let herself into her townhouse building, after stocking up supplies at the local 24-hour convenience store, and climbed up the large encircling staircase to her fourth-floor lab, all on base brain. Still stinging from humiliation and the pain of loss, she was totally preoccupied with thoughts of revenge. She knew that they were trying to steal her work. That's why they had fired her, so they could take all the credit and reap all the rewards. That's why that new girl, Debbie something or other, had been picking her brain for the past three months, trying to get her to document everything, snooping around, looking over her shoulder every minute. It wasn't only her work that they were trying to take, for the microscopic computer was more like a child to her than a machine, more like something she had birthed with her own sweat and pain, than some mere piece of hardware. No, they weren't going to steal her child, not if Dr. Linda Rayburn had any say in the matter.

Linda had done much work in the intervening hours and days since her visit to her ex-employer, QuantumCorp. Fifteen, sometimes eighteen hours at a time, she toiled in her penthouse lab, hunched over the displays of her various computers and electron microscopes, tapping out lines of commands and instructions in some complex programming language faster than most executive secretaries can type a form letter. She was building her own version of the Quantum computer, simpler but equally as powerful as the one she had left behind, this one containing the missing components she had removed during her earlier visit.

The computations were brutally complex, a mind-boggling sequence of recursive multi-dimensional equations that would have left most mathematicians quivering, but Linda dealt with them as if they were freshman math problems, hardly stopping to use a notepad.

Once built, she used her new machine to develop a program to fabricate and activate the genetic code she had left sleeping in her ex-employer's Organic computers, the genetic blueprint of the Bubonic

Plague germ she had stolen from the biological archives. What she was doing was beyond the realm of normal science, even in the day and age where the mysteries of the universe were being unraveled at an ever dizzying pace. Modern science, however, was not quite ready for what Linda Rayburn was about to unleash on her unsuspecting ex-employer.

As extraordinary and complex as her plan was, the individual steps themselves were really quite straightforward. First, using her quantum machine, she decoded the sequences of enzymes and proteins needed to synthesize the blueprint of the Plague germ she had left behind in the company's Organics, storing the decoded model temporarily in an old Organic she had borrowed from the company years ago. Utilizing the optical fiber's entire bandwidth, she planned to transmit her massive synthesis program over the network to QuantumCorp's main computer. Once activated, it would start building the bacteria coded for in the host computer, using the biological soup of the machines themselves. Searching out and combining the various trace elements - carbon, oxygen, nitrogen, and hydrogen that formed the stuff of life – it would form the necessary ingredients, mixing them with the free-floating molecular fragments and RNA that made up much of the thing's internals. In this way, she would fabricate the germ she had implanted the blueprint of, in the master Organic those many days ago.

Her computers whirled away madly, computing the equations needed, building the packets of electrons that would carry her program through the cables and circuits of the fiber-optic network to its intended destination.

Someone watching her work would have had to wonder how she did it, how she could drive herself at the exclusion of everything else, how one person could know so much. One would also have had to wonder how someone so intelligent and gifted could have let themselves come to such a point, consumed with such an overwhelming burning for revenge. Linda probably couldn't have explained it herself. Perhaps more fueled her rage than work issues, like a life of neglect and abuse, but she wouldn't let herself think of those things, only the present.

The Black Death, Altra Mors, call it what you will, the tiny bacillus Pasteurella Pestis, a single-celled creature whose genetic code is comprised of only a few thousand instructions, lay sleeping in the belly of the Organics, waiting for Linda's program to wake it.

For days she had slaved over the manipulators of her quantum super-computer. She had just finished her first set of tests, using the old Organic huddled in the corner of her lab like a fish tank, as a guinea pig. Now it was time for the real thing.

Linda smiled a haggard grin, not of joy, but of grim determination. The time had come. The days of toil and sleepless nights were about to pay off!

She checked her program one more time. Everything was ready. Using the security breaches she had lain down a few days before, still undetected and active, she connected to the QuantumComp main computer over her apartment's fiber link. There was nothing to stop her. No expert security system watched the network. No shield of defenses protected the massive bank of computers. All stood unguarded and open to her, the entire system long since compromised by her tiny serve-lets.

Once the deadly virus was activated, it would literally begin to feed on the Organic computers while it propagated itself, gaining access to the vital resources of the machines and using them for its own purpose. All would be accomplished in a few days.

Linda established the network connection, made certain that everything was ready on the host end, then unceremoniously executed the transmit command with a quick click of her glove device. It was done in a millisecond. She felt a rush of heat and a momentary wish to hit the undo key to take it all back, but it was too late. There were no keys to undo this act.

Her hesitancy passed quickly when she remembered her humiliation at the hands of her ex-employer. She had taken all precautions necessary to prevent the virus from spreading beyond the intended target. The disabling of their Wide Area network to the outside world was the first task her virus performed. Linda believed in focusing her enmity on the party who had done her wrong, like drawing a bead on a hunted prey, not like some nuts, lashing out indiscriminately at any innocent bystander that happened to be walking by. She had no wish to harm anybody but the people who had tried to steal her work. That included anybody and everybody who worked at QuantumCorp. In her heart, in that part of her consciousness kept just below the surface, was the feeling that by unleashing the virus she was getting back at life itself.

The blueprint of the germ waited passively in the bowels of company's master Organic like an egg waiting for a sperm donor, while the virus to activate it flew through the Fiber, carried along on a beam of light, hurtling toward its target. On it flew, over city blocks and concrete highways, under streets in cavernous spaces, her message flashed through the intervening miles in microseconds, like a guided missile, unerring, unstoppable.

The package of instruction-carrying electrons arrived at the other end of the link, and surged through the communication ports of the host computer like germs invading a living organism, moving along the data pathways just like any other piece of information. It all came to rest in the belly of the organic machine, and began activating the genetic code embedded in its molecular chips.

Once lodged in the cells of the first Organic, each packet of instructions started copying itself along with the Pestis DNA to all the other Organics on the company's network. Then, as instructed, it went to work, using the soup of the computer to create the living germ.

There were so many places things could go wrong, so many false paths and detours to get lost in, so many potential points of error that could frustrate things that only a miracle or a mad genius could have pulled it off. Everything clicked into place like a fine-tuned drill team, however. Every requirement was met, every contingency thought of in advance. It all worked like a charm. One step after another in lock-step precision, the production of the Bubonic Plague took place in the bowels of the machines.

Throughout the next day, molecule by molecule, the tiny microbes were constructed, as strings of amino acids were linked to form the protein chains like the DNA of a living cell, to first create the nucleic acid, using the abundant phosphorus and other trace elements found in the machines, and then the watery cytoplasm that comprised the body of the single-celled microbe, until by the time people were beginning to come in for the day, the insides of every Organic computer in the company was crawling with germs. As people drank their coffees and stood at the water-cooler talking, thousands of the tiny creatures were squirming blindly around the insides of the machines, seeking warmth and nutrients, alive.

Slowly but surely, the germs worked their way down the circuits and pathways of the machines toward the light of the outside world. Out they groped, extending their pod-like membranes in front of them, searching for a home. Homes they would find, but these germs weren't destined for the fleas and rodents infesting the underworld of sewers and back alleys. No, they were destined for far better domiciles. They were going directly to the top of the food chain.

It wouldn't be long before the tiny invaders would have come into contact with human hosts - hands as they touched screens or clicked a key and rubbed tired eyes that had scanned output devices too close; human lips as they talked into microphones or touched infected hands or breathed the air circulated by fans and blowers.

The molecular computers would freeze up, having the effect of bringing even more humans nosing around, prying the insides of the bio-machines to see what was the matter. And as soon as these germs made contact with human skin and hair, they'd slither and slide into pores and crevices to invade the human bloodstream directly, without the need for any flea or rodent middleman. By then, many would be infected with the invisible microbe.

Everything went like clockwork, one incredibly complex series of instructions after another bringing together the precise components, at exactly the right time, flawlessly executed, to perfection. That is, all except for one small detail, a tiny timing problem hardly noticed in the complexity of the moment, but one which would have huge consequences for the future.

SALT SPRAY MOUNTAIN, JAMAICA, JULY 30, 10:00 PM

Peter Danvers sat with a few friends in the warm tropical night, under a wide canopy of stars. The crescent moon hung in the sky as if suspended by its two upturned tips. A large star – or was it a planet - hung next to the moon like a diminutive diamond.

Despite the happy mood of his guests, Stephen and a few of the guys from his rental shop, who were chatting away among themselves, Peter was flooded with memories and regrets, ranging from his failure as a businessman, to his failed marriage and deserted kids. This was happening more often lately. Always one to look forward, to the next experiment, the next discovery, he had never looked back, until recently. This past year had been an exception. It was the kind of soul-searching that's normal under the circumstances and not altogether un-healthy given his almost nervous breakdown of a year before. For the most part, he was convinced that his move to the islands was the only thing that had saved his sanity, his life for that matter. Sometimes, however, when memories of past happiness crowded out the memories of pain and disappointment, he wondered if what he had done had been for the best.

Images of his wife Sandy and the kids came unbidden to his mind. How had he come to this? How had he strayed so far from the dreams and aspirations of his youth? Whose dream was he living now?

As his mind wandered toward the past, another image intruded on his thoughts, the day of his Ph.D. dissertation, where the dream had begun.

It was warm day in May. Peter was late, running down the hallway toward the chamber where his doctorate dissertation was being held. His rapid footfalls clambered off the hardwood floor of the venerable building on the Charles River, at MIT, where he had spent the last five years of his life.

He arrived out of breath and disheveled, almost three minutes late, his light brown hair in his eyes, his face flushed. He was hot and sweating from his sprint across the campus. Pulling his sweater over his head, he flipped it onto the back of a chair and faced the table of distinguished and powerful academics, the wall he would have to scale this day if he wanted that coveted degree. They stared at him stonily. These five individuals held his uncertain future in their collective hands. To Peter, it felt as if they held something else of his on a meat hook.

His thesis advisor, Dr. Andy Turner, was there, on loan from his post at IBM's Watson Labs - his only friend among the pack of hungry wolves thirsting for his academic blood. Also present were the heads of the math, electrical engineering, chemical engineering, and AI departments, as well as a visiting professor from Stanford University. The young woman, whose name was Dr Linda Rayburn, was lecturing on some advanced subjects related to his topic of study and looking at Peter in a peculiar predatory way that he found a bit disturbing.

A few friends and interested observers sat in leisurely postures in chairs scattered across the rear of the room, spectators to the slaughter. His inquisitors began bombarding him with questions even before he had a chance to catch his breath and cool down. They were on him like piranha in a feeding frenzy, tearing at his thesis arguments like so much hamburger.

Peter's theory of molecular logic attempted to demonstrate the programming of a biological computing device, much like genetic code is programmed in the nucleus of a living cell, using structures such as proteins and amino acids. The application of biological functions in this way, to build a chemical computer whose working parts would be individual molecules, had long been a dream of computer scientists at the end of the century. Peter Danvers' theory of producing computations using DNA had the potential of moving the field forward by leaps and bounds. He demonstrated his thesis using the Traveling Salesman problem, a standard method employed in computer science to explain the concept of complexity.

"The goal of the Hamiltonian Path Problem, as it's formally known, is to find the shortest route that passes through all the cities in the game," explained Peter to the audience, so that even a sophomore could understand. "It's one of those NP-complete problems where the time to solve it increases prohibitively as the number of cities and paths increase."

Peter chose a simple arrangement of seven cities and thirteen connecting streets, which he drew on the board, representing each city chemically as a single strand of twenty base pairs of DNA, using four letters, A,T,G, and C, similar to the base-pairs of amino acids that make up a real molecule of DNA. He then showed how all the possible sequences for the strands could be represented, drawing his little strings of letters like alphabet worms on the board. Finally, he demonstrated how the partial overlapping of the twenty base strands representing the cities with their complements, denoted streets literally joining the cities together.

Peter explained, "As in nature, the letter C always pairs with G, and T always pairs with A, so that a given multi-city tour becomes a piece of double-stranded DNA, with the cities linked in a random order by the streets."

Through a series of equations, he went on to prove that if a few hundred trillion molecules were tossed together in a test-tube, they would naturally combine to make multiple copies of every possible path in the game, all in a blink of an eye. Of course, there was still the problem of recovering the answer. How was the shortest path visiting all the cities extracted from the jumble of all possible paths? While there were chemical techniques for doing this, developed a few years earlier at Stanford, there was no known programmatically-based method for dealing with trillion word pattern-matching problems. This is where Peter made his ingenious contribution to the puzzle, developing a genetic algorithm to do the job. He demonstrated how it worked.

"We first extract all the paths going from start to end, then of those, all the paths going through the seven cities. Next we isolate all those paths with seven different cities. Any paths left are the answers. Making use of the inherent parallelism in the process, this last task can be accomplished in linear time," Peter explained, finishing up the supporting formulas with a flourish of chalky symbols.

The room was silent. He could hear the sounds of the city intruding once again like a long forgotten song. The late afternoon sun filtered through the windows, giving the place a soft golden hue that reminded him of his many hours in the library while the rest of the university partied and played. Linda Rayburn, the visiting lecturer from Stanford, looked at Peter with an expression of surprise and admiration. Her thin eyebrows were arched over her wide brown eyes, her mouth slightly open in thought. She was seeing him in an entirely new light, and to Peter's discomfort, looking at him as if he were something edible. They thanked him and told him they'd let him know the results.

Forty minutes later, exhausted and drained, he dragged himself to his apartment on upper Commonwealth Ave in a daze. He had been living with Sandy for almost two years by this time. She worked as a waitress in a nightclub on Kenmore Square, and wouldn't be home until after two am. He fixed himself a supper of steak and eggs, and tried to read.

Unable to concentrate, he started pacing back and forth across his small living room, walking in time to the music of *Aerosmith*, blaring defiantly in the background. Going over each question, each answer and utterance, spoken and unspoken, during the four and a half hour ordeal, he looked for places he might have messed up, points he might have missed. Peter was a far cry from the older, happy-go-lucky man who would be sitting in his villa by the sea with his friends in Jamaica twenty years later.

His thoughts had been interrupted by a knock on the door. "Who could that be?" he wondered out loud, looking at the clock above the mantle, mildly annoyed. It was eleven-thirty in the evening and he wasn't expecting company. Sandy wouldn't be home for a couple of hours yet. Turning down the stereo, he went to the door and opened it. To his surprise, there with her pageboy haircut and her large brown eyes, was Professor Linda Rayburn, wearing the same predatory look on her face she'd had earlier that day.

"Hello, Peter," she said in a husky voice, handing him a bottle of red wine. "I wanted to be the first to congratulate you. Good job!"

LOS ANGELES, CALIFORNIA, JULY 31, 10:45 AM

Stan Bellows had just gotten off the phone with one of his suppliers. They had been promising the delivery of a breakthrough new quantum computer for the past year and a half, and he still hadn't seen hide-nor-hair of it. This latest excuse for a delay was the last straw. Breakthrough technology or not, if they didn't deliver something by the end of the month, he was having his lawyers tear up the contract. He had put his own reputation on the line, and he'd be damned if he was going to take the fall because of their incompetency. He fumed silently until his phone unit buzzed. He answered absentmindedly.

"Hello," he said, surprised to see his far eastern partner on the console display. "Feng, what can I do for you?"

China and the rest of Asia were scheduled to connect to the global fiber network a few months after the European link was established. The Chinese economy had grown by leaps and bounds in the first two decades of the new millennium. It was partly their tough trade and tariff policies that precipitated the trade-wars in the first place, a situation which helped them grow even more in the end. Not only were they the biggest market in the history of the world, their manufacturing and technical sectors had made them a super-power overnight, second only to the US. It was the massive influx of Chinese yen that made Stan such a dominate force in the global economy.

"How are things, my friend?" said the Chinese minister in clear, clipped, well-educated English. "I am getting a little concerned by the recent delay."

"Nothing serious, Feng. We're back on schedule. Just a momentary snag. We got the little bastards who tried to shut us down, couple of malcontents from Boston. We'll take care of them. Don't worry. By the time we're done with these saboteurs, people will think twice about messing with us."

"I am gratified to hear you have it all in hand, my friend. I did not doubt your ability to deal with this problem. That is why we joined you. I just want to make sure our mutual interests are well protected. I stand at your service."

34

"Thank you, Feng," said the chief executive of OptiComm. "We couldn't have come this far without your support. What we're about to do will change the world forever."

"Yes, let us hope that all mankind will benefit from our work."

By all mankind, of course, he meant himself and Bellows.

"The riots in New York are troubling," said Feng. "I hope this does not interfere with our plans."

Recently there had been severe rioting in the slums around the megacity, where huge shantytowns and cardboard villages had been erected to shelter the growing population of homeless from around the world. The teeming slums filled with garbage and human waste was more than anyone had bargained for with the opening of the borders after the trade-wars. Now Stan Bellows led the growing chorus of voices calling for stricter handling of the problem.

"The more trouble they cause, the easier it will be for us to get tougher new laws passed," stated Bellows. "They're playing right into our hands. All we need is another outbreak of typhus or dysentery, and we'll get the whole dammed mess cleaned up real quick."

"I hope so," said the mildly agitated Chinese official. "We would never allow such things to happen here." Despite China's open capitalistic economic system, it was still the most repressive society on the planet, where the accused were guilty until proven guilty.

"I don't see many people breaking down your doors trying to get in." He had meant it as a joke, but was sorry he said it as soon as the words left his mouth. Regardless of the fact that it was true, it may have offended someone who was critical to his success. Stan Bellows was not one to guard his words, however. Why should he, when he controlled a good part of the global economy?

The powerful minister of Science and Technology for the People's Republic stared back unperturbed, his polite smile never leaving his inscrutable face, as if he hadn't gotten the jab.

"Sorry," said Bellows, attempting a laugh. "I was thinking about those damn Indians and Africans."

"Your racist humor is patently American, my friend, but I think you are funny nonetheless. Just as long as you remember who your friends are."

They both laughed. "As one bastard to another, eh?" said Bellows between snorts.

"Yes, as one bastard to another," said Feng.

After a few more moments of mirth, Bellows spoke.

35

"The Democrats are lashing out at each other like a pack of hyenas. It's like Jimmy Carter all over again. The president's completely discredited and they can't find anyone to take his place. Burns and the Republicans are a shoe-in. The more trouble leading up to the elections the better it is for us. Trust me Feng, I can't say more at this time, but everything is going to plan."

"I have no doubt you are in control of things there, my friend. I just wanted to let you know personally that we are completely behind you. You have my fullest support."

"Thank you, Feng. I knew I could count on you."

With the FBI and SNA in his pocket, Bellows had little reason to fear eavesdropping or phone surveillance. Like J. Edgar Hoover back in the nineteen-fifties - even if he didn't dress in women's clothing - Bellows was the one who determined who got watched and who got arrested. The two would-be saboteurs caught recently in Boston weren't the first to feel the brunt of Stan Bellows' ire. Like Newton, who became a magistrate in the seventeenth century so that he could prosecute counterfeiters better while he ran the mint, Bellows had judicial authority in matters of computer crime and theft.

Things had turned out better than he could have imagined. His early huge investment in Organic technology and fiber-optics had paid off in spades, but it was the power that Bellows craved more than the money. The ease with which he acquired it had been the big surprise.

The whole country depended on his network and Organics for work and play, to entertain them, teach them, balance their checkbooks and pay their bills. Life without the new machines, which did not require anywhere near the electric and power requirements of a normal light bulb and released no pollutants into the air, was unthinkable. They were as efficient as they were clean, besides having quadrupled the computing capacity of the largest silicon based machines. No wonder Stan Bellows was so wealthy and powerful. The person who controlled this technology, controlled the country, and that was only the beginning. Knowledge was power in the twenty-first century and Stan controlled a good proportion of that knowledge.

As soon as his man Burns and the Republicans were elected, which seemed about as certain as these kinds of things can be, especially if the troubles in the slums kept flaring up during his opponent's watch - trouble he had more than a little to do with - there would be nothing to stand in his way. He had been planning this for a very long time, before his first fiber cable had been laid. Now the time had come to make it all pay off.

Soon all of Europe would be linked up to his massive network, under subsidiaries and licensees that he controlled. Soon after that, the world!

MINIMUM SECURITY FACILITY, BULGARIA, EASTERN EUROPE, JULY 31, 4:45 PM

Eddie Pavloski paced back and forth in his dorm room, waiting for a phone call from his agent. The warden had been particularly difficult these past few days, refusing to send Eddie's last disks to his publisher, until a portion of the profits had been directed to his own bank account, even though Eddie was doing it for charity.

"You're not fooling me, Pavloski," the Warden had said. "I know you've got access to those funds, no matter what you say."

The warden had been right, although Eddie would not have used his backdoor access to the funds unless it had been absolutely necessary. Now it seemed it was. Well, that was the price of doing business. Now the only thing that mattered was making his comeback. Timing was critical.

Since the hour a few days ago when he had finished the last piece of his virus, smuggled out of his prison cell hidden like pins in a haystack in the files of his memoirs, he had gone over every nuance of the problem in his head. Given half a bit of luck, it just might work.

His Trojan-horse worm, once unleashed unwittingly by his publisher, would propagate through the Fiber looking for any Organics to infect. When it found one, it would alter the cellular rules of the molecular machine, turning its well-ordered sequence of genetic operations into a chaotic mess. But none of his plan would work if the last piece of code wasn't delivered on time. Thus his agitation as he paced back and forth in the confined space.

"Pavloski!" yelled a guard from the open doorway. "The warden says you can have your phone call. You've got twenty minutes."

He threw the cell phone onto Eddie's cot, and stood waiting a short distance down the hall.

Eddie punched the dial key to call the pre-programmed number of his agent. After a few rings, a suave voice answered in English.

37

"Hi, Eddie, is that really you? My God, I was beginning to wonder what happened to you. I haven't heard from you in days. How are things going in there?"

"Could be worse," said Eddie, not willing to divulge his real thoughts, knowing his conversation was more than likely being listened to. "The warden just released the last disk. The publisher should get it by tomorrow."

"Good! About time," replied his agent, glad the project was finally completed and he would be getting his commission. "Say Eddie, I been meaning to talk to you about your book."

"Yes," said Eddie, feigning interest.

"Well, the publisher is a bit disappointed. They were expecting a little more, er, I don't know, something more revealing. They're not sure they can sell it the way it is."

"Tell them with my name on it the thing will sell itself. I'm famous, remember, public enemy number one. A good Polish boy gone bad, one lone hacker against the world, it's a great story. What's their problem?"

"Well, they're having second thoughts."

"Tell them the last chapters are the best. I make some very interesting predictions that are sure to intrigue them."

"I hope so. I'd hate to have gone this far only to have the whole thing fall through."

"Don't worry. Just make sure they get them, OK?"

"Sure. Will do," answered his agent, unaware that as soon as they did so, Eddie's virus would be propagated through the network and begin to infect the Organics, shutting them down one by one like so many illegal whore houses. "How are they treating you?"

"Oh, just fine," said Eddie. "If you call dodging large, hairy Russians in the shower a good time."

His agent didn't laugh, and after an embarrassing silence filled him in on the latest news from the outside.

"All everyone's talking about is the upcoming link up with the US. It'll be the largest, fastest network of supercomputers in history, all at your fingertips."

"We'll see," replied Eddie cryptically. "Did you take care of that other matter I asked you about?"

"Yes," said the agent, not liking in the least his involvement in an illegal financial transaction. "I'd just as soon not know anything more about it."

"Good," said Eddie, clicking off the phone.

Lying back in his cot, with his bare arms flung over his head, Eddie smiled as if he had just had sex. Everything was working as planned. A few more hours and his final disk would be delivered and processed. Then it would just be a matter of time. All he had to do was lie back and wait.

As he thought about his comeback, Eddie could hardly contain himself. If he pulled this off, it would be the greatest feat in hacker history, a supreme demonstration of his skill. Only a handful of people could have done it even under the best of conditions, but to do it from his cell, watched like a bird in a cage, well, that was something else entirely. Too bad the world would never know, at least not for a very long time.

The complexity of his program, written in the language of the living cell, was staggering, designed to attack each layer of the Organics in turn, opportunistically looking for weaknesses as it unraveled itself. From the hybrid communication ports, to the internal cellular arrays, it would spread, until the nucleus itself would be infected, the innermost heart of the cell. And in that deepest level of his virus, weaved into the code like a stitch in time, stood his calling card, emblazoned like a gold tablet in stone

He closed his eyes and calmed his breathing. There would be plenty of time to gloat. For now he just had to wait and see what happened. Then he thought about the possible repercussions of his actions, a thought he had been able to somehow put off until now, until after the deed was done.

The smile left his handsome, bearded face as quickly as it appeared. He sat up suddenly. Standing, he went to his small desk and opened the ancient laptop, checking the system yet one more time for any trace of his recent activity, purged the day he had sent out the final disk. Of course, the only way to completely clean up after himself would be to restore the system to its original state, resetting it to the way it was when it came out of the box twenty-five years ago, but Eddie didn't have the means to do this. He'd have to figure out another way. Opening up a search program, he started typing furiously in the language of the universal browser

"Doing some last minute work there, Pavloski?" the warden's voice said directly behind him. Eddie jumped in surprise. "What are you doing?"

"Nothing, sir," said Eddie, gaining his composure in a heartbeat. "Just making a few last minute corrections on the manuscript."

"I thought you said you were finished?" said the Warden, a little piqued.

"I am, but my agent said the publisher wanted a few things changed. You know how they are. I was just typing it up when you came in."

"We had an agreement, Mister Pavloski. I'm afraid I can't accommodate you on this one. The court said you could have a computer to write your, er, your confessions, six months or ten disks, whichever came first. Your time is up. I'm afraid you'll have to go back to court if you want to change the contract, and well, Mister Pavloski, you've already had your day in court. I'm going to have to confiscate that machine. There are a lot of other deserving inmates who have a right to use it. It's not fair you hogging it all this time."

"Didn't you get my payment, the fifty thousand dollars I had my agent wire you? I just talked to him." Eddie said these words in a whisper so that only the warden could hear.

"Yes, that's all taken care of, thank you," said the warden, having Eddie right where he wanted him. If he could get that much money from him so easily, who knew how much he could make if he really tightened the screws. "But I hope you don't think that gives you the right to keep that computer longer than the court allotted time."

"OK," said Eddie. "Have it your way. It's no skin off my nose."

The ease with which the warden, who had expected a scene, had gotten Eddie to give up his beloved computer, gave the prison official some pause. Turning to one of the two guards accompanying him, he spoke a few words of command.

"Bring me the restore disk for this machine. It's the master disk in the lab. Ivan knows where it is."

The guard turned and hurried down the hallway to obey his commander's orders.

"What are you going to do?" asked Eddie, with a feigned concerned.

"You don't think I'm going to carry that thing out of here and plug it back into the prison network where it belongs without cleaning it up, do you? I'd just as soon release the plague."

"But warden, that has the only other copy of my manuscript outside of the disks. If anything happens to them, the whole thing will be lost."

"That's not my worry, Pavloski. My problem is to make sure you don't cause any damage to the outside world, and I intend to do just that."

Eddie's search for any incriminating evidence he may have left behind, which he had initiated on the tiny PC only seconds before the warden intruded into his privacy, had finally completed. There on the screen was his calling card, the string of characters that spelled out his handle, as it had been left in the belly of his Trojan-horse virus, displayed for the world to see.

Somehow missed during his final attempt to clean up the machine, it had been hidden in an operating system init file. The only way to remove it permanently would be to completely restore the system. He held his breath as he shut down the computer.

"Help yourself," he said as he did so. "But if you think you're getting any more money out of me you're crazy. I'm not going to let you rob people who already have nothing. The rest of the money is going to the orphan relief fund, as the court stipulated."

"Whatever you say, Mister Pavloski," smirked the warden, his keeper and his curse.

Eddie watched impassively as they inserted the CD and restored the system to its pristine state, completely erasing every last bit of Eddie's activity. He breathed a sigh of relief as the final set of screens finished displaying.

"Don't blame me if my publisher sues you," he said, barely able to suppress his jubilation, as they ceremoniously carried the computer out of his room, completing the task he had been unable to do himself. "Thank you very much, jackass," he muttered under his breath as they departed.

Eddie lay back down in his cot with his face to the wall as if bummed-out at losing his computer. The smile on his face, however, looked anything but sad. Eddie, the *Great Enigma*, Pavloski was about to strike again.

CHAPTER 3

HARVARD, MASSACHUSETTS, AUGUST 1, 2036, 11:22 AM

Sandy Danvers stood on the front steps of her large rural home rereading the postcard from her ex-husband. The smell of pine trees permeated the clear morning air. She was steamed as usual when it came to anything concerning her ex-spouse, the schmuck she had put through graduate school; the jerk she had sacrificed her own promising career for; the selfish ingrate she had wasted away her youth for; so he could spend all his time - days and nights, weekdays and weekends, holidays and birthdays - at the office and the lab, away from his family.

Sandy Danvers' mood stood in deep contrast to the serenity and beauty of the green New England landscape around her.

"If he thinks he can pull that crap on me, he's sorely mistaken, no matter what god-forsaken piece of earth he tries to disappear on," she raged out loud. His excuse for why he couldn't wire the money was pitiful. "In this day and age, whoever heard of not being able to transfer money because the telephone lines were down? Telephones! Where the hell is he, in the middle of New Guinea or something?"

She stood there tapping her foot angrily while her two daughters played in the expansive yard that fronted their three-story, brown Colonia. She was tempted to crumple the card up and throw it away, but thought better of it, deciding to show it to her lawyer, good old Fred, instead.

Stomping inside, she called the girls impatiently to come in and get ready for supper. Today was the housekeeper's day off. They would have to do with some frozen dinners, better than the regurgitated leftovers Anita served.

"If we could get some more money from that cheapskate father of yours, we could get a real cook," she said under her breath as she watched the two girls traipse past her into the house.

"What'd ya say, mommy?" asked Melissa, the youngest at seven, two years younger than her sister Abigail.

"Oh, nothing, sweetie. Go get ready for lunch. I was just thinking out loud," she answered distractedly, as she reread the postcard for the third time.

While the girls were upstairs cleaning up for dinner, Sandy went to her office off the kitchen.

"On," she said as if speaking to the wall. Immediately, her OptiComm unit sprang to life. The video console sitting above her desk connected to a central unit located in the living room, which combined TV, DVD player, computer, video arcade, and telephone services all within a single framework. Through a box attached to the side of the house it was linked via fiber-optic cable to the Worldwide Telecommunication network.

"Computer on," she said in a commanding tone, as if she were disciplining one of her children.

"Computer on," an automated voice echoed back in a flat, emotionless tone, lacking that subtle change of pitch - caused by slight alternations in the position of tongue, lips and mouth - that humans color their spoken words with.

Sandy hated to type even more than she hated pointing devices. The only machines she would use were ones she could command in a loud, imperious voice. It was ironic that someone who disliked computers so much would decide to live with a person whose whole life revolved around them. She sighed to herself. They did have their good points, like generating the wealth that made all this luxury around her possible.

Sandy, like most upper-middle class housewives in the third decade of the twenty-first century, could activate any appliance in the home by voice, not to mention the lights, thermostat, and doors. In most cases, the appliances responded back with polite acknowledgements. Some, like the coffee-maker, even greeted her in the morning when she spoke them on.

"Application menu," she commanded, directing her statements at the microphone hidden in the voice activation unit of the console, even though it was not necessary to speak directly into the highly sensitive device.

"Household Bills," she announced after perusing the menu for a few moments. Immediately, the window for the Electronic Billing system appeared on the 52-inch, flat plasma screen. When she spoke the words, "Auto Checking", an electronic checkbook appeared on the bottom right-hand portion of the window, complete with blank checks.

Sandy called up the appropriate displays, speaking slowing and distinctly into the screen. As she did, the software embedded in the speech recognition unit translated her spoken commands into the appropriate set of statements in the computer's memory. Since Sandy's service did not include continuous speech recognition, her unit did not understand full-blown conversational speech, but only those commands needed to interact with the operating system and the software products and applications layered on it, mostly menu selections and button options, some of which invoked remote network services. That was enough to get the job done.

She went through the list of unpaid bills, each one automatically marked paid when she wrote out a check for it using her graphic checkbook editor, which also debited her checking account balance, a running total of which was displayed on the screen. When she spoke the command, "Send", and answered, "Yes" at the confirmation, the funds would be transferred from her bank to the payee.

In spite of the fact that she had been very selective in her bill paying, there was still not enough money in her account to cover all the expenses. With her balance flashing red and warning messages popping up all over, it was obvious she had overdrawn. Hastily, she brought up her daughters' college fund accounts, only to find she had already borrowed substantially from these. No money here she thought, feeling the panic rise in her gorge. She would have to get more cash somehow and fast, before next month.

Sandy had spent prodigiously over the past year and a half, traveling to expensive resorts, shopping at the most exclusive stores, gathering up jewels like they were seashells on a beach. This, together with her many unwise investment schemes, some of which were downright hare-brained, which she had gone into in the vain attempt to generate the wealth she felt she was entitled to, only worsened the downward spiral. She just wasn't making it with what her ex-husband had given her. Why did that jerk have to up and leave like that, she asked herself for the hundredth time.

She called up display after display, looking for some way to make ends meet, analyzing options, tradeoffs, doing what-ifs, but it didn't take a quantum physicist to understand the results being displayed through the graphs and charts. Her expenditures far outstripped her income. She couldn't afford to continue like this for much longer. She could always sell the summerhouse, live cheaper, get a job to try and make ends meet. But these prospects filled Sandy Danvers with dread and loathing.

Reluctantly, she called up the Travel Consultant option from the Service menu and connected to the on-line Worldwide Airline

Reservation system. Pulling up her reservation to Majorca, Spain, she sat staring at the picture-postcard display. Choosing 'demo', she watched as the screen presented a slide-show of the island, while from her stereo speakers a commentator with a deep Latin accent extolled the virtues of the scenic paradise to the lush background music of Spanish guitars. Sandy sighed as she spoke the commands that would cancel the trip she had been planning with her friend Joanne for a year. Joanne may be a royal pain in the neck, but she attracted men like flies. Too bad but she just couldn't afford to go. The $25,000 refund would be deposited back into her account by the end of the day. At least that's what she hoped, but the tour companies could be a real pain in the butt when it came to refunds. Canceling her trip was the last straw. This was war, and Sandy was determined to use whatever weapons she had at her disposal to win.

She was busy working on the monitor when Melissa, the seven year-old, walked in wearing her new blue party dress.

"What are you doing? Take that dress off immediately!" she ordered.

Instantly, the entire OptiComm unit shut itself off, turning the picture on her display screen into a tiny white dot.

"Oh crap!" she shouted in exasperation.

Telling her oldest to get her younger sibling out of the party dress and into a clean set of play-clothes, Sandy activated the OptiComm unit yet again and called up the Phone Utility – after first giving the fake oak-paneled cabinet housing the unit a sharp kick. The machine wheezed and banged as if complaining about being hit, and took a long time to get going again after the sudden shutdown. She'd have to call the service company and have it checked. The last thing she needed was her OptiComm to conk out on her.

In her extremity she decided to call Todd Daniels, an old friend and business associate of her husband's. He always did want to get into her pants again after the one night stand that cost Sandy her marriage. Now he just might be able to make up for all the trouble he caused. Before she called him, she went to her room and hurriedly changed into a light, see-through summer dress. The air was a bit cool for such flimsy material but it would serve its purpose nicely, thanks to the wonders of videophones.

Back at the console, she selected the number from a virtual Rolodex display, which was immediately dialed by the system. At the first ring, her automated downstairs vacuum-bot rolled into the room on its twenty-four hour a day search for dirt and dust, making a whirring, chattering noise as it crossed the floor.

"Out!" she yelled at the time-saving contrivance. "Get out of this room!"

The small, round robot, activated by the loud tone of her voice, bumped into walls and furniture in its haste to vacate the premises.

Quickly viewing herself on the monitor as the phone-unit rang a third time, she checked her image on the screen. A lithe figure returned her gaze, her slim, tanned body peeking through the white material of the dress. Her black bra and panties only vaguely visible, showed a faint promise of things to come. A well-shaped head of golden-blond hair topped a pretty face. Yes, she thought, he didn't have a chance.

The connection made, another image filled the screen, a masculine form with dark, wavy hair and a mustache, framed by a youthful, tanned face, out of which looked two admiring brown eyes. The light-blue sports shirt he wore showed off his broad shoulders and well-developed chest. He had an unmistakable air of sophistication about him, the practiced charm of a politician or movie star.

Todd Daniels smiled brightly as he recognized his caller, and stared boldly at her image with obvious pleasure. The smile Sandy Danvers flashed back at him across the miles of cable curled his toes.

Todd Daniels was not only her husband's ex-partner, he had taken over the business on Peter's departure - and if he'd had his way he would have taken over Peter's bed as well. From the very beginning, Todd had paid special attention to Peter's vivacious wife. Things finally came to a climax at a Christmas party she and Peter attended at a friend's house in Harvard. Todd spent the whole evening on the couch talking animatedly to Sandy, who was ignoring everyone else in the room, much to Peter's annoyance. Todd drove her home from the party after her husband had been obliged to remain. She was feeling exceedingly good that night, high on vodka gimlets, in her new sleek, low-cut black dress, and had been exceptionally miffed at her husband, for what she couldn't even remember afterward. One thing led to another and before she knew it, she was naked on the couch with Todd's tongue probing every inch of her body. By the time her unfortunate husband walked through the front door - the children were visiting her sister Kathy - she was riding the stud like a cowboy on an unbroken filly, having the orgasm of her life.

Of course, as enjoyable as her little romp had been, it was hardly worth the trouble that it caused; the heated arguments and violent recriminations; the painful separation and divorce; the guilt and anguish at screwing up her marriage and losing the father of her children. She was soon on her feet again, however. She had been good and faithful until that incident. It was only one time. Why did Peter have to react so stupidly and blow the whole thing out of proportion? So she crucified him in the divorce settlement, not that he contested any of it.

If Todd wanted to step into Peter's shoes, why not let him, she reasoned. After all, he was better than most of the flesh-bags she'd been sleeping with recently, including her useless lawyer, Fred.

Peter Danvers had left the bulk of his considerable estate in the hands of his life-long friend, ex-roommate, and lawyer, Fred Peterson. Fred had power of attorney and was also occasionally bonking Sandy - after all, he had gone out with her first. In spite of her infidelity, Sandy got both houses - together worth several million dollars - and a substantial lump sum settlement of a million and a half, which she proceeded to exhaust in less than two years. He also provided a large monthly stipend for both of his daughters, in addition to a substantial college fund. Sandy Danvers, however, felt cheated, deprived all the years of pampering and luxuries she had so looked forward to, of all the promises she had made to herself. The settlement was not nearly enough. She thought herself and her children robbed of their future.

Not that she didn't have her share of the good life for the last sixteen years, trips, furs, diamonds, big cars, and homes, but it had always seemed only the preliminaries, not the final prize, which always loomed just outside her reach, a greener pasture forever ahead, that once obtained seemed pale next to the one further on. Now it was gone forever, slipped between her fingers like a wet jar, just when things were finally starting to get good.

"Hello, Sandy. To what do I owe this singular pleasure?" Todd said in his smooth, husky voice.

"Todd, I was just thinking about you. Wanna have sex?"

QUANTUMCORP COMPUTER ROOM, PALO ALTO, CALIFORNIA, AUGUST 3, 4:50 PM

Ted Samasoto, lead field-tech for OptiComm, checked the molecular boards of the intelligent network hub, a large, special-purpose, hybrid computing device that managed the connection between QuantumCorp's Organic computer banks and the global fiber-optic network to the outside world.

He had never seen anything quite like this before. Cellular chips exploded as if from the inside, boards and chemical circuits seized and covered with a gooey substance, and no explainable cause. He scratched his head in perplexity and took another reading.

This was all he needed. The European link about to go on-line and this bull-crap starts to hit the fan. Of course, now that the Fiber had gone live, it's the first thing they think of when things go wrong. By the looks of it, though, whatever caused the disruption had come from within the local environment, from the Organics, not the network.

He pulled out the bad boards, with their jelly-like components, and replaced them with new ones, doing the same with the various molecular relays that the network hubs utilized, which unplugged like Lego blocks. Ted wore gloves, for contaminants were easy to transmit through hand contact. But the gloves he wore weren't meant to protect the wearer against microscopic organisms, only the organic computer against dust and body oils. He pulled out a few modules and plugged in others. It was something any idiot could have done. The idiot they had sent on this call, however, was a senior technician who had worked together with Ted when they had first joined the company almost twenty years before. When he saw the strange symptoms at the customer's site, he called his old friend Ted Samasoto, head of Field Service, immediately.

Ted looked up at the group of technicians and scientists crowding around him as he worked.

"Looks like something from inside, maybe a corrupted Organic. You say your network went down on the morning of the thirty-first?"

"Yeah," answered Andy Beckman, fresh from his run-in with Walter Townsend, the ECO of QuantumCorp, Linda Rayburn's old company. "What'd ya mean from inside? It can't be from inside. Don't try to tell me it's from inside."

"Something closed all the ports and shut down the net. All the bio-circuits in the hub have been damaged. Only an Organic could cause something like that." Ted spoke with quiet assurance. "I've traced it to this machine here," he went on, pointing to a node on the schemata displayed on his network console. "Looks like an overload, maybe caused by a run-away processor, which in turn could have been caused by the network being shut down. I'd say you have an internal problem, not a virus."

"It's not internal. Someone hit us with a virus," answered Beckman, ready for this one. "It's gotta be the goddamn Fiber."

"That's impossible. It's not the network. The WAN checks out. There's no trace of anything coming in from the outside. The ports and input channels are clean. It's just your local hub that's affected. It's got to be the Organics," said a perplexed Samasoto.

Although the OptiComm field tech was right, the system had been attacked from within, he had no idea of the extent of the horror hidden before him.

"Don't worry about our Organics," said Beckman. "Just get the network going again. How long before you replace those parts?"

"We should have you operational by the end of the day, by six at the latest. I'm not making any promises, though. With Organics, anything can happen. I'd like to know what caused this myself."

"You and me both," answered the haggard head of the computer department, where all the garbage seemed to flow. "I tried to tell them something like this might happen, but they wouldn't listen to me. Andy, get me this software. Andy, my desktop doesn't work. Andy, I need access to this file from home. Andy, wipe my ass. But when I really try to do my job and run their systems the way they're supposed to be run, all I get is abuse."

A few of the technicians who had heard it all before, left the clean room snickering. Ted Samasoto went back to work, replacing burnt out circuits in the back of the Organic hub. It was late in the afternoon. He would now have to deal with rush hour traffic on the freeway, still a nightmare despite forty years and billions of dollars spent on automated highway systems and public transportation. He blocked out the incessant whining of the fat little administrator and concentrated on the problem at hand.

If there was a new bug out there, it was even more important to get the Organics operational again so that the necessary analysis could be performed. In a way, he knew how Andy Beckman felt, for he too had tried to warn his superiors that implementing the worldwide fiber-optic network with fully functional Organics was total folly. They were opening themselves up to all sorts of unknown and unforeseen problems. Much more testing and research was needed to ensure a safe and well-understood system. Of course, no one, least of all his superiors at Global OptiComm, wanted to hear any words of caution.

As the employees of QuantumCorp worked through the day, unseen, unfelt, unsuspected, the tiny bacillus that were already on their hands and faces and clothing and hair, made their way into any openings they could find, mouths, noses, ears, and eyes, pores and mucus membranes, seeking nutrients and nesting places, silently, irresistibly groping toward the light.

SAN JOSE, CALIFORNIA, AUGUST 3, 5:30 PM

Deb Murphy, research assistant turned project leader for the QuantumCorp computing lab, had all she could do just to get home to bed, even with the help of an auto-pilot capable car and her doorman.

Deb had always been the healthy one in her family. Vibrant and full of life at twenty-seven, she was in excellent shape, as her tight thighs and slim waist attested. Today she felt like death warmed over.

She was feeling normal enough this morning when she arrived on the job, bright and early at 7:00 am, to work on the Rayburn project so it would be ready in time for Mr. Winters' meeting, only to have the system conk-out on her after half an hour. She had been able to download most of the necessary information and continue working on her office Organic, but by 2:30 in the afternoon she started to feel ill, just a scratchy throat at first, then coughing and chest pain. By 3:15 she felt so bad she asked permission to go home. It felt like a good case of the flu. Well, she knew how to take care of that.

As soon as she got home, she called her doctor and got a prescription for some antibiotics. He diagnosed her over the video-monitor. After all, he'd been treating her since she was a child and had seen hundreds of cases of the flu over the past few months. Modern anti-viral drugs, which arrived within a half-hour from the pharmacy in her high-rise, would make short thrift of any flu bug.

Before putting on her flannel pajamas, she made herself a hot concoction of tea, lemon, ginseng, vitamin C, and honey, together with a generous helping of brandy, an old family recipe that was sure to cure what ailed you. It had always worked before. She had every confidence it would do so again.

Just as she was getting into bed, feeling weak and drained, the phone system rang. She activated it with the remote control unit from her bed, and yelled in a weak voice across the room to the image appearing on the bedroom console's monitor. It was her boss, that proverbial twit, Jack Veldt.

"Hi, Debbie, how you feeling?" he said, ignoring her alarming appearance. "They told me you'd gone home sick. I was just concerned and thought I'd call."

That's a laugh, she thought to herself, as she laboriously pulled on a thin bathrobe and walked unsteadily to the video-unit. "That's very thoughtful of you, Jack. I must have caught a dose of the flu. It came on pretty quick."

"Well, that's not good. Have you called a doctor?" he asked, feigning concern.

"Yes, he prescribed some new super-antiviral thing. I just took some. As a matter of fact, I thought you might be the doctor. He said he'd call back."

Now that she had moved closer to the camera, her appearance was even more alarming. Her eyes were sunken and bloodshot, her skin sallow and blotchy, her voice husky and congested. She looked as if she could hardly stand, as she grasped the back of a chair for support.

Ignoring her dreadful state, he went on. "I just came out of a meeting with Jeffrey. He was really concerned with the project results, very disappointed we didn't have them ready for his staff meeting. I was wondering...?"

"Have they fixed the computers yet?" Debby asked, anticipating his next question.

"Er, no, but we're making the backup system operational. It should be all set in a short while."

"Well, there's no sense me coming in until the system's up. Anyway, I feel lousy. I don't think I'd be much good to you, I can barely see straight."

She started coughing violently. Unable to stop, she turned away from the screen, covering her mouth with both hands. Embarrassed, the persistent manager of the research lab waited for her to recover. She barely made it to her bed without collapsing, and grabbed some Kleenex to wipe her mouth and teary eyes. She had never felt this bad before. Her chest felt as if it were on fire. Her throat was so constricted that she could hardly breathe. She was on the verge of passing out.

Jack Veldt tried to continue with his pre-composed speech. He prided himself on his persuasiveness, a combination of charm, good looks, psychology, and threats, but he was cut off in mid-sentence.

"I'm sorry, Jack. Tell Jeffery I don't feel so well," she managed to croak out. "I'm going to call my doctor. I think I've got pneumonia or something. I'm going to have to call you back. Bye."

With that she disconnected the line and tried to get her doctor back. His answering service said he had left for the day and took a message. She lay back down and tried to rest, but was feeling worse by the minute. Her breathing became more difficult and labored, the pain in her joints and neck more acute. She was long past being worried it might be something more than the flu.

Tossing and turning this way and that, she tried to get comfortable, but no position was good for more than a few moments before she was forced to move again. She was sweating profusely, her breath coming in labored pants. Her eyes seemed glued shut in their throbbing sockets. By the time the phone-unit rang again, she was breathing in shrieks, forcing air down her aching lungs, making them work by sheer willpower, as less and less oxygen reached them.

She tried to sit up and answer the voice activation unit, but was unable to move or utter a sound. She groped desperately for the remote control, which lay at the foot of the bed, but it might as well have been ten miles away. It was as if her arms and body weighed a hundred tons. Her chest heaved with the effort.

She fought for air, her once pretty face horribly contorted and covered with tears, snot, and spittle. The effort to answer the incoming call had gained her nothing but more coughing spasms, this time accompanied with the vomiting of a thick, black, bile-like substance that filled her with disgust. The smell was so bad it made her retch again and again. Filled with an overwhelming terror, she shrieked repeatedly, arching her spine in agony. No air was getting down her constricted windpipe.

Bouncing on the bed, her back arched like a levitating psychic, the young scientist's body contorted with pain. Tearing at her clothes in her misery, she ripped off her pajama top. All thoughts of the buzzing phone-unit were forgotten, all memory of quantum physics research projects obliterated in the single, all consuming need to draw just one more breath.

With effort akin to scaling Mount Everest, she raised her head and opened her eyes. The room spun and turned as she mouthed the air like a dying fish. Her hands grasped the bed sheets to keep her from falling off, as it seemed to toss about like a raft in a stormy sea. Her finely tuned muscles were rigid with tension, flexed isometrically as if straining against a great weight. She died like this, terrified and alone, with her pelvis arched toward the ceiling as if it were a lover.

Walter Townsend, CEO of QuantumCorp, let the phone ring a few more times before disconnecting the line. He would have to send security to pick her up.

"If I need to, I'll bring her here in an ambulance," he vowed to his subordinate.

Jeffery Winters, the head of research, had no doubt that Deb Murphy would be here within the hour, dead or alive.

CHAPTER 4

SALT SPRAY MOUNTAIN, JAMAICA, AUGUST 7, 2036, 8:45 AM

After weeks of rain, the sun was finally out, bathing the wet landscape with much needed warmth. After many days of trying, Peter had finally gotten through to his wife.

"Hi, Sandy. It's Peter. I'm calling from Jamaica. How are things going?" he yelled over the static.

"Yes, Peter, hi. Good. I can hardly hear you. God, are you hard to get hold of. I've been trying for weeks, and now when I finally do hear from you, it's on a bad connection."

"Yeah, I've been trying to get hold of you too. I don't have a computer and the lines can get really bad here, especially during the rainy season. Did you get my letters? Why didn't you write?"

"Write? Letters? You mean those hand scribbled hieroglyphics you call communication?"

Peter could tell by the strident tone of her voice that it was going to be a bumpy conversation.

"Peter, what's happened to you? You used to be such a forward-looking person, always thinking of how to make life easier for people. Now look at you, still using pencil and paper. Why don't you get with it and live in a normal place like everyone else, so people can get hold of you when they need to? I'm really having a tough time here, bringing up your two children, you know."

"Yes, I know Sandy. I'm making arrangements to take care of that now. As soon as I get off the phone with you, I'm calling Fred. We'll have the necessary paperwork releasing the first batch of stock options to you by next month. They'll be worth, oh, between one fifty to two hundred thousand."

"How am I supposed to live on that?" she yelled. "That's not nearly enough. I don't know what things are like on the islands these days, but it's damn expensive living here in the States. I'll hardly be able to make ends meet with that."

"Well, you'd better learn," he said, hearing a complaint he was only too familiar with. "There isn't a limitless supply for you to dip into whenever you want. Once it's gone, that's it, there won't be any more.

Besides, I don't know what your problem is. I gave you more money than most families see in a lifetime. It shouldn't be that hard to get by comfortably on. No, that's the best I can do, take it or leave it. I don't have to give you anything more. We settled our affairs a year and a half ago. Since then you've managed to spend more money than we spent in all our previous years of living together. This is it Sandy, don't push it."

Peter Danvers seldom raised his voice, but when he did, his wife knew he meant business.

"I need $50,000 by next week. I can't possibly wait until September."

"I don't have $50,000 to give you, and even if I did, I couldn't get it to you by next week. You should have planned better. You'll have to wait for the stock options. Borrow the money in the meantime if you have to."

"Peter, how can you be so mean to your own children? What am I supposed to tell the girls? They're already a laughing stock at school because they had to wear last year's wardrobe. You just don't give a damn, do you Peter, that your little girls are going without?"

"That's not fair. They shouldn't have to go without. I'm paying $4000 a month child support. I left you millions, both houses, what the hell more do you want?"

"Don't you care what we're going through? Don't you care about their future?"

"We've been through all this. They have their trust funds and college funds, they'll be OK. You haven't touched those have you?" he asked, his voice rising with nervous concern.

"Don't worry, Peter, but we'll do what we have to, to survive. Now are you going to help us or not?"

"OK, I'll see if I can't have Fred sell some of my other investments, but fifteen or twenty grand is the best I can do."

"OK. It's not nearly enough, but every bit helps. Thanks."

Peter sighed audibly. "Sometimes I think all you ever cared about was the money."

"What do you mean by that?"

"Well, you haven't so much as asked me how I am. All you care about is where your next fifty thousand is coming from. I don't think you ever really cared about me." Peter felt her attacks were unjust, especially about him not caring about what happened to his daughters.

"Well, *excuse* me!" she said, in an exaggerated tone. "I was so busy trying to take care of our two children, who you so callously left, I forgot to ask his royal highness how he was doing. So how you doing, big shot? Are you getting enough dope and beer there on the beach? Huh? Getting laid enough are we, big guy?" Once she started to speak her mind, after weeks of frustrating silence, the flood-dam of pent-up emotion gave way to a torrent of anger and resentment.

"Come on, Sandy, there's no need to get nasty." Peter was sorry for the argument. He had only wanted to make her happy, and had actually been looking forward to hearing her voice.

"No, there's no reason to get upset. Just the fact you ruined my life and the lives of your two little girls, that's all." She was obviously crying at this point, but then she always had been good at this.

"That's nonsense, Sandy, and you know it. If anybody's ruined anything it was you," he said, sorry as soon as the words left his mouth

"I'm not the one who left!" she screamed. "I'm not the one who deserted his family, neglected his kids, ignored his friends. Do you know what people are saying about you? Do you Peter?"

"No," he said weakly. "And I don't care."

"Well, you better care, because your daughters have to grow up hearing it. They're saying you're crazy. You should've been institutionalized. They think you have a mental problem, Peter."

"Like who, that little weasel Todd Daniels?"

"You leave Todd out of this!" she demanded, as if the telephone were a bullhorn and Peter a holed-up kidnaper.

There was a long, hostile silence, as both parties were lost in angry thoughts.

Peter broke the ice, taking a surprising and risky gambit. "Say, why don't you come down? Bring the girls. You sound like you could use a vacation."

"If I take a vacation it won't be with you and it certainly won't be with a couple of screaming kids."

"Hey, if that's the way you feel, I'll be glad to take them off your hands," he said angrily, giving up trying to appease her.

"That'll be the day," she fired back. "You'd have them living on fish and beer and sleeping in a shack. Do you want your daughters to grow up like that?"

"I don't know, maybe it wouldn't be such a bad idea. They might grow up to appreciate life a little rather than going through it thinking it's one big shopping spree. Anyway, I have my rights. I'll see them whenever I want."

"So come up and see them, Mister Mom. Like you'd ever live up to your responsibilities. They'd be brought up by wolves if you had your way. I'll see you in hell before you get my little girls." She was getting downright hysterical now.

"Calm down, Sandy. No one's going to take the girls from you. I agree, they're better off with you and I'm doing everything reasonable to take care of you all."

Again there was a heavy silence, again broken by Peter.

"How are the girls, anyway?" he asked.

"They're fine, no thanks to you," responded Sandy relentlessly.

Another silence, this one even heavier with venom.

"Hey, I didn't mean to upset you," he said finally.

"Well, you did."

"Sorry. Can we at least part as friends?"

"I'll be expecting the money by the end of the month."

"Can I talk to the girls?" he asked hopefully.

"They're not here right now. I'll have them write to you. Maybe I can find an old ink pen in the attic. Bye," she said, disconnecting the line before he had time to respond.

Peter banged the receiver down, fuming at his ex-wife's behavior. He only had to talk to her ten minutes to be reminded why he had left. He had a good mind to call her back and cancel the whole stock transaction but decided against it. That would only hurt the girls. Anyway, he had enough troubles without his irate ex-wife trying to sabotage him behind his back. He hoped naively that his daughters would get the benefit of the money, and worried that his wife had already broken into the college funds he had set up for them. He would have to check into that.

Making a drink, he tried to calm himself, as he placed another call, this one to his attorney and old roommate, Fred Peterson. It was now almost nine o'clock in the morning. Peterson's secretary answered the phone, and after a few moments Peter heard his friend's booming voice on the other end of the line.

"Peter, how the hell are you? I was wondering when you'd get around to calling us from that deserted island of yours. How's everything hanging?"

"Great, Freddie. How's the wife and kids?" Peter pictured Peterson's petite, well-built wife and two rambunctious, over-sized little boys.

"Oh, Madeline's doing fine. Busy with the new job. Teddy and little Bill are both in school now."

"That's good. So are the girls."

There was an awkward pause with the mention of his daughters. Peter Danvers trusted Fred Peterson as much as he did any man, even though he was Sandy's friend too and had dated her before Peter met her. Fred had been his lawyer since they roomed together when Peter was still at MIT. Fred not only assisted him from time to time with legal issues, but helped set up his company when Peter went into business for himself, also investing a good amount of his own life's savings in the new venture.

"I, er, just got off the phone with Sandy," Peter informed him. "Things didn't go so well. I guess she's having cash problems."

"So what else is new?"

"I'm just calling to make sure all the arrangements I made regarding the yearly transfer of stock options from my portfolio to Sandy have been taken care of. We need to have the papers signed and finalized as soon as possible. I'll also need an additional sum transferred to Sandy's account from my investment funds. See if you can let go of two or three hundred of those stock options maturing this month. Get that to her by next week at the latest. It should amount to between thirty to forty thousand dollars."

"Right'o, got it," responded the lawyer agreeably. "That shouldn't present any problem. Very generous of you, Peter, considering the situation and all. Anything else I can do for you?"

"Yeah, I was wondering how the girls' college funds are doing. Could you check into that for me and let me know. Drop me a line, you know, a letter with an envelope and a stamp, remember those things you lick."

"Oh, yeah. Say, didn't they go out with video stores and penny arcades?"

"Maybe, but that's the only way you're going to get in touch with me. OK?"

"Sure, I'll look into it first thing. Hey, how's the fishing down there?"

"Great. When you coming down? I got plenty of room in the bungalow for guests." Peter was always trying to get one of his old friends to come and visit him. So far, he had been surprisingly unsuccessful. Maybe his wife was right and they thought he was crazy after all.

"Oh, I don't know, maybe someday, I could really use a vacation about now. My court load has been tremendous. I could retire soon at this rate, from exhaustion. I may take you up on that offer real soon, partner."

"Good," responded Pete.

"Say, Peter, have you heard the latest news from Europe?"

"No, what's up? I'm a little out of touch down here," he replied, neglecting to mention it was mostly by his own desire.

"Well, there's word from Eastern Europe about a new computer virus that's shut down systems in several cities. And Peter, get this, the infected systems were Organics. I guess it's a real big problem over there right now."

"What? That's impossible," objected Peter. "Are you sure it was Organics? One of ours?"

"That's what the article said," answered Fred Peterson. "There's a big hullabaloo about it. Scientists and computer experts from around the world are meeting to discuss it. I'm surprised you haven't heard something about it. No one's tried to contact you?"

"Not that I know of," answered a perplexed Peter Danvers. "I'm not exactly in the thick of things anymore, but there must be some mistake. Somebody's confused and got their story wrong. No known computer viral techniques will work against an Organic."

Fred Peterson said he didn't know anything about computers, although he had made a fortune in the early decades of the new century defending accused peddlers of computer-based child pornography. He went on about other news events and the latest industry gossip, his usual enthusiasm fueled by the knowledge that his listener was deprived of information. As he listened, Peter thought about the implications if what Fred had told him were true. Could someone have penetrated the secrets of his massively-parallel molecular device? Of course they could. He understood the weaknesses of the Organics better than anyone. There were several things, from electrical impulses to chemical disruptions that could affect the proper operation of the bio-machine. It was even conceivable that the molecular structures themselves could be altered somehow.

Before hanging up, Fred Peterson mentioned one more bit of strange news from the States, an outbreak of a highly contagious and virulent form of Bubonic Plague, occurring in the vicinity of Silicon Valley. News was sketchy, but it appeared that several people had already died, many overnight in their homes before they could be brought to the hospital. No one was sure how it started or where exactly it was located, but a near panic had set in. The media was blaming the outbreak of plague, not seen since the mid nineteen-nineties when it broke out in India, on the teeming slums surrounding the metropolitan areas of Palo Alto and San Jose, vast breeding-grounds for disease and pestilence.

Peter listened to the news with a kind of dull numbness, the words affecting his brain's emotional centers more than his intellectual ones, which denied the information he was hearing. By the time he signed-off with his old friend, he was thoroughly depressed and disheartened.

The weather outdoors accurately mirrored his mood. Just as he made it outside to enjoy what was left of the day, the clouds, which had been massing for attack in the eastern sky all morning, broke over the mountains to block out the sun, casting a pall on the land. Soon the rain, which had been Peter's constant companion for the last three weeks, returned with a vengeance, bouncing off the empty white tables and chairs of the small veranda like the feet of a million angry flamenco dancers.

PALO ALTO, CALIFORNIA, AUGUST 13, 1:15 PM

The first morning after unleashing her virus, Linda had lain on her bed where she had collapsed soon after the deed was done, feeling all the accumulated exhaustion she had somehow managed to put off until her quest had been reached. Now, her task completed, she had been hit with overpowering tiredness, like she could lie there forever. In spite of the irresistible urge to sleep, however, Linda had been unable to drop off, her brain buzzing with unwanted equations and molecular symbols, burned into its circuits over days and nights of repetitive use, like an old computer monitor without a screen-saver has an image burned into it forever.

Finally, some time during the early morning hours of the next day, too exhausted to care any longer, she drifted into a half-conscious state between wakefulness and slumber where visions of DNA couplings danced in her head. This eventually gave way to deep sleep and real dreams, where animated appliances moved menacingly through a dreary dreamscape of crooked streets and Kafkaesque buildings.

That had been over a week ago. She had slept for fourteen hours straight, waking up disorientated and abruptly, around four o'clock on the morning of the first. The news broke a few days after that.

The results had surpassed all her wildest expectations. The first reports were sketchy, mentioning the deaths of several top scientists from a local but undisclosed Silicon Valley high tech company from a rare form of Bubonic Plague. At first everyone thought it was an isolated case, having something to do with the work they were doing, but when more people began turning up at the local hospitals with the disease, people who had nothing to do with the company or its work, the mild concern turned to all out panic.

At fist Linda was a bit shocked when the names of the deceased were published, people like Debra Murphy, who she had known and worked with closely. Her distress soon turned to elation, however, as she remembered how they had tried to steal her brain-child. They deserved to die horrible deaths for what they had done to her. Unfortunately, her slime-ball boss, Jack Veldt, wasn't among the list of the dead. Well, there was still time.

It didn't take long for the media to determine where the first batch of deceased workers came from, and the name QuantumCorp was published on the first page of every news report in the country. Not exactly the kind of publicity the company had been looking for. The report also spoke of a sharp decline in the value of their stock.

There was much speculation how it had started. To make matters worse, QuantumCorp had attempted to cover-up the outbreak, causing several days of critical time to elapse before health officials could begin taking action. In that time, several people had died and many more had fled the city to stay with relatives, spreading the disease over the surrounding countryside, making the identification of its source and cause that much more difficult. Over thirty people were reported dead already, some from as far away as San Francisco and LA. Most of these were employees of QuantumCorp or their relatives, but it was feared the plague was spreading to other areas.

Linda listened to report after report, story after story, each day for as long as it remained in the news. Now that it had actually happened, she was a bit taken back, the finality of her act hitting her like a sledgehammer. In defense, she held her ridicule and humiliation steady in her mind, using it as an ember to keep her hatred hot, although she was somewhat concerned that the disease had spread so quickly to other cities. So what if a handful stupid fools had tried to get away and consequently infected a few friends and relatives. Too bad, but they had all got what they deserved. Someone had to pay for her pain and misery, for her life of loneliness and heartache. Someone had to suffer as she had suffered. What better target then those who had stolen her life's work, and along with it, her sanity.

Of course, everyone was quick to blame everyone else for the outbreak. City officials blamed the state. The Republicans blamed the Democrats. The CDC blamed the city, and everyone blamed the massive cardboard shantytowns and slums encroaching on the city like a mold, carrying untold disease and violence with it. Each day, more and more of it was spilling onto the enclaves of the privileged, the bureaucrats and technocrats that kept the global economic engines running.

There was a rising cry, despite official disclaimers that they still did not know the source of the outbreak, for something to be done about the growing slums and huge garbage dumps that accompanied them, a smoking, festering no-man's land where women and children lay huddled in the worst conditions.

Amid the jubilation at her unqualified success, there was something gnawing at the back of Linda's mind. Something about the way the plague had spread. She had anticipated a few outbreaks in the surrounding area as employees of the company tried to flee, but something about the speed it moved to the adjoining cities was troubling. More to occupy her mind than anything, she built a small simulation package, modeling the action of her fabrication program on a virtual network of Organic computers programmed to duplicate her ex-employer's local network. Of course, since this was only a simulation, no plague germ would be created, only its propagation from machine to machine, with each Organic represented as a tiny rectangular box on the screen.

She watched with detached interest as her model replicated the movement of her virus through the company's local network. The pixels on the screen turned red to indicate the infection, as the simulation showed the disease invading machine after machine, then one office after another. Days were shown in minutes, so that she could see the birth of the Pestis in node after node until the screen was covered with them, the display totally obliterated with red dots. Soon the whole diagram representing the QuantumCorp facility was colored out. Figures appearing below each rectangle denoting bacteria numbers were increasing faster than Linda could count, like an altimeter gone haywire.

Linda was watching the simulation in this way, when she noticed something on the edge of the screen, in an area outside the local network, in a part of the model representing the worldwide Fiber, an entry ramp to the information super-highway.

"No," she said half to herself. "That can't be. It must be some sort of modeling error."

After all, she had built the simulator in a quick and dirty manner. She could have easily made a mistake. Shutting down the QuantumCorp network hub to the outside world to prevent her bug from escaping should have been the first thing her programs did. Could something have prevented this part of the code from executing until after the virus copied itself over the gateway computer to the global network? If so, it would travel over the Fiber like a vacationer on the Fourth of July.

She halted the simulation and backed it up to the beginning. Rechecking her work, she started it again, stepping through each clock tick, one instruction at a time. It was then that she noticed the glitch, packets of her virus being copied to the worldwide network just moments before the hub was shutdown by a subsequent instruction.

She stopped the simulation and played it back again, then again, until she had replayed it twenty times. Each time it was the same. Her virus was propagated to the outside world before the hub was disabled. She went back to her original program and checked it again. It was murderously difficult, but she finally found the bug, a subtle timing issue between two independent threads of massively-parallel neural pathways. It was true. The unthinkable had occurred.

She sat staring at the display, mouth open, head shaking in disbelief and dismay, much like she had that hot summer day long ago when her father had molested her, all her senses seeing that which her heart denied. She couldn't deny what her simple simulation program was telling her, however. Despite all her efforts and superior intelligence, the unimaginable had happened. Mr. Henry Rayburn's little girl had made a mistake. She had failed again.

Linda was stunned. After all, she had only meant to infect her enemy. She was sure that with modern medicine and antibiotics the plague would be controlled before it did any harm to the population at large. Still, she felt a sudden dread. She prided herself on the smart bomb-like accuracy and precision of her revenge. This was something she hadn't counted on. For she understood better than anyone the true potential of the germ, its speed of contagion as it propagated itself along the network in nanoseconds; its insidiousness, as it rapidly, invisibly, infected machine after machine, then humans, with the Petis germ. The utter inconceivableness of sending such a thing through the network would make it that much more difficult to detect. They would be totally unprepared, without cure or prevention. Yes, her little virus could easily destroy mankind.

As luck or instinct would have it, Linda had already disconnected the network link from her apartment house to the Fiber, more to cut herself off from the outside world than as a precaution.

She had savagely torn out the wires, using a pair of pliers like giant scissors to sever the cables, and soldered the connections to the outside world with lead, completely closing off and insulating her apartment against anything that might come its way over the Fiber. It was a good thing she did, although she didn't think she'd be in any danger, isolated has her Plague germ was in her ex-employer's system, or so she thought.

If what she suspected was true, it might already be too late to stop it, but she had to try. She went back to her model. If her simulation was correct, it was only a matter of time before the thing got out of control. She had to verify the effect on the slim chance that she was wrong and it somehow would die out on its own, like one of those quick-lived populations in the computer Game of Life.

Hoping against hope, Linda expanded her model's parameters to include the entire country, inputting a representation of the Fiber network from well-publicized schematics. She also programmed in the appropriate set of government responses, with antidotes and medical activities to quarantine and treat the public. Linda could only assume that even the current herd of elected officials would get this right, not that she thought it would matter. She made sure to enter the most optimistic scenario in terms of the medical responses. Then she ran the simulation. Now, however, instead of representing organic computers on the local network of QuantumCorp, the pixel-sized dots stood for cities hooked-up by the global Fiber.

She started the simulation and watched in fascinated horror as her virus, sure as the coming of day, spread from west to east across the graphical representation of the United States. Slowly, inexorably, city by city, in a matter of a few simulated weeks, the screen was covered with red dots of death. No response scenario seemed to make the slightest difference to the spread of the disease, as it hopped over vast distances like giant, leaping frogs. There were just too many paths, too many gateways, too many ways it could move to infect the millions of organic and hybrid units that tied the whole thing together, twenty years and billions of dollars of human activity.

Linda let the simulation run, sitting in numb shock, without moving, until the entire screen was reddened. She did not turn on the lights when it grew dark, nor did she have her usual Healthy-Choice Vegetarian's Delight frozen dinner, but continued to sit in the darkness, watching the now red screen as if it showed her favorite movie. Linda Rayburn was looking at the death of the world.

LOS ANGELES, CALIFORNIA, AUGUST 15, 7:00 PM

"What do you mean, there's been a delay?" said Stan Bellows, chairman of the board of Global OptiComm, yelling through his satellite hookup. "The European linkup can't be delayed, you understand?"

The voice on the other end of the line went on in futile self-defense for a few sentences more, before Stan interrupted.

"I don't care if Ted Samasota is dead. Is he the only one who knew how to get anything done around here? Just do it, or don't bother coming to work tomorrow," he said, flipping off the connection.

He had a late dinner at the office, but the recent reports from his field operations had not done much for his appetite, neither had the recent headlines about outbreaks of Bubonic Plague in major cities across the country. That was just a minor nuisance, soon to be dealt with. What really irked him was news of a new computer virus in Europe that had caused indefinite delay of the planned linkup between the US and European network. Stan Bellows bristled at the disruption of his great achievement. Feng, his Chinese backer, had already called and expressed his concern. That's all he needed on top of all his other worries and pressures. Now this damned plague thing.

"What the hell is the world coming to?" he fumed.

The new computer virus reportedly came from Germany or the Russian Republic, and strangely enough infected organic systems, the backbone of his worldwide computer network scheme. His people were confident they could deal with this new issue and get the European operation back on target before the schedule slipped too much, but time was running out. At the very least, they would have to isolate the virus and make an antiviral program for it and quick, or their whole operation would be in jeopardy. Stan Bellows was determined to let nothing get in the way of his plans. There was just too much riding on the outcome. If Bellows didn't know better, he'd of thought someone was targeting him personally, trying to ruin his business.

The worst setback had been the death of Ted Samasoto, his chief field technician, of the Plague. Without him, they would be severely handicapped. He made a note to send a letter over the Net to the grieving widow.

He had blamed that idiot, Walter Townsend, head of QuantumCorp, for starting the epidemic, at least at first. Then when it broke out in other cities like Chicago, St. Louis, and Houston, he had realized along with everyone else that it could only be one thing, a terrorist attack, probably organized in the slums around the cities where it occurred, ready breeding grounds for subversion and violence. But the Bubonic Plague? Whoever thought of this was a monster beyond belief. Stan was not the only one to think this way, as his man Burns made clear in his many campaign speeches across the country, always one step ahead of the epidemic, which was breaking out in places as far away as Spokane, Washington and Los Vegas, Nevada. No one bothered considering the network as the carrier. There were too many other likely vectors, like the massive slums surrounding the cities.

If he couldn't get satisfaction concerning his Fiber, at least he could take care of this damned plague thing. He knew where it was coming from, and even if it couldn't be proven scientifically, one way or another, for the good of the country, these festering slums, breeding grounds for disease and terrorist, would be cleaned up once and for all.

Bellows cursed the fact that the last thing Ted Samasoto did after visiting QuantumCorp, was order all OptiComm hybrid hubs and Organics taken down. He never explained his order and died soon after, but it pretty near single-handedly put them out of business. If it wasn't for the satellite backups, Bellows didn't know what he would have done.

"The sonofabitch must have gone crazy with the disease at the end," Bellows had said, when he heard the news.

Now he had to work practically in the dark, little knowing just how lucky he was that Ted had realized what was happening in time to disconnect the headquarter offices. It wouldn't stay disconnected for long, not with Bellows cracking the whip.

His mind wandered unbidden back to the mysterious outbreaks of Bubonic Plague that had been appearing across the country, as if spontaneously erupting from the very ground itself. It was obvious to him what was going on, even if no one else could see it. Those damned immigrants flooding the slums were responsible, with their diseases and dirt, their garbage and filth, breeding pestilence and death wherever they went. It was an organized conspiracy, it had to be. How else could the disease crop up full blown in so many places so fast? He was going to see to it that the problem was cleaned-up once and for all. In the meantime, he would move his family to the summerhouse in Oregon, just to be safe.

CHAPTER 5

MINIMUM SECURITY FACILITY, BULGARIA, EASTERN EUROPE, AUGUST 25, 2036, 4:15 PM

Eddie Pavloski walked the small rectangle that passed for one of the minimum-security prison's outdoor recreation areas, his hands in the pockets of his denim jacket in defense against the cool damp air coming in off the Black Sea. It was time for his afternoon walk. Most of the inmates were in the main hall, playing cards or Ping-Pong, lifting weights or reading, the perennial pastime of prisoners everywhere, warmed against the bleak overcast day. The thick fog he walked through blinded him to his surroundings and wet his eyes with little watery droplets.

Eddie loved the fog. It hid him from the constant surveillance and eyes of his guardians. Not that he could really do anything or go anywhere, he was seen sure enough. It was just that being cocooned in a blanket of clean, white mist made him feel shielded from the world's hostile glare.

Eddie walked along reveling the feeling of solitude and privacy, something so totally lacking in prison where everything you do, from taking a dump to dreaming, is observed by someone else. To Eddie, the feeling of privacy afforded by the protective fog was like a healing balm to his spirit. Not that he needed it, for Eddie Pavloski was celebrating his victory over the powers that be, over the very ones who had put him here. He enjoyed the feeling of triumph that accompanies a job well done. That pride of accomplishment that goes with a challenge surmounted and the defiance of the impossible.

He had succeeded beyond his wildest dreams. Machine after machine had been compromised by his worm, which searched out and disabled all the Organics it could find, that collection of parallel, molecular logic arrays and processors that stood guard over the information and assets of Europe, just like his jailers did over him. His victory had been complete. The authorities and experts not only didn't know where the worm came from, they didn't know yet exactly what it was doing or how. Soon, if they didn't catch on quickly, the entire continent would be shut down. Eddie almost jumped with joy.

Anyone seeing his face would have been struck by the look of self-satisfaction that beamed from it. There was something not quite right about someone who's supposed to be undergoing punishment for crimes against society looking so happy. But then Eddie had a secret, a little gem of knowledge that kept him protected against the slings and arrows that life flung at him. The computer resources of the entire continent were about to be shut down like a bankrupt car dealer, every action taken to try and recover only aiding and abetting the worm, and Eddie Pavloski, the *Dark Enigma*, was the one who had made it happen.

In spite of his elation, he was uneasy about the news from the States, where an outbreak of Bubonic Plague had occurred in several major US cities. Nobody knew exactly what was happening, but it sure was strange. Things like this just didn't happen anymore. It was like something out of the middle ages. He had heard the horror stories about the slums surrounding the new mega cities, the high crime rates, the filth and disease. Something weird had to happen eventually, but it disconcerted Eddie, despite the distance and his own victories. The Plague was something that made everyone worry, especially when no one knew its cause. With modern global travel it was only a matter of time before it spread to Europe. Then there was the terrorist theory, but how were they doing it? Eddie's reveries were rudely interrupted.

"Heard your book isn't selling so well, Pavloski," sneered the warden, standing just a short distance away in a black raincoat and wide-rimmed hat. The disembodied voice coming out of the fog, and the sudden appearance of the disturbingly dressed man, momentarily confused Eddie, who forgot where he was for a moment, suspended in the clouds as he was.

"I don't know," he answered, gaining his composure. "You have to talk to my agent about that."

"I don't have to. I downloaded it over the internet. If you sell five copies of that hogwash, I'd be surprised."

"Well, good thing you made your money up front, eh?"

"Ya, good thing your precious orphans have other sources of donations," said the warden, not looking at all happy. "You make some very interesting predictions towards the end there, about a new kind of computer virus attacking the Organics. Quite a coincidence, considering what's happening, wouldn't you say?"

"You mean that someone could invade the Organics? Not really, it was only a matter of time. You can lock me up, but there'll be ten other hackers who will come after me. You can't stop us all."

"Oh, we'll stop them, just like we stopped you, Mister Pavloski," replied the warden, eyeing his prize prisoner suspiciously. He had the strongest feeling, almost a certainty, that the unassuming young man standing before him was responsible for this current trouble, but he didn't know how. He'd find out though, if it was the last thing he did.

NEW YORK CITY SLUMS, AUGUST 25, 10:00 PM

When the country finally reacted to the threat, it did so with a vengeance. An immense mobilization of medicine and manpower flooded the stricken cities, planeload after planeload of vaccine, medical experts, and troops. Massive aid camps were set up and citizens were subjected to house-to-house searches. Round-ups and forced vaccinations were a common occurrence, not that many people needed an added incentive to seek the anti-serum. Thousands of National Guard troops were flown into the areas of epidemic to cordon off those parts of the cities considered the source of the infection, which everyone knew were the teeming shanty-towns of cardboard hovels surrounding the major population centers.

The outbreak of the plague put still more pressure on the authorities to contain the slums. Most in power failed to appreciate the fact that the majority of incidences of the disease occurred in the offices of high finance, technology, and business, where the fiber network was most heavily used, far from the tin and box houses of the homeless. They ignored the evidence indicating no cases of the plague had been found among the rats and mice caught there and tested by the hundreds. Everyone knew it must have come from these filthy wastelands, somehow secreted through the barricades and defenses of the rich. There was no other explanation.

The Center for Disease Control in Atlanta was completely baffled. At first they treated it with smug assurance. Certainly such an old disease as Bubonic Plague could pose no threat to modern twenty-first century medicine. There was the usual finger-pointing and I-told-you-so from health workers who had long bewailed the conditions in the slums and warned of such an event. The CDC was ready for it, or so they thought. When their initial efforts at discovering its source and the vectors carrying it failed, however, their mild concern turned to high anxiety. The disease seemed to have a mind of its own, not following any of the well-established patterns of infection and spread. So many different strains breaking out simultaneously in such far-flung places was like nothing they had ever seen before.

No one suspected the Fiber as being the disease's vector. Such a thing just didn't occur to a sane, clear thinking person. Any rational mind knew where the plague came from, even if those idiots in the CDC couldn't figure it out.

Each state's response had been total. Immense medical centers, giant tent cities full of doctors, nurses, orderlies, disease experts, and the infected were set up. Massive amounts of anti-plague serum were flown to the infected areas, all in an effort to stop the spreading epidemic. This opponent was no stroker, however, to be knocked out with a single punch. No, this was a wily fighter who had been around a long time, and was used to the worst that human beings could throw at it, cloaked in a new guise that few could recognize.

Totally off balance and fully committed to a doomed response, the authorities were unable to react to the insidious threat as it cropped up behind them everywhere they turned. Before they realized it, they had depleted the country's supply of medicine, money, and manpower, and had nothing left to defend themselves with when the disease popped up anew in some yet unforeseen place. Urgent calls went out to the rest of the world for aid. In the meantime, travel to and from the US, Mexico, and Canada virtually ceased overnight. The Western Hemisphere was sealed off like a steel drum.

Already thousands had died across the nation. The Plague seemed to take the most healthy and strongest, the youngest and most attractive among the population for its victims, as if seeking out the cream of the crop, the best, to be sacrificed. Across the country like a sickle it swept, cutting down all in its path, leaving houses, neighborhoods, towns, and cities, bereft of loved ones and friends. In some places a third of the population died, in others over half. The wail of the survivors disturbed the night, as cemeteries filled to overflowing. Soon even burying and mourning the dead was neglected in favor of a quick and expedient removal, carried out with zealous efficiency by white-suited medical teams in the dead of night. For some unknown reason, few slum dwellers seemed to get sick, at least from the plague, but they died of other causes, as vengeance ran high on those thought to be responsible.

New York's reaction to the plague was typical, as blind and full of panic as any and no more effective. National Guard and army personnel converged in force on the miles of cardboard dwellings and tin shanties surrounding the city. Reinforced to a total of 40,000 strong, the massive army complete with tanks and bulldozers, rolled over the tin metropolis like a hail storm, razing it to the ground, arresting or shooting anyone caught in its net. Still the plague raged on.

NEGRIL, JAMAICA, SEPTEMBER 3, 4:00 PM

After one of Pansy's home cooked meals and a half bottle of over-proof rum, Peter sat alone on his patio looking out over the darkening mountainside below him. The rain had been replaced by a succession of near perfect days and star-filled, balmy evenings. His recent conversation with Pansy about her sons – one a fisherman the other a dope dealer - had started him thinking about his own kids. It didn't take much from there to sink into a painful episode of guilt and recrimination over his failure as a father and the infidelity of his wife. He felt completely alone and missed his family, at least his little girls. He even toyed with the idea of bringing them to Jamaica, but knew in his heart he didn't want the responsibility of bringing up two young women alone.

Like most divorcees with children, Peter Danvers was torn between the need to live the life he had to live to stay sane, and the responsibility of raising his daughters. It became a matter of the lesser of two evils. Living the lie his life had become during the last few years of their marriage was more harmful to them all, he believed, than his leaving. So he left. He didn't regret that decision, although the pain and confusion it caused his two little girls broke his heart. He had always preferred a quick, clean approach to the unpleasant than a drawn-out one, as attested by the shooting of his car-crippled, favorite pet collie when he was a kid.

He was worried by his recent inability to contact anyone back home. He hadn't heard from his lawyer or Sandy since his last short phone calls over two weeks before. He hadn't been able to get another call through, although he had mailed several letters.

Around six o'clock the electricity went out, plunging Peter into complete darkness, alleviated only by periodic flashes of heat lightning on the distant horizon. Lighting a few candles, he continued to stare out at the night, occasionally sipping his rum and coke, getting more depressed by the minute. He sat there a long time, waiting to get tired enough to go to sleep, wondering what was happening beyond the darkness.

Peter had watched developments in the States with growing alarm, as city after city was infected with the plague, which seemed to cluster around the centers of population like ants around a sugar cube. Panic, riots, involuntary quarantines, and use of deadly force, it seemed the whole Western Hemisphere had gone insane overnight.

Even though no cases had yet occurred here on the island, there were scares daily, as panic-stricken people with pimples, rashes, colds, and fevers rushed to the hospitals, medical centers, and doctors' offices in droves. Every cough and sore throat presaged the Plague. Peter stayed cool. He didn't see any cause for alarm, but he wasn't taking any chances either. For the time being, he was as safe in Jamaica as anywhere, but what about his two little girls? News of recent outbreaks in Boston and New York filled him with concern for their safety. Then something happened that made getting home even more compelling.

As he was sitting by the window his phone rang. Hoping it was someone from the States, he ran to pick it up. A woman's voice answered. He couldn't really understand what she was saying. It sounded like an operator asking for information. He asked whoever it was to repeat herself. He thought she said she wanted his name, so he gave it to her. Soon another voice came on the line. The connection was bad and there was a lot of static. He was having difficulty understanding what was being said. It sounded like Sandy.

"What?" he yelled, speaking loudly as if it was the other person who couldn't hear. "I can't understand you."

He thought he heard the woman yell loudly, something like, "Help. Come home. Help. We need you." Then they were cut off.

He frantically tried dialing an operator to find out where the call came from and who it was, but when he finally did get someone after several attempts, it was impossible to trace. He spent the rest of the day calling anyone he knew in the States, including Sandy, but only got busy signals or interminable ringing when he could get through. Not even a machine answered.

It only confirmed his growing fear that something terrible was going on. What chance did his little girls have against the onslaughts of something like the Plague? It was a call for help. What else could it be? He resolved then and there to visit the States and try to find his kids.

Things were pretty much on hold in Jamaica. The business was running itself. He had no ties to speak of. So he put his affairs in order and left his villa in the care of Stephen, his caretaker, who drove him in the Lada down to Montego Bay the next day to get one of the last flights out to the US.

PALO ALTO, CALIFORNIA, SEPTEMBER 4, 12:00 AM

Linda Rayburn looked at herself in the mirror. A haggard image returned her stare - sunken eyes, hollow cheeks, and jaundiced complexion. She looked worse than she had during the sleepless nights and exhausting days building her virus. There was no excuse for her appearance now. She was getting plenty of sleep, however restless, eating enough, taking her vitamins. She should have been in the peak of health, but she looked and felt terrible.

The spread of the virus across the country had been rapid once it hit the information super-highway, which swept it along from hub to hub like good gossip, infecting all the cities along the major US links, LA, Chicago, Houston, New York, Seattle, where Organics dominated. Like a snake it slithered along the network, as Linda watched the terror unfold in enthralled dismay.

She had tried to warn them, tried to let them know what was happening so that they could put a stop to it, but no one had believed her. The numerous anonymous calls she had made from various public phone-units - none of them with video - were treated by the authorities as just one more crank call from a neurotic public that seemed to come out of the woodwork in calamities like these. Short of turning herself in, she was completely unsuccessful in getting anyone to listen to her. In the end, she had given up, leaving the world to its own devices, and good luck to them.

Linda checked the skin under her eyes, pinching her cheeks and pulling them down. Why did she look so bad? She pulled her blouse open and looked carefully at her chest. Were those red blotches? It was hard to tell in the dim light.

It had been almost a month since the night she discovered her blunder. It seemed so long ago, like an eternity. She had spent the intervening time trying to decide what to do about it. Informing the authorities hadn't worked. Whatever was to be done, she'd have to do it herself.

Even though most of her neighbors had fled or been taken to medical centers, she had managed to elude the authorities, who thought the apartment building deserted like so many others, thanks to the information she had planted in the city's computer banks. After that, she never left the place.

Were her arms blotchy? She felt weird, like her head was swimming in molasses. She went into the kitchen to make herself some tea. She was wide awake and had lost all sense of time. Other than knowing vaguely that it was day or night, she had no concept of temporality. It would be awhile before she went to sleep. She hadn't seen her cat, Pepper, all day.

"Wonder where she is?" she said out loud.

Firing up her workstation, now running standalone and disconnected from the net, she started some simulations, using the model she had constructed earlier to play out the virus's progression across the fiber network of Organics. Using her quantum computer, she worked up the genetic codes for several potential antibodies that might be effective against the Pestis, and tested them in the model to see the outcome.

Deep into the night she worked and far into the next day, until she collapsed in exhaustion around eight in the evening. She had eaten only a bowl of rice in the morning and a cup of instant soup that afternoon. The wind outside howled and whistled as it rushed between buildings and rattled against the window. Although tired and feeling slightly sick, she was invigorated and alive for the first time in weeks. She finally had a purpose, a worthy goal, a chance to make-up for her sins and save the human race from destruction. Yes, she would do it. She had to!

She tried simulating antibody after antibody, along with a variety of deployment scenarios, each designed to head-off her original virus and destroy it before it could spread any further. She would succeed in eliminating her incredible monster before the sleeping world even knew where it came from. At least that was her hope, the human race's only hope.

Frantically, she searched the solution space, but try as she might she was unable to find an answer that would halt the deadly epidemic. Oh, she was able to build the necessary antibodies genetically, and her original programs were a suitable vehicle for any genetically coded message, bacteria and antibiotic alike. But the number of organic nodes on the worldwide network and the number of possible links between these nodes, made the number of solutions grow exponentially with each additional unit, and there were new ones being added every day. There were just too many paths to follow, too many ways the virus could go for her to systematically search them all. No matter what she tried or how she simulated the deployment, her antibodies were unable to stop the progress of the Pestis through the massive fiber-optic network of Organics. All her simulations ended with the screen covered with deadly red dots.

Another grueling fourteen hours netted Linda little more than she had when she started. Unable any longer to keep her head up or her eyes open, she succumbed to a fitful sleep. Lying on the floor beneath her workstation, her sweat-shirt for a pillow and a coat for a blanket, she dreamed that she was running to beat some impossible deadline established by a sadistic manager intent on driving her into the ground.

She woke the next day feeling tired and having all she could do to drag herself to the bathroom, where the image that returned her stare through the fogged-up mirror momentarily shocked her. Her complexion was like that of a cadaver's, as if someone had made her up for Halloween, with white grease paint for the face and black around the eyes to give them a deep, sunken look. The skin on her chest, stomach and arms looked blotchy, covered with red, smeary spots and patches of pink rash.

She swallowed a handful of aspirin and supported herself on the basin while a spell of dizziness almost overcame her. Dressing in jeans and sweatshirt, she went to the kitchen and tried to eat, an endeavor at which she was only partially successful. She was determined not to give up the fight, and equally determined that she could not get sick. After all, if anything happened to her, what would happen to the human race?

CHAPTER 6

CLAYMOTH FALLS, CASCADE MOUNTAINS, OREGON, SEPTEMBER 4, 2036, 11:30 AM

It had taken two days for the seed to germinate in the Quantum Corp Organics, and another three before the first human became infected. By the second week it had spread to every major hub in the Fiber network. In a matter of weeks, hundreds of cases of Plague had turned up in cities throughout the country. People stampeded to medical centers and family doctors to get the anti-serum, which grew scarcer as the scare continued. People rioted in the streets, as police attempted forced quarantines of some areas, all to no avail. Still the mysterious epidemic raged on, killing thousands in a matter of weeks. By the end of the month, it was a nationwide outbreak the likes of which hadn't been seen since the middle ages.

Stan Bellows had watched it all unfold before him like a coach on the sidelines, incapable of changing the outcome. Had watched as his friends, neighbors, and relatives died off like roaches after a dose of Raid. He had looked on as business after business, enterprise after enterprise, vendors, customers, suppliers, and competitors folded and went bankrupt or just ceased to be because there was no longer anyone left to do the work. He stood by helplessly as his plans, schemes, and dreams crumbled around him in the chaos and destruction brought on by the plague, which had by now infected the entire northern portion of the Western Hemisphere, from Mexico to Canada, from Massachusetts to Hawaii.

For some reason South America, Europe, and Asia had been so far spared. The fact that they had not yet been connected to the worldwide fiber-optic network should have been a clue to anyone with the where-with-all to catch it, but few did.

All their massive efforts to contain the epidemic had been for nothing. Not only did they not stop the spread of the disease, their efforts to forcibly round up and contain people, together with widespread terror, fueled a level of urban violence that had not been seen before, not even in the strife-torn years of the twentieth century. The terror and violence soon spread to the countryside.

When things became no longer tolerable in LA, Stan Bellows had moved his family to their summer home in the Cascade Mountains of Oregon. When they left LA, there had been rioting in the streets, as National Guardsmen and Army troops tried to round up citizens and escaped slum-dwellers alike. On their way to the airport and his private plane, crowds of people trying to hitch a ride had mobbed their car. Only by accelerating rapidly and almost running over several were they able to continue on their way, the quick thinking and steel nerves of his specially trained driver - an asset to any corporate executive in this day and age - had paid off.

They had been stopped twice by roadblocks where people were being turned back by military police, but Stan Bellows' credentials were enough to get them through. At the airport they were told no one could take off and that their twin-engine Cessna had been confiscated. Besides, a state of emergency had been declared. All airports in the country were closed. There would be no place to land.

It had taken all Stan Bellows' ingenuity and influence, which was significant, not to mention considerable cash, to find a helicopter and pilot to take him the 400 miles to Oregon. As it was, he could have bought a helicopter for what he paid to lease one and someone to drive it. He also bribed officials at the airport so that after a quick medical check-up by a team of military doctors, Stan Bellows and his family were allowed to fly out of the LA airfield.

With the ECO of Global OptiComm were his wife, Tillie, their teenage daughter, Julia, and their eleven-year old son, Timmy. That had been six o'clock in the morning, a week and three days ago.

Stan was one of the few to have gotten out, one of the small number of elite who had been able to breach the prison walls of the cordoned off city. When they reached the serenity and solitude of the Cascade Mountains and landed their craft beside the crystal clear waters of the lake, the deep sense of anxiety that had been plaguing him for weeks, ever since the first outbreaks of the dreaded disease back in early August, started to dissipate. He was sure they'd be safe here for the time being.

Washington was a ghost town, a large majority of the Fiber-dependent senators and congressmen, including the Vice President, having died in the first wave of the epidemic. The remainder of the nation's elected officials fled the city like rats scurrying from a sinking ship, only to bring the red death with them as they connected to the Fiber with their portable hybrids.

The elections had taken on new life with the first outbreak. The finger pointing and accusations flew left and right, as more and more screamed that terrorists were behind it all. New nominees came out of the woodwork, against all the rules of the electoral system, but with the widening of the epidemic, most of these either died off or had long since disappeared. In the end, the country was left virtually leaderless. While the strident press cried it was the end of the world, the CDC was failing miserably, as it frantically tried to come to grips with the mysterious outbreak, looking in all the wrong places.

Stan Bellows was still determined to see his plans through to completion, despite the monkey-wrench that fate had thrown into them. He set up his office in the upstairs guest room of the summer house, a chalet-type dwelling of cedar, pine, and large flagstones, with sky-lights and lofts, set in a clearing surrounded by tall trees.

He had been on his portable satellite unit constantly since their arrival, phoning instructions and obtaining information about the status of his various enterprises. Several key people in his organization, as in most others, had died of the plague or been lost in the following chaos, but there were still enough dedicated individuals, like die-hard Marines on the beach in Guadalcanal, who refused to lie down and stop functioning. These individuals formed the core of Stan Bellows' SWAT team, doing his bidding, being his eyes and ears, all for an exorbitant salary and the privilege of saying they worked directly for the ECO of Global OptiComm, the most powerful man in the world.

Bellows was resolved not to let a little plague get in the way of his plans. As the epidemic spread from place to place, he continued to connect ever more Organics to the Fiber, unwittingly spreading the disease even further. He was also working tirelessly with the vendors of the organic machines on the East Coast to discover a fix for the debilitating computer virus that had hit Europe and caused such a costly loss of productivity and capital assets there, not to mention delaying the final phase of his implementation plan - connecting the European and American Fibers. Without the European Organics, the demands of the vast network would be too overwhelming for the idea of a virtual, worldwide computer to even be feasible, and if those devices were being compromised, the whole scheme was in jeopardy. So far they had made little progress in solving the problem.

He was standing by a large picture window, looking out onto the front yard, which sloped down to the lake, the water reflecting the sun with blinding flashes of light, thinking of his next move, when the phone unit buzzed, disrupting his musings.

"Hello, Bellows here," he answered, snapping up the satellite device with a flick of the wrist.

"Hi, Mister Bellows. Mike Pearlman here," answered his representative on the East Coast. "Got some news on the European recovery project. They may have hit on something."

"Good, it's about time. What is it?" asked the ECO, impatient for some positive news.

"Well, they think they've discovered the mechanism being used by the virus to infect the machines in Europe. They called it a Trojan-horse virus. It comes in as an innocuous service request and then boom. Look's like this worm was designed especially for the Organics, which means that someone has figured out the fundamental workings of the thing and then gone one better. The machine handles the first layers of the virus all right, which are more or less conventional, but takes in the inner core of the thing in the process, which proceeds to alter the structure of the machine's molecular cells themselves. Then it starts to duplicate itself, churning out copies like a cancer cell. Eventually, the whole process accelerates and the cellular components are destroyed from the inside out."

"Can they fix it?"

"They think so, given enough time."

"How much time?" fired the chairman.

"About two or three weeks. There seems to be several levels of virus involved. They've only analyzed the first two and that's taken weeks, but they think they've got the hang of it now, so things may go faster."

"Do they have any idea where it came from?"

"Other than somewhere in Eastern Europe, no," replied the field rep.

"When they find the bastard who caused this, I'm going to make such an example out of him that no one'll ever mess with us again. I'll have him publicly flayed, drawn, and quartered!" yelled the chief executive, losing his composure momentarily. "What's the status in Europe? Have you talked to Carlo?"

"Yes, we're in constant touch with Europe. They've been kept up to date on developments here and vice-versa. Now that we've got a handle on what's going on, we should be able to institute some sort of recovery."

"Good! I want that European link-up established by the end of the month, come hell or high water." Stan Bellows was determined to not let anything stand in his way.

"Mister Bellows, sir, don't you think we had better be a little cautious about this?" warned the young employee. "With the Plague epidemic and everything?"

"What the hell has the plague got to do with any of this? Just make sure you get to the bottom of things over there as quick as you can and relay the necessary information to Europe so we can fight this Trojan thing. Got that? I want the network connection established by October one or we're finished."

"I should tell you. It may sound crazy but..," stammered Pearlman, uncertain how to continue.

"Well, what is it? Spit it out, Pearl."

"Eh, there's a few engineers around here, a couple of screwballs really, no one believes them, but they've, ah, got some, ah, ideas how the plague is being spread. Real far-fetched, you know how, ah, some of these think tank boys are, umm, you know, off the wall."

"Well, what is it? What the hell do they say?" asked Stan Bellows, losing his already thinning patience.

Mike Pearlman let out a long, audible sigh over the other end of the line. "They think the plague is traveling along the fiber-optic network."

There was a long pause, as Bellows digested this latest bit of intelligence. Like the complacent commanders of Pearl Harbor back in 1941, he discarded it as useless.

"That's impossible!" he exploded.

"I know, sir, that's what most of the others are saying around here. But, just to be on the safe side, maybe we shouldn't be in such a hurry to reestablish that European link. Just in case, until we can be certain..."

"Screw that! What are you, stupid? Just get that network going, pronto. I want a solution to this European problem by the end of next week at the latest and I want it deployed on the infected Organics over there by the beginning of next month. Report back to me as soon as there are any further developments. Got it? And for Christ sake, make sure our hubs are clean of that Trojan thing. I don't want it cropping up over here. We have enough to worry about."

"Yes, sir, what ever you say, sir," answered the cowered junior man, knowing full well the consequences of failing Stan Bellows.

MINIMUM SECURITY FACILITY, BULGARIA, EASTERN EUROPE, SEPTEMBER 5, 8:15 AM

Eddie Pavloski had been a bit nervous lately, ever since his last visit to the warden's office, where he had been grilled for hours about his knowledge of the most recent computer virus, which had virtually shutdown European businesses and governments almost over night. Despite the warden's rather vague suspicions, however, they could prove nothing.

"What did you do, Pavloski?" raged the warden. "How did you do it? Tell me and I'll go easy on you."

"I don't know what you're talking about," said Eddie, lying through his teeth. "I knew it was just a matter of time. Somebody a lot smarter than me figured it out. You should be more worried about the plague than about some fool computer virus."

The interview had not gone well after that, the warden leaving a few unsubtle hints as to Eddie's likely future if he failed to comply with his wishes, thus his current anxiety.

He was in the shower room, an area he avoided as much as possible due to the crowded conditions and beastly things that went on there, especially lately with the new batch of inmates that had arrived, mostly hardened criminals from the east, who made the term 'minimal security facility' a misnomer. Things were getting downright ugly. Eddie half wondered if the new prisoners weren't hired thugs working for the warden.

This morning the place was virtually deserted, except for the two guys he had come in with, men he knew he could trust, even if they didn't particularly like him. Even so, he was reluctant to lose his towel and go under the water. Something about the way a couple of the men had looked at him as they passed in the hall, as if they were looking at a dead man. Eddie tarried by the sink and looked at himself as if contemplating cutting his long beard.

Glancing up from the steamed-over mirror, he froze in fear. The showers were still running, but his shower-mates weren't there. The place was suddenly deserted. Turning to leave, he received a further shock. Standing in the doorway were two of the biggest, meanest looking men he had ever seen, eyeing him with hostile intent, their fists clenched, their postures menacing.

Eddie, having nowhere to go, stood his ground and looked frantically about the room for a weapon. The two goons parted and a smaller man, with sharp features and a close-shaved head, walked into the room between them.

"You're going to tell us what we want to know," he announced with a crisp, English accent. "You're going to tell us everything."

Eddied tried to dart to the right, past the big man standing closest to him, but his assailant swung his arm out and knocked Eddie back against the wall. Then he punched him in the stomach, knocking him to the floor, where he lay gasping for breath. The short man kicked him with his sharp, pointed shoes. Eddie screamed in pain and clutched his body with his arms, attempting to shield himself. Soon all three of them were kicking and punching him, as he flailed around the floor trying to avoid their blows. He was naked and bleeding like a helpless baby seal, thinking it was his time to die. Before his attackers could do much more damage, however, a host of other inmates swarmed into the room to overwhelm them, subduing the three despite the size and ferocity of two of them. Eddie just had too many friends and admirers in the prison; had helped too many with their complicated legal cases; had taught too many of them computer skills and how to invest their ill-gotten gains. They weren't going to leave the *Great Enigma* out to dry, not after he had made such a spectacular comeback. For why else would the warden be sic'ing his goons on him?

Things got a bit ugly when the crowd decided to finish off Eddie's attackers once and for all, but the authorities soon arrived, and only the small, English-sounding felon lost his life, although the two survivors wouldn't be bothering anyone for a while. Eddie gained new respect and notoriety among his cellmates, even though he still denied any knowledge of the European computer virus. There would be time enough to crow, for now he wanted to keep a low profile.

News from the states had been downright frightening, a deadly plague ravaging the country. Thousands dead, thousands more locked in detention centers or under house arrest, secluded in their homes. Martial law and lawlessness ruled side by side, the government and businesses closing down as if on permanent holiday. It was like something out of the science fiction magazines he used to read as a kid, about an invasion from outer space, just as far-fetched and unbelievable. Eddie believed it. He was even beginning to have some ideas how it could be done, although he still couldn't admit that someone would intentionally do such a thing.

If Eddie knew anything, it was computer viruses, how they moved, how they spread, how they copied themselves from machine to machine, city to city, until everyone that opened up an email attachment got infected no matter where they might be across the country. This US thing had spread the same way, not like a real biological epidemic, along the major travel hubs, but like a computer virus, along the information highway. The knowledge that had enabled him to crack the inner code of the European Organics gave him an insight as to how someone else might go about doing it.

Back in his room, where he spent most of his time since his computer had been confiscated reading old technical papers from the early years of the century, he picked up Peter Danvers' PhD thesis. It was sitting right where he left it when he had used it to devise his TR virus. The warden had picked it up and thumbed through it not even realizing what it was. In it was the answer to his question.

"Sure," he mused. "Use the molecular structure of the Organic to house the DNA for the germ." But how do you activate it? How could you synthesize the germ itself?

"They must be synthesizing the proteins from the soup of the Organics," he realized out loud. "Ingenious!"

Still he could not believe anyone would do such a thing, unless it was terrorists after all, as all the alarmist were saying.

So far, for some reason, the epidemic hadn't turned up in Europe yet, except for a few isolated cases of people fleeing the plague in the US. That only added to Eddie's conviction that it was somehow being carried by the Fiber of Organics. If that was true, then his own virus had saved the continent from infection by shutting that network down. Still his mind refused to believe the obvious. There had to be some other, saner explanation.

KINGSTON, JAMAICA, SEPTEMBER 9, 9:47 PM

Peter Danvers sat strapped in the passenger seat of a small, single-engine aircraft as it waited on the runway of Kingston airport for clearance to take off. He could hardly believe that he was actually on a plane, ready to fly to parts unknown, after the events of the past few days.

Once he had made up his mind to leave the island, events followed in rapid succession. He hadn't heard a word from the States

84

since the strange phone call pleading for help. Three weeks had come and gone since he had last actually talked to his wife, with nothing but the most horrible news from home about the plague.

After a couple of days to settle his affairs, leaving Lincoln in charge of the business and Pansy the house, he and Stephen drove the tortuous seventy miles from Negril to Montego Bay, taking a little over three hours due to the bad condition of the winding coastal road. They got stuck in traffic for another hour when they reached the city, the streets clogged with every conceivable type of vehicle and pedestrian. They arrived hot and exhausted at the airport. Peter's flight to Miami, the only port of entry into the US that was still open, was scheduled to depart in two hours, giving him an hour less than he had counted on. He spent the next hour and forty minutes arguing with various operators and phone company officials in a vain attempt to reach somebody back home, all to no avail. Then he almost missed his flight and had to run to the plane, only to be told after sitting on the tarmac for two hours that the flight - for that matter all flights to the States – had been canceled.

Peter trudged his baggage off the plane and schlepped it back out of the terminal, where he was pleasantly surprised to find Stephen waiting at the curb with the car. He had stayed to watch his friend's departure. He sat there shaking his head from side to side, smiling broadly at Peter's expression of frustration.

"What's ta matta', boss? Ya like Jamaica so much, ya can't leave?"

"Yeah. I just like this place so much I'm going to sue the airlines for every cent they're worth. How do you like that?"

"I like tat jus fine, mon," said the tall, dark Jamaican, taking one of Peter's bags and walking with him back to the car. "What now, Petar? Want to go home and have a good, long spliff?"

"That sounds good, but I've really gotta get back to the States. I wonder if we can get a flight out of Kingston."

"Yah, mon, you can get a flight out, I'm certain of it," said Stephen, as if he had the latest airline schedules beamed direct-ly into his cranium, something not yet possible even in the twenty-first century.

Stephen looked up the best route via the Airport's Internet hookup, since he didn't know the way – even third-world highways were on MapQuest by this time. Peter used another kiosk to book a room for that evening. Not only did the vintage Lada they were driving not have a Geo-synchronous locating unit, it had no computer whatsoever. They would be on their own once on the road.

The rest of that day they drove along the beautiful north shore of the island as it alternated between unkempt coastal beaches and well-manicured lawns. On the right, mountain pastures and jungle forests dotted with white stucco villas and colorful tenant holdings slid smoothly by. As they drove, the sun slowly moved across the western sky behind them.

A couple hours of daylight still remained by the time they reached the quaint, if gritty, town of Ocho Rios, on the eastern part of the north shore. Kingston lay thirty miles away, southeast as the crow flies, although they would have to travel further east before they could head south over the long, torturous road that led through the mountains. It was a trip Peter would not soon forget.

After a harrowing eight hour journey, where they got lost in the middle of nowhere in a torrential downpour when Stephen took a shortcut that led them deeper and deeper into the mountains, they finally saw Kingston. The largest city on the island, it was spread out before them on the southern coastal valley, sparkling in the early morning sun like a bag full of precious stones spilled across the ground.

At one point, as they sat marooned in the mountain jungle, Peter had despaired of ever getting out.

"If there's one thing I hate," he complained. "It's running around in the middle of nowhere, not knowing where the hell I am!"

"You'll get use to it boss, stick with me," laughed Stephen.

They headed directly for the airport, on the far, left-most edge of their vision.

To Peter's great disappointment, the only flights out of Jamaica were to the southern-most Caribbean islands or South America, places far from the plague-infested centers farther north. He was told emphatically that there were no flights to the US, Canada, or Mexico. Peter was at a loss as to what to do, when Stephen somewhat made up for his mistakes of the previous night. It turned out that he had a sister living in Kingston, who was married to a mechanic who might know of someone that could fly him to the States, for the right price. Peter's resolve to find and help his children had by now hardened into a life or death mission. He was determined to make up for lost time. Nothing would keep him from his little girls.

Stephen made some phone calls and soon came back to the car, which Peter had pulled into the airport parking lot, paying the attendant twenty dollars. Welcome back to the real world he thought, noting the price. Stephen returned with directions to his sister's house, which was across town. He drove, while Peter gazed out the window at the carnival that was Kingston.

At Stephen's sister's house, where they were given dinner and treated like long lost relatives, they were informed by the brother-in-law that he indeed knew someone who might be able to help them. He agreed to take them to meet him after dinner.

At ten that evening, after a few hours nap, they drove back toward the airport to meet the man, an older Jamaican with thinning hair, graying at the temples, but otherwise well preserved. He informed Peter that he did mostly sightseeing trips, taking tourists through the mountains or to the western end of the island. In his younger days, he said nostalgically, he had flown pot into Florida, before it became suicidal to do so. The experienced pilot told him he couldn't fly them into Florida now because the waters along that coast were too carefully guarded and patrolled. Texas was too far to go in his small single-engine plane. The only other place he could fly Peter was the Yucatan peninsula, three hundred miles due west from the western tip of the island, from where Peter had just come. He would fly into a small private airport he knew of near Cancun. He said he would take Peter there for 10,000 US dollars.

"That's too much money!" Peter exclaimed.

"My plane may be small, but it is the only way for you to get where you want to go," countered the wily Jamaican. "Soon this airport will be shut up as tight as a sprung trap. You won't find anyone else to take you. Go ahead and try."

In the Yucatan, Peter could hire another plane to take him to Texas, where it would be easier to get into the country along the long, unguarded coastline. Soon even that would be closed. Eventually, after much haggling, they agreed on $6,500, which Peter withdrew the following day from a local branch of the Jamaican bank where he had his account.

The next evening, his papers in order, they were given permission from the airport authorities to fly out on the private plane to Negril. They were scheduled to leave at 9:15 PM. From Negril, they would fly to Yucatan early the next morning.

So here he was. After what seemed like another interminable delay, as a series of large cargo planes and military aircraft landed and took off before them, they were ready to go. Peter held his breath in anticipation while the small plane shuddered down the runway and wobbled into the air. He was having second thoughts about flying three hundred miles over water with this pilot and his flimsy airplane. He'd have a chance to change his mind in Negril before heading off over the Caribbean. The whole thing was beginning to seem like one bad dream. He had a feeling the nightmare had only just begun.

CHAPTER 7

GLOUCESTER, MASSACHUSETTS, SEPTEMBER 15, 2036, 12:32 PM

Life had become one nightmarish episode after another for the thirty-six year old mother of two. She had the money Peter sent her, although it had come too late to do much good. Oh, if she could only be somewhere else, safe with her daughters, instead of stuck in the middle of this God-awful catastrophe.

The days leading up to the outbreak had been increasingly grim, the worsening reports of the spread of the plague across the US and Canada causing terror in those places it hadn't yet struck. She had been spending more time with her new beau, Todd Daniels, who turned out to be as bad in relationships as he was good in bed, though the girls liked him, probably because he had a handsome teenage son and the newest virtual-reality games.

Sandy's TeleComm unit had been on the fritz ever since she had kicked it that day it told her she was overdrawn. Luckily for her it still hadn't been repaired, although no one appreciated the fact at the time. She still cursed the service provider. A digital cable backup, although slow, provided some TV shows and news services. That unit came on one night with a high-pitched tone indicating that the emergency broadcasting system was transmitting, and announced that all citizens were to stay tuned for important information regarding the current state of emergency. She had tumbled out of bed disoriented, thinking it was a dream.

Turning on the lights with a verbal command, she blinked in the hard, bright glare, as she listened intently, still only half-believing it was all real. The announcer explained that due to the outbreak of the epidemic in the Boston and surrounding areas, people were being asked to stay in their homes and contact the following list of emergency numbers at the first occurrence of illness. A statewide curfew was in effect. The sick would be taken to one of the listed locations for medical treatment, depending on where they lived. As soon as the broadcast was finished, she called Todd, who came to her place in Harvard with his son to stay. By August 25th, all hell had broken loose. No place was spared.

The sickness was followed by panic and violence. Fleeing citizens stole from and mugged one another in a mad frenzy to survive. Soldiers beat, clubbed, or shot anyone found violating the curfews, and herded the sick into holding pens and detention camps where if one didn't already have the Plague, they were certain to catch it. Groups of armed men roamed the countryside plundering and pillaging, while the shelves of supermarkets and grocery stores soon stood bare, stripped of all produce by the terror-stricken mobs.

As things worsened, Todd moved Sandy and the girls to their summer house in the country near Ipswich, and hopefully away from the scenes of chaos and misery engulfing the city, and more importantly, away from any hint of the Net, for rumor had it that the Fiber had something to do with the epidemic.

They had left in the dead of night, Todd driving without the lights, through deserted streets and back roads. Sandy's heart was in her throat the whole time at the prospect of being caught. Nestled in the woods, surrounded by thick trees and shrubs, the summer place made an ideal hideaway, separated from the nearest neighbor by a quarter-mile of wooded seclusion, if only no one looked too closely. As a precaution, Todd pitched a tent back in the woods out of sight, stocking it with essentials. It turned out to be a providential move.

Soon after their arrival, a second wave of the epidemic hit, as backup Organics were brought online to fill the void left by the first onslaught, in turn themselves becoming infected and killing their users. The area was decimated. Hardest hit were the first response teams, rescue workers, police, and medical personnel. Those who remained in command were ill-prepared for the positions they were thrust into. Most were undeserving at best. Some were incompetent or stupid. Not a few were downright evil.

Communication and coordination were practically nonexistent, which was good for those like Todd and Sandy who were hiding out. Unfortunately, this also meant there was little overall authority. Anyone with an armed group of henchmen could do pretty much as they pleased, such as rob and kill all who stood in their path.

It was a cold damp afternoon when it happened. They heard the gunfire and helicopters while sitting at the table playing cards. It was amazing how they had all reverted to a more primitive, simpler time. Sandy hadn't played cards since she was a kid. The girls had never seen a real deck, although Todd's son had a virtual gambling game with blackjack and roulette-wheels that seemed to come out of the walls. Todd was dealing the old pack, found in the attic on their most recent exploration. Everyone had put in their penny, when the faint, *pop pop pop*, of small arms fire erupted in the still, damp air.

Jim, Todd's boy, came running down the stairs from his room where he had been involved in that age-old pastime of bored, horny teenagers since time immemorial, sometimes known as shaking the rug. Interrupted in his activities by the sounds of screaming and yelling, he had spied his neighbors being loaded into trucks by armed men, while their valuables and possessions were being hauled away in the opposite direction. Worse yet was the sight of a man and woman who had decided to run for it being gunned down in the road, not a hundred yards from the house. Jim arrived downstairs out of breath and barely able to describe the events he had just witnessed. It was then that she had called Peter in panic, not knowing what else to do. She was surprised that she got him so quickly, but the connection was so bad she could hardly hear him, and only had time to yell out a plea for help before she was cut off. Her phone went dead soon after that.

They got out just in time, as trucks full of armed men in protective suits swarmed over the area taking away everyone they encountered and everything of value. Todd and Sandy, with the kids, spent a cold, wet, terrifying night in the woods, crowded together in the barely adequate tent, fearful of the slightest sound.

Sandy had trouble understanding what was happening. How could things change so drastically? That everything she knew and believed in could be turned on its head like this was just beyond her comprehension. Her level of disbelief and denial bordered on hysterical. This just couldn't be happening. Yet here she was, huddled in the woods, shivering and scared, a fugitive from whatever law was left to rule the land.

After the main sweep had passed, the area became a ghost town, with only a few sporadic patrols left to look for stragglers. Sandy and the rest were able to avoid detection by living in the tent, only using the house for the most inclement of days, and then only with a lookout standing watch. They lived in the wild, off the land, like a small family of gypsies, attracting little or no attention. In this way they passed the days and weeks. Still, Sandy was having second thoughts about Todd Daniels.

He was good looking enough and personable, at least at a superficial level, and he had certainly proved himself a good protector in their current predicament. But Sandy had learned a lot about him over the past few weeks and was not sure she liked what she saw. Granted he had saved them from capture, but he had a cruel side and a hair-trigger temper that was getting more and more out of control. He often berated her and the girls to the point of physical violence. She was starting to look for a way out, but there was no escape from the situation she was in.

HARVARD, MASS. SEPTEMBER 15, 3:00 PM

Mark Goodwater sipped his beer and rubbed his Buddha-like belly in contemplation, meditating on his navel as it protruded between his corduroys and an old MIT T-shirt.

Until a few weeks ago Mark had been project leader for Organic Computers Inc., Peter Danvers' old company, working with their biggest customer, Global Opticomm, on the European Trojan-horse virus project. That was before the Plague had wiped out all major East Coast computer companies and think tanks, the communication and computer workers invariably the first victims claimed by the horrible disease. That is most of them, all but a few very lucky or very smart ones. Mark Goodwater was both lucky and smart.

Mark had worked for the company over fifteen years, ever since it was founded. He was one of a new batch of engineers and scientists hired by the start-up right out of college. He remembered the good old days when they worked twelve and fourteen hour shifts, eating and sleeping right in the shop to meet a deadline. Despite the hard work, he remembered those times with nostalgia.

Unlike most of that first group of new hires, Mark didn't have a graduate degree from MIT or Stanford. As a matter of fact, Mark didn't have a degree of any kind, having dropped out of Brandeis University as a chemistry major during his fourth year. He was also a self-taught hacker. He had heard about the new company from a friend at MIT who was applying for the job himself, and asked his friend to see if he could get Mark an interview. He did, and Mark, with his knowledge of computers and chemistry, made such an impression on Peter Danvers, the president and founder, that he got the job on the spot. In a way, Mark reminded Danvers of himself at that age, when he had gone to

MIT. What Mark lacked in formal training he made up for in natural aptitude and ability. That, coupled with an unlimited supply of energy, helped him soon rise to a position of some responsibility, in charge of all Organic program development for the blossoming company.

He remembered those late hour sessions with the partners fondly. He had a special regard for Peter Danvers whom he thought of as a true genius. Despite his lack of formal training, Peter relied on Mark more and more as time went on. Mark's innate talent and instincts always seemed to hone in on the solution or approach needed at the time to get the project moving forward. Peter, a shrewd judge of character, appreciated Mark's considerable talents. It was a big blow to Mark when Danvers left the company and an even bigger blow when that jerk, Todd Daniels, took over.

When the Danvers' family built their new home in Harvard, Mark purchased a place there himself, to be closer to the job and Peter, whom he had become good friends with. They spent many pleasant evenings together over dinner and good conversation, Mark's favorite pastimes. He became quite a fixture around the Danvers' household, a fact that unknown to him, added to the already considerable friction that existed there.

Unlike the Danvers' home with its large yards, imposing façade, and expansive view, Mark Goodwater's was small and unassuming. An underground house built into the side of a hill, it was made of pale-green cinder-blocks, only the top front quarter of which peeked from the sloping turf of the hillside. All but invisible amid the tangle of grass, bushes, and trees in which it sat, it was built on the unpopulated side of a place called Oak Hill. You could almost walk over it without noticing it was there.

Mark's latest assignment for his ex-employer had been the investigation of the Trojan-horse virus, which had cropped up in Europe toward the beginning of August. Soon after that the plague erupted on the West Coast. If it's not one thing, it's another. This new worm attached itself to the Organics, turning them into one big amplifier, blasting copies of itself across the European continent like sound at a rock concert. The problem had both intrigued and worried him.

It would have been a good one to work on if the customers, the corporate giant telecommunication company heading up the worldwide fiber-optic network, weren't such blithering idiots and the plague hadn't erupted. Although their man, Mike Perlman, was a nice enough chap, the whole assignment left him sour. He took another swig of beer and wiped his tired eyes, pushing his wire-rimmed glasses up on his forehead as he did so.

That's not the reason he hadn't been able to concentrate on his work toward the end, however. He had never let personal feelings interfere with a project before. No, something else was bothering him, something far more important.

For the past month Mark Goodwater had been, like everybody else in the world, preoccupied with the growing horror of the plague - Bubonic, Pneumonic, every other Pestis variation you could think of - that was slowly, inexorably, spreading across the country.

Modern humans had been just as incapable in dealing with this threat as they had been in the Middle Ages, their sophisticated science and technology just as useless against the ancient microorganism as had been their ancestors' superstition and religion. Twenty-first century man reacted just as barbarically, just as irrationally, as did their predecessors over six hundred years before. Killing and shunning each other like frightened animals, they hurt and neglected loved ones and friends as if they were aliens, just as their forefathers had done.

Mark had seen it all coming, anticipated the plague's path as it made the fast track for the East Coast. He had it all figured out. He knew the plague was carried on the wings of the fiber-optic network, along the backs of the Organics. He didn't know how, he didn't know why, but he knew it, he and only he. No matter how he tried, he couldn't convince anyone else but a few fellow peons. So he had left, packed up his meager belongings, five boxes of books, manuals, programs, and knickknacks, and vamoosed. He also returned all the computers and network hookups he'd been using at home, keeping only an obsolete PC he had picked up back in '09. He still used it for his game writing, which he did as a hobby when he wasn't troubling over some chemistry problem. His home had no network connections. Nor did Mark believe in wiring his house with all the latest cable services. He didn't watch TV or movies, and the music he listened to was on vinyl. Since there weren't many left to carry on a good conversation, he mostly drank, read, played his sax, or wrote computer games for his amusement, and that was it.

When the plague hit Boston and the surrounding area, Mark was safely hidden in the comfort of his spacious underground hideaway, as safe as if he had been in a bomb shelter, living off a freezer full of frozen meat and a storeroom full of beer. Unfortunately for those around him, the rest of the world wasn't so insulated. His research lab along route 128 in Littleton, Mass was decimated in the first week of the epidemic. That had been over a month ago. He had gotten out just in time.

Mark had accurately predicted what was going to happen. Too bad nobody had listened to him. Maybe they'd listen to him now. That is if there was anybody left to tell his theories to. He hadn't been able to contact any of his old associates or friends, and was afraid of contacting the authorities after seeing how they reacted to the outbreak. No, he decided prudently, he'd disappear and hope the world forgot all about him.

When trucks full of soldiers came to search the houses one by one and take their inhabitants away, sick and healthy alike, Mark Goodwater's home was somehow missed. Maybe it was because long, yellow grass and thick tangles of briars and bushes covered the only part visible above the ground, and the door was concealed by thick clumps of large evergreens. Or maybe it was because Mark had left his car up the road at the corner filling station, where a friend who owned the place was working on it. Perhaps it was the fact that he only gave them a PO Box for an address. Whatever the case, his property looked more like a field of deserted ruins than a house, more like the home of mice and woodchucks than that of a computer scientist fast on the trail of the worst epidemic to plague the United States in its history.

Somehow, somewhere, for some reason, someone had unleashed a computer virus that was an actual living bacteria that infected human beings and made them die. Someone had figured out how to move matter through the fiber-optic network. At least that's what he thought at first, but a little research convinced him of the impossibility of that idea. Matter just couldn't be moved along by photons or electrons at the speed of light like that. It was around this time that he first tried to explain his theory to his boss, and had been removed from the project lead as a result. It didn't take him long after that to follow his own advice and disappear. He wanted to be as far away from any fiber-optic network of Organic computers as possible. Horror upon horrors, he had been right!

No, he thought, the virus itself wasn't moving along the network, it must be the code to build the germ that's traveling along the Fiber, the instructions to use the surrounding chemicals and elements in the Organics to construct the living bacteria. As incredible as it seemed, that had to be how it was being done. The genetic code of the germ was somehow miraculously converted to a computer program and then back into a bug. Now that he knew what was going on, what was he supposed to do about it?

CORPUS CHRISTI, TEXAS, SEPTEMBER 16, 4:45 AM

The past seven days had seemed like one long, bad movie to Peter Danvers, as his small plane flew in low over the oil-stained dunes and deserted beaches of southeast Texas. They flew clandestinely, like smugglers carrying a cargo of drugs, wary and alert for patrol boats and search aircraft. The border between Mexico and the US was shut-up tighter than the lid of a pressure cooker.

His Jamaican pilot had landed him at a small, private airport outside of Cancun with no mishap, a little before 1:00 pm on the tenth, after a brief overnight stay in Negril where he resupplied himself with money, fresh clothes, and accessories. On arriving in Mexico he had tried staying in a small inn near the landing strip - little more than a wide, smooth, dirt track with a few out-houses looking on - but the large tarantula in his room convinced him to move on.

Using information supplied by his Jamaican guide, who took off immediately after depositing him on land, Peter was able to get in touch with some old contacts of the pilot's who lived several miles up the coast. After a difficult trek, Peter located one of them, and after a lengthy negotiation, which lasted several hours, the person agreed to fly him further up the coast and then to Texas. After days of delays and false starts, he was woken one morning at his motel by the man, who told Peter to follow him. He drove a beat-up Ford pick-up, and said he would take Peter to the secret airstrip and fly him out. Peter did as he was told.

They drove for some distance before Peter began to get suspicious that he was being set up. His rental car had a full tank of gas and he had plenty of supplies, but he had no idea where he was. It was getting dark. They had climbed quite far into the treeless clay hills, away from the flat coastal plain, which they had been hugging all day, like Peter longed to do his daughters. The sun was sinking below the western mesa, filling the sky with fiery red and yellow streaks.

They rounded a knoll. Below him was a small complex of houses, no more than wooden shacks, and a landing strip, hidden in a pleasant, green valley amid thick cotton trees and cactus.

"I'll be darned!" Peter exclaimed out loud in relief, as he pulled up to the closest building, in front of which was parked a small, single-engine, early-model Piper Cub. It had probably been a nice one in its day, but that was at least thirty years ago. Now it looked flimsy and frail, dilapidated and fragile, a wreck waiting to happen, hardly airworthy.

Peter got out and walked over to the short Mexican who had so mysteriously led him there.

"Hi, my name's Peter. Are you the pilot?"

"Si, amigo. My name's Pedro, Pedro Ornelas. Hola!"

"Hola, Pedro. Have you done much flying?" he asked, shaking the man's hand.

"A bit. I've been known to fly gringos in and out of the States now and then. Of course, I haven't done nothing like that in a long time. No need since they opened the borders, but then that was before the terrible sickness. Come inside and have something to drink, while we discuss business. We shouldn't stand out here in the desert sun."

"Si, that's a good idea," agreed Peter, following the shorter, older man into a whitewashed adobe dwelling.

That had been twelve hours ago. Following several more hours of long and involved negotiations, a quick dinner of beans and tortillas, and a brief wait until the dilapidated plane was fueled and ready to go, they took off into the night, the stars and moon acting as the only light to guide the way.

Now they were flying low over a stretch of beach Peter assumed was somewhere on the southern coast of Texas.

"Where you going to land?" he asked, seeing only blackness below. The pilot, who had been quite garrulous the whole trip, hadn't said a word in the past twenty minutes.

"We'll put down on the beach," he announced, concentrating on the dark scene below him and banking the plane sharply into a 180-degree turn. The engine whined with the effort.

"On the beach? Are you sure? Looks kind of rough down there." The idea of landing on the soft, driftwood-strewn, pocked-marked sand, in the dark, did not appeal to Peter in the least.

"You got a better place? Maybe you like to land in the water, eh?" said the amused pilot, lining the plane up for a landing. The wings of the aircraft wobbled wildly as they descended toward the beach. All Peter could discern was the white spray of the surf as it surged up to the sand and the moon reflecting off the choppy waves of the sea. All else was complete blackness. "I could always drop you off if you like."

"No, that won't be necessary. I'm not a bag of cannabis," Peter responded, not at all amused.

"Then hang on amigo, here we go," said the Mexican, giving a little yippee yell as they dove for the undulating ground.

"I hope you know what you're doing," Peter replied, as he grabbed a handhold for support.

The plane sputtered and spurted as it bounced and pitched down the beach, spray and sand flying as it leaped in ever decreasing arches along the shore. Peter felt like he was on a runaway carnival ride, and expected the fragile aircraft to break apart on each bone-jarring contact with the uncertain ground, or tip sideways and go cart-wheeling down the surf in a ball of flame.

They came to a halt on a flat piece of hard sand somewhere in a wide expanse of beach. The surf crashed off to their left. Low dunes disappeared in the darkness to their right. The pilot left the engine running high and smiled at Peter with a wide, yellow-toothed grin. "Eh, amigo? What I tell you? Pretty good, eh?"

"Yeah, that was just great. You're a regular Charles Lindbergh," replied Peter, slapping the short Mexican on the shoulder. "No really, that was good, Pedro. Thanks."

"Glad to help, gringo," said the pilot, shaking Peter's hand. "These are bad times. People need to stick together." He didn't mention the substantial additional fee he had managed to negotiate for his services.

Pedro looked around warily for any signs of approaching vehicles. There was nothing to disturb the stillness of the night. Their landing had apparently gone unnoticed, but one could never be too careful with this sort of thing.

"You'd better get a move on, amigo," said the Mexican, who was very familiar with this stretch of beach. He knew it was usually deserted and not patrolled because of the oil spills, and that it was quite wide at spots during low tide, which it was now, consisting of hard-packed, flat sand, perfect for a clandestine landing strip. Nevertheless, the authorities could be here any moment and he didn't want to be caught on the ground.

Peter opened the Piper Cub's door and jumped out, leaning back in to remove his bags, and shook the friendly pilot's hand one more time.

"Remember what I told you, amigo," said Pedro. "Good luck."

"Thanks," answered Peter, removing his bags and waving. He watched as the plane moved slowly forward and made a wide turn on the expansive beach, heading back in the opposite direction. Soon it was just a speck, moving down the shoreline at high speed. Peter expected it to crash any moment. Instead, it lifted suddenly into the air with a noise like an angry bee, and disappeared into the star-filled horizon.

He looked nervously up and down the coast, which was so far still clear. He couldn't believe what he was doing, hitting the beach like a Navy SEAL. The only thing lacking was camouflage and black face paint. Oh yeah, and some kind of weapon would have been nice. If someone had told him he'd be doing this a month ago, he'd have thought they were crazy. Yet here he was acting like a commando raiding some terrorist camp.

Looping the straps of his knapsack over his shoulders and grabbing his duffel bag, he made for the road Pedro had told him about that would lead him to Corpus Christi. There he hoped to find lodgings for the night and maybe get a car for the next part of his journey – so little did he know of the true situation. He'd find out soon enough.

As nervous as he was, as hungry and tired and dirty, he was exhilarated, full of energy. He was doing something at last. It seemed that he had just been marking time all his life, treading water, waiting for his real purpose to unfold. He would wait no longer.

He couldn't explain it but he felt good. After all, walking in the night, beating the system, on a mission to save his loved ones, was a lot better than vegetating on some tropical island out of touch with the world. At least that's what he kept telling himself, as he walked like a man possessed, briskly through the dunes and down the sand-covered road toward the main highway and his meeting with destiny.

CHAPTER 8

PALO ALTO, CALIFORNIA, SEPTEMBER 16, 2036, 4:30 PM

Faced with the failed attempt at stopping her virus, Linda's mind went blank. She could not face the results of her actions any longer. For a while she had lain in bed all day and night, hardly moving from one position to the next. Now she paced the floors of her apartment like a caged cat in heat, her body twitching with uncontrolled tics and nervous spasms, as she walked back and forth with stumbling half steps, as if chains bound her feet. Her manic brain, caught in an endless loop between self-castigation and self-righteous anger, where the present tangled with the past, was an incomprehensible whirl of meaningless images.

Linda meandered through her apartment, walking aimlessly from room to room, floor to floor, searching for a peace she could not find. First lying, then standing, next sitting, then walking. Nothing gave her release from her torment.

Her meandering eventually took her to the lab where the display screen of her quantum computer glowed eerily from the corner like a green-scaled jewel, the colored patterns of its logic dancing like a psychedelic lightshow on the monitor. The light and bright movement caught her eye and she stopped dead in her tracks to stare dumbly at it, dropping down on her haunches, her head tilted as if she was trying to recognize something.

Linda looked at her creation as it danced in the gloom before her, with no more comprehension than a child of two. A ragged smile formed on her chapped lips.

"Pretty," she said in a voice barely audible, so hoarse and laced with phlegm it had become the harsh whisper of a throat cancer patient. "Pretty lights."

Her shaking hands reached toward the display screen of the quantum computer, supplicating, beseeching, pleading, as if it held all the love and compassion that had for so long been denied her, as if it alone could assuage her burning pain. In a way it did, for while she was captivated by the pulsing light of the computer screen she forgot her misery and suffering. She saw herself as she had once been, a bright, not unattractive young woman full of passion and dreams. Her vision quickly faded, as she saw the wide, unbridgeable chasm that separated her from what she had once been. Despair descended on her again like the false night of a full eclipse, sending her reeling to the floor in a swoon, taking her roughly into the bliss of forgetfulness.

MINIMUM SECURITY FACILITY, BULGARIA, EASTERN EUROPE, SEPTEMBER 18, 4:40 AM

Eddie Pavloski lay on his back in his minimum-security prison cell, with his arms under his head, listening to the rhythmic snoring of his new cellmate. With each noisy inhale and exhale Eddie felt his blood-pressure increase by a degree. He hadn't bathed since his narrow escape from the shower room twelve days ago. He was beginning to smell a bit gamey but decided he could go a few more days without washing, especially if it annoyed his new roommate.

The guy was a mole, planted by the warden after his last failed attempt to question him, as sure as Eddie was a Pole. The skuzzy-headed twenty year-old with the pointed nose and jaw - and a gold earring and a diamond in his nose - wouldn't leave Eddy's side. He hounded him with questions about virus writing in general and the Trojan-horse virus in particular. Just what Eddie needed! Well, he'd been through this all before. He didn't break then and he wouldn't break now.

According to news reports, experts in the US had developed a new program for the Organics that was immune to his virus. He knew it was only a matter of time before they deciphered the final layer of his worm and discovered its source. Soon the European Organics would be brought on-line again and finally connected to the US network, where the Fiber-born plague still raged unabated. Eddie knew that couldn't be allowed to happen. He had one more card up his sleeve, a little surprise to confound his pursuers just as they were about to solve his viral puzzle. If only it could be played in time.

If the reports were correct, and they had indeed found the antidote to his virus, they were no doubt close to deciphering the inner-most layer of his code wherein lay his handle, that pandering for recognition that had put him in prison in the first place. As Eddie lay staring at the bunk above him, that string of characters, hidden in the depths of his Trojan-horse virus, blazed in the darkness before him as if burned into the bed-board - *Pavlov's dog*.

It wouldn't be long after this that they'd trace the germ to his Bulgarian prison. The thought caused him no little anxiety, but it also caused his heart to beat in wild anticipation. For in deciphering that final string of characters embedded in the kernel of his worm, they would unwittingly unleash his final act of revenge, a little snippet of code that would infect the very anti-viral software they were installing to catch his Trojan-horse worm. Thus, as soon as the new protective program was turned on, it would begin propagating his virus with renewed energy, just as they thought they had conquered it.

As he lay on his cot despairing of sleep - long ago tiring of shaking his snoring cellmate awake - in the wee hours before the break of day, when his imaginings and fears grew like balloon creatures in his mind, he could see the plague closing in on him along with his pursuers.

So far Europe had been miraculously free of the disease, but there were daily scares and false alarms from England to the Russian Republic. Unknown to everyone but Eddie, his virus was the only thing standing in the way of the death and destruction of the continent. After a respite of 700 years, all that was needed for the Black Death to revisit her old stomping grounds again was the rebuilding of the Fiber of Organics and linking it to the US, and that could happen any day now, thus the real source of his anxiety.

Eddie's popularity, not to mention his reputation, had grown considerably since the scuffle in the shower room, some might even say because of it. Somehow a story had entered the prison rumor-mill that Eddie the *Dark Enigma* Pavloski himself, was responsible for the recent European computer virus. Its devastating destructiveness and ingenuity earned him mountains of respect, at least among the sociopaths and deviates that made up the majority of inmates.

There were still others, however, their strings pulled by the warden, no doubt, who weren't particularly fond of Eddie and were out for his blood. He had just returned from two days in the infirmary after an altercation with the prison's largest inmate, a 280 pound Russian Physicist who had been incarcerated at the turn of the century for selling homemade atom bombs to the highest bidder. He jumped Eddie in the gym where he was pumping iron. This time he had the presence of mind to slam a set of twenty pound dumb-bells off his assailant's temple, but not before the Russian had broken two of his ribs and fractured his jaw. Too bad the guy wouldn't suffer any permanent brain damage. At least Eddie had gotten a few nights sorely needed rest.

Obviously, the warden was increasing the pressure in his search for answers to questions he couldn't quite formulate. He was far from giving up, however, as witnessed by the Chinese snoring torture Eddie was currently undergoing.

The days, which had flown by while he was working on his computer worm, when he had so much to keep him occupied and look forward to, now dragged on like a bad play, as he waited for the final act he hoped would never come. Prison had become unbearable, a claustrophobic place where the walls breathed hatred and the floors simmered with despair. All he could do was sit helpless, while his fate crept in around him like vultures around a stricken calf.

His most recent interview with the warden led him to believe that they were already closing in, hot on his trail. Though it didn't bode well for him personally, it was of vital importance for the human race, for it also meant his final thrust would be made in time.

"Well, Mister Pavloski," the warden had gloated last time they talked. "It seems you've attracted the attention of our friends in the States." His tormenter's smile of vindication said it all. "I knew you were up to something. They should never have given you that computer. Now your troubles are just about to begin. They're sending over a couple of their folks to talk to you. I'm afraid you'll find they're the type of people you won't be able to say no to. Have a nice life, Eddie."

Now all he could do was lie here and wait, unable to flee the long arm of the law. He had no place to run and nowhere to hide. It would all be worth it, however, if only his final stroke arrived in time.

SOMEWHERE IN NORTHERN TEXAS, SEPTEMBER 19, 4:20 AM

After his harrowing touchdown someplace on the beach near Corpus Christi, Peter had walked northward through most of the night, along the shore of the southeastern part of the great state of Texas. To his right, a few miles off in the night distance, were the Padre Islands. To his left, several miles away, unseen behind sand dunes and hills, ran route 77.

The knapsack he carried on his back was packed with sixty pounds worth of necessities, things he would need for his survival. The only thing he knew about the situation in the States was that he knew nothing. He had to be ready for anything.

His drop off point had been a few miles southeast of Kingsville, just south of Corpus Christi. He walked briskly along the beach until the sun rose like a red-hot coal from the blue-green waters of the Gulf, as oil-caked and deserted as the northern coast of Alaska. As he made his way closer to the city, Peter was struck by the desolation and silence of the place. Not a dog barked, not a crow cawed. It wasn't the quiet of early morning. It was the quiet of the grave.

An eerie silence ruled the world, a bone-penetrating quietude that filled him with increasing dread the further he walked - suburbs with no activity, houses with no people, trees with no birds, roads with no cars, a sky with no planes. Where was everyone?

Wherever he went, he could see signs of the violence and vandalism left in the wake of the plague, the blackened shells of buildings and the smoldering ruins of cars and buses, some of which were thrown across streets like hasty barricades. Other intersections were still stained with blood. Through the entire scene, nothing stirred in the warm morning air but a few stray dogs.

Peter hadn't seen a soul all night. If he had he would have instinctively hid, for he somehow knew he didn't want to be spotted. Staying on the outskirts of Corpus Christi, he worked his way northward around the western edge of the city. He had snacked lightly earlier, while he walked along the beach, wanting to get to this point by daybreak. Now he was tired and hungry, and things looked much worse than he had imagined. His plan had been to move northward along the coast, then up through Mississippi and Tennessee following US route 59, either hitchhiking or using public transportation. Now, on seeing the total lack of any recognizable sign of civilization, he was having second thoughts.

He decided to stay in the open country and avoid the cities as much as possible. The prospect of having to walk all the way to Massachusetts filled him with dread. Could he find a car? Would someone spot him? What would they do to him if they did? And where was everyone? They couldn't all be dead, could they? These questions and others buzzed around his head like black flies around a carcass, while he walked through the silent, sleeping streets of the city's suburbs.

Still later that day, as he rested and had a frugal dinner behind an abandoned farmhouse, he heard gunfire not far off in the distance. That evening as he prepared to resume his hike, the night was pierced with yet more gunshots and what sounded like a fleet of helicopters that flew low overhead. In the distance, as he started on his way shortly after sunset, he saw what looked like huge bonfires lighting up the sky to the southeast, back toward the city. The whole scene seemed eerily unreal, like he had fallen through a looking glass into a world of nightmare shapes and murderous sounds.

After checking his compass and getting his bearings, he made his way furtively along the highway north toward I77 and Victoria. From there he planned to travel northeast.

He made good time, his long strides propelling him quickly along the sandy, pebble-strewn roadside, like a native nomad. He was thankful for all the long walks he had taken along the seashore and up the mountains of Jamaica to keep himself in shape. Still, he saw no sign of life, either vehicle or pedestrian.

Peter found himself in a desert-like land comprised of low grass intermixed with sand and cactus. Cold and lonely, he walked all that night, resting in a gully under a press of trees and boulders a few hundred feet off the road at daybreak. After what seemed like a hundred hours of lying in the shaded heat waiting for the darkness, the night finally arrived. By the time he stopped to rest the next morning, he had made almost fifty miles and was approaching the town of Victoria.

Going to sleep in the shade of a cypress tree beside a small stream that meandered behind a deserted farmhouse, he was abruptly woken by the wet nose of a large, brown German Shepherd. Not far behind the dog was the barrel of a twenty gauge shotgun.

"Don't shoot," Peter yelled, as the dog barked and nipped at his upheld hands.

The man holding the gun appeared to be in his forties, with short-cropped hair, his large frame sporting a well-developed beer belly. His fingers were dirty and his clothes greasy. He turned out to be the cousin of the local sheriff, and informed Peter he was going to take him in. When he wasn't arresting people, he was a mechanic at a local truck stop.

Ordering Peter into the back of a pickup truck parked out by the highway, he informed him that everybody in the state had to report to one of several holding areas to be vaccinated, and quarantined until it was determined if they were sick or not. He was going to take Peter to the nearest facility in Houston, despite the scientist's pleas that he needed to get to his family in Massachusetts. There was a little girl about nine or ten sitting in the truck, with a pageboy haircut and a blue sundress, who reminded Peter of his oldest girl, Abigail.

"That your daughter?" asked Peter, trying to strike up a conversation. The man said nothing in reply. "My oldest is about her age," he continued. "I'm trying to get back east to see her."

"Shut up and get in that truck!" yelled his captor, pointing the gun at him. "And don't get any funny ideas or I'll sic my dog on you."

The man then got into the cab, joining the girl and the dog, who eyed Peter like he'd much rather chew on one of his extremities than his rawhide bone. Peter sat in the back of the truck holding onto the sides tightly as it started up abruptly and jostled down the road.

Barreling up the straight highway, they headed toward route 59 just above Victoria, at no time slowing down below fifty. There was no way for him to jump out without being killed or seriously maimed. Not that it would have done him much good. There was no place to go in the flat, empty landscape, and Peter wasn't tempted to try either the shotgun or the dog.

They followed the river, which ran along their left, sometimes disappearing around a bend of trees or a hill, sometime marching right along the road beside them. It looked brown and muddy, fast and high. About fifteen minutes after they started out, the clouds, which had moved up fast from the south, emptied themselves in torrents on the river-swelled landscape. Peter, sitting in the exposed rear of the truck, got soaked, despite the tarp he had pulled over his head.

For thirty minutes they rode through the downpour, which seemed to come down harder the further they drove, while Peter huddled as far beneath the canvas covering as possible. Despite the blinding rain, the truck never slowed down. The driver, who could not have seen more than two feet in front of him, must have known these roads by heart.

Suddenly, they came to a halt. The sky was dark-gray, the midday sun blocked out by a mass of large thunderclouds that seemed to be painted black. The driver had the lights on, but they illuminated little in the gloom. As Peter peered over the cab to see what was going on, he noticed that the road ahead appeared to disappear into the river, which was raging now like a flood. He could vaguely see the tops of the white concrete posts marking the edge of the highway.

To Peter's utter dismay, the truck started up again and headed across the river as if it were an amphibious vehicle of some kind. Unfortunately, it wasn't even a four-wheeler and stalled in mid-stream, where water began lapping its sides and splashing into the back where Peter sat. He banged on the top of the cab, but they were already stalled in the middle of the river.

Then the truck gave a sickening lurch and seemed to turn on its axis about forty degrees. He heard the little girl scream and the dog bark, as they sank another few feet into the swollen stream, which pulled and tugged at the vehicle like a cat with a rubber mouse, prodding it first this way then that, each time sinking it a little deeper into the muddy, swirling current. Before he knew it, they were in the middle of a large mass of water that seemed as wide as the Mississippi, being swept downriver like a piece of driftwood.

Peter's heart was in his throat as the vehicle became an unstable two-ton raft. With water splashing in on all sides, he had to hang on for fear of falling in and being swept away. He could see looks of surprise and shock on the faces of the truck's other occupants, as they frantically looked back at him through the rear window. The little girl was screaming continuously now, one loud, high-pitched howl that froze the blood in Peter's veins. The dog, frantically trying to get out, was biting and clawing the desperate driver as he tried to extricate himself as well, hanging on to his arm with its jaws clamped tight.

Despite his fear and precarious position, Peter tried reaching a door to help them out, but the passenger door was locked, the window rolled up tight against the rain, and he could not get to the other side of the truck no matter how hard he tried. In two more seconds, which felt like tiny eternities, the truck nosed into the stream and sank like a lead weight. Water flowed over the cab in a cataract as it started to submerge.

Clinging to the sinking vehicle, Peter desperately tried to free the little girl, who pasted herself to the windows like a snail, her lips pressed against the glass as if sucking air through it, while the truck sank quickly out of sight. Unable to hold on any longer against the current and water pressure as it swirled and eddied around him, Peter floated off and away from the truck, and made his way with difficulty to shore. He was having trouble keeping his head above the surface of the slashing waves, and didn't know if he could make it.

Feeling himself going under, he fought to get his head back above the water. Then he sank a second and third time, his recent strenuous activity and deprivations draining him of every last ounce of strength. He couldn't believe he was going to die like this, drowned only yards from a shore he should never have ventured from. As he went down for the forth and last time, he thought of the absurdity of it all, and the daughters he would never see again. Just as he was about to sink out of sight and be swept down river, however, a strong pair of gnarled hands grabbed him by the shoulders and pulled him to the bank.

"No, ya don't, buddy. Don't worry, I've got ya," said his savior, an old man with graying hair and ruddy features. He seemed to be smiling in amusement despite the drama of the moment. Peter, recovering quickly, stood up and thanked him, then looked desperately back to the river.

"There're two others. In the truck!" he shouted, running along the rocky shore.

There in the middle of the raging torrent, balanced precariously on a sharp boulder, was the pickup. The driver had finally gotten the window down and was starting to clamber out, but before he was halfway free the truck started moving again.

Peter and the old man watched in horror as it bobbed and weaved in the wild flood, now floating, now submerged, rushing downstream at a rapid clip, the man hanging out the window like a rag-puppet. Peter tried to keep up with the floating deathtrap, hoping against hope that it would come to a stop again and reemerge. Then his heart sank with the truck, as it capsized on its side and disappeared completely out of sight for the final time.

Running frantically back and forth along the shore, Peter considered his chances of making it to the sunken vehicle. Despite the odds, he started wading out, though he knew the strong current would only sweep him away as it did before.

"There's nothing you can do now," the old man counseled from behind him, putting his hand on Peter's shoulder and guiding him back to the shore. "It's not your fault. I saw the whole thing. That fool should've never tried to cross there. There's no way he could've made it."

"There was a little girl in that truck," Peter said frantically, thinking of his own two daughters.

"Well, that can't be helped," said the old man, who was now standing next to Peter as he stared out at the empty river. Despite his seventy-some-odd years, he stood straight and erect, his frame strong and tall, though a little bandy-legged. "Nothing we can do unless you got diving gear and a crane. That river's ten feet deep there when it's low. It's probably over twenty by now. The current'll take you away sure as shooting. We don't even have a rope."

Ignoring the old man's advice, Peter stripped to his underwear and dove into the raging river, only to be quickly swept downstream. He had all he could do to struggle out again, and probably would have drowned for sure this time without the old man's help. As it was, he had gotten nowhere near the sunken vehicle. Instead he lay on the rocky bank, exhausted and beaten, sobbing like a child.

The man, who turned out to be a retired high school teacher named Arthur Berry, comforted Peter as best he could and helped him into his clothes. On hearing he was making his way to New England, he asked Peter if he could join him, since he himself had relatives there. For some reason Peter trusted the stranger and decided to go with his instincts. The old guy seemed healthy enough. At least he didn't have the plague. After all, he had just saved his life, twice. Peter agreed and without further delay, they headed off with Arthur in the lead, each step taking them closer toward the unknown.

CHAPTER 9

GLOUCESTER, MASSASHUCETTS, SEPTEMBER 22, 2036, 12:32 PM

Sandy walked alone along the beach. The sun was at its peak in the bright midday sky. Things had been quiet since those harrowing days a week ago when the military trucks had rounded up all their friends and neighbors. They were still hiding in their small tent in the woods behind her summer house in Ipswich. Today she had gone further than usual, far from the house, as far as she could get from that overbearing know-it-all who tried to control her every move and thought. Sometimes it felt like he was smothering her. His treatment of her and her girls bordered on abusive, but then they were all under a lot of stress. Some people just handled it better than others.

Suddenly, as she was nearing the mouth of a small river leading inland, where a path led to the highway, she heard the unmistakable sound of gun shots. Tuning around, she saw the thick, black smoke from several large fires.

"Not again!" she shouted out loud.

Racing back down the beach toward the house, she arrived in time to see several military trucks filled with people, some of whom she recognized, who had been missed by the first sweep. They were being guarded by armed men dressed in white protective suits, and driven off amidst the smoke and ashes of what was left of their smoldering homes. Staring in mute astonishment, she crouched behind a hedge and watched the unreal scene unfold before her. There were signs of violence everywhere. The bloody forms lying in the road and lawns hardly registered on her frazzled senses, the sight was so unthinkable.

Then her heart stopped in her throat as she glimpsed a familiar figure in back of one of the nearest trucks, her oldest daughter, Melissa, holding on to her younger sister's hand. Todd crouched in fear nearby with his son.

Her terror now overtaken by concern for her children, Sandy flew from behind her cover and ran down the empty road after the retreating trucks, which turned up the sand like a dust storm, partially hiding her from sight.

Frantic, all thoughts of her own safety driven from her by the sight of her helpless little girls, Sandy sprinted toward the highway, following the trucks as best she could, but they were soon out of sight. Disheartened, not knowing what to do, she sank to her knees sobbing by the roadside. Her flagging sense of survival, however, was raised by the sound of approaching vehicles. She had enough presence of mind to throw herself behind some bushes just as another group of trucks rushed passed. They too were filled with frightened, bewildered people being escorted under guard to parts unknown. Sandy hid unmoving until night began to fall. Then she made her way slowly back toward the beach and away from the highway, walking along the shore until she could walk no more.

She didn't know what to do. Her mind was in total confusion. Where had they taken her girls? Should she follow? Should she hide? Sandy couldn't seem to settle on an answer for any of these questions, as her mind jumped back and forth between the unacceptable and the inconceivable. This just couldn't be happening. Maybe they would be safe with Todd, although the expression of abject fear on his face didn't bode well for their future.

HARVARD MASSACHUSETTS, SEPTEMBER 22, 6:00 PM

The sun shone pinkish-orange as it set behind a band of purple clouds in the western sky. The gray-clad slopes of mount Wachusett, visible in the hazy distance, stood in stark contrast to the colorful sunset. The end of a perfect day, thought Mark Goodwater, errant engineer, fugitive from the law.

He walked back into his underground house, pulling out a cold beer from the fridge on the way through the kitchen - something he always managed to supply himself with no matter what the circumstances. He reviewed his list of names, his dream-team of computer experts and biochemists who he hoped would save the world.

He'd been trying to contact the three people who he thought could tell him how the Bubonic Plague had been transmitted through the Fiber, and even more importantly, how the epidemic could be stopped. The writer of the Trojan-horse virus, Eddie *Pavlov's Dog*

Pavlosky, had obviously figured out how to compromise the Organics. His code, which Mark had analyzed while working on the Trojan-horse antidote, showed knowledge of the machine second only to its creator. For this reason alone Eddie Pavloski was needed, as was, of course, Mark's mentor and friend, Peter Danvers.

Unfortunately, Eddie Pavloski was now in prison, although from the looks of things he had struck again, this time from his jail cell, targeting the European Organics themselves.

"That clever bastard," said Mark out loud to himself. Mark Goodwater had always talked to himself. So far no one had answered back.

Eddie's arrest, subsequent trial, and imprisonment had been big news at the time. The problem was Mark couldn't remember the details, things like what prison the guy had been sent to. All he knew was the writer of the Trojan-horse virus had to be the *Dark Enigma*, and he was in prison somewhere in Eastern Europe.

"Now what do I do?" he asked himself. Knowing where Eddie Pavloski was being kept was one thing, getting to him was going to be quite another. Without the proper authority, with himself a fugitive, contacting the *Dark Enigma* would be all but impossible, but then Mark Goodwater was an old hand at dealing with the impossible.

Putting that question on the back burner for the time being, Mark turned his attention to his ex-boss and friend. All attempts in the past month to contact Peter had been fruitless. None of his calls to Jamaica had been answered, none of his letters replied to. It was as if Peter had fallen off the face of the earth, but then that had happened to a lot of people lately.

If he knew Peter, he'd be somewhere on his way here right now, coming to straighten out the whole mess. Then he'd go back to Jamaica and drop out for good. Maybe this time he'd go with him, thought Mark dreamily, live on a boat in Montego Bay. He made another mental note to visit Peter's house on the top of Harvard Hill to see if there was any sign of his friend.

Finding the last member of the dream-team was much more of a problem, for in this case Mark didn't even have a name, only a vague hunch. From his investigations of the plague's progress across the country, he knew it had originated somewhere on the West Coast. He needed someone from that area with knowledge of the disease and how it could be fabricated and propagated across the Net, someone with deep knowledge of chemistry, biology, and physics – a tall order indeed.

Serendipity lent a helping hand, as did Mark's habit of keeping mementos of the past. Rummaging around some boxes of old books and papers given to him years ago by Peter, looking through the stuff more out of bored curiosity than the hope of finding anything useful, he stumbled upon a college textbook on the very subject he was interested in, biological and genetic engineering. He picked up the book and started leafing through the pages, when a small piece of folded paper fell out and floated to the floor. Mark groaned audibly as he bent down to pick it up, and whistled softly to himself as he unfolded and read it.

"I'll be darned!" he exclaimed, as he digested the contents of the letter. It read like a page from Lady Chatterley's Lovers, with graphic references to body parts and remembered caresses, and the hope of more to come, a love letter signed, LCR, by the looks of it from Peter's student days.

"The lucky stiff. Looks like little ol' Pete was carrying on hot and heavy with some chick. I wonder if Sandy knew about this."

That would have explained a lot of Peter's marital problems. Maybe she figured what's good for the goose is good for the gander, mused Mark, as he looked at the textbook with renewed interest.

The author's name was Dr. Linda Rayburn, from Stanford University. He slid his finger down the book's many-paged table of contents. It was immediately obvious that its scope was immense, covering topics from Genetic Engineering and biochemistry to the possibility of Quantum computing machines. Toward the end of the book was a small, forth-level appendix called 'Using Free-Floating RNA to Construct Single-Celled Organisms for a Self-replicating Computer.'

"Sounds like she knows her stuff, partner," said Mark, doing John Wayne to the wall. "And she has the hots for our main man, Peter. She's exactly the one we need!"

Mark quickly turned to the back jacket of the book and noted the small bio about the author that gave her address in care of Stanford University in Palo Alto, California. There was a small, black and white head shot of a not unattractive brunette, with straight bangs, thick-rimmed glasses, and a rather pretty but down-turned mouth.

"OK, beautiful, now how do we find you?" pondered Mark verbally, scratching his head and pacing the length of the rectangular room. "Dr. Linda Rayburn. Where are you now?"

Mark's musings were interrupted by the sound of someone trying to get in the front door. He froze in panic, his heart beating against his ribcage like a runaway pump. Walking to the bottom of the steps leading to the front entrance, he peered up listening intently. Then his heart stopped beating completely. Someone was trying to break in!

EMERGENCY GOVERNMENT CENTER, BOULDER, COLORADO, SEPTEMBER 22, 3:00 PM

Stan Bellows convened the emergency meeting of the committee of corporate heads that now ran the government of the United States. Where before these bureaucrats had acted behind the scenes to control the legislature and executive, they now governed directly, with no pretense, without lobbyists or front men, an event that went mostly unnoticed in the chaotic, uninformed daily struggle for survival, which for most people in the country now passed for the norm.

The president of Mexico and the Prime Minister of Canada had both succumbed to the plague, as had a good portion of the United States government, including most of the cabinet and the second in command. There would be no elections this year, while the Democratic incumbent had fled to Europe, where he vainly tried to organize a government in absentia.

The ski resort that had become the center of Stan Bellows' emergency government high in the snow-clad mountains, had no fiber-optic connection to the outside world and so stayed mysteriously plague free, although the coincidence was still lost to most of those in power. The good news was that with the disruption of the fiber-optic network caused by the plague, the epidemic had subsided for the moment, though it festered in the bowels of those Organics still functional. The bad news was that every effort was being made to restore the network as soon as possible.

Europe, although still free of the plague for the most part, was having problems of its own, in the form of a major financial collapse. This was caused by the disruption of the continent's Organic computer banks by the Trojan-horse worm, the first computer virus of its kind targeted at the biological machines themselves. Each day the infected

114

computers were out of commission cost the countries involve millions of Euros, resulting in falling prices, unemployment, and fiscal chaos. In the midst of their troubles few took the time to notice the almost coincidental absence of the plague.

"Gentlemen. Ladies," said Bellows, addressing what was left of the most powerful leaders of industry and government in the country. "The first meeting of the emergency committee is now in session." Stan Bellows' voice boomed out over the subdued din of individual conversation. "The first order of business is reestablishing of the fiber-optic network system and the link-up with Europe. To achieve this we have..."

Stan Bellows was interrupted in mid-sentence by a storm of protest.

"What about the plague...?"

"People are starving..."

"We need a nationwide approach..."

"The banks have to be stabilized..."

"Why should OptiComm's problems take precedence...?"

And so on, in one loud outburst of fear and anxiety, as each one claimed a special need or emergency, or promoted one area of the country or some segment of industry over another. The discord in the room mirrored the contention and disharmony at every level of government and society as a whole.

"Order!" bellowed the chairman, banging his fist on the table. "Everyone shut up! We're not going to get anywhere like this."

It soon became obvious that stopping the plague was everyone's top priority. Also high on the list was the problem of Europe's terrorist-induced economic recession, which threatened the US economy as well.

Bellows went on quickly and decisively. "We cannot solve one problem without solving the other. They're inter-related. We can't stop the plague without European aid. We can't help Europe recover from its current economic situation without stopping the plague. We cannot defeat either the plague or the European problem without the capabilities made possible by the fiber-optic network. To solve one, we must solve them all. To solve them all, we must be free from the type of terrorist activity that would destroy our very way of life. People like the inventor of the Trojan-horse virus, must be found and punished.

There was a period of prolonged silence. Several committee members, supporters of Bellows, nodded their heads in soundless

115

agreement, while many others sat pondering his words with furrowed brows and downcast eyes. A few sat fuming in frustrated anger, unable or unwilling to express their thoughts. Finally, key members of the committee voiced their reserved agreement, and the decision was made. There would be a three-pronged effort, each working on a specific imperative, but all coordinated through the committee. Since Stan Bellows would head that committee, the likelihood that his personal agenda would be focused on was all but assured.

Someone at the far end of the room voiced the growing rumor that the plague was carried along by the network itself and grew inside the organic computers. The room burst into another chorus of loud objections and cries of agreement.

The battle lines were drawn. The best minds in the world had looked at it and no one could agree, so how were these bureaucrats supposed to figure it out? When reason fails, instinct takes over, and Bellow's gut was telling him the slums were the source of the plague, just like it was telling him the European virus was a terrorist attack. Then he had a sudden, to him, brilliant revelation. He waited until the room quieted down."

"Ladies, Gentlemen, I have reason to believe the terrorists who attacked Europe's economy with the Trojan-horse virus and the ones in our own slums unleashing the plague are one and the same. It's a conspiracy and I have the proof.

The room was stunned into silence, a silence Stan Bellows did not break.

PALO ALTO CALIFORNIA, SEPTEMBER 22, 3:45 PM

Fear gripped Linda Rayburn, fear and loathing at what she had become, at what she had done. The streets outside were a war zone, a no-man's land where one could not move undetected during the day, and dare not go out at night. Disease and death strode the land like handmaidens, bringing misery and despair wherever they went.

Linda's mind had snapped long ago, long before her thirst for revenge had overwhelmed her reason, long before her failed attempt to halt the epidemic drove her to distraction. She created her demons out of her own malice, like gnarled weeds from a poison garden. Her soul had been warped by years of neglect, her conscious strangled by a lifetime of hurt. The pain she felt had been so intense, she had just

116

stopped feeling altogether, and an unfeeling thing of Linda's intelligence was a dangerous animal indeed.

She moved about her apartment house frantically searching for something she could not find, looking everyway, behind bookcases and cabinets, beneath chairs and tables, for that elusive thing she would recognize if only her eyes gazed on it. Time was running out. She didn't know why, she didn't know how, but the clock was ticking, she could hear it just behind the sound of her own beating heart.

"Oh, where is it?" she intoned in a pleading voice, as she ran up and down the huge staircase, along the wide-paneled hallways and sparsely furnished rooms, her bare feet making a light patter on the hardwood floors.

Fresh outbreaks of the epidemic had broken out in LA, Phoenix, Salt Lake City, and Denver, wherever the network of Organics was reestablished. Where it broke out, it raged like an out of control brush fire consuming all in its path, since there was no longer any means to combat it.

Linda's searching brought her into the penthouse laboratory where her powerful quantum machine continued to compute the last equations she had fed it, only some three weeks before. The pixel representation of its computations danced on the display board like a psychedelic light show. It reminded her for some reason of Christmas lights.

Her meandering mind wandered from there to her last Christmas with Jack Lambross, the last man in her life. It had been a warm, balmy evening in California, where she never got used to seeing Christmas decorations among palm trees and bikinis. It was on that night, after they had made love for the second time under the fake evergreen tree that her lover-teacher-father told her about his dream of creating and programming artificial viruses and microbes that would do man's bidding, fighting disease and performing myriad tasks from mining to colonizing the planets.

It was the ready access to all his notebooks and papers, which he had left her on his death a week later, that allowed Linda to construct her ingenious virus in the first place. No matter that he had died of a heart attack while making love to another one of his students. He had left her the huge sum of money that made it possible for her to start research into her quantum-computing device. Too bad it hadn't been enough money to prevent those bastards in quantumComp from stealing it. Funny how something that had started out so noble and grand, so pure and exhilarating, had turned out to be so ugly and corrupted in the end.

Just as quickly as they had come, the images from the past disappeared, to plunge her into despair again, as she realized that she had still not found that very important something she had lost some time ago. She started running down the stairway as if the Plague itself were after her. On she ran, past the first floor landing down to the huge, many-roomed basement, where she had intended starting her own company once her invention had allowed her to branch out on her own. Still unfinished, it was dark and full of shadows. She had not been down here in months, since that day they had tried to steal her baby. She stored most of her old things here, items her parents had shipped to her when she graduated from college. Instead of a graduation present like most of her friends got, they sent Linda everything she had ever owned, every picture, every doll or teddy-bear, every book, every article of clothing, as if they didn't want to be reminded that she ever existed.

Her lonely past haunted her like the empty eyes of a homeless child. Could what she was looking for be down here? Frantically, she started rummaging through the boxes and crates. Time was running out. She had to find it soon or something terrible would happen. She forgot what that terrible something was, but she knew she didn't want it to happen. If only she could remember what it was she had lost.

CHAPTER 10

MINIMUM SECURITY FACILITY, BULGARIA EASTERN EUROPE, SEPTEMBER 29, 2036, 8:00 PM

Eddie was surprised that they still hadn't traced the Trojan-horse virus to him yet, at least as far as he could tell in his self-imposed isolation. He talked and spoke to no one. He was even more surprised that the hinted at visitors hadn't shown up. Although if they were coming from the disease-ridden States, where fresh outbreaks of the epidemic were occurring daily, he wasn't too surprised. After all, there probably wasn't anyone left to come and get him, and that suited Eddie just fine. The European Union was almost as concerned about their economic collapse as they were about the plague, but it was hard to tell by the chorus of strident voices raised at the mention of either problem.

Eddie was convinced that his virus had prevented the plague from occurring on the continent. From the looks of things, that was only temporary. There were daily reports that a fix for his virus was only hours away, as new batches of Organics were being manufactured with the preventive measures encoded, but the new machines never arrived. Another day without the modern conveniences the world had come to depend on turned into another week. Perhaps, Eddie thought, his last minute jab had worked after all. One could only hope.

He was somewhat heartened by the late night radio chatter, talk against the Fiber and the Organic machines that comprised it, of how much nicer the world had become without them. People were beginning to rise up against the machines, at least a few of them. Some were even arguing for a moratorium on whether or not the Fiber of Organics should even be started back up again. There were a number of competing technologies using satellite communications and old silicon machines beginning to make a comeback, despite the obvious limitations. However, for some, going back in time twenty or thirty years was like asking someone in the 90's to live without electricity.

His first task was to get rid of his irksome roommate. That problem was about to be taken care of once and for all. Eddie checked his face in the mirror and got ready. The nosy little snitch would be coming back from his session with the warden any minute. Eddie gulped down the awful smelling concoction he had made himself earlier that day in the pharmacy, and lay down on his bunk to wait. He didn't have long.

The room was dark, only the light from the hallway filtering in through the small meshed window in the doorway. He could hear his roommate's telltale footfall as he sauntered, feet shuffling, up the hall.

"You asleep already?" he asked rudely, flinging open the door suddenly and switching on the harsh lights. "I want to write some notes up for the warden."

Eddie didn't answer, but turned toward the wall and groaned.

"What's a matter, you don't feel good?" said the snitch worriedly. Eddie knew his roommate was a hypochondriac with an understandable - given their filthy surroundings - fixation on the epidemic in the US.

Eddie would have answered, but the vile-tasting, black liquid he had drunk just moments before was starting to come up on him. He threw off his blankets and turned over on his side. Leaning out over the bunk, he tried to fight back the nausea.

His roommate stared at him in alarm.

"You don't look so good!" he observed, noticing Eddie's pale complexion and red, blotchy face. Eddie was sweating profusely, his hair plastered to his forehead.

Unable to hold it in any longer, Eddie threw-up violently, gushing black, awful-smelling bile across the floor in a spectacular series of heaves that left him breathless and teary-eyed. For a moment, he wondered if he had gone too far. The unwanted roommate almost dropped dead with fright, but before he could get to the door to flee, Eddie stood up and approached him with outstretched arms, revealing his bare chest. His throat and underarms were swelled with large, reddish lumps the size of almonds. His terrified tormenter almost flew backward in fright, plastering himself against the wall. Eddie staggered toward him croaking, "Help me! Help me!" as he grasped the petrified man by the arms.

The snitch screamed in terror, flailing his hands in the air, and ran out of the room and down the hallway, raising such a ruckus that a riot broke out. They had to shut down the entire section of the prison until order was restored late the next day, after medical teams had assured everyone there was no plague. It had all been a false alarm, they said, caused by yet another neurotic individual who thought they had every disease they ever read about; just an overactive imagination caused by the strain of living with someone like the mad Polack, Eddie Pavloski. Eddie, of course, had cleaned himself up, removing the flesh-colored lumps of putty he had glued to his neck and underarms. Cleaning his room of the liquid he had regurgitated on cue, everything looked normal when they came barging in with their protective suits.

"I don't know what you're up to, Pavloski," the warden said. Eddie stood there like a model inmate feigning complete confusion. "I don't think mister Manly would make something like that up, and I certainly wouldn't put it past you to pull some sort of scam like this. That's what you do, isn't it, Pavloski, scam people?"

"You don't have to be so formal, warden. You can call me Eddie. Or you can call me the Great Enigma, if you think I'm such a big mystery."

"That's very funny, Pavloski, but I wouldn't be so glib if I were you. Your old friends have been asking about you. Remember, the guys who put you here in the first place? The people in the US involved in helping us solve this Trojan-horse thing seem to have taken a renewed interest in you. They want to make sure you're safe and sound until they can, eh, have a little talk with you."

Turning to the two burly guards he had with him the warden continued. "I think we should put Mister Pavloski in solitary, for his own protection."

As they led him out of his semi-comfortable room to the cold, bare cell in the damp basement of the facility, Eddie smiled pleasantly, as if he were a monk on another plane. At least he wouldn't have any more roommates to worry about. If his last little bomb had triggered as planned, it would be quite awhile yet before there were any Organics working on the continent, and longer still before they were hooked to a Fiber, and that suited Eddie just fine.

SOMEWHERE IN NORTHERN KENTUCKY, SEPTEMBER 30, 5:00 AM

Much had happened in the eleven days since Peter had met Arthur. They had covered a lot of ground and not a little personal history, most of it Arthur's, who was as talkative as he was knowledgeable.

For the first few days they wandered through the plains and deserts of eastern Texas, heading in a rambling way almost due north

121

toward Dallas. Following Arthur's advice, they steered clear of Houston, not that Dallas promised to be much better. They traveled at night. Their plan to stay well away from populated areas was made all the easier due to the fact that the countryside was practically deserted.

Eventually, after a few days like this, they were able to commandeer a truck from a small filling station just outside the middle of nowhere. An early model Chevy with dangerously exposed gas tanks, it was sitting at the station with the nozzle still in the tank. They drove north along route 79 toward Buffalo, which Arthur assured him would be deserted as well. They saw no patrols on the roads or in the air at night when they traveled, or during the day when they rested beneath a tree or behind some building or sign. Driving north to Texarkana, they then headed east across southern Arkansas on route 82 all the way to Columbus, Mississippi, before striking northeast through Tennessee and Kentucky toward Lexington. Most of what they passed was wasteland and desolation, but there were many signs giving hint of the mighty plague ravishing the land.

Driving across four states, they had seen how each one handled the epidemic in its own way. The towns and cities in Arkansas, like their counterparts in Texas, seemed to be deserted, all the inhabitants presumably taken to the so-called medical centers. In Mississippi they encountered roadblocks at the entrances of cities, so that they could not leave the lonely highway, the villages, towns, and municipalities of that state sealed off from the outside world like a boy in a plastic bubble. Though the roadblocks appeared to be guarded, no one bothered the travelers, who drove only at night with the lights out.

Tennessee had been a battle zone and their trip across the state a harrowing experience for both Peter and his companion. It was obvious as soon as they crossed the border from Mississippi that things were out of control. First were the burnt-out buildings and vehicles, not just a few scattered here and there, but whole neighborhoods, entire towns, complete counties, without an untouched edifice. Then there were the huge, red, glowing bonfires, burning God knew what, that raged on the distant hilltops. Finally, the bodies started appearing. First one here by the intersection, then another one there by the street sign, then two, then a half-dozen, until eventually they saw mounds of them wherever they looked.

They had little luck sleeping during the day because of the constant chatter of small-arms fire that filled the air, interrupted occasionally with short bombardments of heavier mortars or rockets, as marauding bands of indistinguishable factions competed for one place or another

One tense moment occurred on their second night traveling through the state, about halfway through their nightly run. Peter was driving slowly with the lights out as usual, the full moon hiding behind high trees, which crowded both sides of the highway. Arthur, who had slept poorly the last two days, was asleep in the seat beside him. Suddenly, a group of men surged out of the woods a short distance in front of the pickup. Peter instinctively sped up. As he did, so did the men, running across a field to intercept them. He could see several of them out of the corner of his eye as the car sped past. Some shouted things he couldn't hear. Some waved their arms as if hailing him. One leveled something in his direction. The truck, now doing sixty, zoomed past the mob, which merged on the road behind it. Breathing a sigh of relief, Peter heard several faint pops that sounded a little too much like gun shots.

"Jesus! Are they shooting at us?" he yelled in alarm.

"What's that? What happened?" asked Arthur, shaken out of his stupor by the commotion. "Why are you going so fast? For God's sake slow down!"

"I can't. I think we're being shot at," Peter informed his now wide awake passenger.

"And I missed it?" said Arthur with a wry smile. "Well, if you're going to drive so fast, you'd better at least turn on the lights. It might be nice to see whatever it is we hit. I wouldn't worry about being spotted by the authorities. I doubt there's anybody in authority around these parts. Don't stop for anyone."

They drove on in silence the rest of the night, twice more narrowly escaping running encounters with armed gangs of ill-looking ragamuffin men. That had been two days ago.

They were now moving through Kentucky, which like Mississippi seemed to be barricaded behind their cities and towns, using the light of the waning moon to see their way. Arthur hadn't stopped talking since they started out that evening.

"I'm telling you, Peter, this plague is retribution for a human race who thought it could live without God. Who thought their technology would make them free of their creator. And look what good all their technology did them, all their great medical science."

"That's pretty funny coming from a teacher," yawned Peter, responding more out of boredom than any real desire to participate in a philosophical discussion.

"Oh, just because I teach how to use something, doesn't mean I give my humanity up to it or stop believing in the spiritual side of things."

"Well, Arthur, you should know you can't turn back the clock," observed Peter, the great technocrat turned dropout. "You can't stop progress."

"Oh, Yeah? Well this here plague has pretty near stopped civilization dead in its tracks. Anyway, at what price is our progress obtained, the price of our souls?"

"Now you're being melodramatic," chided Peter.

"No, I'm being a realist. Science believes it has all the answers, even to the point of proving or disproving the existence of God. Science has come to the opinion that it no longer needs God, not to explain the universe, not to create life, not to perform miracles. All these things science has taken over. Now we find ourselves faced with the inexplicable and our science is as helpless in the face of it as a puppy against a hungry lion."

"You're starting to sound like some evangelist. I thought you said you didn't believe in religion."

"I said the old religions have broken down. They're no longer relevant. They no longer fulfill the needs they once did. They don't hold any credibility for most of your scientifically sophisticated folks now days, and nothing has been able to replace them. Oh, there've been attempts, some good ones too, but every time someone speaks of spiritual things, things that can't be measured and analyzed by scientific methods, they're ridiculed and laughed at. Even those who think they're religious are just going through the motions, never really seeing its true meaning. These things have been neglected by society for too long, a society that can think of nothing but its next gratification, its next time-saving device."

"Are you through?" asked Peter laughing, not agreeing with Arthur in the least. As a matter of fact, you couldn't have found two more diametrically opposed points of view regarding science and religion. For while Peter had turned his back on technology itself, seeking to get as far away as possible from computers and their networks, he still believed science was the savior of the human race. To Peter Danvers, science was religion, the ultimate expression of an intelligent, creative energy. Arthur wasn't through.

"At the end of logic, at the end of reason, at the end of all your scientific gyrations lies mystery," he said, as if that summed it all up, case closed, end of story. He was about to go on when he suddenly yelled.

"Watch out!"

HARVARD, MASSACHUSETTS, OCTOBER 4, 2036, 7:00 AM

Mark had crawled out a back window that terrifying day in late September, and hid beneath a flowering lilac bush as men in protective white uniforms broke down his front door. Not knowing what else to do, he made his way furtively to the Danvers' house on the top of Harvard Hill, moving along hiking trails that connected it to Oak Hill where his underground home, until then undiscovered, had been. That was almost two weeks ago. He had been living in the basement of the Danvers' home ever since.

Mark had spent many happy hours here in the old days, working with Peter late into the night on one project or another. It, like all the other well-heeled homes on the hillside, were now deserted and boarded up, as if a level-5 hurricane was expected. The wind that beat these houses, however, shook no leaves and battered no shutters. This wind flew on the silent wings of the pestilence.

Mark was no closer to putting together his dream-team of experts to fight the plague than he'd been two weeks ago, but at least he was still alive and free. But for how long? The authorities were obviously conducting exhaustive sweeps to gather up all those who had somehow escaped the first pass. Mark's name must have been high on the list. He was surprised that they still had the manpower to do such things, and wondered who was running the show now.

He had set up trip wires around the house and attached them to the doors and windows, so that anyone trying to break in would cause an elaborate chain of events culminating in a number of pans crashing to the floor, a sound sure to wake him up even from a deep, beer induced slumber. Now he wiled away his time thinking about a good stiff drink and how to get one, that is when he wasn't busy worrying about the plague and how to stop it.

Recent events had only confirmed his suspicions. The plague had receded with the disruption of the Fiber. No net of Organics, no epidemic. It seemed obvious to him. Why didn't anybody else see it?

The fact that Europe's Organic net was dysfunctional and they were virtually without plague, made it even more obvious. Whatever the *Great Enigma* had done to those machines, it had saved the continent. If only Mark could do the same thing here, before they installed the newest batch of biological computers and began to link them up again. Even more importantly, where was his good friend Peter Danvers?

Mark spent much of his time reading from Peter's rather substantial library, now buried in boxes in the corner of the basement, along with old computer parts and antiquated test equipment. It didn't take Mark long to construct a working, although antiquated silicon-based computer and satellite receiver, which he used to scan the airwaves and radio frequencies for news and intelligence - what little of it there was - listening to the chatter, but not taking part in it.

From the sound of things, time was running out. A new bank of Organics had been scheduled for installation at the end of the previous month. Something must have happened to delay things, but they couldn't be far from completing the task and bringing the new machines online.

"How can they be so stupid?" fumed Mark, picking up the transmission one morning. "They'll start the whole thing all over again, the idiots!" Unfortunately, there was no one listening except the bare walls, for Mark was too timid to try to transmit his warnings to anyone on the outside, not after what he had seen.

In his capacity as an employee of OCI, working for the mighty OptiComm, he had been exempt from the strict curfews and roundups. However, he had seen enough to know the depths the human race could sink to when dealing with such extremity and fear. He had once visited one of the huge tent cities that passed for medical camps, more detention centers and deathtraps than any kind of succor or aid for the stricken. The experience left him shaken and ill. No, he wanted no part of that, thank you very much.

If only he could get in touch with Peter and that Pavloski character, or contact Peter's old flame out there on the West Coast, then maybe he'd have a chance of stopping this thing. But what could one man do alone against world?

BOULDER, COLORADO, EMERGENCY GOVERNMENT CENTER, OCTOBER 4, 12:00 NOON

Stan Bellows grunted with satisfaction as he surveyed the latest reports from the field. Everything was back on track. The epidemic was under control. The weekly death toll was decreasing for the first time since early August. New banks of Organics were being established each day. Soon he would have his Fiber back, connecting them all together, and soon after that, the US-European link.

He had been ruling by emergency decree since late September, despite the strenuous objections of an absent president, who had squandered much of his credibility in the first days of the epidemic by fleeing the country. At least Bellows had kept the military under control.

Using the plague as an excuse, most of the slums across the country had been razed to the ground, the inhabitants killed in the onslaught or taken away to even larger camps, something no elected official had been willing or able to do. Instituting these draconian measures, which his Asian backers had insisted upon to curb the plague and the panicked population, was one of the first things he did on taking power.

"We don't need your help," he had insisted to Feng of the People's Republic, during their last conversation.

"Then you must get your people under control. I cannot take the chance that one of your fleeing citizens will infect my country."

"Don't worry, Feng," shot Bellows, angrily. "No one's going to infect you. We've taken all the necessary precautions. The plague's under control. We'll be back in business in no time."

So the forced detentions and roundups continued.

Stan waited impatiently for word from his man on the East Coast, Mike Pearlman, regarding the latest news on the Trojan-horse virus. Final tests of the fix had been completed, but the scheduled implementation deadline had been missed, with still no word of progress. Pearl was bringing the latest results to report in person.

If what he feared the most had come to pass and the TH virus had struck in the US, it could mean his ruin. That must be prevented at all cost. His own bank of Organics had just been installed, the newest and most powerful yet, all immune to the European virus, or so he was told. Soon they would be connected with his bunker in the mountains of Colorado. With these brains and his army of workers, Stan Bellows would rule the world.

CHAPTER 11

PALO ALTO, CALIFORNIA, OCTOBER 5, 2036, 1:35 AM

Linda Rayburn no longer paced the floors of her apartment building searching for something she could not find. At times she had all she could do just to raise her head from the pile of dirty rags she used for a pillow. Only her blue algae pills and vitamins, which she swallowed by the hand full, and a few cans of fruit and raw vegetables, kept her alive. Seldom leaving the confines of her basement, where she wandered among the relics of her sorrowful past, she had not been to the penthouse lab in days. There, her quantum computing device was still silently running the equations from her last attempt to stop the plague.

Linda's mind was no longer her own to control, but flew this way and that of its own accord, like a grain of pollen moves in zigzagging jerks in the air. First to the past, then to the future, now in the present, then outside of time, her brainwaves fluctuated from alpha to beta states as if a switch were being thrown back and forth.

Occasionally the sting of having her work taken from her came back on her as if it were happening all over again, and even in her weakened state, she'd throw a short-lived tantrum, lashing out with kicks and slaps at anything nearby. Other times, she'd be plunged into heart-rending sorrow, remembering what she had done, and all the misery and death it had caused. If only she could somehow make up for it all. But her every attempt to halt the horror had ended in failure. Then she would gnash her teeth and pull her hair in anguish.

Fear of the Plague had become an overwhelming obsession, obliterating at times, her ability to function. She knew what she had been looking for when she had frantically canvassed her apartment house, the Plague, lying in wait for her. It was behind every corner, under every chair and table, the malignant death she so deserved, yet dreaded.

She was lying in the darkness, her mind agitated in this way, when she heard the sound, a soft scratching and chewing noise, as if something were eating the wall next to her head. She sat up in alarm and banged her fists on the floor. Then she listened again. The sound had stopped. Maybe it had just been her imagination. After all, her senses had played tricks on her before, more than once. She lay her head back down again and heard the sound anew.

This time Linda stood up. Momentarily dizzy from her rapid movement and lack of food, she steadied herself on a nearby chair. There it was again, louder now, as if the thing had been emboldened by her pounding. Then she heard a similar noise, this one above her. And another! Whatever it was, they were all around her now, chewing and scratching their way toward her, like her Pestis germ, crawling toward the light.

Linda switched on a lamp and looked about the room. She thought she saw something disappear behind a box. The sounds grew louder. Grabbing an old broom, which had been lying in the corner for eons, she began to bang on the walls and ceiling with the handle, bringing down plaster in the process. She ran to the corner where she had seen something move and punched at the wall with the broom handle, poking holes in the thin plaster-boards. Suddenly, out of the quarter-sized openings jumped black, furry rodents, common mice the size of film containers.

Screaming and jumping on a chair, Linda looked on in horror as more and more mice came pouring out of the holes, running crisscrossing patterns across her floor. Worst of all, Linda knew that the mice had fleas. All critters that live outdoors have them, and everyone knew that fleas carried the Plague. But Dr. Linda Rayburn wasn't going to go without a fight.

Jumping from the chair, she pounded the floor with her broom, chasing the furry creatures around the basement and up the stairs through the rest of the house, screaming in a chilling war cry torn from her pre-human past. The battle was on.

EMERGENCY GOVERNMENT CENTER, BOULDER, COLORADO, OCTOBER 5, 9:00 AM

"I don't care if all the records have been destroyed, I want you to find her," yelled Stan Bellows to one of his local security agents. "She could be the answer to all of our trouble. I want her found and soon."

Mike Pearlman's report, which he had relayed through encrypted electronic mail - having changed his mind about delivering it in person due to this most recent emergency - had been very troubling. The new software, which was supposed to be immune from the virus and was highly anticipated in Europe, had been delayed indefinitely due to the discovery of the TH virus during final testing. Their worst-case scenario had occurred. At least Pearl had been able to discover who had written it, but that could wait. Bellows had more important fish to fry. In any case, the culprit wasn't going anywhere.

Bellows, who hadn't gotten where he was by being stupid or timid, had recently been thinking of some way to get beyond his current impasse, when he came upon what he considered a brilliant idea.

Before the epidemic had hit, one of his suppliers, QuantumCorp, the company where the deadly plague had first broken out, had hinted they were on the verge of a technological breakthrough with the design of a new type of computer. The company had been pretty tight-lipped about it, but Bellows had informants in all the right places. They told him the firm had been secretly working on a quantum computer, something decades ahead of its time, but that one of the lead researches, a Doctor Linda Rayburn, had had a mental breakdown and the project had to be canceled. Then the plague had hit.

Recently, with all the setbacks and attacks on the Organics, Stan began to think of this new computer as an alternative, something to break away from his present predicament. If he could somehow find this scientist and harness her knowledge to build this revolutionary new machine, immune from hackers and viruses alike, he just might be able to get out of this jam, and be one step ahead of his competitors, including the Chinese, who he grudgingly had to sell the Organic technology to.

"Yes, it just might work," he said out loud to no one in particular.

"What?" replied his confused subordinate on the other end of the satellite hookup.

"Nothing," yelled Bellows. "Just make sure you find that woman. Sweep the Palo Alto area. That's where she was last reported living. Don't call back until you've found her, got it?"

"Yes, sir," said the security official. This was one boss he didn't want to cross, not if he valued his job or his life. One word from SB and he and his family could end up on the wrong side of a wire-fence.

All around them had been pandemonium that terrible night over two weeks ago. Peter and Arthur had been making their way across country in their commandeered pickup truck, when they hit a roadblock in Kentucky. Despite their protests, they soon found themselves in Lexington's Commonwealth Stadium Detention Center. Soon after that they found themselves in the middle of a riot. Searchlights flashed. Helicopters hovered. Guns were fired and people ran screaming everywhere. The smoke and flames bellowed to the sky. It was only through their cunning and Arthur's knowledge of the place, picked up from his week in its deepest recesses caring for the sick, that they made it out alive, and then only by the skin of their teeth. Two specks in the chaos, they scurried away from the inferno that had been their prison, and made it to the relative safety of a deserted wooded suburb.

Heading northeast toward Maysville along route 88, avoiding the major population areas and many patrols, they hiked across country in clear weather. Staying away from the highways, they walked mostly at night. Aside from a lone helicopter here and there, a scattered patrol on the road, and a few signs of life in the woods, there was nothing. The countryside was virtually depopulated.

They passed fields full of dead cows and horses, perished because there was no one to tend them; past stores gutted and bereft of so much as a crumb of bread; past bodies left to rot in the street. Just outside the town of Paris, Kentucky, Peter broke into a sporting goods shop, which for some reason had not been vandalized yet, and helped himself to a deer rifle, a Winchester 30-30, one that reminded him of an old bolt-action twenty-two he had as a kid. While Arthur pulled down sleeping bags, wool clothes, and camping gear, Peter grabbed boxes of shells from the shelf and stuffed them into his pack. It was obvious to him now that if he was going to make it home to his kids and be of any use to them, he would have to arm himself and be prepared to use violence.

Peter Danvers had always believed that any confrontation could be solved with a little reasoning and a lot of understanding. The last few weeks had been enough to severely test that theory, as well as his faith in human nature. He had seen man at his worse, man not much better than a snarling, bipedal, hairless ape, and was determined not to be at the mercy of the first predator that came along.

"Aren't you going to take one for yourself?" asked Peter, putting a couple shiny bullets into the chamber of his new high-powered rifle.

"Naw, I'd have more chance of shooting myself or you than of anything else with the damn thing. One gun-toting idiot between us is enough, thank you," said the ex-school teacher.

"Suit yourself," replied Peter. "But I'm not taking any chances."

"Oh, but you are. Your chances of being shot have just sky-rocketed."

"You won't be so smug when this thing here saves our lives."

That had been a week ago. They continued on their way well supplied with food and camping gear, Peter's new gun slung over his shoulder.

Later that same day, they crossed the state line into Ohio and commandeered a lithium battery-powered Ford they found on a suburban side street. After checking the self-charging batteries, they headed northeast.

Traveling this way, they moved across the state without incident. They made good time, traveling in the early mornings and evenings, sometimes in broad daylight, sometimes at night by the light of the moon. Nowhere did they encounter people. It was as if they were on Mars, although this was an area devoid of traffic a good deal of the time even in normal conditions.

Reaching the northeast corner of Pennsylvania, they entered New York and headed across the Catskills. As they neared Wayne County their Ford gave out. Without the necessary repairs, they had to abandon the car. It was a good thing they did.

The entire metropolis of New York, comprising the whole southeast tip of the state, had been cordoned off, from New Jersey to the Catskills, across Massachusetts and Connecticut. They would never have made it in a motored vehicle, regardless of whether they traveled by day or night.

Over the next few days they made their way on foot across the state, walking through the wooded hills of the Catskills. Sometimes they crawled on their bellies past armed guards. Sometimes they hid for hours from search parties in some bush-filled ditch or crevice. Everywhere they went there were soldiers and roadblocks, the skies alive with helicopters and small planes, the roads crowded with troops and state police vans. There were surveillance teams on the top of every mountain, spies in every town, eyes in every farmhouse. The only thing the companions had going for them, except for Arthur's knowledge of the terrain, was the fact they weren't trying to break out of the city, but were coming from the opposite direction, across the rear of the cordoned area. Still, it had been touch and go. More than once they had escaped detection and capture only by the skin of their un-brushed teeth.

They were now at the border with Massachusetts resting in a deserted house, in a small village just outside West Sturbridge.

Massachusetts' response to the plague had been belated and mixed, some areas establishing curfews, with people staying in their homes, others like the metropolitan Boston area, rounding them up and concentrating them in large medical camps. In some places armed bands of vigilantes roamed the countryside. Travel was prohibited, especially across the state line. It was here, after successfully going so long and so far, that luck finally deserted the two companions.

As they left the farmhouse heading for route 2, they were spotted by a group of civilians manning a roadblock just outside the village. Things became ugly when the travelers tried to get past the surly band of scruffy men. It was obvious the two had come from across the state line. A couple of the men wanted to shoot them then and there, which they had a legal right to do, or so they said, but others wanted the bounty on violators of the 'no travel' law, $250 a head. Since there were no central holding facilities in western Massachusetts, it meant the prisoners would be shipped back where they came from, not a prospect either of the travelers relished.

Peter tried to explain who he was and that he lived in the state and was trying to locate his missing children. His pleas fell on unsympathetic, if not hostile ears. Things got tense when the spokesman of the group asked Peter to hand over his rifle. They were outnumbered six to two. Peter regretted Arthur didn't have a gun. At least then they'd have had more of a fighting chance.

Loath to give up his only means of defense, Peter lowered the barrel of the weapon and pointed it between the eyes of the lead man. Simultaneously, the barrels of six assorted rifles and shotguns snapped in their direction. Several of the men cocked their rifles. The Mexican standoff had begun.

Just when it seemed the night was about to explode in gunfire, Arthur stepped forward and spoke. How he obtained his information and reached his conclusions from the bits and pieces of scattered hints and snippets of their conversations, Peter would never know, but he did, and he used it to startling effect.

"Gentlemen, I take it you don't know who you're talking to. This is Dr. Peter Danvers from MIT. We were told not to divulge this information, but you people are acting extremely foolish. I trust you'll realize the gravity of the situation and the importance of helping us once you hear the facts, so I'm going to override our orders and tell you boys the truth. Dr. Danvers is on his way to Boston to help discover a cure for the plague."

"A medical doctor?" several of the men exclaimed in unison.

"No," responded Peter truthfully. "I'm a doctor of computer science."

"What the hell's that got to do with the plague?" asked the leader of the group.

"Did he say he was a doctor?" asked another.

"Everything," responded Arthur brightly. "The plague has been traced to the computer network and Dr. Danvers here is one of the leading experts in the field. His getting to Boston in time is of critical importance for the future of the country."

"Is what he's saying true?" asked the headman, looking hard at Peter, who still pointed the gun between his eyes.

"Yes," said Peter, following Arthur's lead, although he wasn't sure where it was going. "Ah, I've been in touch with a group of medical and computer researchers at MIT, who, ah, have determined the source of the plague and how it's, umm, propagating itself across the country."

"That's why it's defied all our attempts to stop it," broke in Arthur. "It isn't an ordinary type of plague."

"Why don't you have a government escort then?" observed the leader.

"Because it's top secret," answered Arthur, anticipating the question. "If the plague has been sent out across the computer network, then this may be an act of terrorism on a massive scale. Only a few people know this information. We're breaking all kinds of rules by telling you, but we've got to be allowed to go on our way. If anything happens to Dr. Danvers here, there may be no way of stopping the epidemic."

"Is he a doctor?" asked one of the men who still hadn't gotten it. "If he's a doctor, I got a sick child at home."

"We need medical help," said another, emphasizing the dim-witted one's point.

"No," replied Peter again. "I'm not a medical doctor. I can't help your sick people. The best way for me to help you is to get to Boston."

The group of men stood undecided, talking among themselves while still pointing their guns at the two travelers. Peter for his part kept his rifle aimed between the eyes of the headman.

"OK, boys, let 'em go. They can't cause no harm," said the leader finally.

"What about the reward?" asked the surliest of the crew, a gray-haired hillbilly just itching to pull the trigger and blow the fast-talking, smart-ass stock-jobbers away. "That's 500 dollars you're pissing away there."

"If what they're saying is true, they're worth a lot more than 500 bucks," said a second one, a short, fat younger man dressed in a brand new hunting outfit and carrying a shotgun.

"I got sick kids at home," interjected a third.

"Why should we believe what you're telling us?" asked the leader.

"You better believe it," answered Peter, staring hard into the other man's eyes. "If you think I'm going to let you stand in the way of me getting to Boston and stopping this thing, you've got another think coming. We're talking millions of lives for every minute we stand here arguing."

They stood staring each other in the eye, each trying to gauge the others thoughts, while their respective weapons threatened to splatter their respective brains into jelly.

Finally, the leader of the group lowered his rifle, seeing something in Peter's eyes that convinced him he told the truth.

"Come on, boys, let 'em go. They're tellin' the truth."

"Aw, what ya wanna do that for?" asked the surly one.

"Just do it!" yelled the leader. No one wanted to contradict him, so the travelers were not only let go but given written clearance, which would help immensely if they were stopped by other such vigilante groups as they made their way eastward across the state.

CHAPTER 12

PALO ALTO, CALIFORNIA, OCTOBER 22, 2036, 11:45 AM

What once had been Dr. Linda Rayburn slurped water from the toilet bowl as if she were a thirsty house cat. Luckily this particular piece of porcelain was no longer used for its original purpose, which Linda carried on wherever the urge took her. The broken unit ran like a bubbling brook with more or less fresh water. The mice, who had been fleeing some rodent holocaust the night they burst into her apartment, had disappeared as suddenly as they had appeared, although Linda in her mindless state still saw them just behind the next corner.

To one looking at her, she would have appeared emaciated and haggard, alarmingly so, but not the horrible image that she saw when looking in the mirror. No, Linda did not carry the germ that she had so thoughtlessly unleashed upon the world. No Pestis swarmed in her blood. Linda carried something much more horrible in her soul, the germ of her own guilt.

Linda's fall had been complete. Despite her metamorphoses, deep within the recesses of her mind, in some compartment of her brain still functioning, there burned a glimmer of her old self. It was no more than a sliver of gray matter, but it still bore a resemblance to human thought. This is what sustained her and kept her alive during these dark hours between humanity and bestiality.

For the rest of the day she scavenged her apartment for food, eating what was left of her blue-green algae and vitamins, scattered in cabinets and boxes throughout the apartment, opening a jar of apple sauce she found in the storage pantry, all that was left of the supply of goods bought months ago for the long siege.

Linda found her way into the penthouse laboratory, where her powerful quantum computer continued to crunch away on the last equations Linda had fed it, only some two months before. The pixel representation of the solution danced on the computer's display board like a Disney light-fountain.

"Pretty lights," she murmured, mesmerized. "Pretty lights."

The brief sliver of thought flickered out as if snuffed between the finger and thumb of some invisible hand, plunging her again into the darkness of the animal present, far better than the lonely pain and silent desperation that plagued her conscious mind.

MINIMUM SECURITY FACILITY, BULGARIA, EASTERN EUROPE, OCTOBER 23, 6:35 AM

Eddie had been rousted out of solitary late one night and hustled into a holding cell where he was interviewed by four hard-eyed interrogators, who used every cruelty in the book short of outright torture to extract his confession. He still wasn't sure exactly what was happening to him or who was in charge. All he knew was that he was being escorted under heavy security, with minimum belongings - basically the shirt on his back - out of his minimal security home to parts unknown.

He was now in the back of a padded van chained to the floor, with surveillance cameras and armed men watching him as if he were a side of beef going to market. Unlike his incoming journey, he was now pushed, prodded, shoved, and yanked with rough hands, boots, and billy-clubs, making him totally miserable and equally submissive. At this point he would have done anything they asked no matter how sickening and depraved. His one and only question on being taken suddenly from his solitary confinement got his two front teeth knocked part way down his throat. Stripped and hosed down, he was dressed in clean, orange prison fatigues and marched out of town pronto.

After what seemed like an eternity bouncing around in the back of the van, carsick from lack of food and vertigo, the vehicle slowed down at what appeared to be an airport, where he was unceremoniously pulled from the back of the truck and dumped on a runway. Facing him sat the silhouette of a large commercial supersonic aircraft. From the prodding and poking it was clear that they wanted him to go up into the plane, which he did with more than a little trepidation. There were many places they could be taking him, each one worse than the last his active imagination conjured up for him.

Eddie Pavloski moved his lips in silent supplication. It seemed natural for him to pray now, though he hadn't done so since he was a child of ten. His soul was vibrating in tune with the cosmic, plucked by the fingers of adversity. Eddie Pavloski needed all the help he could get.

He climbed the stairs at the rear of the aircraft and entered the large fuselage, his four armed guards - enough for a company of prisoners – accompanying him up the gangway in a tight, constricting knot. Going up was all but impossible given the shackling together of his feet, but two of the men helped by half dragging, half carrying him up to the hatchway. Once inside he was handcuffed to the last seat. Two of the goon squad sat down opposite him, a third sitting in the row across the aisle. Another went forward to the front of the aircraft, which was curtained off.

Eddie sat there trying to avoid the harsh stares of his guards, who sat facing him like two stone-faced gargoyles. His mind turned like a tornado between fear and anger. Then a small voice whispered in his ear, "As long as you're sucking air, there's still hope."

"Where are you taking me?" he asked, emboldened now that his tormenters were belted in and the plane taking off.

One of the men sitting facing him smiled ominously, while the other ignored him completely.

"You've been extradited to the United States, Mister Pavloski," answered the smiling one, looking at him as if telling a good joke. "For terrorist activity against all free and democratic countries."

"What?" he exclaimed over the din of the take-off. "I admitted this European thing, but what does that have to do with the US? You have no right to take me to the States." The fear was rising in his gut. This was by far the worst of the scenarios he had been able to conjure up.

"Ah, but I'm afraid you're mistaken, Mister Pavloski. The computers you so callously sabotaged were licensed to the Europeans by a US Company, which has been nationalized by the government during this grave emergency. This is very much our affair."

Eddie's terror rose in waves, but he wasn't that surprised. He had seen it coming. He just didn't think the United States government - or what was left of it in the form of Stan Bellows' emergency committee - would be coming after him itself.

"Don't feel so bad," said the smiling one, who looked at him as if contemplating his torture with great satisfaction. "In a way we're saving you. When the Europeans find out it was you who disrupted their entire economy, your life won't be worth a plugged nickel."

As much as Eddie hated his captors, he had to admit they had pretty much summed up his situation. Eddie's life was now worth about five stinking cents.

Mark had been sleeping soundly when his trip alarm went off, the pile of tin cans and pans clanging to the hard basement floor with a resounding crash. He jumped up with a start, his heart pounding like a Japanese drum. He had had to flee his underground house just a month ago under similar circumstances, now the same thing was happening all over again.

By the sound of it, someone was breaking into the house above. He stood in the dark, terrified and uncertain, anticipating the worst.

"Damn!" he whispered in the dark. "They've finally found me."

Whoever it was would soon be inside.

Mark listened intently, trying to determine who or what it was, an army or a lone fugitive like himself. He had thought plenty about what he would do in just such a circumstance, but now faced with the reality of it he found he was tired of jumping out of windows and running. Instead, he looked around the basement for a weapon. Then he heard the shattering of glass in the back of the house and almost had a heart attack. It sounded like someone was climbing through a window. He listened but could hear only a single intruder. Except for the noise of broken glass and scuffling above, all was total silence.

Mark decided to stand and fight. He was going to get his own licks in. Whoever it was wasn't going to get him without a struggle. If they killed him, so much the better, he was getting sick of the whole damned thing anyway. Mark readied himself. They would now find out how dangerous a cornered chemical engineer could be.

He grabbed the most lethal thing he could find, a heavy steel poker resting by the fireplace, and stood waiting behind the wall at the foot of the basement stairs, hoping his beating heart wouldn't give him away.

He could hear the unmistakable noise of someone moving around above, going from room to room. What was going on? Was this another sweep? Was the place being robbed like so many others, stripped of every form of essential or valuable, food, clothing, and furniture? Or was someone looking for him?

Mark stood frozen in his stance like a cigar-store Indian, poker in his hand, his arm raised over his head, his back against the wall. He held the heavy iron rod so tight he got a cramp and had to put it down to massage his arm. While he was doing this, the intruder, who he had momentarily forgotten in his pain, opened the door at the top of the stairs leading to the basement and started down. Instantly, Mark had his weapon up and ready to strike.

Slowly, cautiously, the prowler crept down the stairs, one creaking step at a time, while Mark flattened himself against the wall and stopped breathing altogether. Well, this is it he thought to himself, in a surprisingly matter-of-fact manner - time to get ready to die. He almost did expire when the barrel of a high-powered rifle poked around the corner.

Instantly, with a speed and ferocity surprising even to himself, Mark sprang from behind the wall, slashing his weapon wildly but effectively at the rifle and the arms holding it. It fell to the floor with a heavy thud while the intruder fell backward from the last stair yelling in pain.

Mark stood over the huddled figure ready to bring the heavy fireplace implement crashing down on his skull, when he was grabbed roughly from behind by a strong pair of arms.

"Whoa, there! No you don't!" whispered a voice right behind his left ear.

Mark, momentarily disabled, struggled vainly for a short time in the steel-grip of his assailant, fearing for his life as the first intruder slowly got to his feet and picked up the rifle. How had he missed hearing the second person? He was so focused on the gun he had blocked out everything else. Well, it was too late to worry about that now.

The man with the gun turned around slowly and pointed the rifle at him. When he saw who it was Mark almost jumped out of his skin and breathed an audible sigh of relief. Staring at him with suppressed pain and equal shock was his friend and mentor, Peter Danvers.

The two old friends looked at one another in astonished silence for a short time then Peter yelled for joy

"Mark, my God! What are you doing here? It's OK, Arthur, he's an old friend of mine." Arthur slowly let go of Mark's arms and took a wary step back, nervously eyeing the heavy steel poker Mark still held in his right hand.

"Peter!" exclaimed Mark, still in a state of shock at seeing his old friend. "I, um, I, ah...," he stammered unable to articulate his feelings.

"Boy am I glad to see you," gushed Peter. "I didn't expect to find anybody here from the old days. And to think, of all people, here you are. Fantastic!"

Danvers leaned the rifle against the wall and went to embrace his friend, who returned the hug as if sleep walking. Even though he had speculated that Peter might in fact turn up, actually seeing him here in the flesh was almost too much to believe. Mark was having trouble adjusting to the reality of the situation.

The last person Peter had expected to find in the basement of his house was Mark Goodwater. On seeing him, however, the first sight of a familiar face from back home in years, he was overcome with powerful emotion. His eyes teared up as he hugged his only connection with the world he once knew.

After more exclamations of disbelief, backslapping, and high-fives, Peter and Mark got down to business, telling each other their respective stories. Mark pulled out a couple cold ones, much to his guests' surprise, and it wasn't long before the trio was lost in warm conversation.

Mark informed them of his fugitive status and the events leading up to his run-in with the law, although he was unable to tell Peter much about the whereabouts of his ex and the children. Peter and his traveling companion related their adventures coming up from Texas.

It didn't take long for Mark to explain his theory about the plague and the fiber-optic network of Organics. It was surprisingly close to the story Arthur had contrived to talk their way out of the situation in Stockbridge.

It was late. They had talked far into the night as they sat by the low fire burning in the basement's hearth, sipping beer.

"The plague's traveling through the fiber-optic cables infecting Organics," observed Mark.

"That's impossible," countered Peter for the twelfth time.

"No it's not," interposed Arthur. "It's the only possible explanation that fits the facts."

"Yeah, if you ignore the fact it's impossible to physically move matter along a fiber-optic cable. End of discussion. Case closed."

"Then they're not moving the virus across the network," admitted Arthur. "They're doing something else to the same effect. Whatever it is, they're doing it over the network through the Organics. It's the only thing that makes sense."

"That doesn't make any bloody sense," replied Peter in exasperation.

"Here, look at this," said Mark, working with Arthur like a Joe Lewis one-two punch, as he pulled out a map of the United States from under the couch where he sat. It was annotated with heavy red and black-inked lines, circles and dates. Flicking on the little reading lamp standing on a low glass table, he spread it out before them.

"If you take the dates the plague was first reported in each area as it made its way across the country, you see this pattern emerge."

He traced the heavy red lines across the map, connecting them to the ever-widening concentric circles in a pattern that showed a clear sequential effect. The epidemic seemed to move like dominoes, in ever widening parallel lines with double-backs and loops, following the communication hubs.

"A normal epidemic wouldn't spread like this, if it had spread at all, which is doubtful in this day and age," observed Mark. "It would have leapfrogged from one location to the next, along the major transportation routes. It would have popped up here and there, not like a lava flow or army ants following a scent trail. No, this epidemic traveled by some unknown means."

"It's just not possible," said Peter, shaking his head in perplexity. This type of technological certainty had been the plague's greatest ally.

"Rather than state the obvious although unhelpful negative, why not ask how you would go about doing it if you had to," suggested Arthur to his stubborn friend.

"First of all, who would want to? Second of all, I would never do such a thing."

"Oh, come on, Peter, speculate."

"Yeah, humor us," said Mark.

"OK. I guess you could send the instructions across, you know, the genetic code for the entity you wanted to transmit. Maybe you could somehow execute a program of protean formulas, but you'd need to have the necessary chemicals and molecules conveniently ready at the receiving end. No, it's just not possible. The calculations would be too difficult," he concluded, after a short struggle.

"I got news for you, pal," said Goodwater, getting frustrated with his old friend's skepticism at something that to him seemed so obvious. "Someone's figured it out. Those Organics are pumping out Plague germs across the fiber-net like there's no tomorrow.

"Well, it should be easy enough to verify," said Arthur, raising his bottle in a toast. "Let's set up a few little experiments, shall we?"

Talk of the plague brought home to Peter the uncertain plight of his family.

"Any idea what might have happened to Sandy and the girls?" Peter asked during a lull in the conversation.

"No," answered Mark. "Though I'm sure they're safe. You're probably not going to want to hear this, but last I heard Sandy was spending a lot of time with that a-hole, Todd Daniels."

The mention of the man that had taken over his business and his bedroom filled Peter with anger and made his face go instantly red.

"That creep! I hope he's at least taking care of them."

"I'm sure they're OK, Peter," his friend Arthur assured him. "After all, they're not alone."

"Do you know where Daniels lives?" Peter asked.

"No, but we can find out easy enough," replied Mark.

"Good, let's do it first thing in the morning. I've got to find them."

"Sure, Pete, don't worry," said Mark amiably, liking the feel of having his boss back demanding the impossible.

CASCADE MOUNTAINS, OREGON, NOVEMBER 5, 2:17 PM

"No damn cockamamie, hair-brained theory is going to jeopardize this project. If you can't handle it, Jacobs, I'll get someone who can," yelled Bellows hanging up the phone.

"That sonofabitch won't be National Security Advisor for long if he keeps advising me like that," Bellows announced to his new assistant, who stood nearby waiting for him to get off the phone. "The network is the only way this country's going to recover."

"But what if they're right about the plague being communicated over the fiber?" asked the concerned subordinate, Bellows' fourth technical advisor in the three and a half months since the epidemic had broken out. The way his assistants had all died, despite the most stringent precautions, would have made sense in light of this new information to anyone but a person consumed with his goals like Stan Bellow, at the exclusion of all other input. Nevertheless, as a precaution he made a point to postpone connecting his home to the Fiber, which was scheduled for installation in the next few days. He'd be damned if he was going to let it stop his plans, however.

144

"How can they be serious? I've been working in this business for over thirty years, and there's no way in hell you can send a virus like that over a network. It's just not possible."

"It's not a virus, it's a bacterium."

"Yeah, which is even bigger. So there, Phil, it just can't happen. OK?"

"Yes, sir, if you say so, sir," answered the confused assistant. "So what do we tell the CDC?"

"You let me worry about them," replied the chief executive.

There would be no slowing up of the network project. Europe would be going back on line in a matter of weeks, thanks to the patch they had finally developed and the pressure his people were exerting on the European community. The Asian connection would be delayed by months, but that was unavoidable under the circumstances. He'd be able to recoup those losses if he could get the US and Europe back on line.

"Another subject," the new assistant said. "Our people are headed back from Eastern Europe after picking up the hacker responsible for the computer virus over there. They've agreed to allow us to extradite him to the US. They should be in the States by late this afternoon. I'll keep you informed of any developments, sir."

"Good. That stupid sonofabitch didn't learn his lesson last time he screwed with us. He had to try it again. I'll make sure he never messes with anyone as long as he lives, which won't be into old age," promised Bellows, dismissing his subordinate with a wave of his hand.

He made a phone call after his assistant left the room, to another of his underlings in Nashville, Tennessee, who contacted two of his acquaintances in Macon, Georgia, just over a hundred miles south of Atlanta. They made the trip in a little less than two hours.

CHAPTER 13

HARVARD, MASSACHUSETTS, NOVEMBER 5, 2036, 6:20 PM

Peter had been doing a lot of soul searching; replaying every decision he had ever made that had led him to this point in his life, bereft of his family in the midst of calamity. He worried every waking hour about the well-being of his little girls, and dreaded every night the dreams of their suffering. He reproached himself for leaving them alone and defenseless, for thinking only of himself, for his lack of responsibility and courage. He had run away and now they were paying for it. It was only the excitement of the scientific chase, the search for the source of the deadly virus that kept him from total despair.

Vigilante groups and militia bands roamed the New England countryside. Most of the population had fled the cities or been imprisoned in the large internment camps. These circumstances, along with the fact that a third of the state's inhabitants had died, made once populated areas seem like ghost towns. Still, there was a constant danger of being discovered and sent to a medical center, or worse, for under the present conditions violence and death were the rule of the day.

Over time, Peter became convinced that Mark and Arthur were somehow right, the plague was being manufactured and transmitted through the Fiber. But how? Peter had a few ideas, which he explained to his partners during one of their many brainstorming sessions.

"It's gotta be some kind of synthesis program, using the genetic code of the disease and the surrounding molecules and elements of the Organics to construct it. While I have some vague notion how you would build a computer model of a DNA molecule or a protein, I haven't a clue as to how you would use that model to manufacture the actual molecular structures required, let alone how you'd do it outside a laboratory setting full of Petri dishes."

"That's why I was trying to locate that chick from Stanford," yelled Mark from the kitchen where he rummaged fruitlessly for the makings of a snack. "That area's the most likely source of the epidemic as well."

Hunger had become their fourth companion. The results of two earlier expeditions, which had netted a good supply of canned-goods and other non-perishables from deserted homes and stores, had just about run out. They would have to go further afield on each successive run, increasing the risk of capture and wasting valuable time.

They were discussing Mark's plan to contact Eddie Pavloski and Linda Rayburn to elicit their help in stopping the plague. Peter had confessed to knowing Linda, although he denied any sexual encounter with the brilliant professor while at MIT.

"She was really something," Peter admitted after a little prodding from Mark, and not a few beers. "She was a genius in molecular biology. I learned a lot from her. Then without further notice she dropped the whole field and took up quantum physics. I guess she wanted to skip biological computers and go right on to the sub-atomic ones. You're right, Mark, I'm sure she'd be able to help us."

"Even if we locate the people you suggest, how do you propose we contact them?" asked Arthur. "Travel's impossible and the network's out of the question."

"There's always satellite," answered Mark. "They're slow but sure and appear to be clean."

"Yeah, but without the fiber ground links it's patchy at best," observed Peter.

Mark reflected on Peter and Arthur's words.

"Why do you say traveling's impossible? You two did OK coming up from Texas."

"Yeah, but now you're talking about going across country," replied Peter. "Not to mention the fact that to contact Pavloski you have to cross the Atlantic. You don't know how difficult it was just coming up from Texas. We almost didn't make it several times. Things aren't getting any better."

"There are ways to get places if you really have a mind to," observed Arthur with a mysterious grin.

"What about food?" said Mark, heading back toward the kitchen to forage. "I'm starving."

The three friends spent the next few days gathering evidence to confirm Mark's theory about the source of the plague and formulating their strategy, which was rapidly taking shape – and scavenging for food. They also did their best to disrupt and sabotage the slowly recovering Fiber wherever they could. Peter's concern for the well-being of his family had resolved itself into a quest to seek out the whereabouts of Todd Daniels in the hope that Sandy and the kids were safe with him. In the trial of their lives, the three found comfort in each other's company and courage in each other's words, as they hurtled toward their unseen destiny, the fate of the world in their hands.

MILITARY DETENTION CENTER, POWELL AIRFIELD, KNOXVILLE, TENNESSEE, NOVEMEBER 7, 6:00 AM

Eddy's twenty-three hour trip to the States, eight of which were spent sitting on the runway in Bonn, had seemed like an eternity. If there had been a way for Eddie to jump out of the aircraft, he would have done it without hesitation, parachute or not, but he couldn't even go to the bathroom without a duet of goons by his side.

His worst fear had materialized. They had taken him to the plague-ridden US of A. What did they want with him? He hadn't done anything to them. Was this Europe's way of getting even, deporting him to this godforsaken place, where if the plague didn't get you some gun-toting fool would?

The first few days were filled with long hours of interrogations and psychological torture, where he was not allowed to eat or rest for long periods. Once he confessed, however, which didn't take long, his situation improved considerably.

Eddie was beginning to feel like his old self again after a few days of more humane treatment. He was housed alone in a clean tidy, if not overly spacious cell, and allowed to shower twice a week, also alone. As a matter of fact, other than his prison guards, of which there seemed to be an even half dozen, and his two interrogators, he saw no one, no other prisoners, no civilians, and no officials.

He was getting his spirit back, leading the dunderheads who questioned him daily on a wild-goose chase through theo-retical mathematics. No, the situation really wasn't that bad. The only thing that bothered him was the plague. It seemed to lurk behind every container and cubbyhole, and probably accounted for the lack of other human beings. For all that, however, it wasn't such a bad place.

Eddie was able to spend some time out of his cell in a small forty-five by fifteen foot fenced-in courtyard. Because it was surrounded by high, gray brick buildings, he was unable to see the green, rolling countryside on the outside, but the sun splashing on a small patch of concrete and weeds in a corner hinted at what was beyond. That's all he needed to feel alive. He had his shirt off and was lying on a bench, soaking up some early morning sunlight.

Suddenly, a knee descended into his stomach like a jackhammer, forcing the air out of his lungs. Before he could open his eyes to see what was happening, a fist slammed into the side of his head, so when he finally did open his eyes all he saw were stars. He tried to suck in air, but his windpipe was constricted by two very large hands. As he was being choked, still unable to see, with tears flooding his eyes, he heard the voice, soft and close to his ear. He tried to breathe, while his assailant repeatedly bashed the back of his skull into the hard wooden bench. Struggling vainly, his feet kicking in frantic rhythm as he was being choked to death, he heard the voice droned on.

"We've been patient with you, Pavloski, while you've been leading us around by the nose, but now we're done playing with y'all. There's no one who can help you, nowhere you can hide, nothing you can do. We'll make you suffer for every minute you've lied to us. You'll pray to tell us what we want to know, even when you'll no longer be able to."

The seconds without air ticked by like an eternity in which Eddie Pavloski's useless life spun before him like an old Edison movie box. A few more seconds and he would have no conscious thoughts at all; a few more seconds after that and he'd be dead.

"Now you're going to suffer, fool. You're going to pay the piper and the piper's me. I've got things in store for you they ain't even written 'bout yet."

Just as Eddie's eyelids began to flutter shut and his mind reached that alpha state close to sexual arousal, the hands were removed from his throat and he was whacked in the side of the head with a large callused palm, knocking him off the bench to the ground. He managed to suck some air through his already swelled windpipe with a painful gasp, his body racked with spasms. Instantly, he was rolled onto his stomach and cuffed with his arms behind him, then yanked to his feet. He could still not see his assailants through his half-closed eyes, as blows rained down upon him from all angles. Knocked down again, he was dragged into one of the buildings by his feet, hitting his head on the concrete doorway in the process, closing his left eye with an ugly wound.

Eddie was now in the hands of the most ruthless group of people he had ever encountered, throwbacks to another, more brutal and merciless age when life wasn't worth the mucous to spit on it. Men who would in normal circumstances have been in prisons or running some street gang, were now, in the aftermath of the epidemic, in positions of authority. They seemed to be in the majority. What he knew was incidental to them. Oh, he would spill his guts all right, that was a forgone conclusion, but they seemed to want more than the information he had. They wanted to see him scream.

Stan Bellows had what was left of the government's most secret and powerful agencies at his disposal, and as in most times of extremity, when a third or more of the population has died and the rest are struggling to survive, the worst seemed to rise to the top. Eddie Pavloski was now at their mercy.

CLAYMOTH FALLS, CASCADE MOUNTAINS, OREGON, NOVEMEBER 7, 3:20 PM

Stan Bellows disconnected his satellite phone after hearing the first good news he had heard in weeks, after months of stop and go progress his main hubs where about to become operational again. The worldwide fiber-optic network was all but reestablished. On top of this, his guest had arrived from Europe after interminable delay and red tape. Even now his goons were interrogating the prisoner. He was going to make him fry in front of the world, an example of what would happen to future hackers. The only negative news in the otherwise optimistic reports, were vague rumors of network sabotage in the northeast, around the Boston area. That place always had been a hotbed of discontent. He would deal with that nuisance later. For now all systems were *go*.

He leaned over the bed and stroked the naked back of his latest playmate, a twenty-two year-old long-legged beauty named Beverly, with straight black hair, slanting oval eyes, and dark skin that made her look Polynesian, although she was of Slavic descent, from Chicago. She moaned in lazy response, but couldn't quite open her eyes. Stan padded to the oversized bathroom and stepped into one of the twin shower stalls, keeping the water cold to help wash the lethargy away. Even his favorite Colombian brew couldn't seem to keep him awake, and he had so much to do.

Chaos still reigned in much of the country. The death toll was staggering, 500,000 in Los Angeles alone The dearth of skilled labor and technical personnel was a constant handicap, but Bellows was slowly, surely gaining momentum. Already he had a cadre of people, from farmers and truck drivers, to physicist, and engineers, doing his bidding.

He stepped from the shower, which he had run on cold for the last several minutes, into the hot tub, which had been filling with water since he started his shower. Wasting no time, he submersed himself in the hot liquid even though it seemed to sear his skin. He actually relished the pain, as if it were purging some unknown, unfelt guilt. He called for his playmate, until she stumbled into the room naked and slowly entered the tub, first her dainty foot, then her long, shapely leg, next her choice thighs and pubic area, then her washboard stomach, until lastly her delightful breasts were submerged. He began to fondle them playfully.

Yes, he had been smart to send the family to Geneva to stay with his sister. He certainly hadn't been lonely, going through a succession of eager young beauties, much like he imagined it had been for those successful movie moguls in the golden years of film, a different starlet for every night of the week. This latest one was the best so far, an exotic thing with a flare for the kinky. Still, his middle-aged libido wasn't reacting like it should have to the overwhelming stimulus. He must be working too hard.

His mind wandered to the prisoner who had arrived in the back of a chartered Lufthansa luxury liner six days ago, now safely in Kentucky, his East Coast headquarters, for intense debriefing. There, experts were gathered from all over the world at his behest, to interrogate the prisoner and analyze all that he said concerning the Trojan-horse virus. Unfortunately, all attempts to locate the missing inventor of the Organics, Dr. Peter Danvers, had so far been unsuccessful. Now that they had the Dark Enigma, however, they wouldn't need anyone else. After they learned his secrets, he would go on trial. No one had ever sought and obtained the death penalty for computer-related crimes, but all that would change with the execution of Eddie Pavloski on worldwide public television. What he had done amounted to terrorism on a mass scale. If they played their cards right, the sap might even serve as a scapegoat for the plague itself. Yeah, this would work out perfectly.

Thoughts of the public execution of the computer criminal and the reestablishment of his network - leaving him more powerful than ever - filled Stan Bellows with elation, such that his manhood began to swell like his ego. It wasn't long before the young nymphet was equally stimulated and the banquet was renewed. Just before he was swallowed in ecstasy, however, Bellows was visited by the most disconcerting thought. Someone or group on the East Coast was actively sabotaging his sacred Fiber. If this movement gained momentum and grew, it could be the end of everything he had been working for. As suddenly as it had appeared, his elation was gone, leaving both he and his mate frustrated and embarrassed. After a small scene she left the room and Stan was left alone with his dark thoughts.

Gritting his teeth, he choked back a cry of pent-up rage.

"No one is going to stand in my way," he swore, "No one!"

GLOUCESTER, MASSACHUSETTS, NOVEMBER 8, 11:20 AM

Sandy Danvers looked out over the Bay, which sparkled brightly in the late afternoon sun. Standing on a deserted stretch of sand known as Coffin Beach, her mind a jumble of memories and emotions, she wondered what had happened to the world she knew. Even more important, where were her children?

It had been over a month since her girls were taken. Now she lived the life of a fugitive, in one abandoned house or another, scrounging for food like an inept aborigine. All she could do was despair over the unknown fate of her little ones. If it wasn't for the small cache of supplies left in the tent, which she had the presence of mind to go back and get that terrible day, she would have starved long ago.

She had been thinking more and more of Peter lately, wondering where he was and what he was doing. She remembered with fondness his good-natured manner and cheerful disposition, his calm way of dealing with things, his kindness and generosity. Smiling, she recalled his awkwardness in bed and the gentle way he used to caress and kiss her. For the first time in many years she actually missed him. Maybe she had made a mistake there. Perhaps she should never have let that one go. After all, if her experience was any indication, a good man really was hard to find. She had always thought that there were plenty where that one came from, but she had been mistaken. Todd had been fun for awhile, but living with him, especially under the stress of the approaching plague and its aftermath had been less than pleasant.

152

The beach was devoid of life, strewn with debris and driftwood, the houses boarded up or with gaping holes where windows and doors should have been. Millions of dollars in real estate left like a vacant Love Canal, Coffin Beach was a good name for the place, a graveyard for washed-up flotsam and jetsam. The unkempt patch of sand looked like it had been hit by the salvo of a dozen battleships.

Sandy hadn't seen a soul since the military trucks had driven off with Todd and her kids, although she had seen aircraft overhead and heard vehicles in the distance. She found plenty of abandoned places to live, most of them with busted windows and missing doors. Those that weren't burned-out shells were gutted of furniture and personal belongings, or stripped of wall paneling and floorboards. Joining the menagerie of small animals and insects that called these once elegant houses home, she made herself as comfortable as possible, something she would not have thought of doing in her previous life.

Somehow she survived on her own, learning from necessity and desperation what others learn through patient example and practice. All the while, like the constant cry of the hungry seagulls, the fear for her daughters gnawed at her mind.

For some reason over the past few days, Sandy's anxiety had been increasing, as if someone inside her were turning up a knob, slowly but steadily. Nothing she did could assuage the sense of loss, the feeling of helplessness, of utter futility and despair. As she stood looking out to sea she began to cry. She became the primal female, mourning for her fate, for all the dead, for what she had lost, for her two missing children alone and far from home.

She cried until no more tears would flow. She sobbed until all desire to do so left her. The cleansing tears and therapeutic pain did their job. The body's own release and restoration mechanisms were repairing it like no manmade computer could ever do even in a hundred thousand years.

Sandy made her way warily back to the old summer house, confused and disoriented, not knowing where else to go. Just as she was within sight of the dwelling, as it began to peek out from the surrounding trees and bushes, she noticed movement. A group of men were standing on the front lawn talking and surveying the area. The moment she spotted them, one of them looked up and pointed in her direction. Sandy froze for an instant. The dreaded had happened. She had been found. She turned and fled in panic, not knowing where she was going, only that she had to get away. As she looked back in fear, she saw two of them starting after her down the grassy path.

CHAPTER 14

LITTLETON, MASS, NOVEMBER 16, 2036, 4:00 PM

The time had come for all good men to come to the aid of their country. That thought had passed through Peter's head more than once in the last few days, as the imminent date of their departure approached. The plan was absolutely insane. He could hardly believe that he was following it, let alone helped devise it, but then much of what had happened these past four months defied his senses, like for instance finding his wife, Sandy.

After visiting Todd Daniels' home in the suburbs and finding it boarded up and empty, Peter remembered their summer camp near the beach in Essex. He hadn't been there in years, but perhaps they had gone there to hide. Deciding to journey to the area and look for them, the companions trekked out by foot, taking several days. Sleeping on the ground at night and staying along back roads and trails as usual, they avoided the few people they saw. Luckily, the weather had been mild, but that could change at any time.

Arriving in the morning, they found the place apparently deserted and partially destroyed. Signs of long-past violence were everywhere. They were standing on the front yard speculating when Mark saw a woman approach. She looked surprising like a young Sandy Danvers. They yelled her name and waved, but she took off like a frightened doe. They had to chase her several minutes before Peter finally ran her down. Even looking right at him, she refused to recognize her ex-husband. The reality of seeing him there like that was just too much for her disheveled mind to grasp. She stood unsteady, wide-eyed and mute, while Mark and Peter tried to get a spark of recognition out of her. Finally, accepting the truth, she broke down with large hysterical sobs, which scared Peter more than anything she had done so far.

When she had calmed down enough to reason with, they brought her back to the house where Arthur made a pot of tea from fresh leaves he had brought along. They sat on the floor in front of the still intact brick hearth, sipping their tea while Sandy told her story, much of which left Peter shaking with rage and fear. He was overjoyed at finding his estranged wife, but desperate with worry about what might have happened to his little girls. For Sandy's sake, he tried to keep calm, for he recognized his wife's delicate state of mind. In spite of all odds, he had miraculously found her, although she had changed somehow. She seemed younger and more vulnerable than she ever had been before. He found that appealing.

That had been a week ago. Peter and Sandy had much to talk about, not least of which was how to locate and rescue their children. During this time Mark had been able to gather information by hacking into the city's non-organic emergency computer systems, learning the locations of the detention centers where the inhabitants of the North Shore had been taken. With this information, a second plan was hatched, even more audacious than the first.

Where before Peter might have objected strenuously to such a scheme on the grounds that it was impossible and would more than likely get them killed, he now went along eagerly, now that the lives of his girls were at stake. When everything you love is at risk, you have to risk everything, he told himself.

Last minute preparations completed, they headed for the take-off point, a large field in the adjoining town of Littleton, where their first trials had been held a few days ago. The small caravan moved along the tree-lined, country back road, Mark and Arthur in an late-model pickup truck they had found in the garage near Mark's old underground house. Peter and Sandy followed in a small, lithium-powered mini that would not last another day. Arthur's solution to their travel needs still had Peter shaking his head in disbelief. Was he living in a dream? Could all this be real?

They took a right at an abandoned service station, past a post office overgrown with weeds and vines. A few rusted hunks of what had once been cars or trucks sat dead along the road. Passing over a small bridge and stream, they turned left at an old cemetery, not used since the turn of the nineteenth century, with ancient tombstones rubbed down to a nub from the soft pencil-strokes on rice paper of enthusiastic Civil War buffs.

Peter was still having trouble believing that his ex-wife was really here. He hadn't wanted her to come on the dangerous mission, but didn't want to leave her behind either. In any case, she insisted. There was really nowhere else for her to go. Besides, she didn't want to be left alone again. She knew the dangers and had promised to follow his orders.

They followed the country lane as it turned to dirt and curved slowly to the left, along a long copse of tall fir trees. Rounding the bend and mounting a small rise, they got their first glimpse of the object of their drive, resting in a long field of low grass fringed with willows.

Peter remembered the first time he saw it sitting in the middle of the meadow like a thing ripped from the page of some storybook. There, rippling in the breeze was what could only be described as an undersized dirigible, a customized miniature airship. It looked like a tiny Goodyear blimp with a battleship-gray balloon and a matching green and brown basket.

"It's a lighter than air helium dirigible," Arthur had informed them, "propelled by twin ultra-light, hydrogen engines. I built it myself," he announced proudly.

With that, Arthur had walked over to the odd-looking contraption and climbed into the small cabin, which floated a few feet from the ground under a larger cigar-shaped balloon. The cabin, made of lightweight plastic, fibrous material, was obviously the shell of a small, late-model minivan, while the balloon above it was about the size of a mid-sized truck, approximately thirty-feet long and fifteen wide. Over the top of the dirigible was a light wood frame, which enclosed the balloon in a net-like skin held firmly in place by ropes and wire that also reached to cables on the ground.

"How does this thing work?" Peter had asked. "Isn't Hydrogen explosive?"

"It's filled with Helium," Arthur had answered. "The motors employ hydrogen, but are quite safe, I assure you. Just don't smoke near them," he said with a twinkle in his eye.

"Hello, Hindenburg," quipped Mark.

"Don't worry, it's safe, more or less," Arthur assured them through the cabin's small sliding window, as he started up the smokeless twin engines.

"This thing actually flies?" Mark asked astounded.

Arthur explained how he had made it. He got the idea from when he used to sell used cars to augment his meager teaching salary. The dealership decided to float a blimp over the highway with their name on it, a real eye catcher. Ever since he was a kid, one of his hobbies had been hot air balloons, so Arthur was assigned the task of putting it up. When Peter mentioned the need to go cross-country, this was the first thing Arthur thought of. He actually found the balloon at a car dealership. The rest was just good old, down-home American ingenuity, along with a little do-it yourself chemistry and physics. He found Helium in several abandoned factories and labs along route 128.

"Does it have a name yet?" asked Mark.

"The Albatross," answered Arthur.

With that, he released the handbrake, simultaneously releasing the tethers holding the balloon to earth, and floated away on his maiden voyage.

As he started moving forward, he also began to rise, at just the speed he had calculated based on his weight and the balloon's momentum. The whole thing was the result of a long gestation period, during which Arthur had studied just about everything there was to know about lighter-than-air flight. This included the capabilities of every form of balloon and the gases that propelled them, as well as the intricacies of gliding through the thermal layers of the atmosphere. Now it was time to test his theories. So far, everything was working as planned.

Peter, Sandy, and Mark watched the funny-looking airship rise through the sparkling blue sky, clearing the surrounding tree tops by dozens of feet, to soon disappear from sight. They stood staring, their hands shielding their eyes from the bright autumn sun as it became an ever smaller dot in the distance.

Arthur spent the rest of the day learning and practicing the complexities of flying the small zeppelin. Mark took to it readily, like a natural, while Peter could hardly be convinced to sit in the basket, which he and Mark did for the final test. Even he had to admit, once they were in the air, how absolutely beautiful it was. Arthur was right after all, this was the only way to travel, far above the earth, free from hindrance and obstacle. By the next afternoon even Peter was taking his turn at the wheel, feeling the air in his face and the wind in his hair as he maneuvered the light craft over fields and forests, houses and barns, hills and valleys. Soon they would be ready for their journey. They practiced flying it every day for the next week, which involved a combination of adjusting gas-release valves and hydraulically-controlled rudders. It steered like a ship in a wavy sea, although the basket-like cabin was roomy enough, where four could sit comfortably with plenty of space left over for supplies. They were ready.

Tonight, before they began their mission, they were going to take a little detour to the North Shore Regional Medical Center in Lynn, Massachusetts. They had destroyed the area's main fiber-optic hub the previous evening, using a simplified version of the Trojan-horse virus concocted by Mark with some critical help from Peter. The disruption of the facility, which also housed the region's largest Organic computer bank, was something they had waited until the last minute to attempt. They would have put it off indefinitely had the giant plant not publicized that it was about to come back on-line with so much fanfare it was impossible to ignore. It was the first East Coast Fiber hub to be re-established since the plague had disrupted all operations.

They finished loading the supplies then took their places in the airship as Arthur started up the engine.

"And they're off," shouted Peter in a cartoon-character voice, as the balloon lifted into the air.

No one responded, as they nervously watched the earth recede. They were headed on a dangerous mission, an act none of them would have even contemplated a few months before. Their chances of success were so slim that no one had bothered to calculate them, but much depended on the uncertain outcome.

In spite of his skill flying the machine and his confidence, the night flight toward the giant buildings of the north shore city left even Arthur's heart in his throat. Soon their target was in sight, a large open field at the edge of the city, filled with tents and campfires, adjoining a large expanse of empty swampland near the shoreline.

They let the dirigible coast out to sea, to approach the brightly-lit facility from that direction under cover of an otherwise cloudless but humid night. The warm air aided their buoyancy, as they maintained a thousand-foot altitude. After surveying the surrounding area, comparing it with maps they had obtained earlier, they floated back over Nahant Beach, deserted at this time of night.

"See where you want to go?" asked Arthur, as they glided over the lights of the target camp like a silent butterfly. Arthur shut down the engines and used the wind currents to float them forward, another advantage of their form of travel.

Guiding the aircraft toward the coastline where it approached the camp to within a few thousand yards, Arthur brought it down over a desolate piece of swampland that crossed the encampment's perimeter.

Peter dropped from the balloon over the fence separating one piece of dreary bog from the other, into the camp, and made his way toward the holding area, a tent-city filled with sick and healthy alike. The squalor was unspeakable. The stench of it filled his nostrils long before he saw it. It chilled him to the bone to realize his daughters might be somewhere inside this giant house of death and disease. He quickened his pace.

Luckily, once inside the camp, there were few guards, and few of the healthy took any notice of him, all too consumed with their own misery to pay him any mind. As he moved through the camp, past groups of emaciated, filthy, half-clothed men, women, and children, he was struck by the blank, hopeless expressions on their faces, the hollow visage of despair. The groans of the sick and the screams of the dying filled the night.

He ran frantically here and there, calling out his daughters' names, shaking people awake, looking in every sleeping bag and tent. As he gazed out over the sea of squalor his heart quailed. How would he ever find them in this immense field of humanity? He fought down the terror and continued his search, calling out their names quietly as he did so. Finally, after he had searched everywhere and had started back toward the other end of the camp, his heart in despair, he spotted a familiar face. It was a sick looking and emaciated Todd Daniels, sitting listlessly by a low log fire. It took only moments to determine that Todd's mind had snapped, as he rambled on incoherently in answer to Peter's questions about his little girls. At length, after much urging, Todd led him to a small tent where Peter found them sleeping soundly inside. He could hardly believe his good fortune, as he softly roused them and led them by the hand to the pickup point, the unoccupied swampland just outside the glare of the prison lights.

They had some difficulty in the swampy ground. Peter and Todd - who was sane enough to realize a way out when he saw one - carried the girls on their shoulders as they made their way through the stagnant pools and mud-filled eddies. At last they came to the fence, where the Albatross — for the name had stuck - waited, just a few feet off the ground, just inside the barrier.

As Peter lifted the youngest girl up to Mark and Arthur in the balloon, Daniels' last tenuous tie to sanity left him. He jumped in front of Peter and attempted to pull himself into the balloon. Peter tried to stop him and calm him down, but there was no reasoning with Todd now. He wanted to get away from the horror of the camp as fast as he could. Nothing short of violence could prevail against his fear.

They struggled for a short while, and even though the guard was light and surroundings deserted, they quickly attracted attention. The alarm was given. Soon the whole area was bathed in lights and resounding with sirens.

Peter knocked Todd to the ground and quickly lifted his daughter into the balloon. Somehow getting in with help from Mark and Arthur, they escaped unseen into the darkness just as the guards burst onto the scene. Todd Daniels wasn't so lucky. They could plainly see him in the harsh glare of the searchlights below, as he was gunned down by a half-dozen security men, who unleashed a torrent of bullets into his jerking body. The shots echoed in the night long after the sight was mercifully hidden from view.

A short time later they landed back at their field in Littleton, where they intended to spend the evening before departing on the second part of their quest in the morning. The reunion that night was joyous, although they were all still in a state of shock at events.

In return for helping him recover his imprisoned children, Peter had agreed to help Arthur and Mark in their wild plan to find Dr. Linda Rayburn and Eddie Pavloski. Now that he was again united with his family, however, Peter was having second thoughts.

He was loath to leave them to their fate after so recently finding them. On the other hand, taking them with him on this impossible mission, where the odds of survival were miserably slim at best, was equally out of the question. The only sane thing to do was to get his family to safety as soon as possible. But where was that? Back in Jamaica? In the woods of Maine or the mountains of Vermont? In a dirigible?

Both Mark and Arthur had counseled leaving Sandy and the girls at Peter's house in Harvard, Massachusetts. After all, they had lived here for several weeks without molestation. They would be safer there than on a balloon flying to who knew where. Sandy, on the other hand, insisted on being taken along no matter what the danger. She did not want to be left alone again, the victim of any party who happened to come along. Peter could not make up his mind, for the final decision rested with him. Now he wanted out of the whole thing.

Conveying his desire to get his family to safety before he'd partake in any harebrained schemes to save the world, he asked Mark and Arthur to help him take them to Sandy's parent's home in New Brunswick, Canada. As far as they knew, the plague hadn't broken out there, and the distance by balloon wasn't far. Reluctantly, after much argument from all concerned, but especially from Sandy, it was agreed, and they charted their course northward to that destination and whatever adventure might await them.

While Peter and his friends flew northward in the Albatross, the germ of Linda Rayburn's plague awoke anew and stretching its yawning tendrils, reached ever outward. The stalled fiber-optic system was finally semi-operational again. Slowly, relentlessly, the main West Coast hubs were becoming active, the vast network of interconnecting cables and Organics alive once again with electric pulsing signals. And on the heels of the reactivated systems came the Plague, as if it had been an ember smoldering unseen beneath the surface of some brush, ready once more to erupt into a raging blaze.

Unlike the first time, however, there were now voices, a few at first but gaining in number and strength, that raged against the Fiber as the harbinger of death. While some of these were wild and groundless accusations, little more than fantastic superstition, some were surprisingly accurate in their prognosis, especially those emanating from an unknown satellite source in the Boston area.

CLAYMOTH LAKE, CASCADE MOUNTAINS, OREGON, NOVEMBER 17, 10:00AM

Stan Bellows glared around the table at his top security experts, counting to ten before he spoke.

"Do any of you have the slightest idea what this means?" he began in measured tones. Only his chief of security, Joyce Haywood, looked him in the eye. The others had their gaze cast downward in dejected submission or faked perusal of some document. No one sitting around the large, oval mahogany table answered.

"Someone out there is targeting the Fiber. It's terrorism, that's what it is, and it's aimed directly at the heart of the country. This is sabotage on a national scale."

He started pacing about the room while his security team exchanged nervous glances.

"Now what the hell happened out there in Boston?" he demanded. Again, only Joyce Haywood could hold his gaze. Everyone waited for her to speak.

"Sir, it looks like a form of the European virus. We're checking into it now. I should have something more for you in a few hours."

Before her boss could start ranting, the security chief went on, feeding Bellows what he wanted to hear, learned from years of hard experience. She looked around the table and noted that she was the only one of the old-timers left, the others all being long-since fired or dead from working the frontline in the trenches with the plague.

"We've located the entry point for the virus at the Regional Emergency Center in Boston, via a satellite hookup. Some sort of stripped-down version of the worm we saw in Europe." She paused again for effect, but not quite long enough for Bellows to gather his thoughts to speak. "We'll need your best computer guy on this one, Stan."

"You've got 'em," said Bellows, turning to his right-hand man. "Mike, make sure it happens."

"Yes, sir," replied Michael Pearlman, who had flown in from the East Coast on a special government jumbo jet just for this session.

Bellow's security chief went on with her analysis.

"Sir, I wonder if the prisoner we extradited from Eastern Europe has anything to do with this. Whoever did it has an intimate knowledge of the Trojan-horse virus. Remember, he launched his initial attack while in prison."

"Yes, look into it," said Bellows. "As you all know, we had Pavloski shipped over here from Bulgaria. He's in custody now in one of our Tennessee facilities, where I should add, he has no access to computers. From what I understand, he's lucky if he gets a piece of paper to wipe his ass with. I have a report here on the status of his interrogation. It seems he's been giving us the run around for the past few days, leading us down false trails, the usual wise-ass stuff. We've been treating him quasi-legal, you know, keeping the gloves on. Well, all that's changed. By the time we're done with him, he'll wish he was never born."

Bellows continued, working himself into a rage.

"I want whoever the hell's screwing with us out in Boston caught, and I want them caught quick. I'll make such an example of these computer pukes it'll be a hundred years before anyone dares screw with us again. Who do they think they're playing with?"

The room cleared without much more conversation, except for the one-sided tirade from Bellows. Joyce Haywood called her people in Tennessee and gave them explicit instructions concerning their prisoner. No one was going to stand in the way of the Fiber.

SATELLITE TRANSMISSION FROM SOMEWHERE IN EUROPE

APHA::CLIFFY::userGreen@Geneva.tangl5 11.18.36 14:40.14[SIG PeS]

Armageddon is upon us. The insidious organic computer, that plague-ridden, death-dealing monstrosity of progress, that offense to Life and the Universe itself, that abomination and its spawn, the Fiber, have plagued us long enough. This is a call for all free thinking men and women who have not been brain-washed into believing in the sanctity of technology, to come to the aid of their species and free us from the yoke of dependency that binds us. Wherever a vestige of these machines exists they must be ripped out and destroyed. Wherever one single obscene Organic pretends to live it must be annihilated, along with the insidious network that carries its diseased message. Wherever those who strive to reestablish the Fiber toil they must be stopped dead in their tracks. This is the time for action! This is a time for sacrifice! This is a time for war!

CHAPTER 15

MILITARY DETENTION FACILITY, POWELL AIRFIELD, KNOXVILLE, TENNESSEE, NOVEMBER 19, 2036, 6:00 AM

Eddie Pavloski had lost all sense of time. Pain had become his whole life, his entire reason for being. He looked forward to it with mingled dread and fear like a child anticipates getting a tooth pulled. He had almost learned to welcome it as a diversion from the more torturous mental anguish of constantly blaring loud speakers and the megawatt searchlights flooding his tiny space like a too-close sun.

After days of torment Eddie still didn't know what his captors looked like, his eyes being either covered or too full of blood and tears to see. His hands were dangerously numb from being tightly tied behind him for so long. And through it all the dreadful, monotonous voice droned on.

He had told them everything, had tried to tell the truth. As predicted, he even volunteered information about the virus that he had forgotten he knew. His tormentors were having too much fun to stop now, getting too much enjoyment out of his suffering to be much concerned with his story, although they recorded every bit of the blubbering gibberish for later analysis by the experts. After all, their area of expertise was only in getting him to talk. What he said was of no concern to them whatsoever.

He had been alone for some time, returned to his closet-sized cell a short while before, after spilling his guts during several harsh hours of interrogation. He had been trying to rest, even though the hot glare of the searchlights burned through his closed eyelids. In spite of this and the marching music blaring through the loudspeakers, he had almost succeeded in reaching a state approaching sleep, drifting in that realm between consciousness and dreamland where his thoughts mixed with fantasy. He saw himself floating in space, softly like a feather, away from his prison on wings of air.

There had been one last secret that he had managed to keep from them, more out of befuddlement than conscious intent. What he had given them so far would take them awhile to digest, and they would have to analyze it completely before they realized there was still a missing piece. That one secret drifted through his mind like a mote of dust blown in the wind, until it took on a life of its own and became a dark mystery that only his half-conscious mind could delve.

For all concerned, perhaps they would realize that to get the rest of the solution to the complex equations they would have to treat him with kid gloves. They would have to support and sustain him for the effort, not break him down so that he could hardly think. A few more hours of torture and deprivation, and he would lose all threads of his detailed knowledge of the virus, maybe for good. After all, brain cells didn't replenish themselves like other cells, and Eddie Pavloski was coming dangerously close to losing most of his allotment.

SOMEWHERE OVER WEST VIRGINIA, NOVEMBER 22, 8:35 AM

The past six days had been exhilarating, even though Peter could hardly believe it was actually happening. Soaring above the tree, between wood-topped mountains and green-covered valleys, the whole experience was more dreamlike than real.

After a two-day journey northward, they dropped into a field along the Bay of Fundi not far from where Sandy's parents lived. After determining that all was safe and quiet in the small seaside community, Peter left Sandy and the children to make their way to her parent's home. It was a difficult and heartrending decision for Peter, who once again almost decided not to leave. In the end, it was Sandy's entreaties that persuaded him to go with Arthur and Mark, if not for the sake of mankind, at least for the sake of his daughters.

After leaving New Brunswick, they traveled south back to their starting point. Turning westward to fly along the border between Massachusetts and Connecticut, they continued west across New York State until they were just below the city of Binghamton, where they veered southwest. They were following much the same path in reverse that Peter and Arthur had taken on their trip up from Texas.

Three days after leaving Sandy and the kids, they were flying over central Pennsylvania into West Virginia, over the Monongalia National Forest. Every minute of the adventure, although uneventful, had been anything but boring, filled with wonderful vistas and adrenaline-pumping excitement. Peter even took his turn flying the Albatross, though most of the time with his heart in his mouth, clinging to the controls like it was a lifeline. Only a few hours exhausted him to the point of collapse.

They spent their days flying and their nights sleeping on a field, which they were constantly in search of and always gratified to find amidst the thick forests and mountains. Avoiding large populated areas as much as possible, they passed through Ohio, well to the east of their previous visit, Arthur pointing out spots of interest on the way.

Their supply of helium was holding up fine. Arthur assured them there was plenty more where that came from, in abandoned factories and laboratories along the way, although it was a time-consuming and risky business to procure it. So they did everything they could to conserve the gas, as well as his modest stock of homemade hydrogen for the motors. They planned on at least four stops to make hydrogen along the route to LA, and a half dozen more forays for helium, but that was the price you had to pay to fly the skies in the Albatross.

They were heading southwest instead of due west because of a satellite transmission they had intercepted using Mark's homemade dish before leaving Massachusetts, a phone call between the West Coast offices of the giant network consortium, Global OptiComm, and its East Coast base of operations in Tennessee. Several keywords in the otherwise innocuous conversation triggered Mark's instincts in a big way.

"Compromised Organics... Trojan-horse virus...Dark Enigma...Pavloski...in Knoxville... Will soon have information to reestablish network against sabotage..."

Before long yet another plan of sorts had been hatched that now had them flying like a crow toward Knoxville, Tennessee.

Peter, of course, was skeptical of the whole thing, but that went with his training. He had become the group's conscience, counterbalancing the others' confident exuberance with sober and sound consideration, which however it moderated their opinions, never won out in the end against their optimistic decisions.

"We'll have to do some preliminaries, set things up for our arrival, but I think it'll work," said Mark confidently, as Arthur flew the dirigible.

"We have just the combination of skills we need to pull it off. It'll be like taking candy from a baby," said Arthur.

"Yeah, some baby," commented Peter, less than optimistically, with thoughts of their likely failure playing in his mind. "More like mission impossible."

On a second's consideration, however, he realized that Arthur and Mark had been right so far. He didn't have any better ideas, so what the heck, nothing ventured, nothing gained. After all, they had helped him recover his children. He couldn't forget that. At least the weather was holding out. That had to mean something, didn't it?

PALO ALTO, CALIFORNIA, NOVEMBER 22, 2:00 PM

For several weeks a SWAT team of medical personnel and paramilitaries had been conducting house-to-house sweeps of the entire Palo Alto area. They had finally made their way to Linda's neighborhood. After several more days they were at her apartment building. Now, after hours of intense labor they had broken into her very rooms. Besides looking for plague victims they were carrying on a frantic shotgun search for anyone with technical expertise in a variety of fields. Dr. Linda Rayburn was number one on that list. Linda had done wonders in obliterating any trace of herself in the county's' computer files, but they were about to stumble upon her by sheer chance.

Six of them entered the darkened apartment like things from outer space, covered in light-weight, white protective suits complete with headgear, booties, and double-layered latex gloves. At least half of them had firearms. There were several reasons it had taken so long for them to reach this spot, not least of which was the pockets of armed resistance they had met along the way. In the new push to obtain skilled manpower, however, all obstacles were being swept aside.

"Doesn't look like there's anyone home," said the lead man, through his built-in radio headset. "Let's check the place out anyway."

The team moved up the stairs, two of them remaining below as a precaution.   As soon as they were at the top, they noticed a strange glow emanating from the far corner of the top floor room.

"What the ...?" the lead man muttered.

They moved to the penthouse lab and fanned out, watching the glowing lightshow in the corner with mixed awe and fear.

"What is it?" asked one of them.

"Don't know," said the leader. "But whatever it is, I don't like the looks of it."

168

Just then, there was a barely perceptible growling noise from the opposite corner of the room, which was darkened and filled with tables and desks covered with test-tubes, vials, and scopes. Again they heard it, a low growl coming from the far shadows.

"What was that?" asked one of the jittery men.

"Over here, there's someone over here!" yelled a third, who had crept along the wall to get a better vantage point. There was a high-pitched wail. A half-naked, dirty form skittered across the floor on its hands and knees.

"Don't let it get away," yelled the one in charge, as the team moved to head off the fleeing figure.

"Don't let it bite you," yelled another in unneeded warning. They all knew the perils if the Plague were involved.

The four men, dressed in awkward protective clothing, tried to corner the scarecrow figure as it scurried and darted around the floor of the lab like a crab, in the eerie, pulsing glow of her super-quantum machine, which watched the scene like an all-knowing green eye. They were having little success catching her, partly due to Linda's frantic and sudden movements, and partly to their clumsy clothing. The fact that they were afraid of coming into contact with her didn't help matters much. A frantic call over the radio headset brought the other two upstairs with a nylon net, which they were finally, after considerable effort, able to throw over the animal-like creature.

"That can't be human," exclaimed one of the SWAT team, as they held the emaciated, hard-breathing, dirty thing down and administered a tranquilizer. They immediately took and tested samples of her blood for the Pestis germ right there on the spot, with a mobile lab they had brought for just such purpose. Finding no sign of the Plague and discovering - from a quick scan of their wrist-unit records - that she was the much sought after Dr. Linda Rayburn, a renowned specialist in the critical fields of bio-engineering and quantum computing, they transported her to a special hospital set up for just such highly-skilled resources

Linda lay in a deep coma. The attending physician, Dr. Fernando Rodriguez, one of the few medical doctors alive and still functioning in California who was not confined to a large medical camp, was himself a product of Stan Bellows' hunting expedition. A Mexican-American in his mid-thirties and a former gastrointestinal specialist, he chafed at being kept a virtual prisoner attending to a few of the pampered

169

experts needed for the Fiber, instead of helping the people in the teeming cities and decimated countryside, mostly his Spanish-speaking brothers and sisters. He had practiced medicine for eleven years in Los Angeles before the plague, and had first opposed and then refused to work in the medical camps, which earned him the ire of the local authorities and his incarceration on several occasions, this being just the latest in the series. He was sour and cynical, and was starting to think himself too mean and ornery to die of the Plague, although he knew better.

"Well, she doesn't have it," he said to the hospital superintendent, a direct subordinate of Stan Bellows, who stood next to him looking down at the pathetic figure lying in a bubble-like protective cocoon. "But she's dangerously malnourished. One of the worst cases I've ever seen. She's also completely catatonic. We can probably take care of her physical problems well enough with intravenous food and drugs, but I don't know about her mind. She has a pretty bad staph-infection and other ailments, including scurvy, but nothing we can't fix. The mental condition is something else again. She may have suffered brain damage. We'll have to do some tests, but even if they come up negative, she may never recover from whatever shock she's experienced. Not that what's happened isn't shocking enough to drive anyone over the edge."

"Just do what you can," replied his boss. "She's one of the only experts in her field still alive. The entire profession, which was mostly out here on the West Coast, was practically wiped out in the early stages of the epidemic. She's the only one left. See what you can do."

"Sure, but I can't make any promises." Rodriguez felt nothing as he looked down at the skeleton-like form partially covered by thin linen sheets, which exposed pasty white skin. Deep purple sockets surrounded puffy eyes placed in a cadaver's face. Fat chance she'll even make it to vegetable, he thought.

CHAPTER 16

MILITARY DETENTION FACILITY, POWELL AIRFIELD, KNOXVILLE, TENNESSEE, NOVEMBER 24, 2036, 9:00 AM

Eddie sat in his cell, still not believing the turn of events. He had been fed, clothed, cleaned, and coddled as if the days of torture were a bad dream. But they weren't, and the memory of it was fresh and sharp.

He had been told that the people coming to visit him would help him right his great wrong. All he had to do was cooperate - there was that insidious word again - and everything would be all right. He hoped they were telling the truth, but in a way it didn't matter. In his heart of hearts he knew he was more than likely a dead man.

Dressed in a clean white shirt and dungaree slacks, he was cuffed and taken out of his cell to another building where he was led to a small auditorium. It was just lunch time. In the front row were the three visitors, two of them in suits, a third dressed in jeans and T-shirt like himself. One of them, the tall one in the dark-blue suit, looked vaguely familiar. Standing in front of the room next to a podium was the camp's commander, Colonel Taylor. Eddie was brought down the center aisle and introduced to the visitors. His four guards did not leave his side.

"Gentlemen, I give you Eddie Pavloski, otherwise known as the Dark Enigma," announced Colonel Taylor with a sarcastic smile. "Mister Pavloski, this is Arthur Boyle from the Massachusetts State Police, and this young man here is Mark Goodwater, the one who almost cracked your virus for us before he deserted. And this gentleman is Dr. Peter Danvers, the inventor of the organic computer."

"Hey, I thought you looked familiar," said Eddie in English colored with a strong Polish accent. "How you doing? That's a clever little machine you built there."

"Thank you. It was clever of you to bust it. I can't wait to hear how you did it," replied Peter, truthfully.

"That's what we're all here to find out. Isn't that right, Eddie?" said the colonel, clearly the one in charge. Eddie didn't answer, though he somehow felt more confident and safe with the newcomers present, even though they seemed to be on the wrong side.

Arthur had landed the Albatross a few miles north of Nashville where they bivouacked for the night. Their plan was highly unconventional and risky, born more out of desperation than logic. If it worked, however, they would soon leave as they came, but with one additional passenger, Eddie Pavloski.

Using an official-looking vehicle that Mark and Arthur found in an abandoned garage and were able to get going again, they headed for the military base where their target was known to be. Mark was able to obtain much useful information from intercepted satellite transmissions to and from the facility. Arthur was impersonating an official supposedly sent by Stan Bellows himself with two experts, who were to help interrogate the prisoner. Mark had no problem making fake IDs for their purpose, using his digital camera and the photo-processing system on one of the laptops they had brought along. They obtained appropriate clothing on the way, Peter having his pick from the suit racks of the best stores in town. Hiding the balloon under a crowd of trees and making it ready for their return, they drove to the base. They were going to use their enemy's own blind obsession in re-establishing the network, and fear of the plague to achieve their ends.

As they moved to a smaller conference area off the main room to discuss preliminaries, Arthur made a point of asking about the status of the local fiber network, which was centered in Atlanta, the East Coast hub that connected the US to Europe. Scheduled to go on line by the end of the month, it would encompass two entire continents in a single, hi-speed Fiber. Although Peter and his friends knew the basic facts already from their eavesdropping of satellite transmissions, the resident scientists, along with the base commander supplied many more helpful details. Eddie Pavloski was silent and pensive for most of the conversation.

During the discussion, Arthur was able to get their host aside and inform him privately about the problem he was having with his two reluctant geniuses.

"They seem calm now, but they're both extremely nervous about the plague. Who could blame them, eh? I've had a heck of a time getting them to come down here and leave their little sanctuary in New England. To tell you the truth, I didn't want to come myself. After all, the plague has subsided up where we come from. But orders are orders, right? Anyway, we've got to make them feel safe here if they're going to be any use to us. They need to be assured beyond all doubt that this place is secure from the epidemic."

"Don't worry, Mister Boyle. I assure you every precaution and then some has been taken to ensure just that."

For the benefit of the visitors their host obligingly went through the details of their infectious disease control system, explaining the working of the warning devices and air filter mechanisms, precautions and emergency procedures - amply demonstrated by the capable guard who escorted the group. The Colonel even issued protective suits and equipment to them, which appeared to placate his visitors considerably.

After an afternoon of questions and answers, and a brainstorming session that left Eddie extremely impressed with the newcomers but even more concerned with their purpose, they adjourned for the day. Eddie was surprised at the ease with which Peter and Mark had come up to speed in understanding the equations involved, Peter even volunteering some of the omitted parts. It was obvious to Eddie, even though they made no mention of it to anyone, that they suspected key parts of the solution were missing. That suggested to Eddie, at least tentatively, that they might not be wholly on the other guy's team after all.

On their way to the cafeteria where they were to have dinner with their hosts, Mark Goodwater complained of a headache and sore throat.

"You don't look so good," observed Arthur loudly, as they sat down at a long wooden table. Pouring him a glass of juice, he said, "Here, drink this."

"How you feel?" he asked under his breath.

"Lousy," replied Mark weakly.

"Good. Remember, what you're feeling is only the results of the potion I made you drink this morning. It's just going to make you sweat a lot and a little dizzy, that's all. Just act sick."

"That shouldn't be too hard," Mark replied good-naturedly.

Peter looked on with concern as the others came up. The concoction of drugs and herbs Arthur had given Mark four hours earlier was starting to take effect, making him sweat profusely and break out in large red splotches.

When Eddie Pavloski was seated at the table he noted Mark's sick appearance and the blotches on his arms, and immediately became alarmed.

"You don't look too good, my friend," he said, as their hosts sat down and dinner arrived. "What's wrong?"

"I feel terrible," Mark replied hoarsely, telling the truth and feeling worse by the minute. "Wicked sore throat, I can hardly swallow. I don't think I'm going to be able to eat anything."

"Well at least try to get some juice and toast down," said the Colonel, standing up as if he had finished eating, even though his plate had not been touched. "Then we'd better get you to the infirmary. Can't take any chances, you know."

"What do you mean?" Mark asked, panic slipping into his voice on cue.

"Oh, nothing, don't worry. We'll just give you something to make you feel better. I'm sure it's nothing serious, but then wouldn't you like to be sure?" It was obvious to everyone he couldn't wait to get out of the room.

"Do you have plague serum? I need plague serum," cried Mark suddenly, losing his composure and slipping into well-feigned hysteria. He stood up and immediately keeled over, losing what was left of his not yet digested breakfast in the process. At that moment, alarms started going off all over the compound. Sirens howled, bells clanged, lights flashed, and computers beeped.

"Oh, my God!" exclaimed the Commander, running to the door and heading out of the room with considerable haste, followed by the other officials. The four guards, two who had been standing by the wall and two by the entrance, stood there uncertain for some moments, exchanging nervous looks. Finally, the two by the door left as well, following their boss's example.

"We need help!" said Arthur kneeling over the now prostrate Mark Goodwater. "Help me get him to a doctor."

"There is no doctor," one of the remaining guards informed him. Both men were now nervously glancing back and forth between Mark and the far door. Sirens screamed alarm far and near.

"What do you mean, there's no doctor?" replied Peter, sounding incredulous and dismayed, but actually much relieved. So far everything was going as planned.

"Just what I said," answered the tall, pale one, as the short, swarthy one concentrated on the events taking place outside. "All the doctors are in Atlanta or dead, or have high-tailed it out of here."

"Never mind that," said Arthur from the floor. "Just get us the serum. This man has the Plague, the most infectious kind. Everyone in this room has been exposed."

The guards', jaws agape, stared in horror at the scene unfolding before them and cursed their ill luck. Eddie Pavloski, who had been watching with growing concern, stood up and backed away from the table.

"Cripe!" he exclaimed, followed by a few choice words in Polish.

The guards looked at each other for a few moments, then drew their guns and edged toward the door.

"Stay where you are," ordered the biggest one. "Don't move," were his last words as they disappeared out of the room.

Eddie was about to flee too. Trying the door first, which had been secured from the outside, he headed for a window.

"Wait," yelled Peter going after him. "It's all a hoax. We came here for you. He doesn't have the Plague. It's just a trick."

"Are you sure? He looks awfully sick to me," observed Eddie, remembering his own ruse to get rid of his ex-cell mate. "What about the alarms? They're tied to highly sensitive sensing devices designed to monitor for bacteria contamination. You might be able to fake the appearance of the Plague but you can't trick those machines."

"Now Eddie, I'm surprised at you," replied Arthur, looking out the window. "You of all people should know better. Those sensors are tied to computers, are they not? It was quite simple to reprogram them last night to go off at a pre-arranged time. I mean, how else would you explain them all going off simultaneously? That would mean every area of the compound was infected at the same time. Not very likely, is it?"

"We better get out of here before they get wise," advised Peter.

"Yeah, or worse," said Mark, getting up and smiling at Eddie as if nothing had happened. "Before they decide to come back and burn us alive."

CLAYMOTH LAKE, CASCADE MOUNTAINS, OREGON, NOVEMBER 25, 5:15 PM

"What?" screamed Bellows over the satellite phone, beside himself with anger.

The thin, nervous voice of Joyce Haywood, his head of security, came back over the receiver.

175

"There was an outbreak of the Plague at the Knoxville facility where Pavloski was being held. Look's like he got away in the confusion."

Stan Bellows couldn't believe his ears and was at a loss for words, so the voice on the other end of the phone went on.

"All the alarms went off at once. Everyone was scrambling for protective clothing. Some of the men simply bolted. Fighting broke out when there wasn't enough gear to go around. Unfortunately, our prisoner was in the employee cafeteria when all this occurred. Apparently his guards panicked and ran off," she said, finishing her summary. "The team of experts you sent down from Boston with the state cop disappeared with him. They fear a possible hostage situation."

"What?" sputtered Bellows, hearing of this for the first time. "What team? I didn't send anybody down there except you."

"Sir, we received a transmission from you earlier this week, informing us that you were sending some experts to help interrogate the prisoner. You know, that one from Boston who was working on the European virus and deserted just before the Regional Defense Center there was wiped out? All our queries concerning them checked out. Their credentials were good. What's wrong?" asked the confused and concerned security chief.

"You fools!" yelled Bellows, long since unable to control himself. "Any jerk can intercept and fake radio transmissions. You've been had, conned, you stupid idiots! They're probably the ones responsible for wrecking our operations in Boston!"

Bellows screamed at the top of his lungs, spewing forth a tirade of obscenity that left the security chief stunned and holding the phone at arm's length.

"They'll ruin everything! I want every man you have on this. I want you to find those bastards if you have to turn over every rock and sewer cover in the country. They couldn't have gone far. Find them. You find them!" he screamed.

"Yes, sir, we will, sir. We'll find them, sir. I've got air patrols combing the state, along with roadblocks and twenty-four hour, red-alert status at every facility in the area. They won't get far, sir. We're tracking their vehicle north now."

"What about Pearlman? Where is he?"

"We don't know, sir. He disappeared at the first sign of trouble and no one's seen him since."

"When you find him, Joyce, and you will find him, I want you to send him directly to me. Got that?"

"Yes, sir. I..." The connection went dead and with it Joyce Haywood's heart. She knew the cost of failure in the new world order.

LOS ANGELES MEDICAL CENTER, LA, CALIFORNIA, NOVEMBER 25, 5:30 PM

The figure on the bed was no longer skeletal and emaciated, although she was still lying in a semi-catatonic state, fed by tubes of intravenous drugs and nourishment, the best twenty-first century medicine had to offer. Even her drug-resistant strain of staph infection was getting cured, albeit slowly. Still, no gleam of intelligence peeked through her half-opened lids.

She was under the constant attention of a platoon of nurses and the care of Dr. Fernando Rodriguez, one of the few medical specialists still alive. This patient needed a specialist in psychology, however, not infectious disease. Her doctor seriously doubted if they would be able to recover her mind, as his bosses so adamantly insisted on.

Paging through Linda's medical chart on his palmtop computer, he interacted with the hospital's main system, all old silicon-based computers brought up to replace the lost biological units. All the hospital's Organics, needed for advanced diagnostic and analysis functions, were due to come back on-line in seven days. Even in his busy and isolated state, rumors of fresh outbreaks of the plague in other parts of the city had reached him. The medical camps were growing. More people were dying. Dr. Rodriguez had his own things to worry about, however, like getting his patient, a much needed, highly skilled worker, productive again. Fat chance!

He looked down at the pitiful form in her white, flowered hospital gown, beneath the thin sheet and blanket. Her hair was washed, her body and face cleaned, but her figure was frail and thin despite all the nutrients and vitamins they were pumping into her. Her muscles hadn't atrophied yet, and if she woke soon and got a little exercise, she might not come out of this too badly, at least as far as her physical health was concerned.

Linda, far from being devoid of thought, was lost in an inner world of great beauty, a world where there was no pain, no loneliness, and no one had to grow up without love. She would soon be going home, home to a loving father and mother where she'd be appreciated and covered with adulation.

She floated over the earth as if suspended in air, drifting above a landscape of her own making, filled with outlandishly-dressed inhabitants and fairytale architectures, with flags and balloons of all the colors under the sun sticking from every turret and lamppost. A storybook land where everything was clean and there was no death or disease, the world she could have made if they had only let her.

Then a huge shadow, round and soft, drifted into view, partially hidden by hazy clouds of vapor, which she strove to penetrate with her sight. She widened her eyes with effort. There before her was a dark-skinned man dressed in white. She blinked twice, trying to focus her vision as the room spun around her. It was the first human contact she'd had since those days several months before when she last saw Pop Wineman on her midnight mission. She recoiled in shock when she realized she was no longer dreaming.

Dr. Rodriguez talked softly, in his best bedside tone, explaining as clearly as he could what had happened to her and where she was. He spoke slowly and calmly so as not to alarm or upset her even though he was excited almost beyond control.

She was actually conscious! He tried to ascertain what had happened to her but in her confused state she was completely unintelligible, mumbling something about the plague and being infected. He tried to assure her that there was nothing wrong with her that a little food and modern medicine wouldn't take care of, marveling all the while at the miraculous way she had just come out of it like that. She was actually making an attempt to talk, although it was all gibberish, nothing that made any sense. He made a note to tell his boss that the patient had made a marked improvement contrary to all expectations.

CHAPTER 17

SOMEWHERE OVER SOUTHERN ALABAMA, NOVEMBER 28, 2036, 7:15 PM

Peter flew the Albatross over multicolored patches of farmland and wooded swamp, approaching the Gulf Coast near Mobile Bay, while Arthur slept. The last few days had been like a scene from a pulp fiction novel. First the escape in broad daylight from a military base amidst confusion and gunfire; then a race across country to the dirigible, taking off and barely missing the trees to make their getaway. Finally, hiding out like fugitives in the Smoky Mountains where they had parted company, Mark and Eddie making their way by foot to execute their part of the plan, while Peter and Arthur flew south to begin their journey to California. As Peter got used to flying the dirigible his mind was free to wander over the recent days' events.

Smashing a window, they had been able to escape the cafeteria building. No one seemed to give them much notice. They were all too busy trying to save themselves, the guards fighting over protective clothing like a pack of hungry dogs. The vehicle the companions had arrived in was commandeered by a group of panicked workers, one of whom was GOC employee, Mike Pearlman. There were no armed guards in sight.

The escapees limped along with Peter and Eddie helping Mark, while Arthur led the way. Eddie was still trying to decide whether to take his chances alone or stick with the strangers, who claimed they had just broken him out of prison. Well, he was at this very moment walking past an unmanned guard-post. If he had tried that a half-hour ago he'd be full of lead by now.

There were no vehicles in sight not being driven at breakneck speed away from the camp, although armed men in protective clothing were beginning to secure the area. Others began going over the facility with highly sensitive equipment looking for the source of the germs that had triggered the alarms. Someone had managed to organize a response to the situation. Fortunately for the four fugitives, it had come just moments too late.

The Albatross was hidden a few miles north of the airfield, about ten minutes away by car. They made for the dirigible as quickly as they could on foot, running through trees and bushes like woodland Indians. Luckily, it would be some time before their captors realized they were missing and longer still before a search could be organized. Mark recovered quickly and they made good time as they moved over the countryside.

It was mid-afternoon when they reached the field where the small balloon lay hidden, covered with tree branches and camouflaged netting. Unknown to the fugitives, it would be hours before the search would be expanded to this area using vehicles and helicopters. As far as they were concerned, however, the posse was breathing down their backs.

Peter and Mark explained the plan to Eddie, while Arthur readied the balloon for take-off. Every bit of unneeded baggage was jettisoned, including most of the extra food and clothing. Even then it was touch and go as they moved across the clearing toward the forty-foot beeches at the opposite end of the field, only clearing the trees by a few feet. That was enough, and they were soon on their way, flying with the wind on the wings of the Albatross toward a future as unknown as an amnesia victim's past.

Arthur, who seemed to have a knack for this sort of thing, had also worked out this part of the plan as well, reasoning - correctly as it turned out - that the authorities would expect them to follow the highways. Furthermore, any aircraft they might have in the vicinity would have to come from bases and airfields in the western part of the state, from Nashville and Memphis, or Atlanta. He was counting on a margin of time before there would be any type of large-scale organized air and land search. Time enough for them to make their way south.

Less than twenty miles south of Knoxville lay the Great Smoky Mountains National Park, with the Appalachian and Smoky mountain chains rising behind it. It was this area they made for, reaching the park just as it was growing dark, finding a clearing to land in amidst towering peaks and lofty trees. There they waited until the search activities, which were intense, moved off in other directions. The fact that they had rigged their borrowed car's satellite antenna to continuously transmit dummy messages, helped matters immensely by decoying the search efforts northward where the unfortunate Mike Pearlman had taken the vehicle in his flight from the outbreak. They would be on their separate missions before it was discovered they hadn't gone in that direction.

The decision to split up had been almost as difficult as leaving his family after just finding them, but they knew they couldn't accomplish what they had to do in the time required without dividing their efforts. Mark, along with Eddie, would move east over the mountains toward Virginia where they'd attempt to disrupt the reestablished Fiber and the new European gateway. From there they would move slowly northward causing whatever damage they could along the way to make sure few Organics were brought back on line.

Peter and Arthur would take the balloon to the West Coast and search for Dr. Linda Rayburn as Mark's original plan had called for. Their mission would also be to destroy as much of the Fiber as possible along the way, which had already started to function again in that part of the country and was growing rapidly.

They would be flying in a southwesterly direction until over the Gulf of Mexico, then due west to enter the US again along the long, meandering east coast of Texas near where Peter had originally come ashore over two months before. From there they'd fly over the vast, thinly populated state where barren, flat stretches of desert made for excellent landing strips, and onward through New Mexico and Arizona to enter southern California. At least it sounded good on paper, and so far Arthur's plan had worked like a charm. But the prospect of flying over water and desert in a helium balloon didn't appeal to Peter in the least, especially when Arthur started mentioning they were getting low on gas.

Peter was flying near the ground, looking for a place to land for the night. He wasn't having much luck, the land below him full of swamps and bogs and stunted trees. Arthur, who had just woken up and was ever the expert, told him not to worry, but to fly along the coastline, which they were just passing over. There, he assured him, they would find plenty of long, wide sand beaches to land on. Soon his advice was borne out, as an endless white sand strip appeared in the waning sunlight below. All this time, the only thing Peter could think about was Sandy and the girls, who were getting farther away with each passing day. Were they safe? He should never have left them a second time. The only consolation he had was that he and the others were at least doing something positive, fighting those forces that seemed determined, even if unwittingly, to destroy them all.

Peter cut back on the throttle and trimmed the tabs, slowing the dirigible's air speed. At the same time, Arthur released some of the gas, which caused the craft to slowly lose altitude. Soon they were hovering just above the ground. Arthur jumped out, securing the lines with spikes he hammered into the hard sand, and large rocks, which he tied to the ends of ropes. They were down for another night. Tomorrow they'd be on their way westward.

So far the weather had been perfect, with a southwesterly wind to help them on their way, allowing them to conserve their meager supply of hydrogen fuel. Equally pleasing had been the fact that they had not seen anyone since leaving Powell Airfield in Knoxville. Still, despite the good fortune, Peter couldn't help wonder how Mark and Eddie were faring on their adventure.

NANTAHALA NATIONAL FOREST, NORTH CAROLINA, NOVEMBER 28, 7:30 PM

The dynamic duo, as Eddie and Mark called themselves, sat around the fire in a small deserted campground. Normally filled to capacity this time of year, it was now empty. If there was anyone out here they were hiding in caves or skulking about in the forest like wolves, trying to avoid detection and incarceration just like themselves.

Mark and Eddie had not stopped talking since they started their trek over the Great Smoky Mountains two days ago, warming to each other with every step. It had been grueling and exhausting, but exhilarating at the same time, hiking over the mountains along neatly cleared trails amidst tall peaks, along brooks that bubbled with clear sparkling water, through forests of mixed southern pine and fir.

Eddie filled Mark in on how he had built and transmitted his Trojan-horse virus across the Fiber while in prison. Mark in turn described his own network disrupting activities and his theory on the source of the plague, which Eddie agreed with. Together they developed their own plan using Eddie's virus.

"According to my theory," said Mark, as they sat beside the fire, "you actually saved Europe. By disrupting the fiber-based transmissions of the Organics when you did, you stopped the plague from crossing the Atlantic."

"I know," replied Eddie, "although that wasn't exactly my intent."

It was getting dark, the stars bright on a clear sky above them. The fire crackled.

"Even with all you have said, which seems to be irrefutable, I can still hardly believe it possible." Eddie poked the fire with a stick as he spoke, a pilfered cigar, his first in years, clenched in his hairy mouth. "First of all, to build the genetic code for such a virus, then to fabricate it in the back of a computer…"

"An organic computer," interjected Mark.

"An organic computer, whatever," echoed Eddie. "Well, it's just all a bit much. Way out of my area of expertise, I'm afraid."

"That's why it's so important we find and contact that bio-physicist in California. Without someone like her I'm afraid we may never be able to defeat this thing. It'll just sit and hide in the system forever, somewhere in the Net, just waiting to spring up and kill more millions."

"Well, we may not be able to destroy the plague itself," said Eddie with a grin, but we can sure mess up the Fiber. How you say it? Let's kick some butts."

"I was hoping you'd say that," answered Mark. "What are we going to do, exactly?"

"You just leave that to me. For now we just enjoy your American wilderness and keep out of sight. I know how we can do a lot of damage and maybe decoy the authorities away from your friends. In the meantime, do you have any more of those cigars?"

CLAYMOTH LAKE, CASCADE MOUNTAINS, OREGON, NOVEMBER 29, 7:00 AM

Over a week had elapsed since the escape of the prisoner from their base of operations in Knoxville and still there was no word of his capture. The scenario of their dramatic get-away was now reproducible from visual data collected from security cameras and eyewitness accounts, along with the analysis of the warning systems.

After the initial alarms had been checked and restored - not without some difficulty - search parties were dispatched to locate and secure the prisoners. That was when they discovered Pavloski was missing and the three fake-interviewers were nowhere to be found. When it was determined that the alarms had been falsely triggered and there was no plague anywhere in the vicinity, teams and roadblocks were set up at all routes into or out of the city, as well as on all the main highways in the state. In addition, all the available aircraft - which amounted to three Cessnas and a helicopter - were dispatched to help in the search, which was concentrated initially around the city of Knoxville. This was all accomplished in the first several hours. After twenty-four hours had elapsed with no results, the hunt was expanded and major cities like Nashville, Atlanta, and Memphis were notified so that they too could help with the manhunt.

Because of new laws just put into effect concerning computer-related crimes and terrorism, the fugitives were treated as highly dangerous killers. Although there were few available men in uniform, every spare one was dedicated to the search, which was being concentrated mainly to the north of the state after satellite signals believed to be emanating from the escapees' vehicle began arriving from that direction. Then after two more days of frantic tracking the car was found in Pennsylvania driven not by the fugitives, but by Bellows' own man, Mike Pearlman. Realizing that they had been decoyed in the wrong direction, they backtracked, belatedly expanding the search in the opposite area, although still with no results, just as Arthur had foreseen.

Every form of ground sensor and satellite tracking system had been put to the task. Originally installed by the NSA to monitor traffic and movement over the highways, and to help locate missing persons and stolen vehicles, these satellites were now being used to search for the escaped prisoner and his accomplices. Anything moving on foot or car across the land would sooner or later be spotted, or so the theory went.

"Then why is there still no word of their capture after over a week?" fumed Bellows, as he stared out over the scenic mountain landscape of his Claymoth Lake home. The longer they went free, the more his plans were in jeopardy. There were more desertions every day. Every hour his enemies and competitors grew stronger. Time was of the essence. He must put a stop to their games and gain control soon or all would be lost.

Slowly but surely, he was making progress, as the rebuilt Fiber backbones and hubs went back into operation with their molecular components and relays, and the banks of organic computers blinked awake.

The giant, global, fiber-optic telecommunications network controlled by Stan Bellows, consisting of cables, satellites, and computers, on which the entire edifice of modern civilization was supported, carrying entertainment, education, commodities, and services to billions of people, was finally starting to get on its feet again. It may have been staggered, knocked-down, and bashed in the teeth, but it was still functioning. And with it the lives and livelihoods of multitudes were starting to get back to normal. Now here a couple of punks on the East Coast, a few malcontents and net-surfers, were trying to take it out again, annihilate all the work of decades in an irrational orgy of destruction. It made his blood boil, and when the blood of this man boiled other men's blood flowed, as witnessed by the destruction of the slums and the resulting riots, which Bellows had more than a little to do with.

Stan Bellows, despite his unlimited ambition and insatiable greed, was not motivated solely by negative impulses. Like every human being, however seemingly bad, he had a positive side. Motivations like the good of the common man, the economic well-being of the country, social order and work ethics, were not unknown to him, and might even have been dominant much of the time when things were good and he didn't feel threatened. If you talked to him and listened to his vision - and hadn't heard him rant and rave at his subordinates - you would have been impressed with his good intentions, and well you should be for they were honestly expressed. The road to hell, as we've often been told, however, is paved with well meaning intent.

In truth, the good intentions of Stan Bellows were leading the world to the brink of destruction, and those labeled as criminals in the New World order were in fact its saviors. For unknown to all but the few of those trying to stop it, the very network claimed by many to be the salvation of humankind was actually its bane, for it carried in its hair-thin cables the seed of Linda Rayburn's germ.

CHAPTER 18

SOMEWHERE OVER THE EAST COAST OF TEXAS, NOVEMBER 29, 2035, 9:00 AM

The Albatross flew before the wind, approaching the eastern coast of Texas at thirteen thousand feet, the highest they had dared to fly. The weather to this point had been wonderfully compliant with fifteen to twenty mile an hour winds moving west or northwest and clear skies. All this was about to change with a vengeance.

They had been hopping along the Gulf coast of the United States like a skipping stone from Pensacola to the southernmost spit of land below New Orleans, and from there to just short of Port Arthur near Houston. At that point they circled to the south bypassing the city and were now entering Texas just below Galveston.

They had been eyeing the storm for the past half-hour, the thick black clouds climbing into the bright eastern sky behind them like giant, impassable mountain peaks, a stark contrast to the otherwise clear sky ahead. They had been ascending for quite some time now, trying to outrun and get above the storm. Still, the thunderclouds loomed above them, getting higher and gaining on them with each tick of the minute hand on Peter's black-banded Swatch.

"What d'ya think?" yelled Peter over the din to Arthur. "Looks pretty bad."

Arthur was concentrating on flying the dirigible, which was now moving at considerable speed, helped by a powerful tail-wind that was blowing to the northwest at over 30-knots. He was having trouble keeping the nose straight.

"I know," replied Arthur. "I don't think we're going to outrun it. There's too much wind to land safely, especially with the hydrogen aboard. We're going to have to try and ride it out. Maybe we can get above it."

"How high do you think this thing can go?" asked Peter, feeling his stomach go queasy on him as Arthur increased the helium intake to the balloon.

"I don't know, but we're about to find out. I just hope it's high enough to get above that storm."

The balloon rose precipitously and gained speed as the storm clouds rushed in to engulf it. The wind tore at the bindings and hinges holding the dirigible together pushing them forward at ever-greater velocity. What they could see of the earth below receded rapidly and was soon lost in a swirl of gray cloud.

Peter could feel the air thin as they rose in altitude. Fifteen thousand, eighteen, then twenty, Arthur reading the numbers as they appeared on his digital altimeter. Still the storm loomed over them.

Buffeted by strong cross-winds, which shook the compartment hanging below the longish balloon like a cable car below its wire, back and forth sickeningly, they screamed across the sky at a dizzying speed in the rising bag of gas. Just to punctuate the growing danger the sky behind them lit up with a flash, followed momentarily by a thunder-blast that jarred their teeth and seemed to go on forever.

The balloon shuddered horribly but continued to rise through the gray mist. Slowly, the grayness brightened, imperceptibly at first, then with growing certainty as the dark clouds gradually turned white and more empyreal. Then they disappeared altogether to be replaced by intense blue sky and a sunlight that passed little heat.

"How high are we?" asked Peter.

"Don't ask," countered Arthur good-naturedly. "I know how much you hate heights."

They were having difficulty breathing in the thin air.

"We're pretty high. Better relax and try to conserve oxygen," counseled Arthur. "Don't talk unless it's absolutely necessary."

The temperature was dropping. It would soon be below freezing in the small, non-insulated compartment. The cold air would also make the balloon descend, unless more gas was pumped into it to maintain their altitude, gas they didn't have. Things didn't look too good for the Albatross. Perhaps they should have given it another name.

Bereft of navigational equipment, without the benefit of being able to see landmarks on the ground, the travelers had no idea that they were now well past the Texas coast traveling northwest toward Austin, at over fifty-five miles per hour at an altitude topped off at just under 23,000 feet. All they knew was that they were freezing and couldn't breathe, but there was nothing to do now but hold on and pray, which they did, huddled together for warmth.

The huge storm cloud raged its way across the state like an irate mountain seeking vengeance on all who stood in its way, plowing through field and prairie alike with the Albatross perched just above it like a brightly-colored, feathered hat, not quite able to escape its winds. Then, ever so slowly, the dirigible began to descend.

"We can't hold this altitude much longer," observed Arthur. "We're starting to drop back into the storm. Don't have much helium left. We're going to have to take our chances. Hold on."

"Crap, I hate this!" yelled Peter, strapping himself in, shivering from cold and fear. The cabin shook and shuddered with the increasing wind pressure. They were going down. Dark, gray, ominous clouds soon surrounded them. Bright streaks of lightning leaped across the electrically charged atmosphere. Thunder pealed in the blackened sky.

"We're making outstanding time," quipped Arthur, never losing his sense of humor. "At this rate we'll be in California before you know it." His joke was totally lost on Peter, who clung to the seat, his jaws clenched.

"Or dead long before we get there," he said under his breath.

The winds pushed them along, keeping them from descending too quickly into the storm's black mass. But they were trapped in its embrace, unable to land or escape. Their only hope was to ride it out until the winds dissipated somewhere over land. That is if the dirigible stayed together long enough. Already one of the straps holding the passenger compartment to the balloon had snapped. There were plenty more, but that didn't reduce their discomfort much.

On they flew, at great speed, as day turned to dark, starless night. Arthur's muscles and nerves, already strained to the breaking point, were on the verge of complete collapse, but still he clung to the steering mechanism tenaciously guiding the runaway craft as best he could.

"Peter!" he yelled finally, unable to hold it any longer. "I need a hand here, on the double."

Peter crawled on his hands and knees in the swaying, jostling cabin to where Arthur was flying the machine.

"How we doing, Captain?" he asked.

"The aircraft is doing fine," answered Arthur. "But the Pilot's just about had it. My arms are numb and my back and neck are killing me. You're going to have to spell me a bit. Think you can handle that?"

"I don't know," replied Peter, unsure of himself under normal conditions let alone the current situation.

"Just do what I tell you and we'll be OK. First grab the stick here. Now just slip into the seat as I slip out. Good. Now just keep it steady. Don't fight it, let her go where she wants, but just don't let the tail slide out on you too much. You want to keep her straight. That's it. Watch the tail there. There you go. Got it? Good."

He stood behind Peter as he flew the dirigible like a parent teaching his kid to drive, advising him on how to adjust his tabs and stabilizers to counter the effects of the wind.

"Try not to let her drop too much if you can help it. Keep the nose up. That's it. I'm going to try and stretch out on my back, get some feeling back in my arms. If you have any trouble just give a yell. I'll be right back here. Don't worry."

Peter nodded but didn't say a word, his total concentration focused on flying the aircraft. They were at twenty thousand feet. It was still freezing despite the extra clothes each of them had layered on. Peter's unprotected nose and fingers were numbed by the cold. Each prayed for deliverance from the storm in their own silent way. Both felt completely helpless in the grip of nature's fury.

Hurtling along this way for hours, they traveled northwest across the state, trading places several times, one driving while the other rested or had something to eat.

They were slowly losing altitude, and as they got lower they were buffeted more by the wind and threatened by the lightning, although the temperature was getting more comfortable. A wet spray leaked in through every joint of the cabin, soaking their hair, skin, and clothes.

Shortly after dawn, Peter was again piloting the Albatross. The storm seemed to be abating, although it was hard to tell with the wind still lashing the dirigible like a lone ship at sea. A short time later the sky above them parted and they got their first glimpse of the sun since being trapped in the storm the day before.

"Look's like it may be letting up," commented Arthur, coming up behind Peter in the pilot's seat.

"It's about time," responded Peter, tired and sore despite his good frame of mind.

"That's the good news. The bad news is we're almost out of helium and losing altitude. Landing her will be pretty rough in these winds. At least the terrain should be relatively flat and treeless, mostly prairie."

"Got any ideas?" asked Peter hopefully.

Arthur, lost in thought, didn't answer immediately.

"Maybe, but first we'll have to get rid of all our hydrogen and check the balloon. We may have lost some of the cabling holding the basket together in the storm.

"Great," said Peter, forgetting his optimism with the rush of bad news.

While the pelting rain had ceased, and the thunder and lightning had stopped, the winds were still gusting over forty miles per hour. Arthur had seen hot-air balloons attempt to land in high winds, and didn't relish the thought of being dragged along the ground sideways in the flimsy dirigible's passenger compartment, underneath a bag filled with gas, whatever kind it may be. Then there was his hydrogen motor, which could contain traces of the highly explosive gas for hours. He dismantled it and threw it out of the aircraft.

"I'll need to take a look topside," announced Arthur when he was finished, trying as long as possible to put off the inevitable. "Think you can hold her steady for me?"

"You're not thinking of climbing outside are you?" asked Peter with concern.

"You know another way to check out the balloon?" countered Arthur.

"No, but so what if a few cables are loose? What do you think you can do?"

"Like maybe hook them up again. You don't want to have the basket unhook while we're 10,000 feet in the air, do you? Get my drift?"

"Yeah, but how the hell..."

"Just keep her steady and I'll show you," said Arthur, going back in the cabin to get some things he'd need in his daring attempt, including a multi-purpose tool called a Wrench-It.

Arthur had used a variety of methods to secure the cabin to the balloon when he built the Albatross, including bolts, epoxy, and cabling. It was the cables, an even two dozen of them, attached to the balloon's wooden frame and bolted to the top of the cabin, that Arthur was most concerned about.

As soon as he left the cabin, using the rear-side door, and was exposed to the fierce force of the wind, Arthur started having second thoughts. Next to the door was a small metal ladder leading up the side of the cabin. He pulled himself onto it and clung there like a bug on a side-view mirror. From there he was able to get a good look at the dirigible. Sure enough, several of the balloon's cables were loose and flapping dangerously in the wind like live electric wires. Using his miraculous, battery-operated, multi-purpose tool – five tools in one the ad said – Arthur quickly re-hooked one of the loose cables at the back of the balloon, directly over his head, holding on to the ladder with his left hand as he worked the tool with his right. This done, he started pulling himself along the top of the cabin using a long metal rail that was originally used to tie down baggage - that is before the lightweight vehicle was lashed to a balloon. He was able to use the tiny, metal outcropping that ran along the side of the cabin to place his feet. Nevertheless, the thin rungs of the ladder seemed like broad steps compared to the half-inch of metal he now stood on.

It took him some time to work his way along the balloon in this manner, re-securing cables as he went. The last two, major wires securing the front part of the balloon to the passenger compartment, were flying wildly in the wind, slapping the sides of the air-filled fabric like whips. If something wasn't done soon there was danger they would tear the balloon, and that would be the end of it. He would have to do something or they would crash as sure as his name was Arthur Berry. At least that's what he thought in this moment of exhilaration and pique. If he hadn't been so successful in securing the first cables, maybe he wouldn't have underestimated the danger involved. If he hadn't been so angry with himself for not fixing the wiring adequately in the first place, maybe he wouldn't have pushed himself so. But often heroism is nothing more than this, a combination of anger and frustration.

Screwing up his courage, he crawled along the top of the passenger compartment until he was directly underneath the flying cables. He could hear the wire slapping the side of the balloon. He clung there for some time, the wind whipping at him from all directions, trying to peel him off and toss him overboard.

He surveyed the cables just beyond his reach. He would have to scale the side of the dirigible to get to them. Just then the cabin buckled and jumped up toward the balloon like a bee-stung horse. Then just as suddenly it fell away, jerking the whole thing downward in a ragged motion that left his stomach where the balloon had just been, nearly shaking him off his precarious perch. It took him several minutes before he even dared to raise his head again. His heart pounded in his chest. Finally, he made up his mind and started inching upward, pulling himself gingerly by the wires that were still attached, until his feet were on the railing he had moments before been holding onto.

Standing precariously on the rail, he held the nylon netting encasing the balloon with his right hand as he stretched for the dangling cables with the other, but they were still just out of reach. It was so close. With just a little more effort he would have it. Edging himself forward, standing on his tiptoes, the cables just inches away from his fingertips, he started pulling himself up the side of the balloon like a human spider.

Below in the cabin, Peter fought to keep the aircraft steady, and craned his neck in vain to get a glimpse of his daredevil companion.

"Where are you now?" asked Peter to no one in particular.

The cabin rocked and rolled with the strong changing air currents, buffeted about like a cork in a raging river. Still moving at a dizzying speed, it descended swiftly.

Peter fought the controls to keep the craft's tail straight, and maintain altitude and direction as much as possible, hoping Arthur was not having too tough a time of it.

Suddenly, something flashed by the window in front of him. His blood went cold as his breath froze on his lips. It was too quick to make out but not quick enough to disguise. Peter jumped up to verify that the unthinkable hadn't happened. Pushing his head to the window he looked down, leaving the controls completely unattended. Unable to see anything, his heart stuck in mid-beat, he ran to the cabin door and threw it open against the rushing air. Hanging out of the craft, he looked down. Someone had thrown a doll out of the dirigible. It had to be a doll. What else would have a human form and be so small? What else could be falling through the air like that, arms and legs akimbo?

"Oh my God!" he screamed, in a deep, hollow voice.

Unable or unwilling to believe his eyes, his mind refusing the input signals supplied to it by his retinas, he started to climb out of the cabin, calling Arthur's name in harsh, barking tones, his voice choked with emotion. The wind took his words away as well as his breath. There was no answer. He clung to the ladder, half in, half out of the door, and peered upward. He could see all but one of the cables secured to the balloon, but Arthur was nowhere in sight. Still Peter hung there, straining to see every inch of the Albatross. Finally, he came to his senses and crawled back inside. Despite his denial, he knew that he would never see his friend again.

Just as Arthur had succeeded in reaching and securing the closest cable, a gust of wind, as if mad and jealous at being robbed of the balloon, took him instead, in one angry swipe of its atmospheric claw. Off he went, as quickly and as silently as a willow in the wind, to fall past Peter's horrified view in an instant of time. Though it didn't register totally on Peter's consciousness at that instant, that glimpse of the surprised and resigned look of his friend as he plummeted feet first to earth, approximately 10,000 feet below, would forever haunt him.

Somehow Peter made his way back to the steering mechanism of the dirigible, which was now wobbling dangerously from side to side, and got it under control. He sat there numbly peering out into the grayness of the soup-thick clouds that surrounded him on all sides, his eyes blinded with tears. Hardly able to come to grips with what had just happened, he could barely suck in his next breath of air.

Refusing to accept the obvious, numb with grief, Peter put his mind solely on flying the Albatross – a fitting name indeed for all the ill-luck it had brought them - keeping it up and moving, as if to say to his friend - who he would still not admit was gone – "I won't let you down, I won't let you die for nothing". So on he flew, as dawn turned to dark morning, and then to dimmer dusk.

MEDICAL FACILITY, LOS ANGELES, CALIFORNIA, NOVEMBER 29, 3:00 PM

By all appearances Dr. Linda Rayburn was back on her feet and on the road to recovery, but appearances can be deceiving. The patient was far from healthy, although the medical authorities in charge of her were doing everything in their power to help her.

The workings of the human brain, though still largely a mystery, was a mystery that had lost many of its secrets, like a hackneyed movie plot where the general outline is well-known but the subtle twists and turns of the individual sub-plots are still to be guessed. Of course, until the story is ended there is always room for the genuinely unexpected.

Linda walked but did not speak. She listened but gave no outward sign of sensing the meaning of the words she heard. She ate, drank, and relieved herself, but did not relate to anything or anyone around her. To all appearances she was in a classic autistic state, but in actuality she was quite aware of her surroundings, especially of the Organics being installed in the facility's main computer area three rooms away.

"How's she doing?" asked a nurse standing next to Dr. Rodriguez, as they watched Linda Rayburn through the large picture window that looked out onto a small, brick-enclosed patio where she stood and stared into space.

"Not that good, I'm afraid. We still haven't been able to get any response from her other than a few mumbled words that don't make any sense. Jacobs thinks she's suffering from irreversible brain damage due to malnutrition, but we haven't been able to confirm that from the scans. Her brain, at least physiologically, appears to be normal. I think she's suffered some sort of trauma, but I'll be darned if I can get through to her to find out what it is."

He studied his patient as she took a few shuffling steps then stood still again, cocking her head to the side as if listening for something.

What was it, he asked himself. What had she seen or experienced that had affected her so? He would have to uncover it if he expected to cure her, and that, after all, was what this was all about.

He left the window and walked down the few corridors to his boss's office on the west wing of the facility. He needed more help, but knew there was none to be had. He waited in the outer reception area of the spacious apartment-like office, until the boss's automated appointment keeper let him in, the key words, Linda Rayburn, assuring he would get to the top of the queue.

"Yes, what is it, Dr. Rodriguez?" the chief administrator asked, obviously not appreciating the interruption. He had just finished talking to his superior, one of Stan Bellows' staff, and the conversation had not been at all pleasant. "I'm very busy. I hope it's good news about our patient."

"It's about our patient, all right," answered Dr. Rodriguez. "But I'm afraid it's not good."

"Well?" demanded the hospital's head honcho, growing impatient with the other man's hesitation.

"I need more help," Rodriguez continued, although he knew he was wasting his breath. "Her mental condition is very poor. We just don't have the expertise here to deal with it adequately. At least if we could get the diagnostic programs working again we'd have a fighting chance."

"We'll have the Organics working again by the beginning of next week. The diagnostics will get top priority. Is that good enough for you?" asked the administrator with a self-satisfied expression.

"Yeah, that'll be great. Thanks. How are things on the plague front?" he asked, not knowing what else to say, his first request had been answered so quickly.

"Check the news services. I don't have time to sit here and chat. Is that it?"

"Well no," answered the dark-skinned medical man, deciding then and there to speak his mind. "I don't know what you expect to get out of her, but whatever it is, I don't think you're going to get it. She's completely autistic and liable to stay that way. I think we're wasting our time."

"Dr. Rodriguez, all our futures depend on her full recovery. Do I make myself clear? Would you rather be working in one of those plague-infested medical camps, on members of your own family? Is that what you'd prefer, Doctor?" The implied threat was given in a haphazard fashion, while looking at the computer screen, ignoring him completely. For a moment, the even-tempered, peaceful-natured Mexican-American contemplated cold-blooded murder. Then his higher instincts and concern for his own self-preservation kicked in, immediately forestalling any acts of violence with more intelligent alternatives.

Dr. Rodriguez left the spacious office and headed to his own cramped quarters on the first floor. He only had to read the news services to know the plague was on the move again, spreading from the major areas of population to the surrounding countryside. Worse, the epidemic's resurgence was not confined to the state of California, but had broken out again in the entire western portion of the country, from Mexico to Canada, from LA to the Mississippi.

He was torn by ambivalent feelings: on the one hand knowing that he was needed at the camps and could be of help, on the other, glad he and his family had yet been spared that awful ordeal.

It was also clear to him that he would make no progress while he remained here. They had tried everything, every conceivable chemical and therapeutic treatment, all to no avail. Even with the additional help of the Organics, which was a considerable boost, Linda's prognosis under current conditions was hopeless. But they hadn't tried everything. There was still something that might work, and he had been thinking about this possibility more often lately even though he knew it would never be approved by his bosses. It was risky, but there was really nothing to lose. She was already a lost cause. There was nothing to be gained by staying here. If his superiors were too stupid to see the obvious and listen to him, then he'd do it without their approval or their knowledge. He immediately began making arrangements.

Mark and Eddie made their way along the Appalachian Trail to Roanoke, Virginia where they hoped to gain access to the worldwide fiber-network. Along the way Eddie gave Mark a crash course in twenty-first century, multi-dimensional cellular-automata, the basis of his ingenious programming language. He found Mark an intuitive if uneven student. He wasn't sure what Mark did or didn't understand, but his understanding was critical, more so than either of them knew.

There were still signs that their whereabouts was important to the authorities, as evidenced by the frequent roadblocks and low-flying aircraft, but so far they had eluded every effort to locate them. They traveled by night, on foot, along mountain trails and wooded valleys, resting well-hidden during the day. Their success in eluding re-capture was aided by the lack of manpower as much as by the surrounding countryside, which they used to good advantage, although they were still well within the footprint of the multi-state manhunt.

Mark had learned all he could about the Trojan-horse virus and its means of infecting the Organics. Together, he and Eddie had designed a new, improved version of the program that acted faster and would be even more difficult to detect. Now all they had to do was find a way to get it on the Net. Timing would be critical. Too soon and their virus would be lost, ineffectively isolated on inactive machines and deadened lines. Too late and the plague carrying programs would begin fabricating the Pestis germ before their worm could be activated to shut down the network.

It was late afternoon, a little after 4:00 PM. They had stopped at an inviting area beneath three grandfather pines, the forest floor carpeted with their long, brown needles. Close by there was a large boulder, deposited by some unnamed glacier that had passed this way too long ago to remember. The clearing looked out over a flat field of yellow wild-flowers and knee-high grass, with patches of gray-topped weeds that looked like swirling eddies of smoke when the wind blew. It appeared to be a playing field of some kind, long since abandoned.

"This looks like a good spot," observed Eddie, un-shouldering his light pack, all that was left of their meager rations. He jumped on the boulder and looked out over the small field. It was completely flat with grass embankments on three sides that sloped up to pinewoods, which marched right to the edge of the field. On the fourth side, directly

196

opposite him as he peered out like an early explorer at the scene, were the backs of a row of two and three story brick buildings, the dormitories and classrooms of the university, just being painted by the golden light of the late afternoon sun.

"That's gotta be the college," said Eddie, summing up the situation. "I'll check it out, see if we can get the kind of access we need."

"I'm starved," complained Mark, really hungry for the first time in his life and not the least bit interested in the Net. They had been subsisting on instant soup and beef jerky, with stale bread and crackers. The canned goods they had loaded up their knapsacks with were long gone, as was their original supply of water. Although unable to renew their canned goods, they were able to find plenty of fresh water from springs and wells along the trail, which they boiled as an extra precaution.

Eddie fished a stick of jerky out of his bag and handed it to Mark. "Here, gnaw on this."

They hadn't seen a soul since leaving North Carolina three days ago when they stumbled on a family soon after starting out in the early dusk. There was a man and woman with four children, three boys and a girl, all seemingly clustered around the same age, which looked to be about nine or ten, to twelve or thirteen. They were dirty and grimy and had fear in their eyes. The father, in a gray work shirt and matching trousers, had gray stubble and gray hair and was covered with gray dust. He also carried an ugly-looking gray shotgun. The two groups eyed each other suspiciously for a few moments then retreated back in their separate directions, like primitive bands of hunter-gatherers must have treated each other, sniffing and watching, maybe blustering a little, but seldom fighting and killing. It took more civilized humans for that.

Eddie left to reconnoiter the approaches to the buildings while it was still light. Mark hid behind the boulder, nervously peering out every so often for signs of his friend. It was already getting dark. Eddie returned before long.

"Well, how's it look?" asked Mark, as Eddie approached with his long stride, his hair blowing in the light wind.

"Good. I got a good feel for the place," answered Eddie. "Didn't spot anyone."

"And?"

"We should have no problems hooking up."

"Good," said Mark, bending down and opening the cover of his bag.

The campus was barren of both faculty and students, which wasn't surprising given the pervasiveness of the Net and Organics on campus. Things hadn't returned to normal, since a high percentage of both teachers and students had perished in the first phase of the epidemic back in early September. The place wasn't entirely deserted, however. A small contingent of workers was busy reestablishing the European hub, using the university as a base of operations. Several satellite dishes were also operational.

Eddie took the three small computers from the knapsack Mark had been carrying and opened up their thin plastic cases, one of which had a small satellite antenna attached. Connecting them together with hair-width cables, he began to work. With fingers as delicate as a surgeon's, he manipulated the items on the paper-thin screens with amazing dexterity. Mark watched in awe, as Eddie interacted with each machine, using keyboards, pointing devices, and voice commands to relay his instructions.

He was working on each computer simultaneously, like Keith Emerson playing three keyboards at once, all of them responding to his commands with the speed of light. Waves of electrons shot through space and were picked up by a commercial satellite 200 miles above, which relayed them back to earth not more than 500 yards from where they stood, to one of the dishes on the university's main buildings.

The screen on one of the machines beeped with the log-in command for the master control system on the Fiber hub. Mark was good at breaking into systems as he had shown helping set up Eddy's escape in Tennessee, but his methods were conventional. His version of Eddy's Trojan-horse virus was only a poor imitation. Eddie on the other hand, was a true virtuoso. He could make the Net and its accompanying Organics do his bidding, as he had so aptly proved in Europe. Mark had been right to seek him out. Maybe, just maybe, with Eddy's instincts and knowledge, they might make it out of this after all.

All three small machines, which Mark and Peter had obtained from the surrounding high-tech countryside before they left Massachusetts for just this purpose, were working together in concert - like a group of well-practiced musicians, each with its assigned part. The first laptop managed the communication links and synchronized the activities of the other two, while the second performed the access algorithms needed to break into the network security system and cloak their intrusion. The third machine fabricated and transmitted a large portion of the Trojan-horse virus to the satellite, to be downloaded later when everything was ready.

Eddie was soon in, and once in he owned the system. Mark was starting to realize what Eddie had been talking about. Watching him construct the distributed programs and algorithms that embodied his Trojan-horse virus taught Mark a lot. After all, he was much more a hands-on kind of guy, responding to example rather than abstract theories. He was starting to get an idea of how it all worked.

As it grew darker and the time for the dangerous part of their mission approached, Mark grew more apprehensive.

"Tell me again why we just can't do it from here," he asked.

"We need to inject our virus into their system at precisely the moment it's going live. We'll need to be connected to the fiber itself to have the necessary bandwidth, and we'll need a good part of its 1000 million bits per second capacity if we're going to do it at the precise moment required, instantaneously. I've programmed the palmtop to respond to my voice command, which I can send to the small radio receiver here from this transmitter." He tapped the watch-sized device he had strapped to his wrist. "Once activated, it will relay the TH virus to the target organic machine at the precise moment required. In the meantime, the laptop here will be transmitting the main part of our package simultaneously to all the machines in the footprint of the satellite. At my command, they will all be infected and shut down, stopping the plague in its tracks. Or so goes the theory."

"So goes the theory," echoed Mark, wiping his glasses on his dirty T-shirt.

They made their away along the path Eddie had scouted earlier to the main cluster of red-brick buildings. The university was dark with few lights, the moon not yet out. What lights there were cast deep shadows, which the pair clung to like wary night creatures. They approached a building standing alone and to the left of the main cluster. A few moments of observation located the tell-tale yellow cable encasing the Fiber. By sending out their Trojan-horse virus from this location they could flood the entire system simultaneously, just as the network was being turned on. This, together with the preceding downloads would crash every organic computer on the East Coast before it had a chance to manufacture any plague germs.

It wouldn't be easy. With the danger of sabotage amply publicized in the media, and the whereabouts of computer enemy number one, two, and three still unknown, security at the university was tight, at least for these resource-scarce times. There was an armed man patrolling the grounds in addition to an elaborate grid of intelligent surveillance devices scattered about the area, several of which they had already inadvertently triggered. But it didn't matter, for their tiny machines were at work beaming bits back and forth between the satellite and the University's computers. The facility's sensors obediently did their job, but all the messages and alerts were harmlessly forwarded to the computers sitting back on the grassy knoll.

Eddie led the way along an overgrown lawn to the back of the ivy-covered, three-story brick building. It irked Mark that Eddie wasn't only smarter than he was, having an IQ that must have dwarfed a MENSA member's, but in better shape as well. Mark had to trot to keep up with him. He was breathing hard by the time they reached the far corner of the building. Crouching and peering around in the darkness nervously, Eddie followed the fiber cable with his eyes, while Mark looked for signs of the guard they knew must be around somewhere, hopefully on the other side of the campus. Lights were on in what appeared to be one of the main buildings across the street and diagonal from where they hid.

"So far, so good," Eddie said smiling.

"How do you say you're crazy in Polish?"

Eddie said something in his native tongue as he skirted around the corner of the building looking for a way in, finding a locked door with a key-card entrance instead.

"Thank God for modern technology," he said. "Where there's a key-card, there's access. Much easier than busting locks." He whispered two words into his unassuming wrist device and stood waiting behind the outcropping concrete portal that enshrouded the door like a cave entrance. Mark crouched behind the steps leading up to it.

Back where they had camped, behind a small clump of lilac bushes, fragrant and dark purple in the pale moonlight, one of the laptops responded to Eddy's command. Finding the building's access security server and locating the particular key-card device identified by Eddie, it went through simple permutations of eight-digit numbers. Starting a binary search based on the number of students, teachers, and employees estimated for a college of this size, it found a valid code in 3.5 seconds of CPU time, which was actually quite time-consuming by computer standards. The tiny red light on the card system turned green. They opened the door and walked in.

"Cool," said Mark, impressed, though he could have done the same thing himself given enough time. The fact that this last program of Eddy's had been fabricated not by Eddie, but by one of his computers, further added to Mark's amazement

They moved down the dark, silent corridor like two truant kids sneaking out of school. Alarms and warnings were being silently triggered, which if audible would have been deafening, but they were all intercepted and erased by Eddy's programs. They made no noise. Eddie wore the latest air-pumped sneakers, used in the NBA to help them run faster and jump higher than any human beings on earth, the latest craze around the world. Mark wore the same black Rockport Walkers he had worn since fleeing his home on the side of Oak Hill, not being as active in the art of looting as Eddie seemed to be.

"All we need is a machine with enough balls to handle our package," commented Eddie, still leading the way, though now edging along the wall cautiously, all his former bravado vanished.

Soon they found what they were looking for, a small closet-sized room sitting by itself in the corner on the second floor, which held the facility's communication hubs, some controlling the main connections to the European gateway itself.

"This is even better than I hoped for," observed Eddie, surveying the boards and cards that held circuitry and memory needed to handle the intelligent networking tasks. "We'll mainline it."

Quickly activating the tiny palmtop he had been carrying, Eddie sat it on the floor behind the panel of one of the network hubs. The palm-sized computer's massively-dense disk drive was packed with gigabytes of data, the key portion of his Trojan-horse virus, ready to be downloaded onto the University's master Organic the instant Eddie gave the command.

"What now?" whispered Mark, bathed in sweat even though the evening was chilly and the room cool.

"The preliminary work will take about fifteen or twenty-minutes to complete. It's all automated. Once that's done I can transmit the package by voice command in exactly seven seconds, give or take a few nanoseconds."

"Great! Let's get out of here."

They headed down the stairs through the same corridor they had passed before. Using the password obtained earlier, they exited the building and moved quietly along the side of the ivy-covered wall. Instead of going across the overgrown fields that at one time must have been well-manicured lawns, they edged along the building until he could peer at the well-lit structure with all the antennas across the street.

"Now what?" whispered Mark.

"We need to find a place to drop a few bugs so we can eavesdrop," announced Eddie. "We have to listen in to find out the precise time to unleash the TH virus."

"You're kidding, right? Why don't we just announce ourselves and ask them?"

"I've got a better idea," said Eddie, pulling a tiny device from the pocket of his well-worn jeans. "That building across the street appears to be their base of operations. We'll just drop a few of these miniature listening devices around the place, and pop back to our hideaway. I've even got a micro-cam. We can watch them on one of the laptops."

"Can't we just monitor their communications, watch their transmissions? Why do we have to do everything so close and personal like this?"

"Because we may miss it like that. Watching the Fiber itself won't work. By the time the Net is up it would be too late. No, we've got to find a way to watch for the exact moment."

"OK, but for God's sake be careful."

"Don't worry," said Eddie. "You'll be right behind me."

"That's what I was afraid of."

They crossed the street, keeping to the shadows, to investigate in more detail. It was a low, single-story building, more modern than the rest, with large, round windows and a collection of antennas and satellite dishes behind it. It was ablaze with bright light while everything around it was dark. Using the ample bushes and shrubbery that surrounded the place on three sides for cover, they circled to the rear of the structure where a light glowed from a small window.

Carefully, shielded by the night, they peered in. There, in a long, narrow room full of rectangular tables, covered with charts and laptops, were two technicians. One examined lengths of fiber-optic cable while the other laid out what appeared to be a banquet of roast chicken and steaming baked potatoes. A third man sat at a console, in front of an elaborate set of controls and display screens.

"This looks like the spot," announced Eddie, pulling back from the window. "Must be the campus radio station or something. Look's like a good place, eh."

Mark didn't hear a word Eddie had said. His mind was totally taken up with the sight of the food he had just seen. His mouth watered. His stomach made noises as if calling hogs.

"They've got food in there! Did you see that table?"

"Forget the food, Mark. It look's like they're about to go live. We got here just in time."

"They've got food in there."

Mark couldn't get the image of the perfectly cooked chicken out of his mind. It glowed in the soft light like a thing of burnished gold, succulent and juicy. He was ready to crawl through the window. Only his sense of self-preservation held him back and even that was wavering.

Eddie was saying something, which might have been a warning, but before Mark had time to focus on him a figure appeared out of nowhere and walked boldly up to confront them.

"Who are you? What're y'all doin' here?" he asked, pulling a very large handgun from the holster at his side.

Mark's heart dropped to his feet. A small moan of despair escaped his lips. Eddie brought his wrist up to his mouth in a slow continuous motion and yelled into it.

"Activate! Activate! Activate!"

The gun exploded in Mark's ears.

CHAPTER 19

SAN BERNARDINO NATIONAL FOREST, CALIFORNIA, DECEMBER 5, 2036, 11:15 AM

It had happened a week ago, but it seemed like only yesterday. Peter couldn't get the image out of his mind, Arthur flying by just out of the corner of his eye; Arthur dropping to earth at 380 miles per hour. Every moment since then had been like a scene from some mad fevered nightmare.

He had long ago passed denial and was now steeped in mind-numbing grief. His friend and travel companion of so many months was gone. Peter would have much rather it had been himself who had fallen from the aircraft. It was only the thought of his two little girls that kept him going, and kept the horror from overwhelming him.

Peter had ridden out the storm. The dirigible's lightened condition and Arthur's emergency repairs had allowed him to stay above the worst of it until he was far over Texas and crossing into New Mexico. It was there that he rapidly started losing helium and altitude, just as he was approaching a line of jagged rock and limestone peaks. The storm had died down considerably, although there were still wind gusts of forty miles an hour. It was only by sheer luck and the additional boost of the last of the emergency helium that kept him from crashing into the sharp, rocky side of the mountains. As it was, he missed it by only feet.

Whispering over the peaks of the Los Pinos Range, which opened onto a breathtaking view across a deep, thousand-foot gorge, Peter flew in a southwesterly direction. Sailing over the Rio Grande and losing altitude fast, he was able to crash land on a broad stretch of desert in western New Mexico, stopping just short of a twenty-foot gully that would have been his undoing. As it was, Arthur's timely removal of the hydrogen motor and securing of the balloon had saved his life. He suffered only a few minor bruises and scrapes. It was a miracle to be alive.

That had been a week ago. Since then, Peter had trekked overland through the mountains into Arizona. The memory of the crash landing still made him shudder. The loss of Arthur weighed on him like a deadweight drawing all his thoughts down into a pit of depression. Each day since then had been a fight for survival. He hadn't even been able to mourn his friend decently, but had to carry his sorrow with him in his breast, like a soldier carrying a dead comrade.

He thought about Sandy, and how he missed her and the kids. As he walked, the clear desert sky gave way to countless winking stars and the hot air grew cooler. He remembered their last night together, a night of passion and love, as they made up for lost time and stored up emotions.

He found a motorbike and made his way past Lake Havasu City and the Whipple Mountains, desolate, dry, and barren, where he arrived after crossing north of Phoenix through hills and plateaus that make up a dozen national forests. He then followed route 40 across southern California, northeast of LA, and was now entering the San Bernardino National forest.

The plague's second coming was even more destructive and devastating than its first appearance had been, if such a thing can be imagined. Its onslaught had been so sudden, so unexpected, and the population already so weakened with starvation and disease as a result of the first epidemic, that what was left of society in those places where it struck anew was completely obliterated. Any supply of anti-plague serum remaining was reserved for very special officials or stood rotting in warehouses with no one to transport it. Huge bonfires burned day and night, piled high with human corpses, filling the daytime sky with black clouds of soot and the night's darkness with red glowing cinders. Peter knew none of this.

As the sun rose, painting the facing sandstone cliffs with brilliant hues and colors, Peter went to sleep under the shade of a giant cottonwood tree. He had fitful dreams, in the last of which he was at a long buffet table that stretched beyond his sight. There were piles of warm breads, cheeses, and spreads, numerous glass bowls filled with every salad ingredient imaginable, fruits and cold cuts of every type, soups and appetizers of every description, hot, cold, fish, fowl, and this only what was within sight. Peter was last in line, close enough to the table to see the food, but not yet close enough to claim a plate. He was able to get a hint at what lay beyond his field of vision by the heaping platters of the other diners as they streamed by him with happy vacant stares - plates filled with huge helpings of every sort of vegetable, meat, and delicacy. Peking duck, roast chicken, the choicest steaks, tender veal, barbecued ribs, each with its own special sauce. These were only some of the things he saw. Others, who must have been at the dessert line, which he somehow knew was beyond the end of his long table, returned with carts full of Peter's favorite sweets - sundaes, shortcakes, pastries, and puddings, with pots of steaming, strong coffee.

Finally, he reached the start of the table and received a sparkling new dish, oversized to hold as much food as possible. He would be next in line at the bread and salad bowls. Just as he was about to cut himself a piece of freshly baked bread still warm from the oven, the fried dough aroma permeating the air, the person in front of him, a short woman wearing a garish red satin dress and an equally loud red veiled hat, reached for a nice leaf of lettuce and pulled up a large, hairy green spider instead. She let out a blood-curdling scream that made the dream Peter jump and drop his plate.

As he rose to consciousness, somewhere between being awake and still in the dream-state, he thought how absurd it was. Here he was in a dream of his own making, with a banquet about to be eaten, all the things he longed for, and he couldn't even conjure himself a stinking piece of bread. How could he hope to control his destiny in the real world when he couldn't control his own fantasies?

It took a moment for Peter to realize that he was fully awake, but the screams continued. He tried opening his eyes, but they seemed glued together. Squinting against the sun, he raised his hand as a shield. As he did, he saw a shadow in his blurred field of vision. Forcing his eyes open against the blinding light, which peeked through the leaves of the wide Cottonwood tree, he saw a face peering at him from within a tall sage bush at the edge of the clearing. Not a face so much as a cruel deformed parody of one, with bulbous boils where a forehead and cheeks should have been; red, blotchy parchment where skin should have been; swollen slits and pus-covered holes where eyes and lips should have been. It was standing not four feet away. The screaming came from its companion, a smaller form that appeared to be female and hysterical. Her high-pitched cries continued unabated.

Peter stood bolt upright, as if shot from a spring, adding his own shock of alarm to the noise. At that, the thing came through the bushes, a long thin line of spittle hanging from what must have been its mouth. It stared at him like a shark trying to decide if this bit of flesh was worth the risk or not. It looked like hunger was winning out over caution. The thing took another step forward. Peter, without thinking or premeditation, picked up a large, flat rock, and with rage born of terror and surprise, threw it with all his might straight into the face of his attacker, for that's what Peter assumed the figure to be.

The projectile did its damage with brutal speed, crushing the bone of the forehead and driving the fragments deep into the frontal lobe of the brain. Mercifully the thing lost consciousness while its lungs vainly tried to suck in air with a wheezing sound. Peter didn't stand around to see what happened next.

He ran out of the cool, shaded valley, up rough rocky trails to the high ground, under what was now the late afternoon sun. Not used to moving in the daylight, let alone running up a mountain, he was soon out of breath and drenched in sweat. He kicked himself for leaving his bike behind, but there was just no time. Stopping in the shade of a huge boulder to get his breath, he drank the last of his water.

He didn't know what he had seen, but guessed that whoever it was had a bad case of Plague, the bubonic form, which takes a few days to kill and results in horrible pain and insanity. There was nothing Peter could have done, although he felt foolish and sorry for his sudden violent reaction.

At the realization that he had crossed the path of a plague victim, Peter became worried, and checked himself all over until he was satisfied he had not been sprayed with blood.

Moving along the ridges and resting in the shade as much as possible, but not allowing himself any sleep, he walked on until he dropped, a little after the almost full moon reached its highest point in the sky, falling asleep on a bare patch of sand. Peter had decided to bypass LA and head northwest up the coastal ranges toward Silicon Valley, his final destination. He was exhausted and beyond caring any longer if anyone spotted him. An army of Plague victims could have walked over him and he wouldn't have moved a muscle. But his sleep was disturbed, haunted by deformed demons and malformed mutants that groped for him and blocked his path wherever he went.

CLAYMOTH LAKE, CASCADE MOUNTAINS, OREGON, DECEMBER 5, 11:35 AM

Despite incredible odds, the Fiber was slowly being resurrected in more locations across the country, as Stan Bellows and his fellow

207

industrialists focused ever more of their dwindling resources on it. Mile after mile of cabling had been replaced, hub after hub refitted and activated, relay after relay installed. The fact that the Plague had broken out again was less troubling to Bellows than the fact that something disturbingly similar to the European virus had appeared on the East Coast, threatening to stop all his hard earned progress in its tracks.

It didn't take long to put two and two together and realize that the attack emanated from the same computer felon who had recently escaped from their facility in Tennessee. The *Dark Enigma* had struck again, right in the heart of the nation.

If this wasn't bad enough, a second wave of the Plague had hit the west coast, just as things were getting on their feet again. It made it even more difficult to find the trained personnel he needed, which in turn made it harder for him to accomplish his goals. But as hardship and adversity had spawned many great inventions before this, the lack of workers in the field led to the automation of much of the work with computer driven robotics. Some of his new relay stations and routers could actually perform much of the setup work and repairs that once needed human intervention at the location. Still, it was a daunting task. Now someone was trying to break it up. By God, he would make them pay!

Despite his wishes, the Fiber had not yet been installed in his mountain home, nor would it be. It wasn't that he believed the rumors that the network carried the plague. There were just too many other demands on resources and equipment to make it justifiable. Instead, all efforts were now being made to ensure that the National Emergency Center in Boulder, where the contingency government would make its headquarters, was ready. From there he planned to control the entire system, economic, political, and military.

Meanwhile, there had been growing resentment against the Fiber, which some of the more intelligent of the population were starting to associate with the plague. Groups of computer hackers and fiber-surfers were starting to publish their allegations, and there were some groups actively promoting violence against the ever-growing network. There had even been attempts, although amateurish and sloppy, to sabotage and disrupt it, most of these taking place on the West Coast. Then the East Coast attack occurred just as they were about to connect the US and European Nets together. Things were getting out of control.

Still, hackers and saboteurs were in the minority. Most people just wanted things to get back to normal, and that meant the ever-present, all-pervasive network with its army of computers, silicon and organic, doing their bidding, anticipating their whims, catering to their every need, day and night, 365 days of the year. Those were comforts that had turned into necessities for most modern, westernized men and women. Returning to normal meant listening to people like Stan Bellows. To this end, every available official, all police and firemen, all military personnel still standing, and every paramilitary group that could be mustered, were being dedicated to the reestablishment of the Fiber and the apprehension of anyone standing in the way of that purpose.

Stan bellowed orders through his newly installed satellite videophone. The face of a somewhat young and nervous subordinate looked out at him from the console's paper-thin screen. His previous head of security had been fired and incarcerated along with the witless Mike Pearlman.

"And I want him alive. Got that? God help anyone who harms a hair on his head."

"Yes, sir," answered the face on the screen.

The good news was that the intruder who had been shot breaking into their Roanoke facility in Virginia had been positively identified as the escaped East European hacker, Eddie Pavloski. The bad news was that his partner in crime had escaped and was still at large. Worse, they had apparently been able to discharge their virus into the network just as it was being reactivated. In the intervening days, hub after hub of the fiber-optic network in the east had been infected and shut down. Their patches were useless against this new version of the Trojan-horse program. Unfortunately, the West Coast and Central sectors were protected from Mark and Eddy's virus by a fire-wall of gateways and bridges, which were immediately thrown up, preventing the plague-ridden machines in their part of the country from being disabled.

"I want every single man available on this. I don't care what has to give or who has to go. Everything's on hold until we find that criminal terrorist and we've stopped that European virus from spreading."

"Yes, sir, Mr. Bellows," answered the employee, shaking in his penny-loafers. He knew the power and the unpredictable wrath of the man staring at him from the video-unit, with the thick-knit eyebrows and the dark, penetrating eyes. The unit went suddenly blank and the young lieutenant went to carry out his orders.

After the shooting of Eddie Pavloski and the escape of the second man, an intense and massive search had been conducted of the area surrounding the campus, but the escapee had not been found, although the pair's camp was located a short time later, along with their home-made transmitter and computers. While they were attempting to decipher the source code that had apparently been transmitted to the facility's Organics, the program self-destructed, the bits and bytes dissolving into a meaningless co-mingling of data in a constantly shifting pattern that drove the analyst working on it almost insane. Whatever chance they had of learning its secrets evaporated like an early-morning dew, the very action of looking at it - which meant exciting it with electrons - causing its destruction. Now they had a runaway computer criminal on their hands, dangerous in the extreme, and an equally destructive computer virus tearing up the East Coast information highway like an overeager work crew. At least the plague hadn't re-emerged in that part of the country yet.

Bellows pulled up a map of the US on his laptop display and zeroed in on the states of Virginia and West Virginia. The green ridge of the Appalachian Mountains cut across the otherwise white of the map's background, crisscrossed with red and blue lines like myriad veins of oxidized and de-oxidized blood, representing highways and roads. He called up a hiker's guide and set the parameters for trails originating in the Roanoke vicinity outward for 200 miles in a large concentric circle. Several lines appeared on the map like growing black cracks in white ice, from Roanoke, up and down along the rocky spine of the mountain range that slanted across the landscape like a raised scar. The odds were good that the fugitive was sneaking north along one of these trails, lying low and avoiding the search parties. God knows there were enough nooks and crannies for him to hole up in. There had to be a way to smoke him out.

Bellows finished entering his orders directing the massive search, which he was supervising from his rocky fortress in the Cascades. Soon he would be permanently established in Colorado, with a virtual slave army of Organics to carry out the incredibly complicated decision-analysis needed for his plans. A click and a point, and his commands would be beamed at the speed of light along the Fiber to its many destinations, from relay to relay, through every type of medium, all doing his bidding. Now there was yet another obstacle in the way to his goal, which seemed to be slipping from his grasp just as he was getting hold of it. It was almost too much to bear. Was there no end to it? Was he to spend his days like some modern Sisyphus, cursed to repeat his steps over and over again?

Things were too far out of control now to handle alone. He couldn't take any chances. He would need help. With these thoughts in mind, after providing some additional advice to his search teams in Virginia, he called his Asian friend and made special arrangements for the upcoming meeting of the emergency government in Colorado.

CHAPTER 20

PALO ALTO, CALIFORNIA, DECEMBER 5, 2036, 12:15 PM

The pestilence swept over LA. Miraculously, Linda Rayburn was not among the ranks of the dead and dying.. Weary of his bosses' manipulations and orders, and anticipating somewhat the coming of events, Dr. Fernando Rodriguez decided to take matters into his own hands.

It hadn't been difficult to obtain the supplies he needed or the aid of a few well-placed associates at the proper time. Linda's recovery to date had been nothing short of miraculous. Certainly she would be of use to nobody if she were struck down by the plague. The only hope was to get her out of its path, which meant out of the city. But where?

In reviewing Linda's records, Rodriguez discovered how she had been found in the midst of a plague-infested neighborhood, in a plague-free apartment with a complete lab facility. Soon after this, he made a surreptitious visit to her home and found the building filthy but the lab still intact. He spent the next few days cleaning the place and stashing the needed supplies, making it ready for their use.

Dr. Rodriguez was one of those who had become convinced that the reconstituted Fiber had something to do with the spreading of the disease. All other known methods of infection, from traditional vectors to commercial transportation routes, had been exhaustively eliminated, as he well knew. The pattern and speed of the epidemic in its movement across the country, from high-tech areas and communication centers, to outlying regions, and its virtual non-existence in undeveloped areas where the Fiber didn't exist, made it obvious to anyone willing to accept the facts.

Another factor motivating his move, even if the disease hadn't been bearing down on them like a mudslide, was the distinct possibility that the familiar surroundings of her home might help ease her back to some semblance of sanity.

Linda lay asleep in the darkened bedroom, all traces of the strong noonday sun hidden by the thick cloth of dark-purple draperies and curtains that hung across the double windows of her third-story room. Dr. Rodriguez silently closed the bedroom door after checking in on her and found his way back to the now tidy kitchen where he made himself lunch.

The past few weeks had been one long excruciating battle for the reclamation of the mind and soul of his patient. Getting her out of the sparsely attended hospital under cover of darkness had been the easy part. Then came day after torturous day where she made no improvement no matter what he tried, but remained mute and dumb throughout. These periods were interspersed with episodes of extreme emotion, with manic outbursts and crying jags, which left her back in a nearly catatonic state. He never gave up, however, tenaciously forsaking everything for her recovery. Not that he had that much to forego, no wife, no job. His persistence was finally paying off.

The last few days had been particularly rewarding. He was able to carry on a series of ever longer conversations with her that verged on intelligent. She was a far cry from the Linda Rayburn that had forged new discoveries in quantum computing, but no longer the woman he had to bathe and feed like a baby. He was thinking about her well-developed breasts as he banged pots and pans around in the kitchen, cooking up some of the supplies he had procured from the hospital.

Linda's body, which had been emaciated and encased in filth when she had been found, was now clean and filling out nicely, although still on the thin side. The frequent baths he administered made her skin glow with a healthy pink sheen, and her pageboy hair, now long and silky, shone in the dancing rays of sun that stole through the apartment windows. Without the dowdy clothes she habitually wore, perhaps to maintain her distance from men in general, she was positively attractive, as Fernando's libido could attest, even if his higher impulses would not let him act on it, at least not while she was still a mental child devoid of any will or judgment of her own. That was slowly changing.

Luckily, no one had followed them and no one seemed to be looking for them, which was understandable given the devastating effects of the second coming of the plague in LA. While there were house to house sweeps being conducted in the city, where anything that moved was either shot or arrested and taken to the giant medical centers, there were very few left to carry out these orders. There were more protective suits than people available to wear them. Under these conditions, it would be a long time before anyone got around to Linda's neighborhood again, which was thought to be empty anyway. That is if they ever got around to it. Rodriguez had enough supplies smuggled from the hospital's well-maintained coffers to last months. The hospital wouldn't need it now.

He ate without disturbing his patient, and then went to the penthouse lab where he stood looking at the odd object in the corner, obviously some kind of computer, but nothing like he had ever seen before. The colored patterns that played on the device's flat display screen like a kaleidoscopic, drug-induced hallucination transfixed him. In his curiosity about how it worked, he started playing with the surrounding casing - probing it, touching it, examining it like he would a patient - a patient from another galaxy. He was about to start fiddling with the contraption's input device, changing the dancing patterns on the display when he heard a shrill cry.

"No! Don't touch it!" Linda screamed as if he were about to butcher her first born child. "Don't touch it!" she repeated unnecessarily, since he had jumped away from the machine as if it were on fire.

She ran up to him and pushed him further from it, as she stepped between him and her computer.

"Don't touch it," she intoned again, standing in front of the odd machine with her arms outstretched as if reaching for it. Suddenly, she turned on him with wild eyes, her features deformed in rage. As he tried to approach to calm her down and take her back downstairs, she shrieked and attacked him, flailing at him with her fists, which he was easily able to grab.

Subduing her with a massive bear hug, which smothered her into submission, he carried her back downstairs to bed. He had avoided the use of drugs out of fear of causing her to relapse into a catatonic state, but in this case he was forced to administer a shot that knocked her out for several hours. She woke groggy and mute late in the day. Afraid the drug had erased any spark of intelligence she might still have, he was surprised when of her own accord she got up and went upstairs to the lab, back to her pulsating machine. Rodriguez followed at a discreet distance, feeling like a field biologist observing a rare female gorilla in her natural habitat, afraid of disturbing it.

"What is it?" he hazarded after awhile. "Some kind of computer?" Silence. "Never seen one quite like that before. You make it?"

"Yes, I make it."

"What does it do? Is it running something now?"

"I made it," she repeated more grammatically.

"What's it do?"

"Don't touch it."
"What's it do?"
A long pause.
"Pretty lights."

EMERGENCY GOVERNMENT CENTER, BOULDER, COLORADO, DECEMBER 8, 10:00 AM

Everyone spoke at once. The room buzzed and hummed like a living hive with energy and fear, all intermixed in a jumbled tangle of emotion, as the attendees strove to make themselves heard and voice the universal terror welling up inside them. The worst possible scenario had played out. All their best efforts had been in vain. The country lay on the brink of ruin.

Stan Bellows gave up for the moment trying to bring order to the meeting. Stepping away from the podium, he had a few brief words with an assistant, who scurried out of the room like the animal version of what he was, small, brown, and feral. Bellows took a sip of ice water and watched the room through narrowed, ice-blue eyes, waiting patiently for things to die down of their own accord, which they did in time. Much of the noise was directed at him, questions and accusations mingled with recriminations and not a few supplications. He stood there impassively and let the wave of sound wash over him like harmless water vapor.

The plague was again raging across most of the country, and as before, all attempts to stop it had failed. The only positive news to report was that the Fiber was back in operation, except that is for the East Coast where the hub to Europe had been shutdown. In the West Coast, the Asian link would soon be operational, its schedule accelerated in view of other contingencies. A few pilot sites had already been set up in China and Japan. The first cases of Plague had also been reported there.

The bad news was that the link-up of the US and European nets had been indefinitely postponed. Some of the culprits were still at large, although he had the pleasure to report - if they would let him speak – news of the death of the suspected author of the TH virus and the capture of his accomplice, an errant engineer, who had been working for them in New England just before the epidemic struck there.

Bellows glanced in the direction of his Asian friend, Jiang Feng, Minister of Technology for the People's Republic of China, who nodded briefly then spoke to the man standing behind him with a hand-concealed whisper, despite the din in the room. Eventually the hubbub died down to a sputter. The young US Secretary of State, Robert Morris, the only one left of the previous administration still alive and in the country, and thus in line for the US Presidency itself, rose as if by silent agreement, and began to voice the concerns of many of those in the room.

"Mr. Chairman. The plague seems to be our real concern here. All other activity, including activation of the worldwide Fiber, should be suspended until the epidemic is over and its source discovered and eliminated. The world's available resources should be concentrated on this effort and this effort alone. The plague must be stopped immediately."

There was a lone clap from somewhere in the back of the room from a staunch supporter of the speaker, but other than that, almost complete silence, a stark contrast from a few moments before.

"Furthermore," continued Morris after a brief pause. "There is growing evidence that the Fiber itself is responsible for the plague."

With that the room exploded into a chorus of claims and counter claims, accusations and denials, exclamations and expletives. Bellows and Morris eyed each other across the table like two boxers in a ring. Eventually the noise subsided gradually as if someone had slowly turned down the volume. In the silence the voice of Stan Bellows boomed out.

"Mr. Morris, if you had an ounce of commonsense you'd know that was totally impossible, pure fantasy. Every expert in the country will tell you that such a thing just isn't possible. It defies the laws of physics, Mr. Morris. As for your suggestion that we focus all our attention on the plague, that's exactly what's being done. Every available medical facility, hospital, doctor, nurse, and all military personnel are being dedicated to its eradication. The emergency medical centers are being re-instigated and enlarged, and extended to those areas of the country where they didn't exist before. Nationwide martial law is being established, along with curfews, to help fight the epidemic and the lawlessness that goes with it. Strong laws have been enacted to punish those who contribute in any way to its spread. In fact, the most important thing we can do to help stop the plague is to reestablish our organic computer banks and the fiber network that links them, so the full power of these machines can be focused on the problem. But we can't do it ourselves, especially with so many experts in the field of medicine and disease prevention being lost, those brave and dedicated souls who are single-handedly attempting to stem the tide of death and destruction that's being visited on us."

Bellows paused for effect then went on.

"Mr. Morris, your attempts to confuse the issues and cast blame with no facts verge on treason, and are at minimum grossly irresponsible in such a time of great crises as we currently find ourselves. I'm frankly very disappointed in you. I expected more."

These words were greeted with a storm of protest, which erupted spontaneously from the supporters of the young president-designate, stung by the barely concealed venom in Bellows' voice. All pretense of respect and decorum had been dropped. Bellows' anger and momentum had carried him beyond the point where he could control his tone or his words. He spoke in a fever-pitched voice that stunned the room to silence. He swore, he berated, he ridiculed and threatened. He raved like a maniacal dictator with arm gestures and mannerisms right out of some old grainy war documentary. As he spoke to the shocked room, unnoticed by the crowd, a group of newcomers began to filter in, standing along the wall half-hidden from those seated at the table by the throng of secretaries and assistants standing directly behind them.

During his tirade, Bellows explained the pet theory that was to propel his actions for some time to come. The idea - a combination of imagination, desperation, and inspiration - that the plague had been caused by the same persons trying to sabotage the Fiber, who were somehow, intentionally, by some means as yet unknown, infecting the population. Maybe they were contaminating the water supply or the food, or the air-conditioners. Maybe they were unleashing armies of trained rodents to do their bidding, with millions of infected fleas riding on their back, who knows. However they were doing it, whoever they were, there were many of them, an army of secret, cowardly terrorists, dedicated to the overthrow of the American way of life, in our nation's most vulnerable hour. They wouldn't be happy, these nihilists and anarchists whose sole aim was to kill and destroy us, until every visage of our civilization was tumbled into the pits of hell. He, Stan Bellows, was going to make sure that they failed. This would be his sworn mission from this day on.

These statements, so obviously contrary to the facts, delivered with such vehemence, caused even Bellows' most ardent supporters to gape in disbelief and confusion. How was one to reply to a madman? Despite their uncertainty, the staunch followers of Bellows, the power-hungry, the fearful, the subservient and greedy, not small in number considering his immense power, started to clap and shout their approval with broad hurrahs and hear-hears. Foot stomping and table banging, along with well-practiced chants and slogans accompanied this display of support. Others in the room, those with decidedly different views, met this outburst with cries of protest and objections, as people who were sitting started rising to their feet. It was at this point that the participants noticed the newcomers who ringed the room like a living corral of barbed wire, bristling with menace, taut and nervous - more so at being for the most part young and inexperienced, not that this did anything to mitigate their collective threat.

"What's going on here?" cried Morris, sizing up the situation quickly as was his wont and speaking for them all, even the supporters of Stan Bellows, who looked at their leader dumbfounded even as they cheered. "What's the meaning of this?"

"Shut up!" shouted the Chairman at the top of his lungs. "All of you shut up or I'll have you shut-up permanently." He sounded like a gangster in a room full of underlings, like a medieval king in a castle of cowed courtiers. Continuing to shout at the top of his voice for several minutes, he gave a disjointed speech accented with spits and sputters, in language meant to shock and offend. "We can no longer tolerate disobedience...This calls for stern measures...Tough action is needed...Must have total loyalty...Ruthless determination is required..."

Each statement was met by increased protests.

"You'll never get away with this," yelled Morris. "You'll cause a civil war. Is that what you want, more bloodshed? If anything happens to us, you'll have the whole world to answer to. Whatever forces you think you can muster won't be able to stand up against the armies of the world."

"If you want bloodshed, you can have it," answered Bellows barely able to keep from frothing at the mouth. "And you can be the first to bleed. I do speak for the world, you fool. The armies of the world march behind me. Look around you!"

While Bellows ranted, more of the attendees became aware that the uniformed men surrounding them, armed with automatic rifles, were for the most part Asian, dressed in the nondescript green fatigues

218

of the Chinese Army, although there were no regimental insignias. At this point in the proceedings Jiang Feng stood and motioned the room for silence. When it was attained he spoke in tones so quiet even those quite near had to strain forward to hear him.

"Ladies, Gentlemen, please let us keep our senses. There is no need for violence here. We are all of one accord, like the one life that burns within all living creatures. We all want safety for our loved ones, peace and prosperity for our children, health and well-being for ourselves. We only differ in how we propose to attain these things. The Buddha says all life is suffering, but the People's Republic has shown it does not have to be so. For a long time we in the east have watched with concern as the US and Europe, racked by internal problems and calamities, have attempted to solve their troubles by themselves, quite unsuccessfully I might add. We have chosen not to interfere, even though these misfortunes have affected us grievously, just when we had hoped to see our country take its rightful place as a leader of nations. I can no longer stand by and watch helplessly while our dreams and hopes are shattered by incompetence and laziness, as the diseases spawned in your slums reach our shores "

These words, following on the heels of Stan Bellows' self-revelations, were enough to stun even the most cynical in the crowd, some of whom sat back in their seats in shock. Morris looked at the tiny oriental man standing next to him talking, as if he were from another planet. He shook his head from side to side wondering how he had missed it, this unexpected turn of events that now seemed so obvious.

"For months, I have watched this terrible tragedy unfold and spread slowly toward my country," Feng went on, "first striking the Hawaiian Islands last September. Waiting for the inevitable somehow makes it worse when it finally arrives. Now it has, the first occurrence appearing in Beijing, my home, only a few days ago. I have pledged my full support to the chairman, Mr. Stan Bellows. He alone has the courage and foresight to solve the present problem. All the resources at my command, manpower, equipment, medical specialists, computer experts, are at his disposal. We will work with the head of your government until the problem has been corrected."

Feng read the short list of five names that would sit on the governing committee to the stunned silence of the room, with his own name and Stan Bellows as chair. The head of France, a staunch Bellows follower, and two other Asians, an Indian and a Japanese, were also on the committee. Morris was conspicuously absent, as was the Prime Minister of Great Britain, a supporter of the former president who had fled there at the outbreak of the epidemic. There were a few isolated acts of dissension, some of Morris's people arguing passionately for a vote, an election in the democratic fashion. But democracy had vanished like a magician's rabbit, while reason had given way to violent intervention, consensus to brute force. At this moment in time Bellows held all the cards and he had them played face up on the table for all to see.

There were more histrionics, as Morris and his followers were forcibly removed from the room. Breasts were bared to bayonets, oaths were sworn, and not a few heads were bashed in, but in the end the room was cleared of dissenters. The remaining participants, cowed by the forceful removal of their peers, quickly voted to second Feng's proposal into law, voluntarily dissolving what was left of the United States government in favor of the new committee. No longer needed, the emergency governing council adjourned and went home to their respective enclaves and citadels of safety. Morris and his cohorts were detained in the bunker's storage area under house arrest until other more permanent arrangements could be made. Bellows and Feng adjourned to a private room to have dinner and discuss their plans for the future. A new era had begun. The world would now march to the beat of Stan Bellows' drumming.

SILICON VALLEY, CALIFORNIA, DECEMBER 8, 4:45 PM

Peter, on foot again, made his way across the bleak landscape during the night, clinging to the shadows in the twilight. Things had gone from bad to worse in California, one of the places most badly ravaged by the disease. Not a creature stirred on the streets of town or city, farm or suburb, while in the festering camps, crammed with humanity by the thousands, they squirmed and moved and died in teeming hordes. It wasn't so much that insects ruled the earth as it was humans came to resemble them more and more.

Peter had given up all hope. Now at the point of reaching his sought for destination, all he wanted to do was turn around and run. Yet he doggedly went on, driven by subterranean impulses that he could hardly understand even if he'd had the strength to try. Fear smothered his being like a heavy coat in the tropics. It was his constant companion, that and hunger.

He had long ago exhausted his meager ration of food and water. The occasional find or catch along the way - the efforts of living off the land while trying to elude pursuit should not be underestimated - had diminished as he got closer to his target. The signs of destruction and death had become more all-pervasive and terrible. He not so much hid and rested during the day, as cowered and fainted from fear and fatigue.

Dread of the plague kept him awake most of the time when he should have been resting. This last day, Peter had fallen asleep soon after halting and didn't wake up until the sun set, forgetting even the plague in his sheer exhaustion. The lost souls and half-mad beings he had encountered earlier, wandering the land like the living dead, had not been seen for days. All he saw now were stray dogs and cats, which he chased away with rocks and sticks.

Still in the mountains to the east of the city, he looked out over the valley and the gleaming ocean beyond, bathed in the glow of the dying orange sun like a waiting emerald mirror. Then he snaked his way down into the valley along well-heeled mountain neighborhoods and hillside streets.

It was now late afternoon. He was walking along the outskirts of what had once been the heartland of Silicon Valley, feeling a little better after his twelve hours of sleep and a light meal of barbecued lizard. According to the info he got from Mark, Linda Rayburn's last known residence should be on the next street over.

The ruins of houses surrounded him, some charred, some demolished, empty fields where others had been. Abandoned automobiles shared the same fate as the houses, each one a grim reminder of lives lost and forever ruined. The sky glowed garishly in the north from several huge bonfires just out of sight on the horizon. Their meaning gnawed disturbingly just out of Peter's awareness. Not a tree stood standing, as if cut down by superstitious Easter Islanders to appease an angry god. His heart sank at the desolation and at the story it told of what had happened here. His prospects did not look good.

Things improved a little as he moved into Linda Rayburn's neighborhood, the homes of the engineers and scientists who had made the edifice of modern society possible. To Peter it seemed like a scene out of more normal times, a sleeping bedroom community with cars parked neatly along the silent streets and driveways, awaiting the morning commuters and bustling housewives, only the lawns were overgrown, and no one would be arriving.

All about him looked deserted, but looks are often deceiving, for hidden behind overgrown hedges, peeking through half-shuttered windows, spying from gabled roofs, were the mechanical eyes of various sensors and cameras, there to take the place of missing humans. Only these eyes missed nothing. They never grew careless, never got tired, and could magnify their view by thousands of times on demand. Into this web of scrutiny, on guard for the minutest disturbance, walked Peter Danvers.

The disturbance was duly noted, identified, and categorized as human and worthy of attention. The signal, along with the location of its source, was relayed back to a central station where monitoring software awaited the arrival of such messages. There it was interpreted and passed on to the appropriate response station, which in this case was a nearby military installation, populated by teams of individuals trained for just such missions. With the sounding of the alarm, the group of four on duty quickly donned their protective suits and hobbled out at the double-trot to the waiting medical emergency van, more equipped for warfare than medicine. Guided by the GPS computer system in the van, which featured a grid-map of the city with a red flashing light where the intruder was last seen, they closed in on their target.

Peter sensed his error before the results of it were fully apparent, some sort of sixth sense born of urgency and need. He looked around with increased attention and noted the hidden cameras peeking from beneath hedges and the tops of streetlamps, following his movements like robotic vultures.

"Oh no!" he uttered, out loud. "I'm being watched." His wits had returned, but too late. At that moment a dark-gray van careened around the corner and barreled up the street at him with obvious malicious intent. Peter stood rooted to the spot, not that escape was within the realm of possibilities.

The vehicle screeched to a halt at the curb next to him. Like a scene from a B-movie, the side-panel door slid open and three figures in fatigue-colored protective uniforms jumped out and ran toward him. Peter would never forget the unreality of it, as the suited men soundlessly surrounded him and quickly covered him with a thick, mesh net. That was the normal part. The true madness began when from out of nowhere, like skeletal antagonists sprouting from the ground, came an army of figures dressed in rags and glistening half-naked in the pale light of the remaining day. All of them were sick and deformed, with boils and open sores, an army of the walking dead or dying, out for revenge against the hated green-suits, who were nothing more than the worse dregs of society, men who would haul their mothers to the death camps for a mere pittance or hot meal.

They fell on the ill-fated SWAT team like locusts, while in the panic the driver of the van sped off in fear for his life - a wise move considering the alternative. Peter extricated himself from the net as the mob of maniacal sick tore the protective suits from the unfortunate men. Disappearing around a corner, all but unnoticed, he scurried away as fast as he could run. The mechanical eyes watched it all. Before another team could be dispatched to the area, however - probably several teams for such a mission - the mob melted back into the holes and sewers they had sprung from, disappearing into the gathering dusk.

Despite his exhausted and weak condition, Peter, once free of the mayhem, ran as if he were a conditioned athlete competing for the 100-yard dash, except he sprinted quite a bit further than that, until he dropped behind an ivy-covered brick wall. Rolling on the ground in agony, he tried to get his breath back. The pain in his side felt like a knife had been sticking between his ribs for the last half-mile. Flopping around on the ground, he tried to suck air into his burning lungs. Now he knew how a fish out of water felt. He was going to die for sure, right here, right now. With eyes full of tears, he groped his way to a kneeling position and rocked back and forth, trying to get his wind back.

For a moment he thought he had indeed died and gone to heaven. Looking up through his teary vision, he saw an ornate glass window and a steeple, topped with a gold-gilt cross, shining in a last ray of the sinking sun like a golden halo. It was a temple of worship, the church of some long abandoned congregation, from some now defunct denomination.

Gaining his breath in slow stages, Peter managed to get to his feet, and after surveying the situation in more detail, forced himself the last few yards to the building, where he collapsed in another fit of coughing and pain, feeling like a diver who had come up too fast from the depths. Here he was with no food, no water, and no where to go. Now he had no air as well. What more could he be deprived of and still be alive?

He could hear the muted sirens of emergency vehicles approaching from the west, converging on the recent scene of carnage. Peter knew that he wasn't far enough away, but didn't know where else to go, even if he'd had the energy to move another step. Terror and despair hung in his mind like dead leaves. The sound of gunfire and screaming erupted from only a few blocks away, rising and dying on the wind, first loud and near, then soft and distant.

With difficulty he moved to the back of the church where all the windows were barred and shut. The stone structure resembled a medieval castle, with massive stone towers and steel barred windows. Thick, iron-framed doors, made as if to withstand a siege, stood locked and silent.

Suddenly, the commotion and sounds of battle that at one point seemed to be dying down and moving off, picked up, soon boring down on him like a jet coming in for a landing. In a panic, Peter made a dash for the nearest door, a small, nondescript thing of wood, with black iron castings. It stood at ground level and led under a broad, cement staircase to what seemed to be the basement of the church. The gunfire and shouting were all around him now. At any moment one or the other of the warring parties would stumble upon him and kill him outright without missing a beat.

Peter pulled on the door. It didn't budge. He could hear them, almost on him now, one more corner away. Another minute and they would be there. He pulled again. Nothing. He was in despair. Fear coursed through his every fiber. With one more tremendous yank, this time with the strength and effort born of desperate need, the door, which had only been stuck not locked, gave way with a mighty creaking of rusted hinges and metal. He stumbled into the dirt-clogged, bare-walled room not a moment too soon, and slammed the heavy door behind him, bolting and locking it from within. It was pitch-black inside, dank and silent as an ancient crypt. Peter could hear the mob and their attackers as they converged at the rear of the building where only moments before he had stood. The gunfire and screaming seemed to go on forever.

CHAPTER 21

DOBBINS AIR FORCE BASE, ATLANTA, GEORGIA, DECEMBER 8, 2036, 7:45 PM

Time was running out for Mark Goodwater. After the enactment of the new harsh, anti-computer tampering laws, Mark was to be the first to feel their teeth, as he was summarily, with only a military trial, sentenced to public execution by firing squad, the first in the country in a century. Times were a changing thought Mark ruefully from his prison cell, where he had languished in solitary confinement since his capture exactly three days ago.

He had escaped in the confusion immediately following Eddy's horrible death, the shooter just as shocked as Mark at the results of the high caliber bullet and loud explosion. By the time what was left of Eddy's head hit the ground his Trojan-horse Virus was being transmitted through the Fiber to the bank of organic computers just as they became activated. At the same time, back at the knoll where the three small notebooks sat humming silently, commands were issued to the satellite to release its bundle of stored data, and the remaining part of Eddie's virus was distributed over the airwaves to every machine in its path. Within minutes, every single computer on the east coast of the United States was shutdown and the plague neutralized before it had a chance to be fabricated. Eddie, the *Great Enigma*, Pavloski, had struck again - this time from beyond the grave.

Without a thought, anticipating a follow-up bullet into his own head, Mark bolted past the startled shooter, who stood as if rooted to the spot. Expecting a bullet between his shoulder blades any moment, he sped into the night, running as if his feet had wings and his lungs the capacity of a marathoner. He disappeared around a corner even before the dazed murderer had roused himself from his shock, another indication of the lack of training among those government forces still in place.

Pursued without letup from the moment of his escape, with no food or protection from the elements, no one to help him, lost, hungry, sick, and alone, he wandered through the countryside in a vague northerly direction like a sleepwalker, following the trails they had mapped out earlier. Despite his condition, he was making good time, surviving off the land as he had done with Eddie. Luckily the weather held out. Just when he thought he had eluded them, however, after almost a week on the run, they caught him. He was walking along a mountain trail, on the down-slope, moving at a good pace, when he rounded a slight bend in the road. There waiting for him was a ranger on a horse. He had a rifle and smiled as if he was expecting him. Someone must have figured out where he was headed. Brought to Dobbins Air Force Base in Atlanta, he was imprisoned and sentenced by a military tribunal.

His execution was scheduled for the end of the month. Part of him denied it, believing it would never happen, while part of him thought of nothing else. His ability to think straight was rapidly diminishing, like his ability to fantasize, which had always been his one true talent.

When he wasn't thinking about his fast approaching death, he was thinking of Eddie and how he had died, suddenly, instantly, here one minute gone the next, sent to oblivion with a one-way ticket of lead. Christ, thought Mark in anguish for the hundredth time. What was life about when it could be so easily, brutally snuffed out without a thought, as if it were nothing but a slender flame at the end of a wick? Being a child of the twenty-first century, with its combination of Godless philosophies and childish religions, Mark had nothing to aid him against the monstrous nothingness of it all, the total meaningless of life, especially now that his was rapidly approaching its end.

He pondered his own death. Would he die bravely? Would he suffer? Would they have to shoot him over and over again because they no longer had trained marksmen to do the job correctly? Would the onlookers jeer and cheer like the crowds at medieval executions? Would they give him a priest? Would he get an erection? He found keeping a constructive, positive train of thought for any length of time was like trying to hold paper down with a leaf in the wind. His thoughts flittered and fluttered about like nervous feathered friends in the cage of his mind.

Already, thanks to Mark and Eddy, every organic computer on the entire Northeast and Atlantic seaboard had been completely shut down. The last remaining network hub, located in Atlanta and scheduled for reactivation nine days ago, remained inactive indefinitely because of the European virus. Ironically, the East Coast and southern states had also remained remarkably free of the Plague, which was ravishing the western part of the country again and had broken out in Asia as well, adding fuel to the rumors that it was carried on the back of the Fiber. This was a rumor Mark was eager to promote any chance he got, especially since they were trying to blame the whole thing on him. Now all he could do was mark time while life ran on without him and the grim reaper stood waiting in the wings.

PALO ALTO, CALIFORNIA, DECEMBER 22, 3:35 PM

Doctor Fernando Rodriguez was coming back to Linda's townhouse after scouting the neighborhood for news of the plague. He had been going out less often over the intervening weeks and was curious about the situation. He had missed the initial bloodbath in which the three policemen had perished earlier that afternoon, but got caught up in the aftermath, when truckloads of security forces descended on the spot as if they had been waiting for just such an excuse.

He knew about the increasing number of straggling half-dead, the platoons of those infected with the slow-acting and therefore arguably more horrible, bubonic form of the disease, who with no one to care for them or capture them, roamed at will until they dropped in already decaying heaps. That's one of the reasons he avoided going out as much as possible, though they were easy to elude and escape, especially if one were on the watch. He moved about in the shadows during the day rather than at night when they roamed more freely. It certainly helped to know their patterns, and to know something about the disease itself and how it spread, which helped immensely in enabling him to avoid infection. Dr. Rodriguez had also taken the precaution of wrecking and sabotaging anything he found resembling fiber-optic cables, surveillance cameras, and organic computers.

That evening, besides gathering information, he had been out replenishing his store of supplies from stocks he had hidden around the city. He had been delayed in his departure, so had not returned until almost dark, when he was usually safely ensconced in his suburban hideaway. The counterattack by the authorities took him completely by surprise.

He made his way quickly back to St. Mary's, the abandoned Catholic church that served as one of his main stashes. It had a large refrigerated room in the basement and was as secure as Fort Knox. He had the master key to the place, obtained from the last pastor, whom the doctor had nursed in his final hours. He could hear screams and gunfire from the next neighborhood. Running up the front steps like a priest late for mass, he let himself in through a small side door that stood next to the larger, massive main entrance. His rapid footsteps echoed between the lofty arched ceiling and dusty marble floor, emptied of all but hardwood pews and confessionals, not a plaster saint left standing. The large, ornate glass windows were mostly boarded-up, but yellow rays of late afternoon light wafted down through small cracks between the hastily constructed shutters to play on the guilt-laid walls and tiled floors, in which floated the dust of several months.

He moved quickly down the aisle to the front of the altar, then behind it to the priest's vestibule and chambers. Without stopping, he went through another door into a side hallway, and down a short flight of stairs to the basement where the supply room was located. A small wood door with an old-fashioned ivory knob and a small rectangular stained-glass window stood locked in front of him. He opened it with a skeleton key and slipped inside, shutting and locking it behind him. He could hear the noise of shooting and people screaming outside.

Going down the hallway in the dark, he entered the first room on the right from memory, an empty classroom devoid of desks. It in turn led to another short hallway, off of which was the cold-storage room. He would wait down here until the commotion died down. The church was locked up tight and secure. Its sanctity would not be violated. Then he heard the unmistakable sound of a heavy door being slammed shut. It was the rear entrance under the stairwell leading to the storage room in the basement, stuck shut all these years, but apparently not locked. Well, it was unstuck now!

The sound caused Rodriguez considerable alarm. It was the last thing he expected to hear. Either one of the diseased had found their way in or the authorities had. Both scenarios were equal cause for concern

He waited in the darkness, listening intently, hardly breathing, as the commotion outside came to a crescendo. Moving quietly to the far wall, he edged his way to the door of the storage room beneath the back stairs, listening as he went, with his head pressed to the paneling. He was cautious and full of fear, for surely there must be many of them to open that door, which he had thought locked all this time.

He stood in the darkness for what seemed like an eternity. The sounds of violence outside slowly subsided, to be replaced with the breathing and groans of the old building itself.

By now he assumed that whoever had slammed the door was hiding from the authorities like he was, in which case he might be able to help them. Then again, maybe he should just grab his supplies and run. Instead, he slowly turned the knob and opened the door to the adjoining room.

On entering and switching on the light, Rodriguez immediately observed a lone figure cowering in the corner behind a row of stacked metal chairs. The intruder blinked and tried to shield his eyes from the sudden glare of the bare electric bulb.

He was thin and tall, with longish blond hair, and seemed ungainly when he stood uncertainly to his feet from the dirt-filled cement floor.

"I didn't mean to break into your church," he said, obviously mistaking the doctor for a priest.

"Don't worry, I'm not going to hurt you," Rodriguez assured him. "What are you doing here?"

"I'm just passing through. I was caught in some sort of mob scene out there and ran in here to hide. Luckily the door was unlocked."

"That door, my friend, has been stuck shut for as long as I've been coming here. You must be one strong hombre."

"I guess I don't know my own strength. I must have been pretty scared," replied Peter. He held out his hand, smiling. "I'm Peter Danvers."

"Are you sick?" asked the doctor, reserving his name and hand until he learned more.

"No, not that I know of. I've avoided people and the Fiber." The two men looked at each other knowingly across the room.

"Doctor Rodriguez," said the physician finally, extending his hand and shaking Peter's still outstretched paw, meeting him in the middle of the basement room. "Just call me Fernando."

"So you're not a priest?"

"No, I'm a doctor."

"Of medicine?"

"Yes."

"Oh," said Peter. "How'd you...I mean, gee, there aren't many of you...er, I mean, did you...?"

"Never mind that. Let's just say I was lucky."

While they waited for it to turn darker outside, they told each other their respective stories. When Peter mentioned his search for a certain physicist, the doctor grew suspicious and became quite guarded in his speech. Peter, who was perceptive enough to note this and relate it to his mention of Linda's name, decided to open up and divulge the complete details of what he knew about the plague and his plan to combat it. This, together with Peter's belief that Linda was the key to unlocking the puzzle, was exactly what Dr. Rodriguez needed to hear for Peter to earn his trust. Right then and there, the good doctor took him to his hideaway and introduced him to the object of his long quest. Linda Rayburn lay in bed sound asleep.

That had been over two weeks ago. In the intervening time they had learned much about each other. Peter was recovering from his exertions in the doctor's good care, but after much needed food and rest he was still no further along in stopping the plague.

Rodriguez stood next to Peter Danvers in the penthouse of Linda Rayburn's renovated hotel gazing in wonder at her novel machine.

"And this is how you found it?" Peter asked, stroking his chin unconsciously.

"Yes, and when I tried to touch it she freaked out. She's almost normal about everything else, except when it comes to that."

The fortuitous events that brought them together were based on the most slender of coincidences, but here they were, standing side by side. Peter could hardly believe his good fortune. Imagine, to be actually standing in the lab of Dr. Linda Rayburn. What he couldn't imagine were the implications of the machine he was looking at. All he could do was stroke his chin and shake his head in astonished disbelief.

"Jesus Christ!" he said. "It's absolutely incredible."

"I would appreciate it if you didn't swear. Under the circumstances I would not take His name in vain. Now tell me, what is it?"

"Sorry, Fernando, I got carried away there for a minute. It's some kind of quantum computer is my guess. I sure would like to talk to her."

"Give it some time. I'm in the middle of a breakthrough with her."

"Time is what we ain't got, doc," said Peter, emphasizing the word time.

"I know, I know."

"I need to talk to her," repeated Peter as he turned away from the gyrating lightshow of screen pixels, the dancing logic of Linda's

230

quantum computer. "We have a lot of work to do and time is running out. She's the only one who can help us."

Doctor Rodriguez followed Danvers out of the penthouse lab wondering what strange twist of fate or Divine Providence had put them here, at this spot, at this precise moment, to be a mote in the eye of the Black Death.

FEDERAL EMERGENCY GOVERNMENT CENTER, BOULDER, COLORADO, DECEMBER 23, 11:35 PM

Stan Bellows remained in the underground bunker beneath the rocky mountain peaks of Colorado, ostensibly running the country as he saw fit, with a little help from his friends. If Peter and Doctor Rodriguez had noted the spic-n-span streets, devoid of all signs of carnage and bloodshed, empty of bodies, burnt vehicles, and abandoned equipment, they didn't talk much about it. Nor about the size of the clean-up operation needed to pull it off, which must have been massive in terms of manpower and logistics. A new player was in town. If the good doctor and his new-found friend had been imprudent enough to hazard a peek, they would have seen a large number of Asians in the crowd of armed, uniformed men - and women - patrolling the streets, with patches and insignias decidedly foreign in appearance.

Stan Bellows pondered his latest dilemma. The Trojan-horse virus had been isolated in the eastern part of the country. His foreign competitors were threatening to take a considerable lead. Having to ask those very competitors for assistance didn't help his situation much, but the name of the game was expediency. He would do what he had to do, sleep with whomever he had to sleep with, to survive. For now he needed them, the egotistical Chinese, the bloated geriatric Party leaders, and the rest of their intolerant, money grabbing Asian neighbors. They had what he needed most, manpower and equipment.

In spite of his being named chairman of the five-man governing committee, power in the group had been slowly usurped by his Asian counterpart, Jiang Feng. So far, Feng's wishes and his had coincided, except for this latest problem.

With his Asian partner's help, they had been able to reclaim large portions of the city from the armies of the plague-ridden and malcontented, and had rounded up most of those who had until now eluded capture. All their experts on both sides of the Pacific agreed that the latest accusations concerning the Fiber generating the epidemic were scientifically impossible, and dismissed this notion out of hand. In the meantime, everything possible was being done to get the Fiber fully functional again on a worldwide basis, finally fulfilling the promise of generations, and incidentally making them all rich beyond what had ever been possible with twentieth-century economics. To accomplish this, they had to be ruthless and thoroughly wipe out all those who stood in their way, including the hackers and their computer viruses. His latest dilemma and point of disagreement with Feng involved the handling of one of those very hackers, Mark Goodwater.

Bellows was in favor of executing the computer criminal on schedule, as a powerful lesson to those who would deny the new world order. He was confident that his Chinese partner's computer experts, by sheer numbers, would solve the secrets of the ingenious new improved Trojan-horse program before long. Feng was not as confident and more given to practicalities. He favored a reprieve, at least temporarily until they eliminated the virus with Mark's help. They could always have him killed later, out of the public eye, under one pretext or another.

The current disagreement had caused some harsh words to be uttered during their last meeting, where a heated exchange took place between Stan Bellows and Feng's number-two man. Bellows had a bottle of his best cognac sent to the two of them from his private hoard, along with a note of apology. Feng was scheduled to fly back to Beijing in the morning, not that Bellows was especially sorry to see him go. If they expected him to just cave in to their every whim, the world would be one sorry place and his name wasn't Stan Emmanuel Bellows. What could Feng do, invade the country? No, his superiors would certainly rein him in. Still, he couldn't seem to make up his mind. What to do with Mark Goodwater?

It was the plague that kept him in Colorado and caused Feng to speed home. The plague that frustrated all his efforts, marred all his dreams. The bloody, stinking plague, come from some forgotten time to thwart his every step and make his days miserable. At least now the resources of the entire Asian continent would be directed at eradicating the disease from the face of the earth, especially since it had broken out in their beloved countries. The prospect brought him little solace, as he grappled with his problem. He decided to pay a late night visit to his Chinese associate at his airport hotel suite.

As they sat over the intoxicating liquid he had brought, sipping it and exchanging courtesies, Bellows graciously conceded the point of their disagreement, and commented on the wisdom of his distinguished and honorable friend's original position, and his own weakness and error in not seeing it sooner.

"In fact," he went on placidly, finally making up his mind and blithely ignoring his host's expressed wish to avoid publicity. "We'll make the execution a truly memorable event, entertain the audience, give them something to remember and take their mind off their troubles."

Feng naturally seemed less than thrilled with the idea, which didn't bother Bellows in the least. He knew that as long as the final result was achieved, Feng would let him do it his way, no matter how tasteless, crude, and barbaric that happened to be. The execution of Mark Goodwater was going to be like nothing the modern world had ever seen.

CHAPTER 22

PALO ALTO, CALIFORNIA, DECEMBER 26, 2036, 8:35 AM

"Incredible," exclaimed Peter again, as if his vocabulary consisted of that one word alone. "Just incredible!"

Christmas 2036 had come and gone with hardly anyone in the States noticing. Peter and the doctor certainly didn't give it much heed, except to open a bottle of red wine and drink a toast.

He stood in front of the Quantum computer's console trying to decipher its many-patterned logic. "I think I'm beginning to understand, and the more I see, the more fantastic it is."

"Great, why don't you fill me in on it," requested the confused doctor.

"It's nothing I can explain in so many words, not yet anyway. Let's just say we have here a twenty-second century computer in the twenty-first century, a hundred years ahead of its time. Can you imagine what this means?"

"No, not really. How's it work?"

"I'm not exactly sure. The actual computer is too small to even see. This is just the casing and its display unit. You'd need a radio-microscope to see the CPU cluster. It has a million individual, atom-sized processors, together no bigger than the head of a pin, all working in concert. Their memory is comprised of qubits, sub-atomic elements that can take on any one of a half-dozen states. This stuff's still only theoretical. Christ, the whole concept's only a couple decades old. I've heard of machines with a few dozen qubits, but nothing like this, hundreds of thousands of them all connected in a massively-parallel network. Do you realize what this means?"

"No, not fully. What's all this?" he said, pointing to the display screen of whirling, pulsing colors.

"That represents the computer's processing logic. Each pixel is equivalent to a group of qubits all acting together to vote an answer, on or off, or any other of a half-dozen possible states. The states indicate the different spins and positions of the subatomic memory elements, each one shown as a different color on the screen. That purple blob in the center with the green lines through it is a search or pattern-matching algorithm of some kind. This yellow appendage moving in and out is an information retrieval operation. It's like the game of life, you know, the old computer game where the pixels on the screen are programmed according to different rules that elicit patterns of colors as the individual dots turn off and on according to the numbers plugged in. The whole idea was used to demonstrate the firings of neural networks. Each quantum-CPU cluster in the array is shown on a separate display. You can scroll through them like this. There're hundreds of them, all working together. It's incredible."

"Never mind," said Rodriguez. "Sorry I asked." He was already growing tired of the conversation, just as he was growing tired of Peter Danvers - Mister Know-It-All - and his increasing demands. The newcomer certainly was monopolizing all of Linda Rayburn's rational hours, which were increasing slowly with the added stimulus of Peter's company.

Peter pressed her doggedly about the futuristic super-computer. Somehow he knew it was tied to his quest and the ending of the epidemic. For all he knew, it could have been transmitting the plague over the network as he stood there watching it. What he did glean through talking with Linda, however, made him crazy for more information.

Linda still couldn't accept the truth of what she had done, and was only able to deny it with blank spaces and false memories. Yet enough leaked out with Peter's patient probing to lead him to a certainty. Mark had somehow been right. Linda Rayburn had been the key all along.

When he wasn't conversing with Linda, Peter was searching through the voluminous files, tables, graphs, and databases on her conventional computers, looking for clues. The mathematical equations were for the most part undecipherable, but seemed to be related to quantum computing logic arrays that worked at the sub-atomic level. However, there were some parts of it he did recognize, like the biological equations describing amino acid sequences and proteins.

"The building blocks of life," he muttered to himself, as he perused the documents.

Peter also stumbled upon the simulation model used by Linda to test the feasibility of intercepting her virus, although he failed to grasp its significance, as he failed to realize that the source program for the antidote of the Fiber-transmitted plague glowed and danced in front of him on Linda's new machine.

Doctor Rodriguez stood over Peter's shoulder, reading the hieroglyphic-like molecular symbols along with him.

"Ah, this is very interesting," Peter observed. "Part of it looks like the DNA sequencing for a bacterium of some kind. It must be thousands of base-pairs long. See?" He pointed to the sequence of lines and named off the list of genes and the amino acids they coded for. "There are several thousand instructions there, enough to code for a simple single-celled microbe, a bacterium by the looks of it."

"A plague germ?" The doctor was good at asking the obvious, a trait which both infuriated and pleased his professors at Columbia.

"Maybe," Peter hazarded with a shrug. "I'll have to analyze it some more."

He looked at the mysterious code. There was something familiar about it, like a once-known puzzle promising to yield its secrets quickly and obligingly, if only one could remember the trick. In a vague way he knew he was seeing a static representation of what was being created on the futuristic machine behind him. The hair on the nape of his neck stood in silent recognition and saluted his fear.

He turned to look at the pulsating quantum computer. It seemed to be contemplating him in return, sizing him up, judging him fit or unfit for the task at hand.

"I wonder if there's a connection between this thing and the plague," he said, voicing his thoughts.

"Don't touch that!" screamed Linda from behind them, in a high-pitched, hysterical voice.

Unnoticed, she had crept up the apartment stairs and found the duo invading her most secret place, her most private thing, more sacred than a diary, more personal than a confession.

"Get away! Get away!" she repeated witch-like with her back bent and the bony finger of her large hand pointing at them.

They stood and turned in alarm, which only agitated her more. She shrieked and ran into the room, looking about from person to machine, machine to person, a wild animal that some careless human had let out of its cage.

"Get away!" she screamed again rushing at them in her fury.

Peter caught her in mid-stride and grabbed her by the arms, holding her until she grew still.

"Talk to us," he encouraged. "Tell us what this is."

Linda stared at her masterpiece, rocking back and forth in Peter's arms and sucking her thumb.

"Pretty lights," she crooned. "Pretty lights."

FEDERAL EMERGENCY GOVERNMENT CENTER, BOULDER, COLORADO, DECEMBER 27, 12:00 PM

Everything was back on schedule, almost. The Fiber was fully operational in the western two-thirds of the country and opening up in greater areas of the Far East each day. Granted, Europe was still out of commission, as was the eastern US, but the Chinese were fast on the trail of the elusive Trojan-horse virus, which they expected to defeat in short order, especially given the amount of man-power being thrown at the problem, and the intense 'interrogations' they were conducting with the prisoner, Mark Goodwater.

Still, the increased level of sabotage and hostility toward the network in general was causing Bellows some anxiety. Good thing his Asian friend was here to lend a hand. Eliciting his aid had been a stroke of genius.

Feng, as Chinese Minister of Technology, was not supposed to be a military man in charge of armies, but he wielded much power, most of which was hidden in the country's underground where the secret societies still held sway. He could command a small army if the need arose, which he was now proving.

His men had been pouring into the city for weeks. They patrolled the streets, the highways, the beaches, and the airfields, rounding up the populace as efficiently and quietly as possible. They also conducted massive search and destroy missions against the gangs of warlords and thugs who had taken over much of the state. Survivors were rounded up and brought to the medical camps, usually set up in large auditoriums and sports arenas. The armies of the walking dead, when encountered, were mowed down with rapid-fire weapons and burned on the spot with incendiary bombs and giant tank-mounted flame-throwers. Yes, Feng's men were efficient, even if a little overzealous, but they were also experiencing higher than usual casualties due to the plague and the guerilla tactics used by the intransigent rebels. Despite these setbacks, things were slowly getting back on track.

Asian relief money and desperately needed medical supplies were flooding into the country, where they did some limited good in those places the plague hadn't yet taken a foothold. Anti-plague serum and drugs to fight other forms of disease, running rampant in the plague's aftermath, along with food and clothing, was all distributed to the populace. In other places, however, where the Pestis hunkered down and dug in, merging with its susceptible hosts like a mind-meld, nothing could be done to stem the tide of death, no matter what they did.

With the renewed outbreak of the plague, and the devastation of the special medical facilities Bellow had set up for his own people, facilities which made extensive use of Organic machines for diagnosis, his plans to bypass current technology with Linda Rayburn's great invention were crushed. She must have died in the epidemic's second coming with the rest of his people, thought Bellows, and with her died his alternate plans. Now there was only one course to take.

With things being so well taken care of by his ally, Stan Bellows could concentrate on the upcoming spectacle of Mark Goodwater's execution, which the Chinese had reluctantly agreed to, despite their inability to solve the Trojan-horse puzzle, when he showed them how the prisoner had been leading them in circles.

He was in charge of every detail. First there would be the warm-up speeches and preliminary festivities, including the public humiliation of President Morris and his adherents - a little number Bellows had dreamt up all by himself. Next would come the confession and execution of the prisoner, with its bloody and body-splitting climax - the audience would get their money's worth with this one, and the would-be terrorists a warning. Finally, the post-game wrap-up with its commentaries and closing ceremonies would come, replete with instant close-up, slow-motion replays.

He looked forward to the event almost as much as he did the completion of his global fiber-optic network, which had been his life-long dream. The incessant buzzing of his satellite phone interrupted his reveries. Irritated, he flipped open the unit and barked into the transmitter.

"Yes, Bellows here. What is it?"

"Sir," said a weedy voice over the receiver. "We have a report of network disruption in sector 19."

"Where's that?" asked the impatient director, recognizing the speaker as Asian from his clipped consonants and prolonged vowels.

"Palo Alto, sir," answered the subordinate. "We'll need to direct operations in that sector as soon as possible."

"OK. Do it." Bellows had prudently kept a monopoly on those materials, as well as most of the remaining scarce expertise, needed to keep the Fiber in his underground bunkers operational.

"We are seeing an increased level of terrorist activity in this area, sir," continued the disembodied oriental voice over the ether.

"Yes, I'm aware of that. How long before we can make a sweep there? I want house to house searches. Check every single building, apartment, basement, cubby-hole, and box in the city."

"Yes, sir, we're working on it now, sir. We'll be ready by the end of the day tomorrow."

"Good," said Bellows. "With any luck, in a few more days we'll have another batch of traitors to fry."

PALO ALTO, CALIFORNIA, DECEMBER 28, 6:00 AM

She knew him, this baby-faced string bean with the kind eyes, knew his smile, that voice, that easy manner. He was older now, but still nice. When had it been, '07, '08? Boston, LA? MIT, Stanford? She knew that face from somewhere.

At first Linda wasn't sure if the face she saw was real or not. Like all the other things she thought she saw, it could just be her mind playing tricks on her again, hallucinations as she now knew, from sickness and guilt. Whenever she opened her eyes the face was there, with its angular jaw, its deep blue eyes, its thin, beardless lips.

They had talked, at first one-sided, stilted conversations, but gradually growing more intelligent and informative as the days went on. Over time her story came out, but it was a long story of neglect, abuse, betrayal, and revenge, told in spits and spurts, with gaps and omissions, mono-worded, disjointed, so that it seemed it would take forever to say what she had to say. In the end, in the last few hours of a dawn-less morning, it came tumbling out. And even though Peter was primed for it, it still hit him like a sledgehammer between the eyes.

There was much that she couldn't remember, like what logic played on the sub-atomic arrays of her machine, and much that she didn't want to remember, like unleashing the germ DNA. She had conveyed much, however, especially about the workings and programming of her world-changing new computer, so huge in memory, so fast in processing cycles, it made these terms obsolete. She had created a super-brain, smarter than all the computers on earth put together, capable of repairing and programming itself, the dream of computer scientists everywhere for a century, here and now, a reality today.

They sat knee to knee next to the liquid display screen of the twenty-second century quantum computer, teacher and pupil, like two small children sharing secrets.

"What's this?" asked Peter, pointing to a pulsating glob of greenish-blue projecting then withdrawing from within the whirling mass of screen pixels that represented the machine's inner logic.

"Potential activation," she answered cryptically. "A neural primer in your terms."

"Oh. Is your machine fabricating something?"

Silence, while her mind raced through its fragmented, torn memory banks for associations. Was it fabricating something? What? Plague?

"No. Yes. I'm not sure." The light of insight flashed as a thread of memory was found beneath a piece of psychic garbage. "It's an antidote for the plague." This revelation, given without so much as a tone of emotion, shook Peter to his very core.

"The antidote? What do you mean? How does it work?" He leaned toward her, his face not an inch from hers, holding her shoulders tightly.

Linda responded to the simple question from the friendly familiar face, searching the flotsam of her memory to retrieve some more bits and pieces from amongst the wreckage of her reconstructed mind. She felt compelled to please him, as if he were the father she could never satisfy.

"Chemical encodings for an anti-plague serum in the form of macro statements," she stated. "When they're expanded they'll code for specific molecules and elements found in the back of any Organic. The rest is a wrapper of cellular instructions that can be translated to and from machine-readable form for transmission over the fiber network."

She spun on, like a machine spitting out prerecorded instructions. The implications of what she was telling him were almost too much for Peter to handle. He was on the verge of information overload as it was. If he understood her correctly, she had created the antidote for the epidemic! Had she also created and unleashed the plague itself? If so, he was staring into the face of the worst mass murderer since Stalin and Hitler. Yet if she had devised an antidote, then why hadn't she sent it out? Even more important to the big picture, she had figured out how to decompose matter, then transmit and reconstruct it at the other end, using the Fiber's infinite bandwidth and the molecular soup of the Organics' internals. Virtual transportation of matter! Granted, she had only transported a simple single-celled bug, but theoretically the same could be done for any group of molecules, including ones organized as a human being. The very idea was staggering.

"Were you planning to send this antidote through the network to stop the plague?" he asked, still trying to deal with the incredible implications of it all.

"Yes, but it won't work," replied Linda, feeling a vague but growing apprehension.

"How do you know if you haven't tried it?"

"Oh, I know," responded Linda, remembering the simulations she had repeatedly run. Peter finally made the connection.

"The simulation?"

"Yes." Linda stared into space with growing panic, as the realization of what she had done hit her again. Another piece of hidden knowledge had reared its ugly head from the wreckage of her brain.

Peter rubbed his face hard with the palm of his hands, as if trying to wash the whole thing away. Then he stretched his eyebrows as if to clear the cobwebs and stroked his chin, as he always did when concentrating on something perplexing, lost in that inner world where genius often dwells between inspiration and imagination. Just then Fernando came downstairs

"You two been up all night?" Peter thought he detected a note of jealousy in the doctor's voice.

"Is it morning already?" he replied in honest surprise.

Rodriquez didn't answer but went back upstairs. As he went, he threw a few words along with a dirty look casually over his shoulder.

"I'm cooking something for breakfast if you two night-owls are hungry."

"We'd better grab a bite to eat, then get some sleep. We can talk later," suggested Peter, standing up and stretching, letting out a cartoon-character yawn as he did so. Linda stood also and wrapped her arms around him, pressing her head to his chest. Then she crawled up his slim frame until her mouth was equal to his and planted several hot, passionate kisses on it. Peter, being only human, responded at first, although feebly. Coming to grips with his own desires, however, and the memory of her past possessiveness - not to mention the horror of what she might have done - he pulled back and held her firmly by both arms.

"Remember how I used to make you feel?" she moaned. "You've come back to me."

"No, not now," pleaded Peter. "You need to rest. We can talk later."

"No talk," she said softly, sinking to her knees in front of him and fondling his growing erection with her hands through the fabric of his corduroys. There was another momentary hesitation on Peter's part. There was a time when he would have jumped in bed with her on a moment's notice. Linda's mouth looked very appealing at that moment, but again, memories of what she could be like when scorned and the importance of the present situation, not to mention the thought of Sandy and his kids, caused him to pull back. Adding insult to injury, as he pushed her away, he confronted her with his suspicions, to confirm what he already knew to be true.

"Did you cause the plague epidemic? Was it you?"

"No!" she screamed in pain or rage, he couldn't tell which, though it was probably a combination of both. "No!" she repeated as she rose to her feet and flew at him with arms flailing, her full body weight hitting him square on the chest. Peter, off balance and moving backward way too fast in surprise, got his feet crossed up and went down hard on his rump. Linda jumped on top of him, hammering him with well-aimed, tight fists, screaming. "Nooo!"

Rodriguez rushed down the stairs to see what the commotion was about, and ran to Peter's aid when he saw what was happening. As he got to them, Linda had Peter by both sides of the head and was banging it against the floor.

"What did you say to her?" asked the doctor, as he pulled the still struggling woman off the shaken Peter Danvers.

"Nothing. I asked her if she had unleashed the plague."

"And what did she say?"

"Noooo!" cried Linda as the good doctor held her. He quickly administered a shot of sedatives.

Later in the evening, after Peter had sedated himself with a half-bottle of Irish whiskey and slept through most of the day, he and the doctor sat in conversation, talking about Linda's latest revelations. Peter related what he knew, what he guessed, and what he was going to do. Doctor Rodriguez nodded his head in tacit agreement.

"We'll need an Organic, one I can work with," Peter informed him, stating the first requirement of the plan, which was starting to take shape in his head.

"What about the plague?" asked the doctor. "If what you think is true, won't we risk getting it ourselves?"

"Not if it's one that's never been connected to the Fiber. And we won't connect it, will we, doctor?" said Peter with a smile.

"What good is it if we can't connect it to the net?" countered Fernando.

"For what I need, we won't have to hook it to the Fiber. We can use much slower communication mediums for our purpose."

"How?" asked the doctor.

"I don't know yet, but I'm working on it."

As they talked, Fernando picked up the latest reports from the few still operational news services, over a small short-wave radio he had gotten for a steal. It was then that they heard about the death of Eddie Pavloski and the scheduled execution of his accomplice, Mark Goodwater, in four more days.

"Listen to this! Isn't this your friend you were telling me about?" Rodriguez turned up the volume on the small radio so he could hear the announcer better.

"The public execution of Mark Goodwater, confessed computer terrorist, scheduled to take place on January 1st, will be broadcast on national television to a worldwide audience, the first such event in history. The execution is also the first under the new, strict, anti-terrorist laws imposed by the emergency interim government to counteract the threat of growing attacks against the Fiber. Those responsible for trying to disrupt its progress should take a stern lesson from the fate of the unfortunate computer criminal, who was caught red-handed after releasing the highly disruptive European virus into computers throughout the East Coast and mid-Atlantic region, shutting down banks of the machines in that entire section of the country. His accomplice, believed to be the ring-leader of the conspiracy, Eddie the *Dark Enigma* Pavloski, from Eastern Europe, the inventor of the infamous TH virus, was shot and killed during their apprehension after infecting the computers on the campus of Roanoke College."

"Holy cow!" exclaimed Peter, slapping his head in exasperation. "Mark! Eddie!"

CHAPTER 23

FEDERAL EMERGENCY GOVERNMENT FACILITY, BOULDER, COLORADO, DECEMBER 30, 2036, 7:01 AM

Stan Bellows, chairman of the emergency committee that governed the United States of America, chairman of the Joint Chiefs of Staff, and more importantly, chairman of the board of the international conglomerate known as Global OptiComm, his immense and influential power base, tested the new Fiber relay himself for the third and final time.

"Excellent," he gloated. "It's about time. You know how long I've been waiting for this? No wonder I couldn't get anything done. With this and a few Organics, I can lick these computer geeks any day."

"Yes, sir, Mr. Bellow," said the un-amused technician, with an inscrutable half-smile. These days one merely spoke at the deranged corporate giant, always in the affirmative, with the attendant handle of respect. And one meant it if one valued one's head, like one would do to survive the fickle ire of a sixteenth century feudal Samurai.

"You can go now," said Bellows, as the technician bowed curtly and left the room. "Go back to where you came from you stinking little, slant-eyed bastard, and take the plague with you," he added under his breath, as the assistant to Jiang Feng retreated from earshot.

The epidemic ran rife in the west. No place that the Fiber went and was active was spared. There was so much to do, so many orders to give, so many subordinates to manage. Each task and asset was duly tracked and displayed on the many consoles that surrounded his thickly-leathered swivel-chair. He spun and turned about, as he went from this screen to that. Epidemics, terrorists, rebellions, saboteurs, breakdowns, delays, these and many other problems bombarded him incessantly.

Thanks to the efficiency and sheer numbers of his Asian friends, they were close to unraveling the innermost secrets of the new Trojan-horse Virus. They were developing a fix at this very moment. By this time next week he was told, the entire East Coast and mid-Atlantic States would be back on-line, and soon after that, all of Europe.

The taking over of the government by the Emergency Committee and the imposition of martial law, enforced by foreign nationals, was not taking place without objections. The intransigence of some was causing considerable trouble, but most of them could be negotiated with, especially since he held all the cards. He had an ace up his sleeve in the person of the imprisoned President-designate Morris. The growing rebellion in northern California was another matter entirely, and threatened to undo all his latest achievements if not put down quickly. It had started with the murder of two of his representatives who were governing the area at his behest. One of the unfortunate lackeys was lucky and hanged outright. The other was tied in a gunny sack and fed to starving dogs, after first being beaten and mauled unmercifully by the mob. Now the revolt had spread like wildfire, with a rag-tag army of 4,000 in Sacramento and another 3,000 in San Francisco marching toward the south. He relayed the orders that would authorize another 10,000 of Feng's troops to enter the country.

Stan Bellows turned his attention to the final preparations needed to complete the Net. Adjusting the virtual dials on his digitized display yet again, he preprogrammed the desired parameters, the required level of reporting detail, setting up the necessary commands and protocols, which he knew by heart.

Controlling the vast web of the fiber-optic network, its command center, its brain, so important it was guarded like a stack of gold bars, was a bank of Organics sitting in a glass-enclosed corner of the room behind him, humming softly like an expensive roadster. He had finally gotten his fiber-hookup. Electrons and photons screamed down the Fiber with constant acceleration, straining like race horses to get to the finish line, carrying bits of information back and forth, this way and that, and with it the seed of Plague.

PALO ALTO, CALIFORNIA, DECEMBER 30, 7:15 AM

Peter had pulled another all-nighter, or had he worked all day? He couldn't quite tell. All sense of time had left him. He had mentally synthesized everything he'd heard and seen over the past few months - Mark's discoveries, Eddy's revelations, Arthur's theories, Linda's confessions, Rodriguez's exhortations. He had studied Linda's notes and her amazing machine, analyzing them with speed and insight. He was driven, motivated like he had not been since those years of heady discovery back in his graduate school days and shortly after. He certainly had not worked this hard in quite some time.

It all came together in one mindboggling idea, based on Linda's quantum-programmed antibody, of which he knew a little, Eddy's Trojan-horse Virus, of which he knew a little more, and the inner workings of the Organics, of which he knew a lot. These ideas and a few leaps of inspiration brought him over the immense hurdles that stood in his way.

While none of these schemes would have worked alone, as evidenced by Linda's failed anti-viral simulation and the stalled Trojan-horse virus on the East Coast, their combination offered a potentially powerful weapon to combat the Fiber-born plague.

The thought of Mark and the awful fate that awaited him in less than twenty-four hours, filled Peter with dread and constantly battered at his concentration, especially when he was tired, like now, tired to his very marrow. The very roots of his hair cried out in miserable fatigue. Yet he plunged on. Only his bull-dog will kept him going.

The doctor was out gathering the necessary equipment and material, a few functioning but uninfected Organics - a task in itself well near impossible. They also obtained intelligence by eavesdropping on satellite transmissions, about the locations of key communication facilities and central relay stations, troop movements, the spread of the epidemic, and the East Coast situation, among other things. When they weren't occupied doing this they monitored the airwaves for developments in the scheduled execution of Mark Goodwater.

Peter was alone with Linda. She had been relatively quiet since her last outburst, when she had bloodied his nose and blackened his eye. His nose was mending fine, the bruise hardly visible. The eye, however, was still black and blue, an embarrassment he would have to live with for a few more days. The need to have her lucid and talking outweighed the impulse, based on good sense, to keep her sedated or at least bound securely to a chair. This stratagem had paid off, though, as Peter was able to elicit further information from her after she recovered from the initial recollection of her sin, and the rather harsh rejection from the object of her obsessive desire.

Linda's confession of the unleashing of the Pestis DNA on the offices of her employer, and its subsequent escape over the network despite all precautions, filled the two listeners with horror when they first heard it, as much as it did Linda herself. She fell into fits of teeth-gnashing remorse periodically as she told her story, which took much of the day. Although understandably despondent, she seemed to have thrown off a great burden with her confession, and appeared, at least to Doctor Rodriguez, to have made considerable strides toward recovery, both physical and mental. Her legal and social rehabilitation were another matter, but one which neither of them were interested in at the moment.

Linda was bent over the input arrays of her advanced new computer finishing the programming tasks suggested to her by Peter. They had been working together like hive-mates, two workers from the same colony, he to save the world, she to save her soul.

"This just might work," hazarded Peter, envisioning the results of his calculations, "if we can just broadcast the signals to enough locations simultaneously. The ASTAT satellites should have the right footprint."

Linda sat back considering his plan with a lot less optimism, although she admired his enthusiasm and the sheer imaginativeness of his proposed solution. In her heart she knew that there was no cure, no stopping her plague's inexorable progress. Still, she would humor him. Let him continue on in his vain pursuit, blind to its inevitable failure, cocooned in his self-confidence, his immunity to failure, his flawless track record. In the end, she knew there was no hope. Linda Rayburn was, after all, a master of hopelessness in all its shapes and forms.

Peter replayed in his mind again the words of Eddie Pavloski as they talked while hiding out after escaping from the military facility in Tennessee. Eddie had explained the principles of his Trojan-horse program of viruses within a virus, with the innermost one based on a ten-dimensional string grammar. On first hearing, Peter thought it was nothing but slick double-talk meant to confuse and intimidate smart-ass American computer scientists. But now he wasn't so sure. He had pondered those words incessantly since his brief encounter with the now deceased computer genius.

Immediately, his mind drifted back to thoughts of Mark. Those thoughts galvanized him into another feverish bout of activity. Linda sat and watched his back as he worked, like a cat watches its human master, with a combination of contented love and predatory intent.

"This just might work," he said again, running the reprogrammed simulation model. "If we can just locate enough clean Organics."

The main problem with Linda's original plan to stop the plague was that it required the Fiber itself to transmit the anti-virus. This was because of the immense size of the code and the fact that it all had to be transmitted at once, thus it depended on a sequential progression of the antidote program through the network one machine at a time. And it had no defense against Linda's original virus's innate ability to mutate itself as it digested the antidote. This meant it would never be able to overtake the plague virus. But Eddie had shown them how to distribute their virus in manageable pieces that could be independently transmitted to separate locations, yet still work together as a single unit. Even more importantly, he showed them how to embed his worm in several layers of code, so as the plague-infested machines unraveled it, yet another form of the antivirus was unleashed, staying one step ahead of the germ in overcoming whatever resistance it had developed. Linda's anti-plague program would be layered like Eddy's TH program, so that it could be transmitted over the relatively low band-width of stationary satellites, to several machines at once, and thus head off the plague in place. Instead of trying to play catch up, it would unravel and destroy the plague from within. The firewalls and bridges put up by the giant telecommunication company to protect the Net from the East Coast TH virus were likewise, no defense against Peter's improved version.

"It just might work," he told himself one last time for reassurance.

Just then the doctor arrived from his excursion to the outside world, unbolting, opening and closing the townhouse's well-fortified front door. A moment later he came downstairs to lounge in the cool of the basement room.

"Any luck?" ask Peter without waiting for him to sit down.

"Give me a break," answered Rodriguez peevishly. "Cripe, I just got here."

"Sorry, I just... There's so little time."

"Don't worry," interjected the doctor, wiping his receding brow with a white hankie. "I think I found just what you're looking for. Ten functional Organics not connected to a fiber-cable in any way, all clean of infection. Here are the locations."

He handed Peter a crumpled piece of paper with a handwritten list of street addresses.

"Great! Now all we have to do is translate these addresses to GPS coordinates and we're ready to go."

Peter's hands played on the gloved-keyboard of the Von Neumann workstation, tapping in rapid-fire, rhythmic clicks a program for translating the streets to map coordinates. When finished, he scanned in the handwritten addresses for the ten Organic machines Fernando had found, from the crumpled, pencil-smudged paper.

That done, he clicked a few virtual buttons of his GPS application and obtained the desired coordinates.

"Done," said Peter with a flourish. Linda watched him with rapt attention. "Only thing left to do is transmit our programs along with the coordinates of the Organics to the satellite. Then keep our fingers crossed."

"And when are you going to do that?" asked the doctor.

"Soon. Timing is critical. First I have to do one more thing. Doctor, would you please come with me."

"Fine," answered Rodriguez. "Oh Peter, before I forget. I noticed something very peculiar in my wanderings. Everything's really quiet out there. It's downright spooky. I'm not sure what's going on, but all signs of the street people have vanished, not a trace. Nor have I seen any of the usual patrols. Things are just too quiet, like a really low tide before a tidal wave. You know, the calm before the storm?"

"What do you think's going on?"

"I don't know, but something's up. And another thing, I found this near the church where we met. What do you make of it?"

He handed it to Peter.

"It's a patch of some kind," guessed Peter correctly.

"Yes, a patch. The symbol on it is Chinese. I believe it's from a Chinese Army uniform."

"Have they taken over the country?" asked Peter, ready to believe anything at this point. "Maybe they'll shut down the Net. There've been some outbreaks of the plague over there. That must be it."

"I don't know, but my instincts tell me something's goin' down. What I can gather from the signs indicates a build-up of forces all around us, ready to implode. Perhaps your friend told them about you and your plans."

"He didn't know that much. Do you think they know we're here?" Peter was aware of the increased anti-net activity taking place in the vicinity recently, not a little of it carried on by the good doctor and his associates, people accustomed to life on the streets long before the destitute, homeless, and displaced sick of the twenty-first century started living there.

"We'd better get ready to move," replied the doctor in answer to Peter's question "Hey, where's our friend?"

Linda was nowhere to be seen. Peter looked around the room nervously. The last time he had seen her she was sitting behind him like an admiring groupie watching him work. He had been kind of showing off for her. He hadn't noticed her leaving, some time after the doctor arrived, he suspected. He ran up the stairs with growing concern, his long legs taking two at a stride, calling her name, but no one answered.

CHAPTER 24

PALO ALTO, CALIFORNIA, DECEMBER 30, 2036, 7:20 AM

Peter ran up the last flight of stairs to the top floor of the apartment house and searched each room. The last one, the penthouse lab, was empty like the rest, but the double-French doors leading to a small patio were open to the wind, which blew the white curtains like waving gossamer streamers. He approached them cautiously, calling her name as he did so.

She was there on the landing, sitting on the flimsy railing with her feet dangling over the side. The sight sent a slight shiver through him.

"You find her?" yelled Rodriguez from outside the room.

"Yeah, she's in here, but don't come in yet, please."

Peter tried to smile reassuringly. "What are you doing?"

Linda couldn't have answered him if she wanted, for what she was doing was beyond her ability to describe in words. Wishing, regretting, fantasizing, remembering, wondering, atoning, all at once, all at the same time.

Without looking back, wordlessly, she slipped over the side of the railing, sliding into misty space and disappearing suddenly from sight. Peter heard her seconds later, as her head cracked on the cement of the courtyard like a gunshot four stories below.

He ran to the railing, arms grasping thin air as he flung them outward for her. She had already hit the pavement. In the sunless gloom, with the shadows of the surrounding buildings adding to the darkness, he could barely see her, as her blood oozed from the large split in the side of her skull.

Turning and running past the doctor, who had rushed into the room on hearing Peter's scream - a scream which Peter himself did not hear or remember uttering - he ran down the stairs to the basement, which gave out to the courtyard at the rear of the building. The door was locked. Peter, unable to open it, banged on it and yelled in helpless rage, using his head in the process to beat the stubborn obstacle. The doctor was right behind him.

"What happened? Did she jump?" he asked Peter.

"Yes. She went down back here. We've got to get this door opened."

He frantically tried it for a few more minutes then turned and ran up the stairs again to the front of the house. The doctor found him running back and forth outside in the street.

"Here, down this way," volunteered Rodriguez. "There's an alley."

Peter took off at a full run. Then he slowed to a walk as a faint vibration at that moment touched his ears, a low rumbling that hinted of distant machines and wheels.

He stopped and stood, listening more intently. There, over the soft whistling of the wind as it rustled amongst the empty bodies of cars and the silent eves of houses, a clanking, metallic noise. There was another sound too, what was that? A collective shuddering, as if a multitude had sucked in their breath, the silent but audible whisper of a thousand bare feet rushing this way?

Suddenly, the early morning stillness erupted with the sound of heavy gunfire. Only a few streets away, near the church where Peter had taken shelter that fateful night not so many days ago - tanks, cannons, mortars, and automatic rifles pulverizing a pocket of resistance, consisting of remnants of the rag-tag army of San Franciscans, which had succeeded in reaching the city. Their eradication would be swift and complete, as well as brutal.

Even as the cleanup operation was being conducted a few blocks away, advanced teams of commandos were closing in on Linda's neighborhood, with its plush modern townhouses, two-car garages, Jacuzzis and patios, looking for yet another nest of conspirators, the next enclave of terrorists, or any poor soul hiding in his cellar just trying to elude the medical camps.

Several streets down, Peter could hear what was left of the street people, along with the sick and destitute, caught in the open between the teeth of the dragnet, all coming in his direction.

He started running after the doctor, who had just disappeared around the far corner of the building, down an empty, garbage-strewn side street. When Peter turned the corner, Rodriguez had vanished as if in thin air. It was a dark, foggy, overcast morning, making it difficult for Peter to see any distance in front of him. Moving up the alley hesitantly, he looked for signs of his friend, who should have been just around the corner, but was nowhere in sight.

Peter moved along the edge of the brick apartment building to a gap between it and the next one, roughly three yards across, choked and covered with bushes and squat trees. Pushing the outermost branches aside, he discovered a high wooden fence with an iron gate, slightly ajar. It was the entrance to the building's small courtyard. He called softly for the doctor. The noises from the next street were growing in intensity.

At first he saw nothing in the darkened courtyard beyond, until his eyes adjusted to the gloom. Then he saw him, a shadow in the grayness, leaning over the motionless form of Linda Rayburn.

"She's dead," came the pronouncement from the doctor. This was followed by a low cry of anguish from Peter, as he moved toward the voice.

In a patch of fog that hugged the concrete courtyard in the half-light, lay Linda's broken body, long limbs akimbo, torso crooked, eyes wide, hair smeared with dark, putty-like globs of gray matter against a pale, pasty forehead. A bright red halo of fluid arched around her still head, stopping just short of her shattered, thick-lens glasses, which lay broken a few feet away.

As they huddled around the pitiful corpse, the commotion in the street intensified to a fever pitch, as the security force met the cornered rabble of the street - thief, renegade, rebel, hustler, parent, orphan, runaway, squatter, gang member, displaced person. Twenty-first century armaments were unleashed against millions of years of biological evolution, and modern technology won, hands down.

A small group of desperate men and women, some clutching young children, ran around the corner and down the empty side street, clinging to each other and the outer wall of the apartment building behind which the two terrified companions cowered in the darkness of the courtyard. Caught between the a brick wall and a squad of heavily-armed and trigger-happy mercenaries from some Malaysian principality far from home for the first time in some plague-infested foreign land, they were butchered like cattle.

"Die, die!" screamed a terrified boy lieutenant, as he gave the order to open fire. The bodies piled up six deep in front of the camouflaged entrance to the courtyard, covered as it was with thick bushes and hedge. Fortunately, Peter had closed and bolted the gate when he came in. In any case, none of the solders noticed it, although a few stray bullets found their way in to splinter plaster and shower dust on the cowing duo.

Peter and the doctor huddled at the back of the courtyard in the deepest of its shadows, covering their ears from the sounds of the slaughter, which seemed to go on forever. There was silence for a few moments then another blast of small arms fire as the squad finished off the survivors and emptied their magazines into those already dead. A harsh, bright searchlight played back and forth across the scene of carnage, looking for the slightest movement. There was none, so the squad moved on.

What started as a police action to neutralize a small band of rebels who were hampering recovery efforts, degenerated through blood-lust and lack of discipline into a full rampaging massacre, where rape and pillage were the least of the atrocities visited on the hapless populace.

The two friends stayed huddled together long after the sounds of gunfire moved on to other parts of the city.

"How long before they circle back and find the lab?" asked Peter, in a barely audible whisper, at least half an hour after the last shot had been fired.

"I don't know," replied the doctor, moving to a standing position. "I guess it depends on the size of their sweep. If it's the whole city we may have until sometime this evening."

Gaining courage, he moved to the fence and opened the gate, then crawled to the edge of the tangled mass of branches and leaves, and peered out into the side street.

"Jesus and Mary!" he whispered, and crawled back in, visibly shaken even in the weak light of a day that refused to dawn.

Peter didn't ask him what he had seen.

"Can we get back in through there?" he queried, pointing to the door leading into the apartment's basement.

"Sure, I used that door all the time. I had a key, but I lost it. Not sure what happened to it."

"We've got to get back into the apartment if I'm going to do anything in time," announced Peter.

He went back to the body, still sprayed on the ground like a broken doll, and bent over it, as if trying to coax it back to life. His hands played over her as if he were searching for something.

"You can't help her now. What are you doing?"

Peter ignored the good doctor and continued to run his hands over Linda's body, not yet turned cold and stiff, still pink and supple as in life.

"Here, here it is," said Peter, straightening up and holding something in his fist. He looked at the body one last time with an expression of longing and sorrow. "The key. I thought she might have had it."

"I'll be," said the doctor, impressed. "Good instincts."

"Come on." Peter went to the door at the far end of the courtyard. "We don't have any time to spare."

Doctor Rodriguez held back. Peter had turned at the open door, which shed a warm yellow glow on the body in the center of the small patio, accenting the paleness of the skin and the darkened pool of blood congealing around the head. With Linda dead, the doctor's job was finished.

"There's nothing more I can do here," he said. "I'm going to check out what's happening in the city, secure our escape route."

"I'll stay and finish things," replied Peter.

After briefly describing his emergency escape plan to Peter, thought out and tested for just such an occasion many weeks before, the doctor headed out into the now calm overcast day. Following a labyrinthine path through buildings and alleyways that snaked its way, part underground, part above, through the city, he eventually came out in the foothills of the same coastal range that Peter had passed through when he first entered the area.

Peter, reentering the basement, carried Linda's limp body in his arms up to the penthouse lab, where he laid her on the floor beneath her still glowing quantum computer, covering her with a thin blanket. Sitting at the console, trembling slightly, he stared at the lights of the quantum machine's liquid display. It was almost ten and he had not eaten since early the previous day, but food was the furthest thing from his mind. He began to work, the knowledge that Mark was due to be executed in less than thirty hours adding to his distress. Still he focused his mind like a laser on his task, despite the distractions.

It was now or never. With a keystroke he transmitted his program to the aged satellite, to be beamed back to the communication ports of the target Organics identified by Fernando. The ancient orbiter signaled a gracious acknowledgement, fooled by a simple security hack that none of the newer more sophisticated models would have been tricked by. Then one by one the target machines responded to the signal and began fabricating the code for Linda's anti-body planted within their molecular chips, rebroadcasting it to yet more Organics, and so on. A note became a phrase, a phrase a song, first solo voice, then duet, then trio and quartet, until a chorus was singing, spreading Linda's anti-virus like a starburst through the universe.

Peter sat swaying to the unheard music that played in his head like some Beethoven wannabe, while he watched the status display register the successful combining of Linda's antivirus with Eddie's Trojan-horse delivery mechanism. Suddenly, the ground shook around him and plaster snowed down on his head from the ceiling above. Another explosion blasted the house below him away, raining wall boards and two-by-fours on him as he dove for cover. The sky was falling and Peter Danvers was alone beneath it.

DOBBINS AIR FORCE BASE, ATLANTA, GEORGIA, DECEMBER 31, 11:20 PM

The hour of midnight was approaching, that precise hour predicted by astronomical observation and table-driven calculation, and reported dutifully to millions of eager viewers each day by the wire-services and informational bulletin boards, as being especially propitious for the execution of computer terrorist, Mark Goodwater. Mark contemplated the hour of his appointed demise with more than a little trepidation.

He was nauseous and dizzy, his breath coming in short, shallow gulps, his mind totally unable to concentrate. Other than that, and a dull throbbing headache, he didn't feel all that bad. Not yet anyway.

He had made his peace with whatever godless deity he prayed to in the deep of the night, when the twin boogiemen of death and despair gripped him. Now all he had to do was maintain some level of dignity and it would all soon be over.

He heard the clanging of steel doors many corridors away coming inexorably in his direction, each one a comma, an exclamation point, a dreaded semi-colon in the sentence of his life.

As the sound approached, he supposed it was his last meal, and was surprised to find that he was famished, contrary to all expectations. As the noise reached the outside of his holding cell, Mark stood unsteadily to his feet and stuck out his chicken-bone chest in defiance. The door opened.

Mark wasn't sure what they had in store for him. Last he heard it was to be a firing squad, but he had heard plenty of vague hints and rumors since then, even in his confinement, about other possible outcomes, none of them good.

Without formality, the four guards grabbed him and took him out to the parade ground where a helicopter stood waiting in the darkness to take him to the stadium in Atlanta where his execution was to take place.

The night was in full supremacy over this portion of the earth. It would be hours again before daylight. Dark clouds clung to the eastern sky like heavy purple drapes. Mark thought how he would never see daylight again.

The helicopter flew southeast toward a wedge of glowing orange light, which grew larger with each whirl of the blade. Soon he could see other lights piercing the night, man-made beacons arching across the sky, making it glow with eerie phosphorescence. They headed for the lightshow, the coliseum where cameras watched and the crowd chanted, and death awaited him with hungry, salivating jaws.

Mark watched the spectacle with a detached air, as the brightly lit coliseum rose up at him from below. Bathed in the glow of countless search lights, streamers and banners flowing everywhere, his chariot on air glided into the stadium like a mosquito into the mouth of a frog.

As the helicopter landed, a thunderous roar escaped the excited crowd. This was soon drowned out by the blare of the 164-piece marching band, which was in turn eclipsed by the twenty-minute display of thundering pyrotechnics. Mark, handcuffed and shackled, would have given anything to be able to clap his hands over his ears to block out the deafening noise.

As he was roughly escorted from the helicopter with its rotary blades still turning, the crowd surged forward like a swarm of angry wasps. They were kept from flooding onto the floor of the coliseum only by barbed wire and heavily-armed guards. As he moved toward the huge stand erected for his execution, the fireworks and music were drowned out by the noise of the crowd again. Chanting, screaming, crying, yelling, stomping, clapping, hissing, booing, all filled the night air, as each one of the thousands of spectators strove to make themselves heard above the other.

This crowd was angry. This crowd was full of hate. This crowd was out for blood, and represented millions more who had been deprived of their past, present, and future, their livelihoods, their entertainment and services, their comforts and luxuries, all because of the little mole being hauled across the playing field below. Focused by Bellows' cunning publicity campaign, Mark could have been the killer of a hundred babies and still be more loved than the man who was in their midst this night. They wanted to tear him apart with their own hands. Simply dying would be too good for him. These and other like sentiments fueled the crowd's rage.

As Mark was led up the wide steps fronting the execution platform, the full range of torture devices meant for him met his startled eyes. When their purpose and intent registered on his brain, his knees stopped quivering and started shaking violently. He had to fight down the rising gorge in his throat with each gulping breath. The thought of what they were going to do to him flashed through his mind. He fell to his knees and begged for mercy the best he could with arms pinioned behind him.

His pleas went unheeded and unheard, as the crowd and 164-piece band drowned out his pitiful speech. Cameras buzzed and whirled, each one looking for a preferred vantage point, a special angle. Mark's terrified visage was amplified in various levels of size, from tiny to gargantuan, and duplicated all over the stadium on huge billboard-sized displays. The sight of himself on the large screen stunned him to composed silence. His composure and his silence were not to last long.

There waiting on the platform under the glare of countless spotlights were his executioners. Not one, but three of them, wearing white medical outfits and masks, looking all the world like men from outer-space getting ready to see what made this earthling tick. To add to the science fiction atmosphere, Mark was strapped down onto a semi-reclining bed of steel, disturbingly like an autopsy table with its indentations and channels made for neatly handling rivulets of blood. Another figure, this one dressed in a scarlet robe, taller and more imposing than the rest, joined the trio atop the stand. Using a microphone attached to his headset, he spoke through loudspeakers strategically placed throughout the auditorium.

"It's time!" he intoned. "Time for retribution!"

The crowd erupted with a fresh ear-shattering ovation, as if the long-awaited main attraction had finally reached the stage. The tall figure raised his arms in outstretched supplication for quiet, which went all but unheeded.

"Hear this," he yelled over the crowd as it surged back and forth like a tidal pool, jostling and pushing for a better view. "Hear the criminal confess his crimes. Hear him divulge his secrets. Watch his torture and know this could be you if you tamper with the Fiber."

Answering shouts returned from the mob. "Yes, make him talk... Make him suffer... Kill the bastard..."

The red-robed man, with the hawk-like countenance - pointed nose, a birdlike mouth beneath small black eyes, leaned his face close to Mark's and said, "Now, confess your sins to the world."

"I already told you everything I know," said Mark, hearing his words echo strangely back to him through countless loudspeakers. "What more do you want from me?"

The master of ceremonies smiled pleasantly to the camera as if to say, "See, I tried", and motioned to the trio of Martians standing in a knot a short distance away. They approached in a group, not breaking the symmetry of their relationship from one another, as if a single entity with six legs - a white three-headed insect. In their hands were recognizable components of the electrical device, which they had last tortured him with. It looked like they were going to begin where they had left off.

The crowd broke into pandemonium, stomping and shouting even the monster band into submission. Several spectators went down never to rise again in the mini-riot that followed. Many more fell to small-arms fire as they strayed too close to the security perimeter. Some were caught against the barbed wire fence and the press of the mob and suffocated to death in the crush. It took several minutes for things to be brought under control, the entire coliseum resembling nothing more than an overheated pressure cooker about to explode at the seams. In the interim, Mark had time to collect his thoughts. Why suffer? Why let them torture you? For God's sake, tell them what they want to hear, even if you have to repeat it a thousand times!

Mark confessed, he sang, he squealed on everyone and everything he knew. In the end he spewed forth any scrap of information he could conjure up, all in an attempt to avoid being tortured. His words reverberated throughout the auditorium, bouncing off its hard walls and the equally hard heads of its occupants. He told the secrets of the Trojan-horse virus and how he and Eddie unleashed it on the unsuspecting East Coast; told about Peter and the dirigible and of their most detailed plans; told of the Fiber and how it carried the plague - this last piece of information was choked off by fresh jolts of electricity.

Now that his confession and secrets had been disclosed, the crowd thirsted for his blood.

"Ladies and gentlemen. You have heard here today the confessions of a person whose crimes are so monstrous, so evil, of such a hideous nature that only the most brutal, barbaric punishment imaginable would be enough to atone for it." The crowed murmured its assent.

"These troubled times call for special measures. As you all know, the Plague has returned in California. It is only by our most stringent efforts that its spread to this part of the country has been prevented and complete catastrophe avoided. We have reason to believe this crime was perpetrated by this base criminal here before us and his accomplices on the West Coast."

Again, the crowd erupted into thunderous noise. The man in scarlet paused for a well needed rest. So far things had gone even better than planned. The spectacle being beamed around the world would act both as a strong deterrent and a powerful palliative to the masses. He continued.

"In spite of the terrorism and destruction caused by such people, civilization marches on. But before we go, let us deal with this terrorist as he so justly deserves. For your crimes, Mark Goodwater," the master of ceremonies intoned. "You will be hanged, cut down live, disemboweled, and drawn by the four limbs until quartered."

None of this made much sense to Mark, who was still reeling from the electric shocks, his thoughts fragmented and disjointed, his senses clouded and dimmed. The words of his sentence, although recognizable as words, did not register on the semantic processing part of his brain. Only slowly did it dawn on him what they had in store for him.

"Are you sorry for your crimes?" asked the tall man. "Now what say you?"

Suddenly, the image of the humiliated and suffering Mark Goodwater was replaced by the face of Stan Bellows himself, as he peered out from the many display screens throughout the stadium and the world, beamed over a geo-stationary satellite - this part of the country still not having an operational Fiber.

Magnified as it was - his head filled the giant screens - the digitized face of the chairman looked terrible. His skin was pasty. His creased forehead was covered with beads of sweat. His mouth hung open like a tired fighter's. His wearied eyes stared out at the world from beneath caves of dark skin sunken in bony sockets. Wheezing over the loud speakers, the specter spoke to the suddenly subdued spectators. They knew what that face could do if agitated, and who knew for sure if he could see them or not with those giant, bloodshot eyes. The voice, scratchy like an old vinyl recording, was clothed in raspy airless breathing.

"Help me," he gasped.

The bulging blue veins on his temples pulsed and throbbed. His neck swelled and contracted visibly, as if something were in there trying to get out. The hideous mask of a face filled the screen and every other screen that happened to be viewing the spectacle – which was most of the world's video-units. Its terrible scratching breath, like fingernails against a slate board, echoed from every speaker in the place. The plague itself had come in the guise of the Black Death, and looked out at them as it spoke.

"Can't breathe!" it hissed. "Help me!" it rasped.

Stan Bellows was dying in agony in front of millions of viewers throughout the world. In the last stages of his death throes, plague germs swam in his blood, his tears, his saliva. His body swarmed with them, a virtual cesspool of microbes. They choked his air passages, clogged his organs, jammed his arteries, for some reason this variant of Plague doing to him in hours what usually took days to do in its bubonic form. It took approximately four minutes before Stan Bellows - chairman of the board of the most powerful conglomerate in the world, nominal head of the government of the United States, member of the most powerful committee history had ever known - collapsed face first into the array of cameras and microphones facing him on his control panel, with a dramatic flourish and a loud groan.

The unexpected spectacle momentarily froze the over-packed stadium. That is until panic set in and a mad stampede ensued.

"The Plague! The Plague!" they yelled. "It's here. It's here!"

Brother trampled sister, son trampled mother, father trampled daughter, in their mad attempt to flee the coliseum and the invisible Black Death. Lovers were torn asunder, then to pieces in the surging press of the crowd. Some were pushed off roofs and stairwells, some crushed against barbed wire and concrete, and when the terrified security guards let go with a galling automatic rifle fire, hundreds were killed outright and thousands more left writhing on the ground and bleachers in mortal agony. The coliseum became a killing ground, which only a few escaped. Fire broke out in several places at once, adding to the panic and carnage taking place all around the stadium, as if the devil himself had chosen this place and time to show his awful majesty to the world.

Mark, unaware at first of what was happening, was completely forgotten in the pandemonium, as every single person in the stadium watched the stricken chairman fall face first into the camera. Then Mark watched as the mob panicked and stampeded all around him.

Pinioned as he was, spread-eagled and hog-tied, he was neither able to run nor hide. All he could do was and wait helplessly, without hope, as death bore down upon him.

CHAPTER 25

PALO ALTO, CALIFORNIA, JANUARY 1, 2037, 7:20 PM,

Linda's antibody spread from machine to machine, attacking the plague-carrying computers like white corpuscles an invading army of microbes. It would take months before the task was complete, before every computer-carried plague germ was destroyed, but the anti-virus was out there on the Net now, free to devour and destroy its target. Given time it would immunize every Organic in existence.

Doctor Fernando Rodriguez shined his penlight into the pile of wood and brick that had until recently been the apartment house of Linda Rayburn, the last place he had seen Peter Danvers alive. He feared the worst for his friend.

After leaving Peter, he had made his way through a maze of paths to an old church on the hill, proceeding up to the bell tower where he was able to observe the surrounding area. There were no signs of the invaders or the rebel armies. The escape route was clear. It was from this vantage point that he saw the missiles come in, a half-dozen of them, low and fast, to shatter the city blocks that he had only moments ago been running through, in a shuddering blast that shook the tower and made its bells ring.

"Oh, my God!" said the doctor. "What have they done?"

Fernando rushed down the tower stairs, back to help his friend. It was getting late, around 4:00 PM, when he reached Linda's neighborhood. The scene was one of total destruction. Most of the houses on what had been a densely populated suburban neighborhood were leveled. Those still standing were burnt-out husks. Smoke rose lazily from scores of woodpiles that had once been upper middle class homes and offices. Fighting still raged in some unseen neighborhood in the northern part of the city.

Unable to tell one pile of debris from another, he made his way to where he thought Linda's apartment should be and started searching the wreckage for his friend, despairing of finding him alive. With a heavy heart, he shifted through the mounds of plaster and wood, floorboard and ceiling, brick and cinderblock, determined to search until he found Peter or dropped, whatever came first. He hoped it was the former.

He hadn't searched far when he came upon a familiar object, the antique nineteenth century headboard of Linda Rayburn's bed. The discovery filled him with renewed energy despite his lack of food and sleep. Heaving aside debris like a longshoreman he called out Peter's name. Despite the hopeful clue, however, he had found nothing more after hours of frantic searching.

The sounds of battle had long ago ceased when he slumped down exhausted on an up-turned bookcase, his head encased in his palms, his body bent forward elbows on his knees. He fought back the tears, his hands moving back and forth over his face as if trying to wipe away years of grime and grit. Fighting to stay in control, he tried to think the situation through.

About to give up and make his way back toward the mountains, he suddenly heard something in the debris to his left. Standing abruptly and swaying momentarily with vertigo, he made his way toward the noise, which had sounded like metal scraping metal. Nothing, it had stopped. There, there it was again!

He started digging through the pile of rubble, this time finding what he was looking for, an item from the penthouse lab, the shattered display monitor from Linda's workstation. Removing a few more pieces of rubbish, he soon revealed a tiny black hole in the mostly white wreckage, a clear sign of a hollow spot, a cubbyhole where someone might survive being crushed. He flashed his trusty penlight into the crack. A blue unblinking eye stared back at him.

Momentarily startled, the doctor jumped back, almost dropping his tiny flashlight down the hole. Instead, regaining his composure, he started moving it about in the opening. He soon caught sight of another blue eye, this one blinking and full of tears. Before long he had Peter, who had been digging himself out, completely extricated.

The reunion of the two friends was emotional and heartfelt. Both on the verge of dropping from nervous exhaustion, they hugged each other tearfully. Peter was covered with white, powdered plasterboard, and had blood caked on his forehead and chin. Other than that, he was luckily not the worse for wear.

Rodriguez calmed him down and dressed his wounds. It was only after they were heading south out of the war-torn city toward the relative safety of the hills that the doctor asked about the anti-plague virus.

"Did you do it? Did you get it off OK?"

"Yeah, I think so," answered Peter weakly. "Only time will tell if it works or not."

"And if it didn't work?"

"Then we're all in big trouble."

SOMEWHERE OUTSIDE ATLANTA, GEORGIA, JANUARY 1, 9:00 PM

It was the evening of the day of the execution of patriot Mark Goodwater. The scene of the event would be indelibly burnt into his mind. It was one of sheer destruction. The carnage was everywhere, the coliseum a veritable death house. That Mark Goodwater was still alive, sucking air, and would get to suffer another day, was nothing short of miraculous.

Everything after his arrival there was like a disjointed dream that faded in and out of his consciousness, one scene shifting suddenly to the next with no seeming connection between them - giant faces on billboard-sized screens, the menacing whispers of his tormentor, the electric shocks, the cheers of the crowd, the hideous death of the dictator, the riot.

Mark had watched the riot develop before his eyes as he lay half-suspended on his stainless-steel bed. The situation was total pandemonium. Groups of fleeing spectators were chased by knots of armed troops, while lone men in uniformed were pursued by mobs of angry civilians. They ran back and forth across the execution stand, brushing by Mark's outstretched body as if it were an inanimate piece of furniture. God help the object of either pursuit. Once the sole center of attention, Mark was now not even noticed in the general mayhem - almost.

Just when it looked like he might make it through it all in one piece, as the fighting moved out of the stadium onto the parking lot and surrounding area, Mark's luck ran out. From the darkness sprang the tall figure in the long scarlet robe, now ripped and torn in several places, revealing a muscular physique.

"So you thought you would get away," hissed the tall figure, still hooded in scarlet, with a protective breathing apparatus over his face. "That we had forgotten about you. No, no, no, we haven't forgotten you, not in the slightest. You're our reason for being here. No, I came back especially for you."

Mark instinctively shied away from the specter-like form, which he saw was covered in blood, barely noticeable against his long red robe. Whether it was his assailant's or the blood of others, Mark couldn't guess, but was afraid his would soon join the mix. The hooded man grabbed one of the more gruesome of the medieval torture devices intended for Mark disembowelment, obviously intent on carrying out the sentence himself. Mark recoiled in terror. There was sheer madness in the stone-cold eyes that stared out at him from the face of the masked figure. His harsh breath hissed through the breathing apparatus hanging under his chin like a white plastic blister.

"No," Mark screamed in a high-pitched, terrified voice, as he bounced up and down on his bed of steel, tied by his arms and legs. "No!" he wailed, his fear overtaking him before the actual event itself, which was following rapidly on its heels.

Just as the sharp, curved implement of torture reached Mark's quivering body, a short, stocky form rushed the tall, red-clad figure from behind.

"Die sucker!" yelled the interloper, striking at the scarlet-robed man before him with a large, heavy club. "I've been waiting a long time for this, you sick bastard."

As the tall man went down, bellowing in rage and pain, a group of dark-skinned strangers, who had been right behind the first attacker, surged up the stairs to the platform and fell upon the cronies of the hooded man, who had come to his assistance. They too soon lay in crumpled, bloody heaps. And with the death of Stan Bellows and his henchmen, so died the Fiber.

That had been over twelve hours ago. It was now evening again. Mark stretched and moved about in the relative comfort of a room within the massive complex of buildings that were once the campuses of Morehouse, Clark, and Spellman Colleges. He looked across University Park toward the Coliseum, his intended place of execution. Ironically, it turned out to be the scene of mayhem and carnage for all those who had come to see him die.

Mark remembered how his rescuers, after untying him and helping him out of the stadium – the group of six overgrown escorts acting like a phalanx of blockers as they moved across the war-torn parking lot - had shoved him unceremoniously down an open manhole into the city's brand new, multi-million dollar sewer system. From there they moved double-time, swiftly traveling across town to the university campus without being seen.

In the meantime, the city of Atlanta was in flames, as those remaining loyal to Bellows and his minions battled it out with those who weren't, which included Mark's rescuers. He looked serenely out on the tree-crowded campus, clinging to the southern edge of the strife-torn city like an oasis of green in a desert.

He hadn't seen anyone since his harrowing escape, and had woken up to find a light supper laid out for him, which he had just finished devouring.

Mark's reverie was interrupted by a noise behind him, as someone entered his third-floor room.

"So, I see you're up and about," said the deep voice, as Mark turned to see his savior from the previous night. "How y'all feeling?"

"Fine," answered Mark sheepishly. "Thanks for helping me out there. I don't know what I would've done if you hadn't..."

"Don't mention it," interrupted the stranger modestly. The short, stocky black man walked over to Mark and extended his hand.

"Tom Davis at your service."

"Hi, I'm..."

"The famous Mark Goodwater, fiber-buster extraordinaire. Nice to meet you, man." Before Mark could respond, his host continued.

"If y'all did what they say you did, we owe you a great debt of gratitude. Do you know what would have happened if the Fiber in this part of the country had been turned on as scheduled?"

"I'm afraid so. My friend Eddie Pavloski paid the ultimate price preventing it."

"I know, and when this is over, we'll make sure you both get the acknowledgement you deserve. For now, I thank you for all of us."

"I'm the one who owes you the debt of gratitude," replied Mark. "If it hadn't been for you, I'd be chopped-liver by now. Where did you guys come from?"

"Oh, I guess you could say we were waiting in the wings," said Mark's host, taking a seat on a comfortable futon across from Mark.

"We were going to try and rescue you sooner, but had to give it up due to the massive security presence. We had no idea they could get that much manpower together. They must have had every available person on the entire East Coast here last night. Well, I guess that's just as well, that way we could clean 'em up all at once."

"My friends," said Mark, suddenly remembering Peter and Arthur. "I need to contact them."

"You mean the ones you were so quick to rat on when they laid a little pain on you?"

"There was nothing little about that pain," answered Mark, turning red to Tom's amusement.

"I know. Sorry, man, didn't mean to razz you. You went through some bad stuff there. I would have done the same, probably. That is if they was white folk I was ratting on."

They both laughed, Mark harder and longer than he wanted to, as if he were giddy on laughing gas. He soon calmed down after a nervous look from his new friend.

"We'll see if we can make some kind of contact with your friends once things settle down a bit around here. We're in contact with President Morris, who has been released from captivity. Help is on the way. For now just take it easy. You've done your part, brother."

Mark did as he was told, taking the cigar that was offered to him and lighting it up. He liked the sound of that last word, brother, and made a promise to himself. To dedicate his life to helping others, to living as if we all mattered, rich, poor, white, black, male, female. For he knew from bitter experience, to survive on this fragile planet we must all live like a band of brothers. Yeah, he liked the ring of that.

EPILOG

WASHINGTON DC, FEBRUARY 2, 2037, 12:00 PM

Young President Morris of the newly reconstituted United States greeted the visiting dignitaries from around the world that had come to pay tribute to the trio of unlikely heroes seated with him on the viewing stand, Dr. Peter Danvers, Mark Goodwater, and Dr. Fernando Rodriguez. Together, through seeming insurmountable odds, they had saved the country and the world from the most deadly epidemic to visit the planet. The plague, conceived and fabricated by the mad, misguided genius, Linda Rayburn, had killed millions and would have killed millions more had it not been for the three on the dais this day.

Also being honored were two other heroes, one unknown by the public, the other reviled as a criminal during most of his short life. Arthur Berry, the retired school teacher, had perhaps done as much as anyone to stop the deadly disease, with his persistent and kindly needling, his insights and optimism, his wisdom and advice. It could be argued that none of them would have met if it hadn't been for Arthur. Certainly Peter owed his life to the sagely old man. He would be sorely missed in the coming years.

The other unsung hero had inadvertently saved Europe from the plague, and purposely prevented it from reaching the eastern United States. Without Eddie Pavloski's brave, last-minute stand, the entire country would have been re-submerged in the deadly pestilence, rather than just its western half. Both these heroes gave their lives for the cause, and were rewarded with a monument and two bronze plaques near the Lincoln Memorial.

Although the plague had been for the most part defeated, and Europe and the eastern half of the United States were free of the Trojan-horse virus and starting to recover economically, all was not right with the world.

There had been a fierce battle for LA and environs between Feng's forces and what was left of the United States military. However, when Feng's superiors and Party bosses found out what he and his Malaysian allies were up to, they stepped in and removed him and his men, sucking them back to Asia like an outgoing tide. China and the Malaysian Federation, who were so eager to support the errant Minister, were now themselves on the brink of war.

Even with peace restored, the devastation of the western part of the country was overwhelming - mass graves and incinerators; huge sprawling, garbage-infested refugee camps; landscapes strewn with dead humans and animals; a total lack of medical supplies or sanitary conditions; food rotting on the vine and in storage depots; widespread destruction of property, all left much work to do. The western part of the country resembled a war-zone where few humans wanted to find themselves. All this cast a distinct pall over the otherwise festive occasion.

Peter gazed out at the sea of faces mostly unseen through the harsh glare of the spotlights and flash bulbs. While the speeches of the dignitaries droned on his mind raced along the byways of his recent experiences, cutting a groove in the much-played vinyl of his memory - those days in Jamaica before the plague, full of lazy fun in the sun; his rash trip to the States to find his family; his journey up from Texas with Arthur. Arthur. The thought of his friend almost stung him to tears, as he wished he were here to share this moment. Peter could almost see the wry smile playing on his friend's lips at all the hullabaloo. His memory ran headlong as if looking for some great prize, so that after awhile Peter couldn't tell if it was memory or premonition - the pint-sized dirigible from out of some H.G. Wells tale; the audacious prison break with Eddie Pavloski; the cross-country odyssey. Then there was Linda Rayburn and her incredible twenty-second century quantum computing machine, which would have propelled humankind forward into the future like a rocket if it had survived; the unleashing of her equally incredible anti-serum couched in the sub-atomic space of her wondrous computer. Her anti-virus had somewhat made up for her malicious initial act, even if her plague's escape over the Fiber wasn't wholly intentional.

As remembered losses piled up in his mind, his heart grew heavy with the weight of it all. Despite the festive occasion he was plunged into a gloomy mood. It was only momentary. For on looking up his eye caught Sandy's. She smiled a sweet smile at him that would have melted the iciest frown. He smiled back and immediately the gloom lifted like a helium-filled balloon. Sandy had changed profoundly in the past year, as if she had woken from a long sleep. He resolved to never be separated from her again.

It was a glorious day. They were bathed in the glow of love and gratitude from literally millions of people. To be reunited with his wife and children, who beamed at him from the first row of the audience where they sat with Sandy's parents, was all he could have asked for.

Peter wondered what it all meant. What was it that put him at the right place at the right time? What caused him to meet just the people needed at just the correct moments? What was it that drove him forward to this conclusion? That gave him this purpose? Was it accident? Fate? Or the hand of God? Peter would never stop wondering.

Ironically, he had a much better idea of his future than he had of his past. His future seemed pretty much laid out, like a well-drawn equation. He knew where his task lay. For ever since he had seen it humming and throbbing in Linda's penthouse lab, he had been obsessed with her advanced quantum thinking machine. He knew what he had to do. Somehow, even though he knew the task impossible before he even started, he had to reconstruct Linda's creation. He would dedicate the rest of his life to building the super-quantum computer he had seen with his own eyes and helped program with his own hands.

Sandy still beamed up at him. He knew that she felt the same way, and cherished as much as he did the four month old baby in her womb, the future heir to the soon to be growing Danvers household.

So it was with optimism that Peter looked forward to the future, with faith in whatever evolutionary principal was at work in the universe, driving humankind toward its ultimate purpose. He stood to take his place behind the podium to a thunderous ovation that caught at his heart. Once again mankind had averted annihilation and survived the test. We had endured through yet another great trial. The plague and its aftermath had brought out the worst in our species, the lowest most negative aspects of our potential, but it had also brought out the best and the most noble, the highest aspects of our nature. Yes, we are capable of both.

All was not right with the world. Great challenges lay ahead, and the seeds of destruction were still carried in the hearts of many. But a plateau of sorts had been reached and the human race was still here, groping, striving, reaching toward the infinite.

THE END

To P and C

www.ingramcontent.com/pod-product-compliance
Lightning Source LLC
Chambersburg PA
CBHW070901180626
46817CB00003B/862